The Guardians of Allon
Book One

The Great Battle

Shawn Lamb

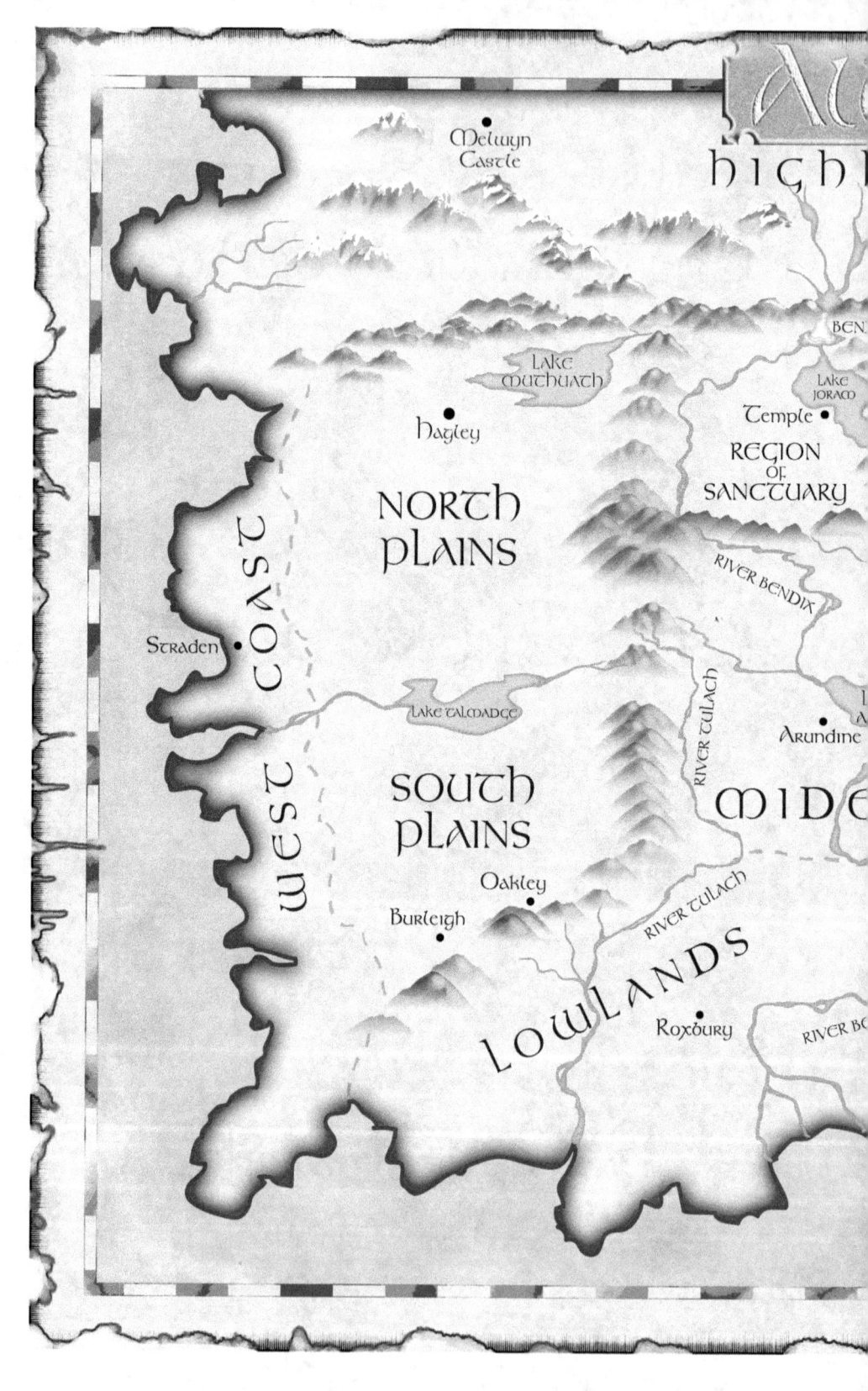

THE GUARDIANS OF ALLON – BOOK 1
THE GREAT BATTLE by Shawn Lamb
Published by Allon Books
209 Hickory Way Court
Antioch, Tennessee 37013
www.allonbooks.com

Cover illustration by Robert Lamb

International Standard Book Number: 978-0-9891029-8-8

Other Books by Shawn Lamb

Young Adult Fantasy Fiction
ALLON ~ BOOK 1
Published by Creation House, a division of Charisma Media

Published by Allon Books

ALLON ~ BOOK 2 ~ INSURRECTION
ALLON ~ BOOK 3 ~ HEIR APPARENT
ALLON ~ BOOK 4 ~ A QUESTION OF SOVEREIGNTY
ALLON ~ BOOK 5 ~ GAUNTLET
ALLON ~ BOOK 6 ~ DILEMMA
ALLON ~ BOOK 7 ~ DANGEROUS DECEPTION
ALLON ~ BOOK 8 ~ DIVIDED
ALLON ~ BOOK 9 ~ IN PLAIN SIGHT
PARENT STUDY GUIDE FOR ALLON ~ BOOKS 1-9
THE ACTIVITY BOOK OF ALLON

For Young Readers – ages 8-10
Allon ~ The King's Children series
NECIE AND THE APPLES
TRISTINE'S DORGIRITH ADVENTURE
NIGEL'S BROKEN PROMISE

Historical Fiction
GLENCOE
THE HUGUENOT SWORD

MORTALS

Curtis
Vicar Avram
Dolan, a farmer
Clare, Dolan's wife
Janel, daughter of Dolan and Clare, age 18
Kerwin, Janel's brother, age 22
Mace, Janel's brother, age 20
Toby, Janel's brother, age 13

Razi, age 18
Ram, Razi's twin brother, age 18
Haggar, Ram and Razi's mother

IMMORTALS

Jor'el, Almighty Deity of Allon
Captain Kell, Commander of the Guardians of Jor'el
Armus, 1st Lieutenant
Avatar, 2nd Lieutenant
Eldric, Guardian Physician
Ridge, Guardian Ranger
Mahon, Guardian Warrior
Barrion
Griswold
Witter
Tor
Dax, Guardian Ranger
Wren, Guardian Huntress
Tegan. Guardian Physician
Altari
Rune
Jedrek
Virgil

TRIO LEADERS

Gresham	Midessex
Priscilla	East Coast
Chase	West Coast
Vidar	Northern Forest
Hunter	Southern Forest
Jayden	Delta
Dagar	Region of Sanctuary
Zanis	Meadowlands
Valmar	Highlands
Sloan	Lowlands
Lilith	North Plains
Raleigh	South Plains

Chapter 1

THE LATE AFTERNOON SUN CAST LONG SHADOWS OVER A SMALL grove. An imposing, intimidating being towered over two frightened teenage boys. Their faces showed the bruising and welts of abuse. The being wore a black and red doublet that could barely contain his broad shoulders, massive chest and bulky arms. His sword and dagger remained sheathed, but his fists clenched. With hateful scorn he stared down at them.

"That should teach you pitiful excuse for mortals a lesson. Show gratitude for the mercy you've been given."

"Mercy?" cried Toby, the younger boy.

"Hush," Judson warned Toby. He then spoke to the being. "He didn't mean it! We are grateful, and will complete our task without another word of complaint."

"If I have to return, it will be the final time." The being's yellow eyes darted to Toby.

Toby paled in fright, which prompted Judson to speak. "You won't! I swear!"

He sneered with a smile of warped pleasure. He disappeared in a white flash of light. The boys shielded their eyes from the momentary blindness.

"I don't want to return to work," whimpered Toby.

"Hush and let me think. We'll go back to camp and speak to Mordecai. He'll know what do." Judson helped Toby to his feet and began the trek back through the forest.

Not until after sundown did they reach the edge of the labor camp. Toby barely stayed on his feet making it difficult for Judson to help. His own injuries compounded his effort. Finally, both collapsed.

"Help!" Judson called in a weak voice yet loud enough to get attention.

Three men took Toby and Judson to a tent at the center of camp where they helped them get comfortable on cots. Henden and Mordecai arrived. They were weathered, hardy men of middle years. Henden served as the camp's spiritual adviser and Mordecai, the camp leader.

"By the heavenlies, what happened?" Henden hurried to examine the boys.

"It was him. The large one," began Judson. "He caught us fetching wood, just like you told us to, Mordecai. We weren't running away again, honest!"

Mordecai's jowls flexed in anger at hearing the news.

"It's true." Toby wept.

"Easy, Toby," soothed Henden. "Reb, I need water. Kirk, Curtis, wait outside. As the men left, Henden sent a prompting look of compassion to Mordecai.

The labor leader spoke to the boys. "I believe you. My anger is for your injuries, not your action. What did he say?"

"He threatened to kill us if he has to return," said Judson.

Toby sobbed, almost uncontrollably. "I want to go home! I swear I'll never do a bad thing again!"

Henden knelt by the cot and tried to calm the boy.

"I'll see what can be done," said Mordecai.

"How? Dagar sent us here," said Judson with bitter complaint.

"I won't do anything bad again! I won't do anything bad again," Toby repeated.

Mordecai placed a comforting hand on Toby's forehead. "Hush. I promise to take you home."

Reb returned with two buckets of warm water.

"Now, let Henden tend to your wounds." Mordecai drew Reb outside. They joined the other men.

"Well?" asked Kirk.

"The large Guardian again."

"Are you going to speak to Dagar?"

Mordecai shook his head. "Every time I do, he says he can't find evidence of who this rogue Guardian is."

"As if he'd say," groused Reb.

"Not all Guardians are bad," said Curtis.

"No, but Dagar is growing less receptive about speaking with me," said Mordecai.

"So what do you plan on doing? This can't go unreported. Toby looks lucky to be alive," argued Reb.

Mordecai's expression grew determined. "I don't intend to. Curtis, when is the next load leaving?"

"I planned for the day after tomorrow."

"Can it be ready by morning?"

"Ay, if we work most of the night, why?"

With compassion, Mordecai glanced to the tent. "I promised to take Toby home. Judson should go as well."

"That's risky. Both still have a year of work on their sentence."

Mordecai's temper exploded. "The risk is worth taking since he threatened to kill them if he returns!"

Curtis' brows grew level at the rebuff. "The load will be ready by dawn." He took Kirk with him as they left.

Reb drew closer to Mordecai. "Home is the first place Dagar will look for them when he discovers they're gone."

Mordecai slyly smiled. "Leave that to me. Just be ready an hour before dawn. I'll need your help.

<hr />

Two lumber-filled wagons, each pulled by a pair of draft horses, backed up to the tent. A hollowed out portion of each wagon was made to accommodate the boys and keep them hidden from view. Mordecai, Henden and others made the boys comfortable in the wagons. Toby and Judson slept through the move.

"Are the wounds so bad they remain unconscious?" asked Reb.

"I gave them an extra dose of poppy juice in their wine. They should sleep for most of the journey," said Henden.

"Good. Time to leave." Mordecai saw Curtis hop onto the driver's seat of one of the wagons. "No, Curtis. I need you to stay here and make certain the schedule is met. Heaven knows Pratt and his crew would take advantage of us both being gone."

Curtis grinned in agreement and hopped down from the seat.

"Reb." Mordecai signaled him to the other wagon then climbed onto the driver's seat. "Any words of encouragement, Henden?"

"May the blessings of Jor'el go with you."

"Ay." He snapped the reins. Reb followed with the second wagon.

By midmorning they reached the crossroads. The main road continued alongside a small river and turned south. The second road went due west. Mordecai pulled his wagon off the main road to stop at the water's edge and let the horses drink. He got down from the driver's seat and moved to the rear of the wagon.

"I want to check on the boys," he said.

"Haven't heard a peep from Judson." Reb did the same as Mordecai.

"Nor have I from Toby. I just want to make sure." Looking inside, he found Toby still asleep. He made his way to the other wagon where Reb reported the same about Judson. "Actually, I wanted to tell you my plan."

"I wondered when you would," said Reb with a grin. "It was obvious you didn't want Curtis involved. I still say he's the one giving Dagar bad reports."

"I'm sure of it. That's why I didn't want him to know we're not taking them home, rather going to the Fortress. With Dagar not being receptive, I'm going straight to the source."

"Jor'el?" said Reb in surprised awe. "You're going to speak to the Almighty?"

"I'm going to speak with Captain Kell. Which I suppose could be almost the same since it's reported he speaks to the Almighty on a daily basis."

"Going over Dagar's head is risky."

Passion made Mordecai motion to the wagons. "This can't keep happening! Whoever this rogue Guardian is, Dagar is either unwilling or incapable of stopping him. He may not have even told Kell. The boys' condition will show the truth of our situation. Two years of hard labor for stealing a loaf of bread is disproportionate. I know them. They are not criminals rather caught in foolish childhood mischief."

"Have you forgotten I know them also?"

"No." Mordecai signed in an effort to bring his temper under control.

Reb clapped Mordecai's arm. "We should continue."

The Region of Sanctuary was the smallest of Allon's twelve provinces. Thus by sundown the next day, Mordecai and Reb neared the Fortress compound.

In a plain surrounded by four majestic hills stood the Temple of Providence. Each of Allon's twelve provinces contributed to the Temple. The pillars of marble came from a quarry in the far range of the Northern Forest where it bordered the foothills of the Highlands. Carved on the pillars were images of Verse. The pillars guarded massive wooden doors hewn and gilded by the craftsmen of the Southern Forest. Twin bell spires of gleaming white marble topped with golden steeples rose to the heavens. The bells were from the sister provinces of the North and South Plains. White marble dominated the entire facade of the Temple with gold accents. Arch-shaped windows contained colored glass blown and assembled in Midessex. At certain times of day, the Temple reflected the sun's rays in a brilliance of white with a kaleidoscope of gold and rainbow effects dazzling the eyes.

Adjacent to the Temple stood the Fortress of Jor'el. The towering battlements gleamed of white marble. Self-contained, the Fortress housed two thousand mortal soldiers, five hundred Guardian warriors and two hundred priests. The position of Vicar of the Temple was the highest honor a mortal could achieve, and reserved for the most dedicated priest of Jor'el. Each man who served was subject to the Almighty's approval.

The major city in each province housed a Fortress for local worship. These also served as the Guardian seat of governing. The construction of these Fortresses depended upon the region's terrain and natural resources. Large towns had smaller chapels under the direction of the regional Fortress.

The magnificent palace of *Jor'el-l`ahair* completed the holy compound. In the Ancient tongue of the Guardians the palace name means *Jor'el With Us*. Here the Almighty resided among the people. From the Throne Room, Jor'el conducted daily affairs. However, only the Vicar and Captain Kell were admitted into the Almighty's presence on a continuous basis. Jor'el granted audiences, but always in the company of either the Vicar or Captain.

Most of the Guardian population congregated at *Jor'el-l`ahair* and Melwynn. Also known as the Castle of the Guardians, Melwynn dominated a mountainside in the Highlands, away from the mortal population. They used the castle for times of refreshing and training. Jor'el's palace served as the place of command and going forth on various assignments.

Since the greatest concentration of Guardians could be found at the compound, they were easy to spot among the mortals. They were beautiful and handsome beings of perfection in feature and form. The shortest stood seven feet tall. At seven and a half-feet, the warriors towered above mortal males, who averaged around six feet by standard measure. Some mortals reached six and half feet. The Guardians' eyes showed another difference from mortals by unusual brilliance and striking colors, capable of evoking heavenly insight when needed.

Neither the Guardians nor mortals paid much attention to Mordecai and Reb as they steered the wagons to the Fortress gate. Two mortal guards motioned for the wagons to stop.

"State your business."

"My name is Mordecai. This is Reb. We come seeking Captain Kell."

A loud moaning came from the back of the wagon.

"Who's back there?" demanded the guard.

"One who seeks sanctuary," said Mordecai quick and anxious. "It is on his behalf, and another, hidden in the other wagon, that we must speak with the captain."

"Why hidden?" asked one guard. The other guard moved to inspect Mordecai's wagon.

"To save their lives from one who would kill them."

At the rear of the wagon, the guard found the safety flap and removed it to reveal Toby. "This one looks badly hurt."

"They were nearly beaten to death. Please, have mercy, they're just boys!" pleaded Mordecai.

The first guard told the second, "Fetch the Vicar." He then said to Mordecai, "Pull through the gate, and stop over there."

With a grateful smile, Mordecai and Reb and followed instructions.

"You four!" the soldier called to fellow guardsmen "We have two for the infirmary, one in each wagon. Be gentle. They are badly injured."

A tall, lean man, of eighty years, arrived. Dressed in his daily robes of royal blue and silver, Vicar Avram appeared spry and agile in step. He kept his full head of white hair neat and trimmed. Keen intelligence shown in the hazel eyes while his grandfatherly features belied a man of stout heart and courage.

"What is the problem, Sergeant?"

"They brought two abused boys for sanctuary. I'm having them taken to the infirmary."

The four guardsmen removed Judson and Toby from the wagon. In a semi-conscious state, the boys squirmed in pain caused by the movement.

"Merciful heaven!" Avram hurried to the litter on which Toby lay. The boy appeared horribly pale and lowly moaned. "How did this happen?"

"Please, Vicar, I beg your indulgence, and would ask for Captain Kell, then I'll explain," said Mordecai.

Avram waved the soldiers carrying the boys to continue before confronting Mordecai. "Kell? Is this a Guardian matter?"

"Ay."

"Sergeant, fetch Captain Kell. You two come with me."

"One of us should stay with the boys. They may become frightened, especially Toby. He's the younger boy," said Mordecai.

The Vicar kindly smiled. "They will be well cared for. You both need refreshment and rest. Now, come. Kell will be here shortly."

The sergeant performed his duty in a prompt fashion. However, keeping pace with the mighty captain of the Guardians proved difficult. He jogged or risk lagging behind. Ageless and knowledgeable, Kell stood just past seven and half feet. His midnight black hair linked with strong handsome features, made an impressive setting for golden eyes. The white richly embroidered close fitting jacket was trimmed in gold and reached to mid-thigh. The jacket had side slits from the hem to the hip for ease of movement. The white breeches were also trimmed with gold and purple braids and tucked into leather boots. A large, gold and purple leather belt held a handsome gold scabbard and sword. He wasn't alone. His lieutenant, Armus, accompanied him.

Also perfect in feature, Armus was brawny in appearance with brown hair and brilliant chestnut eyes. He wore the same uniform as Kell, but with a few differences due to rank. From a fine brown leather belt hung a embossed scabbard complete with a sword. The boots matched the belt. Around his neck he wore his medallion of authority. Both Guardians appeared serious when entering the Vicar's private chamber.

Mordecai and Reb stopped eating and swallowed hard upon sight of the Guardians. The Vicar noticed their discomposure. "Be at ease, you have nothing to fear. This Captain Kell and Lieutenant Armus."

"Captain." Mordecai rose and bowed. Reb mimicked him.

"Do not bow to me, Mordecai," said Kell. His expression softened into a smile. "The sergeant told me something of your disturbing tale. Please, sit while we speak."

Mordecai and Reb sat, though they still appeared uncertain.

Kell sat at the table opposite Mordecai and Reb. Armus took a seat beside Kell. "You are the foreman of the labor camp at the north end of Lake Joram."

"Ay, Captain," said Mordecai with surprise. "How do you know?"

Kell grinned. "I am acquainted with many things that go on in Allon."

"Of course, Captain. I'm just surprised you take interest in the misguided," he said with discretion.

"All mortals are of interest to me, and to Jor'el."

"I didn't mean to imply otherwise." Mordecai became unsettled.

Kell's friendly smile widened. "Truly, be at ease, Mordecai."

"Rather difficult with you being a Guard—who you are," Reb corrected himself in mid-sentence.

"Please understand this is difficult," said Mordecai.

"Since you requested me, I assume the situation involves Guardians."

"Have you spoken to Dagar?" asked Armus.

"He is part of the problem," began Mordecai. "Although, I have tried. He is not receptive, so after this latest incident, I had to protect the boys. The other threatened to kill them when he returned!"

"The other? A Guardian?"

"Ay. Dagar thinks he's a rogue. I'm not so sure."

"Can you describe him?" asked Kell.

Mordecai heaved a shrug. "I've not seen him."

"Nor I," said Reb. "But this isn't the first time he's beaten the boys, and others at camp. We don't know when or where he'll show up."

"I approach Dagar after each encounter, only he claims he can't find him," groused Mordecai, a hint of disbelief in his voice. "That's why I brought the boys here for sanctuary, and to speak to you, Captain. If Dagar can't deal with him then maybe you can."

Thoughtful, Kell's golden eyes shifted between Mordecai and Reb, lingering on Mordecai. "You said Dagar hasn't been receptive to your concerns."

"No," chided Mordecai. He shied away from Kell's steady glance, more from anger than intimidation.

"You don't believe he cares enough to learn the truth."

Mordecai showed guarded surprise, yet remained silent.

"Your encounters with him and this rogue have made you both wary of Guardians," continued Kell. When angry passion prevented Mordecai's reply and Reb appeared uncertain, Kell kindly added, "Your faith made you act despite your fears. Let you hearts and minds be at ease, you did well. The boys will be granted sanctuary."

"Thank you," said Mordecai, relieved.

"Now, for your own safety from this rogue, neither of you will return to the camp. You and your families shall be secretly relocated."

"But I'm the foreman."

"Fret not. Trust us, and Jor'el. Now, finish eating. Vicar Avram will see to your comfort until the arrangements can be made."

Again Mordecai and Reb rose to bow as Kell and Armus left.

Avram followed the Guardians into the hall. "Kell," he began with some disconcertion. "One of the boys is my nephew, Toby."

"What was he doing at the labor camp?"

Avram colored with embarrassment. "They claimed he was caught stealing, but I never believed it. However, when they brought him before a court of mortals and Dagar, I did not interfere and risk being accused of favoritism. The harsh sentence of two years devastated my sister. Since then, I have conducted a secret investigation, and found no evidence of Toby stealing. Oh, he was present along with Judson, only they were in the wrong place at wrong time, and with the wrong people."

"Guilt by association."

"Ay. Now this! He looked awful." Avram gripped Kell's arm. "I have never asked a favor before. But if you could find a way to heal Toby, I would be in your debt."

With a gentle smile Kell replied. "You would owe me nothing. If he and Judson suffered injury at the hands of a Guardian, then it is my duty to see they are cared for and the situation set right."

"Thank you."

"Can you tolerate accompanying me to the infirmary? I want to see the boys. Talk to them, if I can."

Avram told the guards, "Make them comfortable. I'll return shortly."

At the Fortress infirmary, a mortal physician met them. "I finally got the boys to sleep, Vicar. Captain."

"We won't disturb them. I do want to see what wounds they suffered," said Kell.

The physician continued with grave concern. "It is only by Jor'el's mercy the youngest is still alive. He has internal bleeding that I can't stop. I've tried everything and don't know what else to do."

"Merciful Jor'el," muttered Avram in prayer.

Armus laid a hand on the Vicar's shoulder in attempted comfort.

Kell moved past the physician to stand at the foot of the bed where Toby slept. Judson lay in the next cot. Their faces remained swollen and they wore bandages around their heads. Kell's jowls flexed and his brows leveled in compassion at sight of the serious injuries. He closed his eyes and took a deep breath. A moment later, he opened his eyes when a white flash of light appeared beside him.

From the light emerged another Guardian. Eldric, the premier physician, stood a head shorter than Kell with black hair, violet eyes and dressed in a muted blue suit of his station. "You summoned me, Captain?"

Kell motioned toward the cots. "These boys sustained their injuries at the hand of a Guardian."

"Guardian?" echoed Eldric in surprise.

"Ay." He leaned closer to speak in a lower voice. "The younger is the Vicar's nephew. He bleeds inside. Use your skills to heal them."

"Ay, Captain." Eldric enquired of the mortal physician as to the exact injuries.

Kell stepped back to join Avram and Armus. "Eldric will tend to them. No need to fear for your nephew's survival."

"Thank you."

18

At a brisk pace, Kell and Armus left the infirmary to return to the palace. In the captain's office, they found Vidar waiting. The premier Guardian archer was of a trim and athletic build, with auburn hair reaching his shoulder. Brilliant copper eyes gazed keenly at his surroundings. He wore a forester green jerkin with a brown cowl. The breeches were of identical color to the jerkin and tucked into knee-high leather boots. A brown leather belt gathered the jerkin around his waist. A plain-sheathed dagger hung from the belt. Instead of a sword he carried a magnificent bolt-action crossbow for easy loading and firing. A handsome quiver was full of arrows.

Vidar spoke the moment they entered. "I know what happened to the boys."

Armus paused in closing the door to ask, "How?"

"The labor camp is on the border of my province. I sensed trouble and went to help."

"You saw who did this to them?" demanded Kell.

"No, I arrived too late, but the sense of a Guardian felt very strong. No individual essence, just a general presence. I kept watch over the boys as they returned to camp." When Kell scowled with great annoyance, Vidar added, "It doesn't mean I can't find who. I first wanted to make sure the boys arrived safely."

"How could Dagar allow this?" chided Armus.

"I haven't seen him to ask him. Jor'el must be told." Vidar spoke the last sentence to Kell.

"He knows. Dagar started acting strangely over a century ago."

"This shows his behavior is getting worse. You must do something."

"I intend to act. Despite his increasingly erratic behavior, Dagar is one of us. As such he is clever, powerful and—"

"Unpredictable," groused Armus.

"Which is why we must act with discretion. He may not be capable— "

"Unwilling," said Armus with impatience. This drew a look of ire from Kell, who continued speaking, only in a more emphatic tone for Armus' benefit.

"To stop the Guardian terrorizing the mortals!" Kell raised a quick, stern hand, which made Armus clamp his mouth shut. Kell took a deep breath to calm his temper.

"How are the boys?" asked Vidar.

"Bad. The youngest is Avram's nephew, and bleeds internally. I told Eldric to heal them." Kell thought for a moment before speaking again. "Double your efforts. I want this rogue found! Only don't act unless absolutely necessary. *I* will deal with him personally." His set features and narrow gold eyes made his intent clear.

"Ay, Captain." Vidar made the Guardian salute of right fist to left breast. He stepped back and vanished in a flash of white light.

"Will you tell Jor'el about this incident?" asked Armus.

"To approach him again without proof may be foolhardy."

"Why? If he already knows about Dagar's attitude—"

"He says Dagar needs to come to terms with his behavior. I'm afraid of what may happen when he does," said Kell in exasperation.

"Surely Jor'el won't allow that?"

Kell sat at his desk. A weary, thoughtful sigh escaped. "I hope so, but I don't know. Nothing like this has ever happened in our ranks before. Among the mortals such behavior is common, almost expected, but not with us."

"Have you tried talking to Dagar directly?"

"Of course. He either doesn't see the problem, or is in denial. With proof I can convince him before bringing it to Jor'el. Of course, there maybe no connection between Dagar and this rogue."

"And that is what you're hoping for."

Kell regarded Armus with sobriety. "He's not just one of us, he's my peer, as entrusted by Jor'el as I am. Naturally, I hope and pray for the best. We all should."

Armus flashed a pricked frown. "Ay. I guess I'm protective."

"We're supposed to protect the mortals."

"No, I mean of you, of how this could affect you if the worst happens and he outright rebels. His unsettling behavior is already causing you angst."

Kell smiled, touched and grateful. "I want to protect you and the others from the worst—including Dagar." His expression grew optimistic. "And I might have a way to do that."

"How?"

"A meeting of the Trio Leaders to bring the problem into the open."

Armus looked skeptical. "I think that will anger him more than help."

"It will force him to recognize this as a serious problem. With counsel, we can help him deal with the situation. However, before that, I want you to organize a secret transfer of Mordecai and Reb's families. Once they are secure, I'll call the meeting."

"I hope you're right."

"I must try!" Kell stood. "The alternative is unthinkable. Now, go. The sooner the better." He escorted Armus to the door.

"And before Dagar realizes they're not returning," groused Armus, who promptly received a nudge out the door for his comment.

Kell returned to his desk. Indeed, the alternative was unthinkable, yet he had to give it serious consideration. Dagar's unusual behavior had grown worse. A knock, followed by an entrance interrupted his pondering. To his surprise, Dagar arrived. Not that Dagar coming to see him was unusual just awkward timing under the circumstances.

"Dagar."

"Kell," said Dagar with a wry smile. He too wore the warrior's uniform only minus the purple piping. His features stood in marked contrast to Kell. He had sun yellow hair, matching small beard and mustache with bright mahogany eyes. "You seem surprised to see me. Is something wrong?"

"No," said Kell with a forced chuckle. "Just meditating."

"Sorry to interrupt." Dagar sat on the corner of the desk.

Now recovered, Kell assumed a more relaxed posture. "What do you want?"

"Nothing in particular. I happened to notice the way you and Armus made a hasty departure earlier and wondered if something was wrong?"

So that's the reason, Kell thought but spoke aloud, "No. The Vicar needed to speak with me on a matter." Not exactly a lie, nor the complete truth. In fact, lying went against a Guardian's character. They could often tell when a mortal lied. With Dagar being clever, Kell needed to be alert, thus he spoke with discretion.

"Really? Must have been urgent." Dagar sarcastically chuckled. "Or the typical mortal making a mountain out of a mole hill, as they say."

Kell tried to maintain a casual appearance while continuing to gauge Dagar's attitude. "I suppose it depends upon your perspective. Some things they think are urgent, we view differently."

"Please, Kell, don't placate me with platitudes. A mortal thinks the sky is falling if it rains too hard and damages his crop."

Kell leaned forward on the desk to regard Dagar. "What has changed your attitude towards them?"

"I haven't changed. Mortals have grown more fickle and capricious over the centuries. Some play us for fools or magicians, and we let them, doling out our power to satisfy them. Don't you ever get tired of it?"

"No, I find them fascinating creatures."

Dagar laughed. "I mean limiting your power to a lesser creature's whim."

Kell rose to confront Dagar, his expression stern. "Dangerous talk, Dagar. We were created to serve."

"In all your years of existence, have you once wondered what it would be like to freely use your power for whatever you wanted?"

"No."

Dagar sighed with a frown. "I should know better than ask *you*. So dedicated to duty, it would never cross your mind to use your power for pleasure."

"I consider it a pleasure to serve."

Dagar placed an arm around Kell's shoulders. "Kell, my friend, you have a lot to learn about enjoying your existence."

"As your friend, I'm concerned about you."

"Me?" Dagar laughed. "There is nothing to be concerned about. I'm merely enjoying myself. You need to learn to relax. Do like Armus and find yourself a hobby. He says cooking releases tension. Vidar enjoys wine. A little too much maybe, " he added with a snicker. "You are always so serious. Take earlier for example."

"Earlier?" asked Kell, his suspicion returning.

"The Vicar sends for you and you rush over as if it demands your immediate and full attention." He did a mimicked exaggeration of Kell's walk. "Rather than taking time to deal with it. You said it wasn't of great importance."

There! The visit to the Fortress again. Dagar never made idle chatter, and a master at either masking his true intention or using decoy topics to make one think he wasn't interested in a certain subject. Eventually he discovers what he wanted. Not this time.

Kell casually smiled. "No. I needed to get away from Hueil's pestering." True, since he and Armus were with Hueil where the sergeant found him.

Dagar guffawed. "A good reason to walk with such determination, or rather, agitation."

"I'm not one to complain about a fellow Guardian."

Dagar continued to laugh, only now with a mocking tone. "Where Hueil is concerned there is always room for complaint. Or better yet Priscilla, Gulliver, Elgin, or any other vassal or caste not a warrior."

Kell's ire rose when Dagar expressed degrading sentiments towards his own kind. He covered it with a half-grin when Dagar tossed him a probing side-glance. "Well, if there is nothing specific you wanted, I do have work to do."

Dagar clicked his tongue and shook his head. "Poor Kell. So blindly dedicated to duty you can't relax."

"We each function in our own way." He took Dagar's shoulder to steer him to the door. "Still, I will consider what you suggest."

"Glad to hear it." Dagar left and Kell closed the door.

Already troubled by Dagar's deteriorating attitude and behavior toward mortals, his distress deepened at hearing verbal scorn for fellow Guardians. Hopefully Armus would be quick in his task. He didn't want to wait too long to call the meeting.

Kell got a strong sense of summoning in his spirit, and left his office. With long, hasty strides he crossed the compound to the main building. He passed the Guardian warriors standing their posts at various points in the Palace from the front door to inner sanctum of the Throne Room.

A large opulent room gleamed with white marble pillars and floor. Polished gold and silver lamp stands flanked the elevated platform and entry. Six lavishly stained glass windows dazzled with color in the sunlight. A single throne of magnificently crafted gold, inlaid with jewels stood on the platform five steps above the floor.

The throne was empty. Not unusual. Jor'el always appeared after he arrived. Kell knelt at the bottom of the platform and bowed his head.

"I hear and obey, Almighty One." He knew Jor'el arrived when he saw a warm glowing radiance flickering on the steps and floor.

"Rise, my captain."

Whenever the Almighty became manifested, he appeared in glowing heavenly light, creating the appearance of a male, but obscured from any clear view. Only a pair of opalescent eyes was visible. Unlike Guardian eyes, Jor'el eyes saw all, knew all, always invoked the knowledge and power of the eternal to whomever stood before him.

"When were you going to tell me of Toby and Judson?"

"I—" Kell sighed and admitted, "I first wanted to learn if Dagar was aware of this rogue Guardian abusing mortals."

"Dagar always knows more than he tells."

"Ay."

"So do you, Kell."

Pricked, he said, "I didn't mean to lie, just not be caught by his clever speech."

Jor'el's eyes kindly smiled. "I gifted him with cleverness and you with the strength and determination to protect, with both equal to the task required. Dagar needs to be able to discern the hearts and minds of those allowed into my presence, while you possess the iron will to defend. Now he abuses his station by wrongfully employing his cleverness."

Kell began to speak, only stopped when Jor'el raised a hand and said, "I acknowledge your concern. Dagar's heart is becoming hardened. Your plan to call the Trio Leaders is good; only do not be surprised if Dagar is not receptive. His growing pride is affecting his spirit."

"He asked me if I ever thought about using my power to get what I wanted. I told him no."

"Beware such thoughts. They can lead to actions that turn upon comrades."

"No, Great One, never!"

"I mean Dagar. You heard how he scorns those he believes to be of lesser power and importance than he."

"Surely, you can turn his heart! You created us," said Kell with desperation.

Jor'el spoke in a calm and tender reply. "To do as you suggest would take away the ability to choose. I allow the mortals to make choices."

"They make choices based upon the knowledge you give through the scribes. We already know who you are and why we were created."

"Exactly," said Jor'el with emphasis. "Dagar is making his choice with full knowledge."

Disturbed by the implication, Kell gripped the hilt of his sword to maintain his composure enough to ask; "Then, there is no hope if he makes the wrong decision?"

Jor'el's eyes stared at Kell, firm and unyielding. "No."

The simple, unnerving word brought Kell to his knees. "May it not be so, Great One!"

"I gave Dagar life, full knowledge of myself and allow him total access to my throne. I withheld nothing from him, just as I have withheld nothing from you. There is not a single Guardian who cannot claim the same. From the mortals I have withheld full knowledge, for they are not capable, in their present form of accepting the eternal. Mercy and grace is shown them for their frailty and acts of ignorance. Upon the acceptance or rejection of the truth they are given, they will receive judgment or mercy. Upon what can I judge Dagar when he possesses unhindered knowledge and truth? To do so would compromise my holy honor."

Kell winced with intense emotional pain. He could barely speak. "I understand. However, it's not easy to accept that one of my kind could be lost forever."

"I grieve also, my dear Kell. Proceed with the meeting, only be wary of what you discover in its wake."

Kell bowed his head. The fading light signaled Jor'el's departure. It took several moments to gather his emotions, hard to digest the disturbing reality if Dagar chooses wrongly. *Perhaps if I told him the dreadful consequence, he would reconsider. He may not be aware of them.* Bolstered by the thought, he left.

Chapter 2

A ROOSTER CROWED. DEW GLISTENED IN THE EARLY MORNING SUN. Smoke rose from several chimneys at the house of a wealthy farmer. The smell of breakfast filled the air. Soon family members and servants would start the day.

He darted from the trees to the rear wall of the barn. He peeked around the corner toward the house. Even at age eighteen he stood unusually tall for a mortal, close to six feet eight inches. He had handsome clean-shaven features, golden hair and bright blue eyes. He wore a rich burgundy and black brocade tunic worthy of his station. A mischievous, yet winsome smile appeared at seeing her leave the house and head for the barn. A willowy brunette of his same age stood about a foot shorter, with pleasant features. She wore daily work clothes. In each hand, she carried a bucket for the morning milking.

He entered the back door of the barn. The cow lowed. He ignored the animal to hide behind the haystack and watch for her arrival. He drew back when the door opened. Didn't want to give away his presence too soon.

"Easy, Mabyn," she spoke. She put down the buckets to pat the cow. "I'm here to ease your discomfort."

"How about easing my discomfort first?" He sprung out from behind the haystack to snatch her in his arms.

She let out a startled cry of surprise then grunted in mock anger. "Razi! Why scare half the life out of me?"

He smiled. "Just having a little fun." He kissed her; a long, lingering kiss. "Oh, how I've missed you, Janel." He held her close.

"Ay. You were gone longer this time."

"It couldn't be helped," he said with dismay.

"If you told me where you were, I would have written, every day."

He kissed her right hand. "I would have cherished your letters. Alas, I'm not at liberty to say."

Mabyn mooed louder so Janel led Razi out the back door. "Why can't you tell me where you go? Are we not betrothed?"

"Not officially."

"My family would approve."

He avoided eye contact. "You know my father would not."

She touched his face to make him look at her. "If I could talk with him, I know I could win him over."

He let out a sharp ironic laugh. "Impossible."

"Why? Are you so ashamed of me that you won't introduce me?"

"No!" He took her in his arms. "You are the best thing that has ever happened to me! Subjecting you to my father is not something I want to do. For your sake, not his."

Concerned filled her blue eyes. "You make him sound so awful."

He struggled for words. "He's—difficult. All my life I have tried to please him; be what he wants me to be. Since knowing you this past year, I realize what he wants is not what I want." He stroked her cheek.

"You fear he would disown you?"

He cocked a wry grin. "That's putting it mildly."

She withdrew from him, her voice hurt in speaking. "So you're afraid to tell him you've fallen in love with someone beneath your station while continuing to visit me and play with my heart?"

"No! No." He snatched her hands to stop her retreat. "My fear is for you. He is powerful, and the harsh repercussion on you and your family is something I want to avoid. That is why I tried to stay away. Permanently. To protect you, but I can't. My heart won't let me. Your love and faith are a balm to my soul. Without you I am lost and incomplete." He swallowed back his rising emotion. "The problem is I don't know how much longer I can keep our relationship a secret, and when he does learn—"

"My dearest Razi, I'm not without resources. My father is well-respected in the province, and you know my uncle is the Vicar."

He grimaced. "My father would be enraged beyond measure to learn of your uncle."

She compassionately regarded him. "He sounds like a man full of hate."

"You have no idea." He tenderly touched her hair. "For your sake, perhaps it is best ..." Her swift hand on his lips stopped further words.

"Don't say it! Don't ever say it. I love you and I don't care who your father is. I too am incomplete without you. Whenever you say, I will leave my family to marry you."

"Pray it can be soon." He kissed her, more urgently than before.

Upon hearing the insistent mooing coming from the barn, Janel began to laugh.

"Wonderful. After all this, a cow comes between us," he snickered.

"Mabyn running off brought us together. Me knee deep in mud trying to get her out of the bog, and you laughing before agreeing to help me." She playfully struck him.

"Janel!" the voice of her mother called. "What's wrong with Mabyn?"

"Go quickly. I need to be about my chores." She shoved him toward the woods.

"First you scold me for being gone too long, now you tell me to leave," he teased.

"Tonight. The usual time and place." She hurried to the barn door where she paused, blew him a kiss then waved him away.

In deep consideration, Razi wandered back into the wood. What began as a chance meeting a year ago, blossomed into something wonderful and unexpected. He didn't seek romance. In fact, he had no agenda save to get away and wander the countryside unhindered. Those rare times he relished the freedom. Coming upon a girl struggling to get a cow out of the mire was amusing at first. His strength came in handy to help, yet not before both became caked in mud from head to toe.

Finding a pool of water, they cleaned the cow then submersed themselves, clothes and all. Under the warmth of the sun, they sat and talked until sundown. Not until the second meeting did he learn her name. From that day, he took every available chance to leave his seclusion and visit the farm. They laughed and shared childhood stories, those he chose to tell. When they first kissed, nothing else existed. He became anxious for the next time he could see her. When duty interrupted his visits, he grew frustrated by a soulful longing he fought hard against.

During those times apart, he tried to deny his love for Janel. The more he tried to resist, the more he realized how deeply she affected him. To take their relationship any further was dangerous. He came to tell her they were better off apart. Upon sight of her, his heart leapt for joy. Being near her provided a balm to his troubled mind and spirit. Hearing that she felt the same incompleteness and willing to be with him no matter what, bolstered his heart. Unfortunately, it didn't change the situation. Very soon a choice would have to be made. She mentioned her uncle the Vicar. *Right! The Vicar of Jor'el. What irony.*

"Well, you look deep in thought."

Startled, Razi reached for his sword, ready for danger. He snarled in annoyance at seeing his twin brother Ram. The only physical difference between them was the thin goatee Ram wore. "What are you doing here?" he demanded.

"I can ask you the same thing. She is pretty, by the way."

Alarmed, he snatched Ram's arm with a hard jerk. "What do you know?"

Ram removed Razi's hand. "You are playing a dangerous game." When Razi marched off Ram followed. "Father will want to know."

Razi stopped to confront him. "Not a word to him or …"

"Or what? You'll fight me? Your twin? You haven't got it in you."

"Push me and you'll know what I do or don't have in me."

Ram slyly grinned. "So the wench has given you courage."

"Mind your tongue!"

Ram's smile faded into a warning expression. "If the relationship is a dalliance, I will keep your secret. Move to something more, and I will tell Father."

Razi's fists clenched to contain his reaction at the threat. However, the statement told him of Ram's ignorance to the seriousness of the relationship. This meant Ram only observed and didn't hear the conversation. It also meant Ram was sent to spy on him. Not surprising. Their father kept them in seclusion, only allow them to see the light of day on his whim or when they managed to get away unnoticed. Razi thought he eluded anyone following. The fact it was Ram may be advantageous, since his brother considered himself a ladies man. Keeping Ram believing Janel was just a dalliance would protect her, and gain him time before making the final decision. Thus he forced himself to relax and say, "Agreed."

Ram smiled. He tossed an arm about Razi's shoulder to steer him in a certain direction. "Word reached him that her time is short. He has given permission to visit her. Which is why I came to find you."

"I suppose this is his last gesture of good will toward her."

"You can't blame him. She is weak minded and annoying," said Ram with indifference.

"She's our mother!"

"She gave us life. He's given us purpose. Don't forget that."

Razi bit the inside of his mouth to keep from replying. Ram goaded him about their mother to start an argument. Only four times since their weaning were they permitted them to visit her. Over the last eighteen months her health deteriorated to the point of dying. Razi wanted to see her when word first came, only his father forbade it. This change of heart was welcomed, yet also cause for suspicion. His father would hardly turn merciful toward a woman he scorned and only used to give him an heir, or two, in this case.

They arrived where Razi tethered his horse. Ram's horse was there also. Razi asked, "When can we leave?"

Ram's arm came off of Razi's shoulder so they could mount. "When we like, I suppose. He didn't say. I had to find you after you snuck off."

"You could have given me the whole day to be out," chided Razi.

"Oh, you have another rendezvous with the wench?" Receiving warning glare from Razi, Ram put up his hand in mock surrender. "I said I won't mention her to Father, but can't I tease you?"

"Since when is your teasing good-natured?" Razi jerked his horse's reins to turn its head for departure.

"Oh my. You are touchy. I do not let my liaisons get to me. It's easier to deal with them. A lesson you should learn, little brother."

"Stop calling me little!"

"You were born a minute after me, which makes you the youngest. Besides, you are a bit smaller than me."

"Not much. What I lack in comparative brawn, I make up for in brains."

Ram laughed, this time with affection. "That is why Father has great plans for us. With my strength and your brains, we are unstoppable!"

Razi grinned. He may have reservations about their father, and worried about the discovery of Janel, but they were twins. He loved his brother. He sheepishly smiled. "Speaking of stopping, I need breakfast."

<hr/>

When Janel finished milking Mabyn, she placed some milk in a churn for butter and another portion in a curdling crock for cheese. She carried one full bucket back to the kitchen for the day's usage. She found her Uncle Avram in the kitchen with her parents, Clare and Dolan. Her two older brothers were also present: Kerwin, age twenty-two, and twenty year old Mace. Her father tried to comfort her weeping mother.

"What's wrong?" asked Janel.

"Uncle brought bad news about Toby," said Kerwin.

"He was nearly beaten to death," add Mace.

Janel paled with fright at the report of their youngest brother.

"He will recover," said Avram in an attempt to forestall more upset.

"He never should have been sent to the camp!" chided Kerwin.

"Softly! Your mother is upset enough. Uncle did all he could to help Toby," said Dolan.

"He's the Vicar! He can grant clemency and have Toby released."

Avram put up a hand to stop Dolan's reply. He spoke directly to Kerwin; his voice level and compassionate. "I understand your anger at my unwillingness to show favoritism. I did so in order to act independently and not come under suspicion because of our relationship. I have gathered evidence to prove Toby's innocence."

"Why haven't you told us before now?"

"Because I just finished compiling it the other day. I intended to go before Dagar and the judges at the end of the week. Now, after this incident, and armed with new evidence, I can grant clemency without imputing the law. Once Toby is recovered, he and Judson will be free to return home without repercussions."

Clare embraced Avram. "Thank you."

He held her. "You know I love Toby. I love all of you. It has pained me that I could not act before now."

"I'm returning to the Fortress with you to tend to Toby."

He smiled. "Why do think I came in my carriage instead of on horseback?"

"Janel, finish serving breakfast then take a count of the daily egg, cheese and butter rations for the grocer's arrival."

"Mama, I want to go with you."

Clare took Janel's hand. "If there is a need, I will send for you. Besides, someone needs to look after things here."

"Ay. We men folk don't know what to do without our women," said Dolan.

"Then you need to find wives for your sons." Clare kissed Dolan's cheek then fetched her cloak off a peg near the kitchen door.

Once they were gone, Dolan embraced Janel. "Avram said the premiere Guardian physician is tending Toby at the request of Captain Kell. All will be well."

"It'll be well when he's home," groused Kerwin. He poured hot tea into a cup from a pot on the stove.

Dolan sarcastically snickered. "Your mother's right, I need to get you married so you can harass someone else with your complaints."

Mace laughed.

"You too!" said Dolan to Mace. "I was married for two years by the time I reached Kerwin's age, and with a child on the way."

Kerwin took a seat at the table. He flashed a wry grin. "Me being the child. So you've told us over and over again."

Mace joined Kerwin at the table. His teasing gleam mirrored his older brother's expression. "I think you'll have better luck with Janel than Kerwin. Especially with *him* around."

"What?" she gasped in surprise and nearly dropped the platter of eggs onto the table.

The brothers laughed. Kerwin winked at Mace to pick up the teasing. "Don't act so surprised, little sister. Did you think you could keep this mystery man a secret?"

"What man? What are you talking about?" Dolan's gaze shifted between his sons and Janel.

"Nothing! They're making it up." She sneered at her brothers.

"Oh, really?" Mace returned Kerwin's wink. "Then who is the tall, blond man I saw you with behind the barn this morning?"

This time Janel dropped a cup of hot tea, breaking the cup and spilling the tea.

"So there is a man." Dolan said with certainty at her reaction.

Seeing her upset, Kerwin helped her clean the spill. "Come, Janel. We only tease you. You are our sister and we will always look out for you." He put the broken cup on the sideboard.

She dropped the wet cloth next to the sink. "He's someone I met a year ago. He helped me when Mabyn ran off and got stuck in the muddy bank."

"That long?" Dolan asked. "Why not tell us about him before now?"

She ushered her father to his usual place at the table. "Sit and I will explain."

Kerwin returned to his seat beside Mace and across from Janel. The brothers helped themselves to the food.

Razi may be hesitant about his father, but she felt no hesitation about her family. In fact, she fought keeping a secret from them. It would be good to tell them, at least to a point. She sat beside her father, and couldn't help smiling as she began to speak.

"His name is Razi."

"An unusual name," said Dolan. He began to eat breakfast.

"He's an unusual man." Her smile beamed with great fondness.

"You mean because you fancy him," said Kerwin.

"Ay." She blushed.

"What else can you tell us about him?" asked Dolan.

"He's tall, strong, very kind and gentle, with a great sense of humor."

"Bring him by so we can meet him."

Janel became hesitant. "I want to and so does he, but—he is of nobility."

Dolan nodded with understanding. "His family wouldn't approve of him marrying beneath his station."

"We're not far from nobility," chided Kerwin. "He knows our uncle is the Vicar of Jor'el, doesn't he? That should count for something. Not to mention father is a wealthy farmer and well respected in the province."

She nodded, fearing to speak due to rising emotions.

Dolan held her shoulder. "I suppose it is too late for me to advise you not to lose your heart."

"We both have. He told me he is trying to win over his father."

"Who is his father?"

She knitted her brows in thought. "He never said his name—to protect me until he can secure his favor," she added to Kerwin's scoff.

"Some protection."

Irate, she stood. "It's true!"

"Easy, little sister." Kerwin rose to face her and ask a direct question. "Tell me true, is this Razi so worthy of your love and devotion that you defend him to us?"

"Ay! He loves me, despite what obstacle his father presents. He told me so this morning when Mace spied on me."

"Not spying! I was returning from gathering wood and saw you both."

"A year you've kept this a secret, daughter," Dolan reminded her.

Deflated, Janel sat. "I didn't want to. Like he is protecting me, I want to protect him."

"You don't trust us?"

"Not a matter of trust, Papi. A single mistake or loose-lipped servant can cause trouble. I'm only telling you now because of Mace!" She glared at her brother. "If Razi comes to harm because of this, I'll never speak to you again!" Upset, she rushed out the door.

She ran as far as the chicken coop before bursting into tears. She sat on a utility box and buried her face in her hands. She yearned to tell her family, but not the way it happened. She sat up at feeling someone embrace her about the shoulder. Mace sat beside her.

"I'm sorry. I didn't mean to hurt you. I got caught up in teasing. I know," he added, to forestall her argument, "I should have spoken to you privately and not let myself be carried away."

She still didn't speak; she couldn't for anger, hurt and frustration.

He marked her silence. "You love him so much?"

"Ay."

"Then I wish you both the best and hope everything works out. The last thing I want is to lose my sister in a fit of anger." He embraced her and kissed her cheek. "Will you come back to the house now?"

She nodded and wiped her eyes. "Only please, let's not speak of it again. At least not until things are worked out."

"I promise. And I'm sure Papi and Kerwin will agree."

Chapter 3

FOR THE REST OF THE DAY JANEL TENDED TO HER CHORES. Her thoughts wandered between Toby's condition and nervousness at seeing Razi again. Naturally, she felt relief that Toby would recover, but also disturbed by the entire situation. She considered how to tell Razi that her family knew about him. Even though Razi kept his father's identity a secret, she couldn't find fault for protecting her. After all, marriages outside of one's station were rare. Some caused horrid repercussions, even deadly family feuds.

After supper, her father and brothers settled down in the parlor. Dolan read while the brothers played cards. Janel took a cloak off a peg by the kitchen door and left. She didn't need a lantern or candle since she knew the way. Besides, light from the house and the oil lamp near the barn provided enough illumination.

She emerged from the wood behind the barn into a small grove. A stream gently flowed through the grove. Razi rose from sitting on the log to greet her with a warm embrace and lengthy kiss. He held her close against the night chill.

"With winter coming we shouldn't meet at night anymore. It's too cold for you," he said.

He wore no cloak or gloves, so she asked, "Aren't you cold?"

"No, but I'm more than happy to keep you warm."

They sat together on the log. She snuggled next to him. It felt good to be in his arms, yet tonight there was a twinge of regret and worry. "Razi," she softly began. "Something happened today that I must tell you and I hope you won't be angry."

"Why should I become angry?"

"It concerns our relationship. My brother, Mace, saw us together this morning." She sat up, anxious for his reaction. "I had to tell my family, especially after learning about poor Toby."

He became baffled. "Toby? Your younger brother? What does he have to do with us?"

"The news of what happened to him led to a discussion about us. You remember I told you my uncle is the Vicar. When I returned to the house after milking Mabyn, he arrived with bad news. He told us how Toby was nearly beaten to death at the labor camp. "

Razi grew concerned. "Will he survive?"

"Ay. Mama went to the Fortress to help care for Toby. She sent word of the details only it's hard to believe. Most of them I've met are kind and generous. Including Captain Kell and Lieutenant Armus."

"What?" he asked in confusion.

"Toby was beaten by a Guardian."

He reeled as if punched. "Are you certain of this?"

Though curious of his reaction, she replied. "Ay. Uncle said they believe it to be a rogue Guardian. Captain Kell is investigating."

He bolted up to begin pacing.

"Razi? What's wrong?"

He was slow to respond. "I'm sorry. This is stunning news, though I was going to tell you we were seen by my brother."

"You have a brother?"

"Twin. We're nearly identical. Only he wears a goatee. Says he's tired of looking at mirror when he see me."

She lightly chuckled at his humor. "Then you're not angry I had to tell them?"

"No." Razi joined her back on the log. "You said the news of Toby led to a discussion about us, how?"

She rolled her eyes. "Brotherly teasing after Mama left with Uncle. Papi, Kerwin and Mace are willing to meet you. I explained how your father would not approve and asked them to keep our secret until you could convince him. What of your brother? Did you tell him about me?"

Razi flashed a wry smile. "Discreetly. I don't want him blabbing to our father before I can convince him."

"When will that be?"

He shook his head with uncertainty. "I wish I knew. Meeting in the dark or snatching a kiss isn't what I want for us."

"Do you think," she began to make a suggestion, then briefly balked at seeing his questioning glance before continuing. "If we told him *after* the fact he would be more accepting?"

"You mean tell him after we're wed?" he asked with consideration. "I thought of that also. I don't think it will lessen the blow, but I would certainly be a complete and happy man." He held her close.

"Then let's do so."

He tilted her head to gaze deeply into her eyes. "I won't risk exposing you to his anger."

"I'm not afraid. I trust you with my heart, and know you will protect me. My family will protect us both."

"They don't know me."

"They know me, love me and trust me. Kerwin and Mace are horrible at teasing, but would never let any harm come to me. They agreed to keep our secret because I asked them."

His brows furrowed in bewilderment. "Hard to imagine they agreed based only on your word."

She gently touched his arm to get his attention. "Have you ever trusted anyone based solely on a word? Or am I the first?"

"You are the first I have ever loved or trusted with anything. Even with something as simple as keeping your word to meet me."

She grew sympathetic at his confession. "Poor, Razi, to grow up without love or trust. Now, I understand why this is so difficult for you. Be assured, my family will embrace you without question and treat you like a son and brother. That is how much they love me."

Razi embraced her, while struggling to keep his emotions in check. "All I ever wanted was to experience love. We were taken from our mother as toddlers."

"You have not seen her since?"

"Four times in eighteen years. We received word she is dying. I don't know if I'll get to see her before—It depends on him," he scoffed with visible hurt and anger.

"You're of age to make your own way."

"It's not that simple."

"It can be, if you want it."

He kissed each of her hands. "I do, only I'm still afraid for you."

"Don't be. If my uncle marries us, your father will have to deal with the Vicar of Jor'el and not a simple priest to be bullied."

He laughed, more in relief than humor. "What irony!"

"No more hesitation. You can have all you want, me, love, a family, freedom to see your mother again. If we start walking now we can reach the Fortress by midnight."

Razi pulled Janel to her feet. "We'll do better." He whistled. A brief moment later, his horse appeared. "Are you certain about this?"

"I've never been more certain of anything."

He held her gaze, intent and probing. "You won't change your mind if some day you learn who my father is?"

"No, because I believe in my heart that you are nothing like you father." She embraced him.

Razi laughed with genuine relief and nearly shouted, "Indeed, I am nothing like my father!" He lifted Janel onto the saddle then mounted behind her.

* * *

At the Fortress, Avram just got into bed when the captain of the guard entered.

"Pardon, Vicar, your niece is here."

"Janel? I wonder if something is wrong? Can't be Toby." He thought out loud then tossed aside the covers to rise. "Admit her to the antechamber. I'll be there in a moment." Thought it was not unusual to receive guests at odd hours, under the circumstances, Janel's arrival caused concern.

After putting on his slippers and robe, he entered the antechamber. He discovered she wasn't alone. A very tall and good-looking young man stood with her. "Janel? Is something wrong? You shouldn't be worried about Toby. Eldric took him, Judson and your mother to Melwynn for their recovery."

"Melwynn?" asked Razi.

"Ay." Avram stared at the young man. "Castle of the Guardians. Eldric is the premiere Guardian physician in charge of Toby's care."

Razi smiled. "I've heard of Melwynn. Along with Arundine."

Avram's eyes narrowed in concentration. "Have we met?"

"No, sir. I've not had the pleasure of making your acquaintance."

"Really? You look oddly familiar."

Razi blushed. He awkwardly shifted his weight from one foot to another.

Janel linked her arm with Razi. She smiled, wide and happy. "We came with a request of you, dear uncle."

Avram grew suspicious at her speech along with the closeness of the young people. "What request, *niece?*"

"That you marry us. Tonight."

"Tonight? Isn't this rather sudden? What about your family?"

"Not sudden. Razi and I have known each other for a year."

Avram drew to his full height with ire. "Known? How well?"

Razi stiffened at the implication. "Not in that way, I assure you, sir! Our relationship is strictly honorable."

Avram cocked a curious brow. "Then why the rush? And where is your family, young lady?"

"I spoke to Papi, Kerwin and Mace earlier today. Mother was here with Toby and now you tell me they are at Melwynn, so I can't speak to them. This is the only time available."

Avram crossed his arms. "Yet your father and older brothers didn't accompany you."

"I have their agreement," she insisted. At his stubbornness, she left Razi to approach him. "Uncle, I have ever lied to you?"

He huffed a laugh. "You know the consequences if you did."

"Ay," she smiled with sweet confidence. "It is also out of love and respect that I don't lie. So I tell truly, I have their agreement."

Avram addressed Razi. "What of your family, sir?"

"That is a bit trickier, I'm afraid."

Janel returned to Razi's side. "Razi is of nobility, which is why he may look familiar to you. It is a situation you should well understand, *Uncle.*"

Avram scowled in mild annoyance then explained to a baffled Razi. "My late beloved wife was of nobility. Her family frowned upon our marriage. Becoming Vicar, only earned begrudging respect. Your case is similar in marrying beneath your station." For a brief moment, he studied Razi, who withstood the scrutiny. Finally, he asked, "Do you love my niece enough to go against your family's wishes?"

"Ay, sir," he declared. Razi drew Janel close to his side.

"Enough to come to you at this hour, with discretion, as you once did, Uncle."

Avram laughed. "I need to remember certain stories are not to be told in the presence of youngsters. They tend to use them to their advantage at the most inopportune times." He waved at them. "Go to the private chapel. I'll change and meet you there."

"Thank you, Uncle!" She embraced him and kissed him on both cheeks.

"Do you plan on returning to the farm tonight?"

Janel blushed while Razi heaved a hapless shrug.

Avram chuckled. "You didn't think past the obvious. I'll order a guest room prepared. Now, go to the chapel."

<hr />

The following morning, Razi and Janel left the Fortress as husband and wife. Avram lent her one of his horses for the return trip. Their glances and smiles showed they would prefer to ride together. In fact, it surprised Avram that they left so soon. Razi insisted, claiming that being gone too long could cause trouble. He wanted to avoid that, considering what he had to tell his father.

As they rode, Razi became lost in thought. He never imagined the bliss or warmth being with a woman could bring. He loved Janel. After last night, he felt so full of joy and satisfaction he barely contained himself. His feelings became tempered by the thought of his father and brother's reaction to his sudden happiness. However, he would not turn back. What they offered him paled compared to Janel and the future before them. It's as if being with her shielded him from everything.

"Hello?"

"Uh? Oh," he chuckled. "I was thinking."

"About me?"

"Naturally."

"Funny. I was thinking about you. I can't wait for you to meet my family. In fact, the farm is around the bend."

Razi took a deep breath to calm his suddenly racing heart. Not many things frightened him. Being so much larger than most, one look at him and any thoughts of confrontation vanished. Then again, he just married in the dead of night, and about to meet his wife's father and two older brothers. In this case, his size might not matter.

Upon nearing the house, two men led saddled horses from the corral.

"Who are they?" asked Razi.

Janel didn't answer to hail them. "Mace! Kerwin."

Razi swallowed back the lump in his throat when the men responded by leaving the horses and running towards them

"Where have you been, young lady?" demanded Kerwin.

"At the Fortress." Janel let Mace help her down.

"Visiting Uncle?"

"In a manner of speaking," she giggled. She motioned for Razi to dismount.

"He is the man I saw yesterday," said Mace.

Razi stood eight inches taller then either of the brothers. Still, Kerwin let Razi know his wariness by glaring up and down at him.

"Here now! Janel!" Dolan rushed over. "Where have you been, girl? You had us worried sick. We've been up since dawn looking for you."

"She went to the Fortress to visit Uncle," said Kerwin.

"What? Why? And who is this?"

"The mystery man, Papi," said Mace.

"Oh?" Dolan confronted Razi. "Were you at the Fortress with her?"

"Ay."

Janel moved between her father and Razi. "Papi, this is Razi … my husband."

A stunned moment of silence followed her announcement as Dolan, Kerwin and Mace digested the news. Suddenly, Dolan started laughing.

"Papi? What's so funny? She ran off and got married!" chided Kerwin.

"We've known each other a year!" she insisted.

"Then when did you decide to marry?"

"Ay. You didn't say anything about it yesterday," said Mace.

"Last night. Once our secret was discovered, we thought it best."

Dolan laughed so hard, he sat on the ground and fought to breath.

"Papi!" insisted Kerwin.

"She did the same as your uncle, and had him perform the ceremony!" he laughed in explanation.

Janel knelt beside her father. "I told you I love Razi. You're not too disappointed are you, Papi?"

Dolan took a few breaths to calm his humor. "You are so like your mother. Even after we married it took me years to tame her, but a better woman cannot be found." He took her arm and they stood. He approached Razi, who wore a guarded half-smile. When Dolan cleared his throat to speak, Razi jerked to attention. "So you defied your family to marry my only daughter?"

"Ay, sir." Razi thought his size wouldn't matter when dealing with her family. However, size was hard to ignore when he spoke with determination and authority. A hint of intimidation passed over Dolan's brow then disappeared when Dolan grinned.

"Taking such a risk requires courage."

"My father would consider it cowardice," droned Razi.

Dolan stared at Razi to ask, "You have regrets?"

"Not about marrying Janel! I love her. And will defend her even against my father," said Razi in stout reply.

Dolan patted Razi's arm. "Spoken like Avram when the baron confronted him."

"The Vicar mentioned something about it last night."

"He pressed Razi with hard questions, yet still agreed to marry us," said Janel.

"I expect nothing less from Avram." Dolan turned to Razi. "Your answers must have satisfied him." He took Razi's hand in a vigorous shake. "Welcome to the family, *son*."

The gesture and familiar address stymied Razi. "Really?"

"Indeed. I trust my daughter's judgment, *and* you passed Avram's examination."

Razi smiled with genuine relief. He clasped Dolan's hand.

"Well," began Mace to Kerwin. "I guess we have another brother. Bound to happen sooner or later." He held out his hand to Razi. "Welcome to the family."

"Thank you."

"Welcome." Kerwin nodded. He didn't shake hands.

"Come inside for breakfast." Dolan took Razi by the arm to steer him to the house.

"I'm afraid I must decline," said Razi with regret. "I've already been gone too long. I must deal with my father as soon as possible. Please, watch over Janel until I return."

"Razi?" she said in dispute.

"I must go. Alone and immediately." He nodded toward Dolan. "Familiar with the Vicar's past, your father understands what I must do. My father has a fierce temper that I will not subject you to enduring."

"You make it sound final," she said with distress.

"No!" He smiled and held her hands. "I will return for you, I promise. I just don't know when."

Dolan stepped forward to take Janel from Razi. "He's right, you will be safer here." He addressed Razi. "Although I wish you had spoken to me first, we look forward to your return and getting to know you."

"As do I, sir."

"Papi."

Razi's smile quiver slightly as he said, "Papi."

"Jor'el go with you, brother, and bring you back soon," said Mace,

"Thank you."

Janel's smile grew tearful. She blew him a kiss as he rode from the house. This was the most difficult parting Razi had ever experienced. Her family proved to be everything she said. They embraced him without reservation, question or suspicion. Whatever the outcome, he now had a place to call home and people to call family.

46

Chapter 4

TWILIGHT FADED. DAGAR STOOD ON THE PORTICO OF THE Palace conversing with another Guardian. Instead of his warrior's uniform, he wore a white shirt beneath a scarlet doublet trimmed in gold. Breeches matched the doublet. His boots and belt were finely crafted black leather. The other Guardian, Hueil, stood a tad shorter, clean-shaven, yellow hair and icy blue eyes. He wore a scholar's robe of dark blue and silver over his powder blue and gold brocade suit. Hueil served to relay the Almighty's words and laws to the mortal priestly scribes.

Armus' arrival interrupted the conversation. "What is this, Dagar?" He motioned to the suit.

"I thought to spice up my position with a little flare. Like it?"

"Has Kell seen you?"

"Not yet." Dagar heaved a carefree shrug. "Why should I be confined to the trappings of a warrior?"

"Because you were created a warrior."

"All Guardians are created not requiring food to sustain our lives, but you revel in the mortal art of cooking."

Armus' scowl turned to Hueil. "At least you're maintaining decorum."

"My job doesn't entail hob-knobbing with mortals who consider themselves aristocrats."

Dagar clapped Hueil's shoulder and continued with his humor. "One look at Hueil and they could mistake him for any scholar or businessman, while you," he screwed his lips in consideration of Armus. "Well, no one would mistake you for anything other than a warrior no matter what clothes you wore. Even dressed like this, I can maintain the superior attitude befitting a Trio Leader in dealing with mortals while preserving the discipline of a warrior."

Armus frowned in disapproval. "I hope you're joking? We're not superior."

"Oh, no? We're immortal, intelligent and powerful. That alone makes us superior to mortals."

"Not in service."

"Ay, but why can't we enjoy ourselves while serving?" Dagar flashed a toothy grin of retort.

Hueil moved closer to Armus. He spoke in a semi-private tone. "I think you should drop the argument. In case you hadn't noticed, he's in one of his moods."

Armus huffed a laugh. "Not after Kell sees him." He moved to enter the main building.

"Kell's not here." Dagar's irate tone stopped Armus.

"Where is he?"

"At Arundine. The meeting starts within the hour."

"I'll see you there." Armus disappeared in a white flash of light.

Dagar sneered. His ire clearly visible, which prompted Hueil to say, "I warned you about provoking him and Kell. Better yet, don't anger Jor'el. Your attitude has been noticed."

"What? That I like my existence and enjoy the finer things?"

Seeing several Guardians and mortal scribes nearby, Hueil drew Dagar into the shadow of the portico. "No, your degrading and condescending attitude toward the mortals and duty."

Dagar snorted an ironic grunt. "Speaking of degrading, you haven't embraced your responsibilities these last two hundred years."

"Don't change the subject. I'm not the one suddenly parading around in a new suit of clothes while making taunting and insulting remarks about mortals."

"You use your position to subtly challenge a mortal's mind by a clever misuse of Jor'el's own words." Dagar's voice became a harsh whisper. "How would it go with you, if say, Kell learns of your little changes?"

Hueil's eye narrowed in wariness. "You wouldn't?"

"Don't press me, or you will find out." Dagar removed Hueil's hand from his arm. He left the portico.

Cautious and concerned, Hueil watched Dagar's departure. In doing so, he caught sight of Vidar and Wren, the premier archer's protégé. She was stunningly beautiful with long auburn hair, bright green eyes and flawless complexion. Wren dressed similarly to Vidar in forester's clothes and armed with a bolt-action crossbow.

Hueil assumed a pleasant expression as he moved from the portico to greet them. "If you're here at Kell's request, he left word for all Trio Leaders are to met him at Arundine."

"We know. We're looking for Armus," said Vidar.

"He left for Arundine a few moments ago."

"Hueil!" A mortal dressed in similar scribe robes, frantically waved from a doorway across the compound.

Hueil heaved an exasperated sigh. "Excuse me, but it seems I've been away too long. It's a wonder anything can get done without me." He spoke the last sentence as he moved off.

"You don't think it's spreading, do you? He sounded rather put out," said Wren.

"Hueil has always been more caustic in demeanor than Dagar." Vidar's eyes narrowed in watching Hueil enter the other building. He became distracted when the Vicar crossed his line of sight in a rush to approach the building housing the military offices. The Vicar snapped at a person who crossed his path and made him veer slightly off his course. A rather unusual display of anger from the Vicar.

"Return to the province. I want you and Dax to keep an eye on things," said Vidar.

"What are we looking for?" she asked.

"Anything to suggest that discontent is spreading among our ranks."

"And the mortals?"

"If you can get any of them to talk, fine, but I'm not sure it's reached that point yet. Many still remember Radnor."

Wren shivered with discomposure. "Hard to forget."

Vidar gave her an encouraging smile. "Go. I'll join you after the meeting."

Wren took a step back and disappeared in dimension travel.

Vidar went to find the Vicar. Something disturbed the mortal and he might be attempting to call upon Kell. Sure enough, he found Avram outside of Kell's office. He became certain of the mortal's disturbance when Avram seized his arm.

"I was told Kell is at Arundine. Will you join him there?" asked Avram, his voice anxious.

"I was on my way when I saw you. Something wrong with the boys?"

Avram dismissed the question with a wave. "No. Eldric reports they are well." He drew Vidar away from the guards to speak confidentially. "When you see Kell, tell him I *must* speak to him at his first opportunity. I fear the possibility of what I just saw."

"What?"

Avram vehemently shook his head. "Just tell Kell!"

"Very well."

"Now, I must try to calm myself to think clearly." In an agitated state, Avram left.

<hr />

In the forest of Midessex, in the heart of Allon itself, stood Arundine, Council Hall of the Guardians. A small domed shrine of white marble, built similarly to the Temple of Providence. The interior was larger than anticipated by the exterior. Twelve pillars held up the dome while twelve chairs formed in a semi-circle facing the high chair, which sat on an elevated platform reached by two steps. Marble floor titles were arranged to form the map of Allon with the name of each province in front of its respective chair. The closest chair to the platform on the left side occupied a place of honor. This was reserved for the Region of

Sanctuary. On the right was the Southern Forest, the least prosperous of the twelve provinces. Kell stood at the bottom of the elevated platform deep in thought. His gaze shifted between each province marked on the floor map.

Jor'el divided Allon into twelve provinces, Highlands, Northern Forest, Southern Forest, North Plains, South Plains, Lowlands, Meadowlands, Midessex, West Coast, East Coast, Delta and the Region of Sanctuary. Each province was lead by the Trio, three Guardians acting in the best interest of the province. They interacted with mortals to ensure justice, free flowing commerce and protection. Under the command of the Trio, other Guardians served in whatever capacity required. The numbers varied according to the need of each province. Of the Trio, the Leader reported to Kell or directly to Jor'el if summoned into the Almighty's presence. The Trio Leaders formed the Guardian Council.

The Council met once a month at Arundine for updates and exchange of information. Only three times did they meet for something other than the usual business of government. Twice was to repel invaders. The worst time dealt with rebellious mortals terrorizing the countryside in armed revolt. They bore grudges against Jor'el, the Guardians or anyone else who they felt oppressed them. When the number swelled to ten thousand, Kell assembled the Council to inform them that Jor'el appointed him to lead a company of warriors to stop the rebels. The rest would hold in reserve, if needed.

Despite the vast numerical difference, the forces met on the plain outside the city of Radnor. Before the battle, Kell sent a Guardian from the scholar caste with terms to negotiate. The mortals would have none of it. They viciously attacked the Guardian with anything they could and burned him with hot oil. The scholar survived since mortals can't kill Guardians. However, the incident showed Kell that he had to be decisive in dealing with the rebels.

A bloody battle ensued with most of the mortals killed. A few managed to escape, while the Guardians suffered only minor wounds.

The brutal results sent shockwaves through Allon. There had never been a violent and bloody clash between mortals and Guardians. Both sides regretted the actions of the day, though they acknowledged the necessity. The harsh memories of Radnor still lingered.

This would be the first time the Guardian Leadership came together to deal with one of their members. Oh, they dealt with problems, but not the questioning or trouble caused by a Trio Leader. Kell didn't look forward to it. Then again, he consoled himself with the thought that if the meeting went as planned; he may succeed in persuading Dagar to change his attitude.

Kell's gazed lifted from the floor to another warrior by the name of Avatar, who waited near the main door for the Trio Leaders. Avatar had silver eyes, bronze hair and a thin, trimmed goatee. He wore the same white uniform as Kell, including purple piping to symbolize his position as the captain's aide. Avatar was among the second group of Guardians created by Jor'el, and two hundred years younger than Kell and Armus.

Over the course of eight hundred years, Jor'el created a new group of Guardians every two hundred years. Like the Originals, each possessed special powers. However, since dealing with mortals could be tricky due to their passionate and sometimes irrational behavior, Kell instituted a mentoring program. From the day of their creation, Kell assigned the younger Guardians to an elder mentor to watch, observe and learn how to interact with mortals. The duration of the mentoring depended upon the caste: vassal, warrior, ranger, archer, scholar, etc. On average, it lasted two hundred to three hundred years. This ensured that all situations that could occur have occurred. Warriors took longer since they were the most powerful and bore a heavy responsibility for the security of Jor'el and Allon. Usually a close bond formed between mentors and protégés. In rare situations, the initial pairing didn't work out due the diverse personalities of the Guardians. Reassignment became necessary.

Avatar proved an exception, being mentored by both Kell and Armus. Aside from being highly skilled and combat savvy, Avatar proved intelligent, intuitive, very witty and personable. A deep friendship developed between the three of them. The same friendship occurred with Avatar and Mahon during the latter's apprenticeship to Avatar.

Armus arrived. He snickered at seeing Avatar. "Tired of the coast already or did Priscilla's flightiness prove too much?"

Avatar laughed. "For being second-in-command you are behind in intelligence. My assignment was to the West Coast, not the East Coast."

"Sorry. I forgot to tell you I changed his orders to help Mahon establish a new militia for Chase," said Kell.

"Then maybe I'll forget to tell you about Dagar's latest stunt."

"This ought to be good." Avatar followed Armus in approaching the platform

"Don't you have someplace else to go?" asked Armus

"No. I'm here for the meeting remember?" Avatar smirked and sat on the arm of the Southern Forest chair to listen.

White light appeared and faded to reveal Vidar.

"You're early," said Kell.

"I thought you would want to hear what I learned about Dagar before the meeting."

"This is getting better." Avatar slipped into the chair to get comfortable. One leg dangled over the arm.

"Protégés tend to take liberties, don't they?" said Vidar.

"Some more than others." Kell made an upward jerking motion with his thumb.

Avatar rose. "I'll go back to waiting at the door."

"Thirteen hundred is a wonderful time in a Guardian's life. Wren is going through the same awkward phase," Vidar dryly commented on Avatar's departure.

"It will be interesting to see how he responds when Mahon reaches the same age," said Armus.

"It explains Mahon's quirks, like mentor like protégé."

"What does that say about Kell and me with Avatar?"

Vidar mischievously smiled and heaved a shrug.

Kell grew impatient at the humor. "What did you want to tell me?"

"Captain," called Avatar.

The other Trio Leaders began arriving.

"We'll speak in private." Vidar moved to the Northern Forest chair.

Armus flashed an ironic smile as he patted Kell's arm. "Just expect Dagar to make a show." He took his position on the elevated platform standing to the left of the high chair from which Kell would preside over the meeting.

Kell mounted the platform. He didn't assume his seat since that signaled the opening of the meeting. "What do you mean?"

"You'll know at first sight of him."

Avatar moved from the front door to assume his position on the right side of the high chair; a privileged position as the captain's aide and member of the High Trio.

Kell knew the Leaders would be curious since a second meeting in a short time usually meant trouble. Hearing them converse, he loudly cleared his throat for attention. The Leaders moved to stand beside their respective chairs. He watched them, while contemplating what he had to say.

By the South Plains chair stood Raleigh, a redheaded, jade-eyed Guardian with the skills and capabilities to control the elements. Beside him stood Vidar, representing the Northern Forest. Next came Gresham of Midessex, a shrewd vassal with white hair and violet eyes. Jayden of the Delta was a brash, but keen warrior. Valmar of the Highlands was a warrior similar in appearance to Gresham, only his white hair made him look older. Lilith of the North Plains was one of the few female Leaders, and a cunning warrior with bronze hair and gold eyes. Beside her stood Hunter, a ranger from the Southern Forest. Instead of a sword he carried a quarterstaff and hunting knife. His bright forest green eyes spoke of keen observance. Like Avatar, he sported a thin goatee.

Next came Sloan of the Lowlands, another warrior. Chase, a sea Guardian of the West Coast, shared the responsibility of commanding Allon's naval forces with Gulliver. Beside him waited Priscilla of the East Coast, another Guardian capable of controlling elements. She was fair and elegant with long pale yellow hair past her waist. Part of her hair was braided and wound like a coiled crown on her head. Her sky blue eyes held a mischievous glint while the rich pink lips smiled. She wore a dress with various shades of light green. It reached her ankles and was gathered about the waist by a gold belt fastened with a shell buckle. Zanis, an archer from the Meadowlands, used a long bow as opposed to Vidar's bolt-action crossbow.

The Region of Sanctuary chair remained vacant. Dagar had yet to arrive. Kell tossed a guarded look to Armus, who mouthed the words, "*I warned you.*"

As if on cue, white light appeared in the threshold. Dagar. The reason for the warning became immediately obvious by his new suit. One more sign of Dagar's dissatisfaction. Kell fought to contain his displeasure. When he caught Dagar's eye, the latter smiled. Dagar casually made his way to his chair. Everyone watched him, since his change in clothes was hard to ignore.

Once standing beside the chair, Dagar spoke. "Good day, Captain."

Kell's gaze slowly turned from Dagar to address the Leaders. "Let us begin." They assumed a contrite posture of heads bowed. He continued. "We assemble to consult and seek Jor'el's wisdom in the performance of our duty to the Almighty and Allon." Kell sat and so did the Leaders. Armus and Avatar remained in their positions flanking Kell.

"I'm sure you are all wondering why I called this meeting so soon after the our monthly gathering. An unsettling incident involving some mortals in the Region of Sanctuary has come to my attention. It included complaints against governing." Kell noticed Dagar's guarded expression.

"Against me?"

"Not solely, rather the broader Guardian administration."

"Were you not aware of this incident?" Gresham asked Dagar.

"No, I just thought I had taken care of it."

"How?" asked Vidar.

"How else do you deal with misguided, malcontent teenage mortals?" came Dagar's flippant reply.

"That doesn't answer the question," said Kell.

Dagar took a breath to contain his visible annoyance. "By hard labor." Seeing Kell's prompting glance, he elaborated. "I put them to work on building a road to release their aggression in a more positive and constructive manner."

"The complaint mentioned a vicious beating with marks to prove it."

"Not by me!" rebuffed Dagar. He returned Kell's steady stare. "Why should I be held accountable if other mortals choose to issue their own form of justice?"

"They claim the beating came at the hands of a Guardian."

Dagar rolled his eyes. "Oh? And you believed them?" He turned to his fellow Leaders to continue his argument. "How many times have false accusations been made against us over the centuries? It took five hundred years before the mortals accepted the rule of their Creator. Then allowing the compound to be built so we could take our rightful place of authority."

"Rightful place? Jor'el created us for service," said Valmar.

Dagar waved in frustration. "You know what I mean."

"It sounded wrong."

"I apologize for my tone. It's been rather frustrating of late. When I believe I've broken through and reasoned with them, another crops up worse than the last. These two have been trouble for years."

"Some compassion might yield better results," commented Priscilla.

Dagar looked along his shoulder at her. Anger shown in his mahogany eyes. "What do you think hard labor is if not compassion to help effect a change when all else fails?"

Intimidated, she shied away.

"Dagar! Such hostility against a fellow Leader is unnecessary," scolded Kell.

"While the questioning of one is necessary?"

"We ask questions to understand. A serious problem occurred in your province. Like in the past, we meet to help when it grows beyond the ability of the Leader to effectively deal with matters. Priscilla made a suggestion *not* an accusation." Kell's argument did little to dissuade Dagar's smoldering anger. The warrior pressed his lips together to stop a reply. "Now," continued Kell, his voice less stern yet authoritative, "someone beat them. Whether they are using a Guardian as an excuse or not, such violence will not be tolerated. I intend to find out which—"

"No!" Dagar said in vehement objection. "I will learn who did it. There is no need to trouble yourself, Captain."

"My initial inquiries caused enough concern to call this meeting. I would be derelict in my duty not to investigate." Kell allowed his ire to affect his voice.

Dagar barely managed to maintain a level voice. "If you had spoken to me in private, this meeting would not have been necessary, Captain."

"By your attitude, I think it is," said Vidar.

Dagar leaned forward to hotly confront Vidar. "Meaning?"

"The captain is concerned for *you* along with the mortals of your province. We have all experienced the frustration and annoyance dealing with mortals can sometimes bring. Coming together to consult about the issues helps us to cope."

"That is what I meant when I suggested compassion," Priscilla dared to speak.

Dagar's jowls flexed. He sat back in an attempt to regain his temper. He gazed at the group from under shrouded brows.

"You are obviously affected by the situation and understandably sensitive," said Gresham.

Dagar's glowering eyes shifted between Vidar, Priscilla and Gresham. After a moment of heavy silence, he spoke to Kell. "Your intention may have been for my benefit. However, I wish you had spoke to me first."

Kell nodded in acknowledgement. "Perhaps. Be assured, no offense or harm was intended. Open and honest communication among us is the best way to stay on task—and be unified in our duty and efforts to *serve*." He placed emphasis on the word.

"Then allow me to pursue my own investigation first—and *if* I find something that warrants your involvement, I will tell you."

For a moment, Kell contemplated the offer. The objective of the meeting was to confront Dagar's deteriorating attitude among his peers. He achieved that end. Taking it further would be unnecessary. Thus, he assumed a more agreeable posture. "Very well. You have until our next meeting."

Dagar pushed himself up from his chair and marched from Arundine. A flash of light signaled his departure.

"I guess we're done," said Sloan to Hunter.

"It would appear so." Thoughtful, Hunter stared at the door.

"To your duty return," Kell spoke the closing sentence. He remained seated as the Leaders either vanished in the white light of dimension travel or filed outside, talking amongst themselves.

Vidar approached the platform to hear Armus ask Kell, "Did it go as planned?"

"Only his actions will tell. At least his attitude is now publically known."

"I hope it's worth the risk of pushing him," said Avatar. At Kell's cocked brow of inquiry, he added, "Well, I don't like it when you and Armus push me."

With a sly grin, Kell stood. He patted Avatar's shoulder. "Which is why you are going to watch him."

Avatar balked, taken aback. "Me? Watch Dagar? He's an Original, cunning and—"

"You have some of the best covert surveillance skills I've ever seen, including Dagar."

At Avatar's momentary speechlessness, Vidar teased, "Do you need Wren's help?"

Avatar smirked. "No." He started to leave when Vidar stopped him.

"Wait. You'll want to hear what I have to report."

"You found the rogue?" asked Kell, hopeful.

"No, I spoke to Barrion. He's uncomfortable being Dagar's Trio Mate."

"Did he say why?"

"Nothing specific, just that he has his suspicions."

"Does he know the identity of rogue who beat the boys?" asked Kell with impatience.

"He's not certain, however, Griswold has been rather physically threatening of late, even toward him."

"Griswold? I sent Witter to replace him as head of the militia nearly a century ago. How did he return?"

"Barrion doesn't know. Nor has he seen Witter in a very long time. When he tries to speak to Dagar about Witter and Griswold, Dagar makes up some excuse. He claims Witter is busy on assignment and dismisses anything regarding Griswold."

"That doesn't bode well," said Avatar.

"No," agreed Kell then asked Vidar, "Did Barrion say what he believes has become of Witter?"

The archer shrugged. "Only that Guardians don't simply disappear without cause."

"Except if vanquished by one of us," chided Avatar.

Kell stared at Avatar, the statement disturbing. After a moment's pause, he again inquired of Vidar, "What about Tor? Does he agree with Barrion or Dagar?"

"Barrion says Tor *is* leaning towards Dagar's side. You may have to replace the Trio."

"I've argued that possibility with Jor'el. Only he insists Dagar remains Leader with Tor and Barrion as his Mates."

"I don't wish to second guess the Almighty, but that sounds risky."

"So I told him."

"And you're still standing?" quipped Avatar.

Kell didn't reply to dry humor, rather directed his attention to the floor for a moment of thought.

"Are you reconsidering Avatar's assignment?" asked Armus.

Kell shook his head. His focus slowly turned to Avatar. "Be careful."

Avatar flashed a cocky smile. "You said my skills exceed Dagar's."

Kell gripped Avatar's arm in warning. He spoke with foreboding. "If Witter has disappeared, that takes it beyond attitude to subversive action, perhaps treason. Be careful."

Concern replaced Avatar's bravado. "I can't imagine treason from one of our own, and surely not an Original. I'll do as you say, Captain." When Kell released him, Avatar took a step back and vanished.

"*Now* will you speak to Jor'el?" pressed Armus.

"I'll give Avatar time to find any evidence to tie Dagar to this rogue. Although, by the heavenlies, I hope there is none! Avatar isn't the only one who finds this hard to believe. What Guardian would even contemplate rebellion with the knowledge and station we possess?"

"One who wants more," said Vidar flatly.

Kell winced at the truth in the archer's words. "Return to your province. It is the most vulnerable due to its proximity."

"I put Wren and Dax on alert."

"Go. I have exposed Avatar to Dagar's cunning. No need to risk others."

"Avatar can handle it," said Armus with certainty.

"I'm not sure I can." Kell descended the platform.

Vidar moved closer to Armus. "Tell Kell the Vicar needs to speak to him—urgently."

"Why?"

"He didn't say, but is very distressed by something he witnessed."

"I'll give him a few moments before telling him."

Vidar stepped back to vanish.

Armus and Kell found Avram in the Vicar's personal study at the Fortress. Avram nearly jumped out of his chair when they arrived.

"Thank Jor'el! I don't know how much longer I could wait. Leave, and make certain we are not disturbed," he instructed the soldier who admitted the Guardians. He then continued in a vexed tone. "I don't know what to make of it. It's almost too fantastic to believe, but I saw it. As Jor'el is my witness, I saw it!"

"What?" asked Kell.

"Him! Almost the spitting image. It can't be, can it? Tell me it can't. I thought Guardians couldn't produce offspring."

The question and forcefulness of Avram's overly excited state surprised them. "We can't," said Kell.

"Then how do you explain it?" exclaimed Avram.

"Calm down and start from the beginning."

"I've been trying to calm down since I saw him!"

"Well, at least start from the beginning."

Avram took a deep breath then slowly exhaled. "Last night, my niece, Janel, came with a young man she identified as Razi. She asked me to marry them. Since she told me her father agreed, I did so. After all, I defied my wife's noble family to marry her. They seemed to be in the same predicament, I saw no harm. Until this morning, and I saw *him*."

"Who? Razi?" asked Armus.

"No, Dagar! A slight change of hair color and eyes and it is him!"

"You mean Dagar posing as this Razi to marry your niece?"

"No! I mean Razi is Dagar's son."

Kell couldn't help a stunned laugh. "Impossible."

"I tell you it is possible! He is taller than any mortal I've ever seen, just shy of seven feet. He looked familiar so I asked him if we ever met. He said we hadn't, but when I went to Temple for my evening meeting with the scribes, Dagar stood on the portico with Hueil. It was then I knew! The resemblance is too striking to ignore. As Jor'el is my witness, Kell, I swear it is so!"

Although such an affirmation cannot be ignored, Kell found it difficult to accept. "You're claiming something that has never happened before."

"When you see him, there will be no doubt."

"Have you told anyone else?" asked Armus.

"No! The ramifications are too staggering."

"Indeed." Armus gave a long thoughtful look at Kell. The captain considered Avram's claim.

At length, Kell spoke. "I will make discrete inquiry to see this person for myself. Tell no one else."

Avram relaxed. "I won't. If need be, please see to my niece's safety."

"Of course." Kell and Armus left.

Once in the compound, Armus asked, "What do you make of it?"

"I'm not sure. Avram's right about the staggering ramifications—*if* it is true. I'll have to see for my self to be completely certain.

"He wouldn't make up a such a fantastic story. And the way Dagar is behaving ..." Armus stopped when Kell pulled him into the shadow of an outer wall

Kell spoke low and disquieted. "Jor'el told me to be wary of what I might discover in the wake of the meeting. He could have meant this."

"You said it wasn't possible. Was that just for Avram's benefit?"

"No!" snapped a frustrated Kell. "What is happening to the Guardians is unlike anything we've ever experienced. Jor'el warned me there is worse to come. What was unthinkable in the past may well become reality. We must be ready for anything. I need some meditation to consider all the issues."

"I will see you are not disturbed."

Chapter 5

THE SHORT DAYS OF AUTUMN ALREADY MADE IT DIFFICULT to meet the quota deadlines for delivery. Mordecai changing the schedule frustrated Curtis, as it forced him to refigure the workload. However, his greatest annoyance came in wondering if Dagar would accept the new calculations. Then again, nothing pleased Dagar lately. The Guardian grew impatient with the workers' lack of progress. He increased the daily requirements as punishment for incompetence. What exactly the Guardian wanted with all that lumber and bricks he didn't know. Objections or questions weren't welcomed, so he silently went about his chore.

With the camp well lit for the night, Curtis didn't need an individual lantern to find his tent. Before entering, he drew to a halt upon seeing it: the secret signal of an immediate meeting. He quickly entered the tent to retrieve a lantern. He may not need one in camp, but he did for where he headed. Most men appeared to have retired for the night, so he slipped off into the woods unnoticed.

The shedding leaves of autumn fell on top of him or crunched beneath his feet. He traveled about three hundred yards through the woods to emerge into a clearing with two stumps side-by-side.

"My lord?" he called, cautious and nervous. Receiving no reply, he placed the lantern on one stump and sat on the other to wait.

Covert meetings proved the most hazardous part of his job. Other men helped when organizing the loads, delivery or dealing with Mordecai. They too objected to the foreman, and didn't mind making him look bad. However, caution needed to be taken since Vicar Avram favored Mordecai as foreman. Something amiss could start an investigation, and that would not please Dagar. Despite the help against a fellow mortal, these meetings were done alone.

Curtis jumped up in fright when someone touched his shoulder. He heard no approach, yet a very tall, cloaked figure stood next to him. The raised hood concealed the large beings' face in deep shadows. "My lord?" he asked, uncertain.

"Be at ease, Curtis. What is this I hear about a beating?"

"The boys. Toby and Judson. It was him again." Hearing a low throaty growl come from the being, Curtis hastily added, "I was going to tell you once I reset the schedule."

"Why should this upset the schedule?"

"Mordecai left with the load a day early to take the boys homes for their protection. The *other* threatened to kill them if he returned."

"Fool!"

"My lord, I tried to drive, only he took Reb instead."

The hood rose and the lantern light cast ominous shadow from underneath. Curtis swallowed back fear.

"Word reached Kell about the beating. How do you suppose that happened?"

Curtis hesitated, more concerned for a trick question than not knowing the answer. "Mordecai, perhaps?"

"Of course Mordecai, you ignorant worm! He went to the Fortress. Which is why he didn't take you. Have they returned?"

"No. I wouldn't expect them until tomorrow since drivers spend the night in town before returning."

The cloaked being paced a few steps. "Do not be surprised if they fail to return. You may be the new foreman."

Curtis began to smile, but ceased when hearing …

"*If* it is allowed."

"Have I not served you faithfully, my lord?"

"For a mortal you are competent."

With pricked pride, Curtis said, "I can run the camp more efficiently than Mordecai."

He chuckled. "No doubt. Soon more will be required of you than running a labor camp. It will require courage to defy those over you."

"My lord, you know I have no love for the Vicar. Because of him I am here," Curtis said with resentment and disdain.

"You corrupted his daughter."

"We were in love!"

He laughed, loud and mocking. "Love? You had no intention of marriage, only to satisfy your lust. You made her an outcast. So much for mortal love."

"What of you, since Guardians are impotent?" Before Curtis realized it, he dangled off the ground gasping for air. The being didn't touch him rather held his hand up.

"We can do everything mortals can, only infinitely better! In fact, your Haggar has proven to be of value."

Curtis struggled to breathe. Near the point of fainting, he felt a sudden release. He collapsed to the ground gulping for air.

"As punishment for your failure to promptly report this, the next load will be increased by half."

"Ay, my lord," came the raspy reply. "Any other instructions?"

"Do not be late to tomorrow night's scheduled meeting."

"Ay, my lord." By the time Curtis stood, the being was gone, no flash of light, just gone. He sat on the stump to regain his breath and composure. Dealing with Dagar always proved unnerving. At least he believed he spoke to Dagar. It could have been the other, the one called Tor. He sounded like Dagar and they had worked in tandem before. Either way, failure to follow instructions would be dangerous. Curtis returned to camp.

Avatar began his tracking at the labor camp. Since Guardians can sense each other from a mile away, he paused shy of that distance to observe the camp. Guardians possessed keen eyesight capable of seeing as well in the dark of night as in daylight. He noticed an individual leave camp, head into the wood and meet a large cloaked individual. It could have been a Guardian. However, determining that meant stretching out his senses, which meant risking discovery. He chose not to give away his presence by making such an attempt. The mortal hovering in midair confirmed the cloaked individual to be a Guardian. Whether Dagar or the rogue, would only be learned by further investigation.

Suddenly, the Guardian disappeared! Not in the normal form of dimension travel, which produced light—just disappeared! How could that happen? Did Dagar discover another form of dimension travel that didn't produce light? He couldn't take the time to consider the new form of vanishing. He had to follow Dagar no matter how he travelled.

Avatar placed one hand on the ground and another on the trunk of a tree. He carefully stretched out his senses. From the ground he detected movement, while from the tree came direction. He didn't have Vidar, Wren or a ranger's capability to communicate with nature. He obtained a general sense of essence and direction when visible evidence was absent. All warriors knew how to track. He learned from Armus, so his skills were sharper then most.

Avatar sat back on his heels with his brows knitted in curious consideration. The sense didn't lead anywhere above ground, rather below. Strange. He didn't know of any caves in the region. He knew of hollows or carved out portions from the quarry. However, what he sensed was vast and deep underground. In one swift fluid motion, Avatar stood, drew his sword and turned to face danger.

Dax, a ranger of Vidar's Trio, casually leaned on his quarterstaff. He stood a head shorter than Avatar with cat like yellow-orange eyes and brown hair. He widely grinned.

"Having fun playing in the dirt?"

Avatar scowled. He lowered his sword. "I hope you're alone."

Dax looked past Avatar. Wren stepped out from the shadows. She flashed a teasing smile.

"If you cut Dax, I would have shot you. Didn't Armus teach you to keep one eye out for trouble while tracking?" she said.

"What trouble can you two cause?" huffed Avatar.

"We caught you unawares didn't we?"

Avatar laughed with confidence. "If Dax had moved one step closer, he would have sprung a trap, sending him off his feet and knocking you halfway across the province."

She looked skeptical. "Oh, really?"

Avatar took hold of Wren's shoulder and moved her off to one side. He waved his hand to shoo Dax back. Using the tip of his sword, Avatar touched the ground in front of Dax and quickly ducked. A part of the ground lurched upwards like a springboard. A branch snapped over the spot where Wren had been standing. Impressed and surprised expressions came from Dax and Wren.

"Tracking while moving is one thing. When taking up surveillance, I never leave myself vulnerable to an attack from behind." Avatar grinned at Wren. "Remember that next time you try to sneak up on a *well-trained* warrior."

"Vidar told us what Kell asked of you. We just happen to be investigating our own findings when we sensed you," said Dax.

"Just me or someone else as well?" asked Avatar with interest.

"Just you, why?"

"Never mind. How far is the province border from camp?"

"You're standing on it."

Avatar glanced with consideration toward the camp. "Are there any caves in the Northern Forest?"

"A few toward the Highlands."

Avatar frowned in dispute. "The sense leads south."

"Wait," began Wren. "Hunter mentioned a couple of caves in Greenwood just over the Southern Forest border."

Dax shook his head. "I've seen them. Dens used by bears or boars, and only a few feet underground."

Avatar scratched his goatee. "What I sensed is very large and deep."

After a moment of consideration, Dax said, "I can't think of any fitting that description. Vidar or Kell would know."

"I can't take the time to ask them. I've wasted enough time with you two."

"Well, that's a fine thing to say," she groused.

Avatar sent her a skewed glance, along with asking a challenging question. "You want to track Dagar?"

She became instantly regretful. "No."

He wryly smiled. "Watch out for my other trap." He raced off heading south.

"What trap?" She anxiously looked at the ground around her feet.

"The one in your head!" came Avatar's reply.

Dax heartily laughed, which angered Wren.

"I'm going to get him one of these days, mark my words!"

"Get who?" Vidar appeared from the opposite direction.

Wren scowled but didn't answer, so Dax said, "Avatar."

"Oh," said Vidar with amused understanding.

"Dax nearly led us into one of Avatar's traps."

Vidar's humor turned to scolding of Dax. "You snuck up on a warrior and didn't anticipate a trap?"

"No! I stopped short and appeared unarmed. Wren threatened to shoot him."

"My *threat* was sarcastic!" she spoke in defense to Vidar. "Dax didn't identify us when he approached from behind, so Avatar drew his sword and turned. Only he didn't strike upon recognizing Dax."

The explanation didn't sway Vidar's anger. "Did Avatar find anything?"

"He mentioned sensing a very large cave deep underground. South. Maybe in the Greenwood." She pointed.

Vidar stiffened with concern. He issued quick instructions. "Wren, follow Avatar—*if* he senses you, identify yourself. Dax, go north and check out the caves along the Highland border. I need to tell Kell." He disappeared in white light.

Appearing inside a sparsely decorated, damp and dimly lit cave, he tossed back his hood. Tor. His voice sounded similar to Dagar, only Tor had red hair and bright blue eyes.

Dagar accosted Tor upon arrival. "Well?"

"You were right, Mordecai hasn't returned. Curtis told me Mordecai planned to take the boys home for their protection since Griswold threatened to kill them."

"Fool," swore Dagar.

"That's what I said. Only Curtis mistook me to mean Mordecai."

"They're both fools. When Griswold returns, I'll have a few things to say."

"I'm more concerned about Barrion. His suspicion is making him ask questions. I don't know how much long we can keep him from going to Kell."

"If Barrion can't be convinced, he'll join the others. I am going to check on them."

Dagar moved down a tunnel with Tor following. After a quarter mile, they emerged into a large chamber one hundred feet in diameter by fifty feet high. The chamber contained various implements for reconditioning. Cages surrounded a central floor with different levels. Stone stairways led to each level where narrow walkways circumvented the chamber. Guardians of different stations and genders occupied the cages, perhaps a total of two hundred. All of them appeared in various stages of suffering.

Dressed in black leather uniforms, a dozen brawny Guardian warriors stood watch in the chamber. The color of the uniforms served as a sign of an altered personality. They also wore grim and foreboding expressions. Their brilliant eyes were cold and hard, not at all reflecting the kindness and tolerance once common to their nature.

In a center portion of the floor, two Guardians stood between natural pillars bound by chains around their wrists and ankles. They were stripped to their breeches and showed signs of great torture. Their physical size and strength showed them to be warriors. Both had black hair, though one was bulkier, and with hands capable of crushing anything. The slender one appeared to be unconscious, his head down. The cool hazel eyes of the bulky one watched Dagar's approach. Blood ran down his face from a vicious cut above his right eye that crossed the bridge of his nose to his left cheek.

"Well, Witter, how are you doing today?" asked Dagar.

"How should I be?"

"I thought after eighty years you would see reason. Altari has." Dagar lifted the slender one's chin. "Haven't you, Altari?" The shrouded silver-grey eyes opened, revealing a hint of remaining stubbornness. Dagar jerked back Altari's head. "Cup!" He waved to a nearby Guardian.

Dagar forced Altari to drink a greenish liquid. Altari gagged on the liquid being poured down his throat. When finished, Dagar roughly released him. Altari coughed and gasped for air.

"Now, let's try again, Altari."

This time the silver-gray eyes looked placid. "Ay, my lord."

Dagar smugly smiled. "See, Witter, it isn't so hard." He dropped the empty cup, seized Witter's hair, and jerked his head back. "More!" he commanded.

A second Guardian stepped forward with another cup. Witter tried to resist, but Tor helped Dagar subdue him. Soon Witter began choking on the liquid. That didn't sway them to slow down. Only when he fainted, did Dagar stop.

"Do you think he got enough?" asked Tor.

"Ay. With Altari subdued, Witter won't take long." Dagar handed the cup back to the Guardian. He moved from the pillars to look around the chamber in satisfaction. "Soon all will be ready."

"Will we have enough?"

Dagar chuckled under his breath. "I have assurances that when the time comes, many more will join us. Poor, naïve, Kell doesn't suspect a thing."

"Don't underestimate Kell."

"I'm not. I just know his weakness. The thought of harming another Guardian is abhorrent to him. He is doing all he can to convince *me* not to grow more disheartened." Dagar affected a tone of sympathy then scoffed. "He can't see that I have already turned! That I have either captured or recruited Guardians for my army right under his nose." He spread his arms to indicate those in the chamber. "These supposed valiant comrades lost during engagements throughout the centuries, will be my special forces." He smiled with great satisfaction. "Along with the few surprises, it will leave Kell reeling, if not destroyed."

"One of those surprises is growing agitated and erratic."

"Meaning?"

"Tegan sent word that her time is sooner than anticipated."

Dagar rolled his eyes in annoyance.

"All part of your plan. Or did you underestimate the demand placed upon your time and energy?" Tor's humor was met by a throaty growl of warning from Dagar.

"Father." Ram and Razi approached. Ram wore a wry smile while Razi appeared guarded.

"Good. You found him," said Dagar.

"It wasn't too difficult." Ram tossed a wink at Razi. The latter shifted his weight uneasily from one foot to other.

"What have you been up to?" Dagar's probing glance found Razi.

"Exploring," came the awkward reply.

"You know how he likes to take in fresh air on occasion. Nothing to be concerned about. We're ready to leave when you permit," said Ram.

Dagar's pursued his lip in consideration. "Now is as good a time as any." He positioned himself between them and held each by the shoulder. Ram stood ready while Razi appeared hesitant. "I thought you wanted to see her before she dies?"

"I do. I just don't like dimension travel."

Dagar chuckled. "You tolerate it better than most mortals."

"Ay, sir."

Dagar said to Tor, "Continue the preparations," before he and his sons vanished.

Dagar and his sons reappeared in the foyer of a house dimly lit by candles. He waited a moment for Ram and Razi to recover their senses. Dimension travel came easy to Guardians since part of their heavenly nature could transcend time and space. Not mortals. They tended to faint or become ill. Being half-Guardian, Ram and Razi faired better in the fact they didn't swoon. Still, it took a moment to reorient to the new environment.

Voices came from upstairs. The female sounded agitated, speaking words of complaint. Tegan, a female Guardian physician, descended the steps muttering under her breath. Her bright copper eyes looked decidedly put out at spotting them. She hurried down the last few steps.

"How do you put up with such nonsense?" She made an angry upwards gesture.

"All part of my plan," said Dagar.

"Father!" chided Razi.

Despite a frown, Dagar maintained his temper. "I mean, I tolerate her for your sake."

Razi's expression showed disbelief so he asked Tegan, "How is she?"

"Grave, my lord. Although not grave enough to still her voice."

Razi's disapproval made Tegan bow. He passed her to go upstairs.

Dagar signaled for Ram to follow Razi. He spoke privately to Tegan. "I thought you increased the dosage?"

"Ay. However, to avoid detection I can't out right poison her. What would your sons say? Especially Razi."

Dagar glanced at the stairs. Fortunately, Ram and Razi were out of sight. "I should have disposed of her after their weaning."

"Are you admitting to a moment of weakness? That you *did* care for her beyond the obvious mating?"

The intensity in his mahogany eyes made her recoil in fear. "Beware your words, physician."

"I'm sorry, my lord." She made a hasty bow. "It will be done."

72

"After the appropriate time of farewell." He left her to go upstairs.

In the bedchamber, Haggar lay beneath the covers. A good fire blazed in the hearth making the room toasty. She appeared fragile and well beyond her forty years. The graying blonde hair was brittle, hollow cheeks, deep lines about her eyes and an ashen complexion. A weak smile appeared as she tried to lift an outstretched hand to Ram and Razi.

"My sons. You came."

Razi sat on the bed. He took hold of her hand. He tried to mask distress at the sight of her condition. Ram seemed indifferent.

"We came as soon as we could," said Razi.

"You mean as soon as he allowed."

"Hush," he soothed and kissed her hand.

In a weary, jerky motion, Haggar shook her head. "I know the truth. I have all along. Still, I'm glad to see you both for one last time."

"I would not deny you." Dagar stood by the bed opposite his sons.

Haggar's features grew surprisingly harsh for one in her frail state. "Do not play a game of platitudes with me, Dagar. Not at the end. We've played it for too long."

He chuckled. "Your imagination is running wild, my dear."

"Stop!" she snapped, to her painful chagrin.

"Mother, why do you say that?" asked Razi.

"Pain and fatigue," said Dagar with impatience.

"I asked her," rebuffed Razi, which made Dagar stiffen with insult. Razi ignored him to press her. "Mother."

Her weak smile grew tearful. "My dearest Razi, if you don't by now, there are no words to explain in the time I have left."

"Haggar," scolded Dagar.

"Let her speak. What can she say that we don't already know?" said Ram.

Dagar's narrowed eyes and pressed lips told of his complete disapproval. "If you both know, why discuss the matter?"

"Because, I want to face Jor'el with a clear conscience and not take my sins to the grave," she said.

Dagar snorted a laugh of high mockery. "A little late, my dear."

She turned upon him, harsh and condemning. "So tell me, how long until you have Tegan administer the final dose of poison?"

"What?" said Razi in surprised. Even Ram joined his brother in turning to Dagar for an answer.

Although he tried to pass off the question with a sarcastic smile, there was no amusement in his voice. "We have had our differences over the years, but it is going too far to accuse me of plotting your murder."

"Why? You took them from me when they were little. For years you told me of yours plans for them while tormenting me with how I wouldn't live to see those plans fulfilled!" Tears of regret fell.

"Because I knew how ill you were even back then. I took pity on you by relieving you of the burden to spare your failing health."

"Oh, stop!" She spoke in desperation to Ram and Razi. "He's lying. My illness was foolishly believing he loved me, yet knowing all along he used me as a plot of revenge against my father the Vicar, Jor'el and Kell."

Hearing the confession stunned Razi. "Your father is Avram?"

"Ay!" she wept. "Forgive me, Father! Forgive me, Jor'el."

Tegan hastened to the bed. "Enough. She is too weak. This could kill her sooner than … than her time," she corrected at receiving a look of warning from Dagar.

"Out!" Dagar commanded his sons.

"Father—" Razi began to object when Ram pulled him into the hall.

Razi jerked away from Ram. "You heard what she said!"

"She is dying. Her mind may be confused."

Dagar joined them in the hallway. "Ay, she is confused."

"Enough to accuse you of wanting to poison her to death?" challenged Razi.

Dagar struggled to control his temper. "Why do you think Tegan has remained with her all these years?" The questioned stymied Razi, so Dagar answered. "Because of her illness." He glanced back at the door. A twinge of sympathy crept into his voice. "I loved her once. Something a Guardian is forbidden. You two are the product of that love, and proof that Guardians are not impotent. And we are more than capable of rearing offspring."

"She said it was an act of revenge. You can't deny that, not after grooming us all our lives," Razi continued in his stubborn refute.

"I never denied it. You know my reasons. Are you questioning me because of the ravings of a dying woman?"

"She's our mother!"

Dagar shook his head. "You think the revenge is mine alone? She confessed because she joined me in rebellion against her father. A father who spurned her and cast her aside when she didn't do what he wanted."

"What did he want her to do?" asked Ram.

"To dedicate her life to Jor'el," replied Dagar with bitterness.

"How is that wrong?" Razi's his own bitterness mirrored Dagar.

"Because she wanted to be free to love and be loved. To live her own life, but he disapproved then disowned her when she defied him. That is when I found her, wandering and destitute. Back then she was a beautiful woman. I meant what I said about taking pity on her."

"Guardians were created to serve and care for mortals."

Dagar laughed with sarcasm. "Oh, you are so naïve, Razi. And a great disappointment."

Razi squared his shoulder, a brief hint of worry passing over his face. "How? I've done all you asked."

"You still question. Take Ram for an example." Dagar clapped Ram's arm, a gleam of pride in his smile. "He understands and embraces the path I set before him; a path leading to power and the throne! You are distracted by the words of a bitter and dying woman. Let her make her confession to ease her mind, only do not allow it to lessen the great gift I have prepared for you, my son."

"He won't, Father. Too much is at stake to do otherwise." Ram spoke with certainty while glancing at his brother.

Razi understood Ram's meaning. "Ay."

"Then let us return." Dagar positioned himself between them.

"I'd like to stay. If I may, sir," Razi added in voice of submission at Dagar's disapproval. "You said you once loved her. As a last act of pity for that love's sake, don't let her die alone."

"You show too much mercy and pity."

"Only when prudent. Have you not shown the same when necessary to facilitate your plans? Is a king supposed to be devoid of mercy? How can I rule effectively without showing mercy on occasion?"

Dagar chuckled, though dry and humorless. "Well said. Yet everything is almost ready." His cocked his head as if distracted. Neither Ram nor Razi noticed. In fact, Ram spoke.

"Let him stay, Father. I'll fetch him when the time comes. He *will* return, even if she is still alive."

Their eyes met and Razi said, "I will for you, brother."

Dagar's grin filled with pride. "What an unstoppable force you both make. Go." He released Razi then he and Ram disappeared.

Razi entered the bedchamber.

Tegan frowned in annoyance. "I thought you left."

"I'm staying to give her comfort."

"Razi," said Haggar, weak and low.

"I'm here, Mother." He sat on the bed. "I'll stay with you."

Her smile faded as her eyes closed. He felt for a pulse.

"She's just asleep," said Tegan. "Although it won't be long."

Chapter 6

AVATAR STOPPED INSIDE THE TREE-LINE ON THE BORDER of the Northern and Southern Forest. A mile and a half inside the clearing stood a small manor house. This was not where he expected the sense to lead him. Could the cave be under the house with the building a ruse? Why? Suddenly, he gripped the hilt of his sword and drifted back into the forest for concealed observation. No mistaking that sense: Dagar! He hadn't come within a mile so how could Dagar's sense be so powerful and unsettling? Does that mean he was detected? This sense felt different than at camp. Maybe the earlier Guardian was the rogue and not Dagar. What about the cave?

For several moments he pondered the situation. Kell ordered him to follow Dagar; but the rogue Guardian caused physical harm to mortals. Taking the time to send word to Kell about his two encounters may cause him to lose track of Dagar. The rogue would have to wait.

Again he sensed a presence, only this one friendly. Hunter arrived along with one of his Trio Mates, another ranger named Ridge. Except for the color hair and eyes, Hunter and Ridge could pass as twins by the way they dressed. They also had similar facial features with both sporting thin beards. Hunter had dark hair with green eyes, while Ridge was a redhead with light golden eyes.

"What brings you all the way out here?" Hunter asked Avatar.

"Sightseeing."

"Well, if I knew my province would be graced by the captain's aide, I would have arranged a tour," he chided. "Don't try my patience, Avatar. Kell might tolerate your insubordinate humor, but not me."

"I didn't mean to be insubordinate. I'm sorry you misunderstood."

"Your being here deals with Dagar, doesn't it?"

"Possibly." At Hunter's impatience, Avatar added, "No, honest, it's a bit puzzling. I sensed Dagar just now, meaning the earlier presence was the rogue who attacked the boys. I followed that sense here, only this manor house isn't what I expected to find."

"The house is owned by a local wealthy merchant. What would Dagar want with him?" asked Hunter.

Avatar shrugged. "As I said, I'm still trying to find the answers. Yet I felt Dagar's presence before you and Ridge arrived."

"Should I call upon the Sir Cedric to learn if he had a visitor?" asked Ridge.

Hunter shook his head. "If Dagar was here, and I stress *if*, the mortal may not even be aware of his presence."

"I'm certain of what I felt," said Avatar.

"You just said you are trying to determine the answers."

"About the sense leading me here, not what I felt upon arrival."

Hunter narrowed his eyes at Avatar. "I warned you about trying my patience."

"I'm not. I'm carrying out my orders."

The leader stiffened. "If you were my aide, there would be a harsh lesson about insolence towards a superior, with a lecture on humility thrown in!"

Avatar assumed a posture of attention, more for formality than contrition as told by his tone of rebuff. "I appreciate the fact you are a Trio Leader and an Original, but when following Captain Kell's orders, I can do so with or without your cooperation. If you have a problem with my assignment or my attitude, take the matter up with him."

Ridge hissed a breath of surprised concern at the rebuke then flinched when Hunter addressed him.

"Ridge, show him the Midessex border."

"Sir, you can't make me leave," said Avatar in dispute.

"*That* is the way Dagar went." Hunter turned on his heels and left.

Ridge moved closed to Avatar. "By the heavenlies, you are bold."

"Maybe, but I don't recall Hunter being so strict or unfriendly."

Ridge took Avatar's arm to steer him in the opposite direction of Hunter. He spoke in a discrete voice. "This whole situation with Dagar has affected him. Cam and I try to ease his mind, but with little success."

"You think he would listen to one of his own caste."

"When he didn't, Cam added his encouragement. However, being a vassal, Hunter wasn't impressed by his attempt. You're the first one who's made him back down. Probably because you're a warrior."

"I didn't mean to intimidate or be insubordinate."

"All the same, I was surprised when he ordered me to escort you." Ridge snatched a careful glance over his shoulder.

"You think he is following us? I don't sense him."

"As an Original, he knows a few tricks Cam and I don't."

"Have you spoken to Kell about your concerns?"

"No, I'm unable to leave the province. When you see the captain, please tell him what I said. For Hunter's own good."

"Why don't you take this opportunity of *escorting* me so you can speak to Kell yourself? I'm not sure when I'll finish my assignment."

"I want to … no." Ridge looked back again. "We've gone far enough, so it is safe enough to dimension travel to the border."

"I'm not going. I know Dagar is at the manor house. The question is why? And Kell sent me to find answers."

"I'll get in trouble if you return," insisted Ridge

"What would he do?" asked Avatar, curious.

Ridge heaved an uncertain shrug. "Demotion or reassignment."

"Are you afraid of him?"

"No! Concerned. He is my Trio Leader and former mentor."

"I understand," said Avatar with sympathy. "I'll tell Kell when I can."

"Now, please, do as Hunter says and leave. I'll try to learn what I can at the manor house."

For a brief moment, Avatar studied Ridge. If the discontent were spreading then pressing the matter wouldn't help. The sense of Dagar came and went rather quickly. Perhaps only a residual essence remained. Hunter may be correct, and Dagar had left. "Very well. Lead the way."

They vanished and reappeared near the River Conn, some fifty miles from the manor house. The river served as the natural border between Midessex and the Southern Forest.

Ridge winced with discomfort. "An uneasiness stirs in Midessex, only I can't tell what."

Avatar stared across the river attempting to gauge the sense. "Maybe Gresham can tell me."

Ridge doubled over in great pain. Avatar drew his sword and took up a defensive position to shield the ranger. "Ridge?"

It took a moment for the ranger to recover. Ridge took a deep breath and straightened to his full height. "I'm all right now. It's passed."

Avatar observed Ridge. Other than being pale, he appeared whole. "What happened?"

Ridge shrugged with befuddlement. "I'm not exactly sure. A deep cold accompanied by sense of debilitating pain coming from the earth. I've never sensed such a disturbance before, have you?"

Avatar returned his attention to across the river. His expression grew guardedly curious. "Did you go underground?" he muttered to himself.

"Pardon?" asked Ridge, not fully understanding.

Avatar flashed a crooked smile. "Never mind." He clapped Ridge on the shoulder. "I depend upon you to get answers at the manor."

"I will. Jor'el be with you."

"And with you." Avatar took a step from Ridge and vanished. He reappeared on the other side of the river and ran further into Midessex.

<hr />

Kell sat on the floor in a corner of his office by the window. He engaged in Guardian meditation with his legs crossed, hands folded and eyes closed. When white light appeared, his eyes snapped open. Vidar arrived, which brought Kell to his feet. "Do you come with news?"

"Ay, and perhaps quite disturbing," Vidar replied with seriousness.

Made wary by the tone and statement, Kell asked, "How so?"

"Wren and Dax encountered Avatar on the border near the labor camp. He asked about a large *cave* deep underground," Vidar spoke with emphasis. "They told him there weren't any such caves in the province."

Kell's face grew hard with understanding. "Where is Avatar now?"

"Heading toward the Greenwood. I sent Wren after him and Dax to investigate the caves along the Highland border."

The answer confused Kell. "You know there are no such caves in Allon so why send Dax to investigate?"

"Because he's getting too cocky and taking unnecessary risks. He didn't identify himself when approaching Avatar from the rear during his surveillance. It nearly got him and Wren caught in a trap."

Kell studiously regarded Vidar. "I assume he's been taught not to do so with any warrior or suffer the consequences."

"Of course. I reinforced the lesson when you first assigned him to my Trio three centuries ago."

After a brief of consideration, Kell asked a delicate question. "Do you think Dax is becoming discontent like Dagar?"

"No, just high headed about his position. Some tend to do so when being promoted to a Trio. Granted he's manifesting it later than others. I don't think it is of concern, just awkward under the circumstances."

"If you feel certain about him, I'll let him be."

Vidar didn't take offense. "I would tell you if I believed otherwise. The *cave* is of more immediate concern."

"Ay. Did you speak to Avatar?"

Vidar shook his head. "I arrived after he left, which is why I'm here. I could have followed him, but I thought to tell you first."

Kell cocked a wry gin. "You wouldn't have succeeded. Wren is going to have difficulty."

Vidar made a contrary expression. "I am the first Guardian hunter."

Kell's grin widened. "You are aware Armus and I trained Avatar."

Vidar yielded with a nod. "Are you going to send Armus to tell him to avoid the cave?"

"No, someone else." Kell closed his eyes. His brows furrowed in concentration.

Several moments passed before white light appeared in the room. It faded to reveal Mahon, a slender, boyish looking Guardian warrior of nine hundred years with blond hair and bright blue eyes. "You summoned me, Captain?"

"I have an assignment requiring your unique qualifications."

"Oh?" asked Mahon curious about Kell's partial smile.

"Find Avatar."

"He's missing?" asked Mahon in sudden concern.

"No." Kell placed a reassuring hand on Mahon's shoulder. "I sent him on a tracking assignment, only information has come to my attention that he needs to know. Neither Armus nor myself can leave, while Vidar would have difficulty finding him. Being his former apprentice and well acquainted with his skills and methods, you are the only choice."

Mahon grinned, then suppressed it at Vidar's contrary frown. "Of course, Captain. What is the information?"

"Vidar learned of Avatar sensing a large cave located deep underground. He will find no such cave in Allon."

"Then how can he sense something if doesn't exist?"

"Geographically it does not exist."

Mahon blinked in befuddlement. "You lost me, Captain."

"The only cave fitting that description is in a nether dimension and reserved for the most drastic of times. Only the Originals know of its existence and whereabouts."

Mahon listened intently. "Can it be reached by other Guardians?"

"Ay, yet it requires great power to bridge the dimensional gap. Similar to going to the heavenlies or the Fringe. Only it can take several hours to regain strength before attempting a return. You must find Avatar and stop him from going into the cave."

"I'll find him, but he will ask why?"

When Kell hesitated, Vidar said, "They have a right to know."

Kell showed unwillingness. However, Vidar's insisting motion and Mahon's attentive curiosity forced him to speak. "Like strange creatures roam the deep sea, there are creatures in the bowels of the cave which are not meant for mortals. Some Guardians have difficulty with them."

"Gulliver with leviathan," said Vidar about the largest sea monster.

Mahon nodded to the reference then turned back to Kell as the captain continued.

"No need to explain the reasons why Jor'el made such creatures. They exist, are to be avoided and kept in their place."

"And Avatar might not be able to return," added Vidar.

"How so? If the gap can be bridged like the Fringe, why not be able to come and go?" asked Mahon with some confusion.

Kell scowled at Vidar, which made the archer say again, "They should know *everything*. One mistake ..."

Kell put up a sharp hand to stop Vidar. With grave sobriety, he spoke to Mahon. "The cave was created for one purpose, to serve as an eternal prison for any Guardian who would turn against Jor'el. The creatures and labyrinths are for punishment while there is a safeguard to prevent escape. Very few hold the key to coming and going once there. If Dagar manages to gain control of the prison ..." he couldn't finish for the dreadful comprehension on the younger Guardian's face.

Mahon's voice sounded thick in an attempt control his anxiety. "I understand, Captain. Where was Avatar last seen?"

Vidar replied, "Heading toward the Greenwood, an area between the Northern and Southern Forest."

Mahon spoke with grim determination. "By your leave, Captain."

Unable to speak, Kell nodded his permission. Mahon vanished.

"I understand your reluctance but they needed to know, especially if Dagar has seized control," said Vidar.

Kell forced a reply. "Mahon must find Avatar in time!"

"It could be intelligence we need if Avatar does enter the cave."

"Would you risk Wren to find out?" The intensity of the captain's golden eyes and his voice of command made the archer recoil a step.

"No. Like you, I would go in first and spare my protégé. However, since you can't be risked, I'll go …"

Kell seized Vidar. "You know, I am the only one who can counter Dagar if he gains mastery over the creatures of *infrinn*. For now, we wait, and pray Mahon succeeds."

⁂

In a tunnel of the nether dimension, Hunter appeared. He took several deep breaths to recover from the expenditure of energy needed to reach the underworld cave. Once recovered, he went to find Dagar. The warrior and Ram were in the large room serving as the main chamber.

"Dagar!"

The warrior turned at hearing his name then frowned at the speaker. "What are you doing here? I didn't summon you."

"Kell sent Avatar to follow you."

Dagar laughed, caustic, yet amused. "You came here for nothing. I sensed his pitiful attempt at the manor house. Sloppy work."

"Avatar isn't sloppy, you got lucky."

Dagar sneered a warning, "Mind your tongue, ranger."

Hunter heaved his chest and squared his shoulders. "Mind yourself, warrior! We are peers. I've taken a great risk in coming to warn you, not to mention helping to shield your activities. Avatar expressed interest about the occupants of the house."

"What did you tell him?"

"A wealthy merchant lives there, only he insisted he sensed your presence."

"And?"

"I sent him to Midessex."

"What? You sent him here? You fool!"

"Me?" replied Hunter in outrage. "You left too strong a sense to be ignored. If I sent him in another direction he would have doubled back and discovered *who is* at the house. For all I know he already has. I could come under suspicion for leading him astray. Ridge and Cam are already

84

suspicious. Don't speak to me of foolishness. I covered your mistake!" Dagar's angry snarl made Hunter take an impulsive step back. The ranger managed to ask, "How much longer until we implement the plan?"

"Soon. The last hindrance is nearly gone."

"I don't think we're ready for a major conflict."

"You and Tor are too cautious."

"No, realistic. Kell commands all the Guardians, we are but a scant few hundred."

Dagar smiled, clever and pleased. "All you know of."

"Are you holding out on us?" chided Hunter.

"Let's just say, we haven't committed all our assets," he said concerning himself and Ram.

"Dagar!"

"Easy, my friend. When the time comes all will be revealed."

"In the meantime, what about Avatar?"

"I shall deal with him directly."

"His disappearance will rouse Kell," said Ram.

"Who said disappear? Merely keep him occupied and out of communication with Kell for a few days. What happens during that time is of no consequence. If Avatar vanishes; then one less warrior. *If* he manages to elude me, he will be too late to help his captain and mentor."

Hunter wasn't convinced; yet bit back an argument to opt for a more strategic withdrawal. "I better return. I've been gone too long." He stepped away, spoke some Ancient under his breath, closed his eyes, clapped his hands together and vanished.

"What did Hunter want?" Tor appeared from the other entrance.

"To warn me of Avatar. Apparently he is tenacious in tracking."

"Did you expect less?"

Dagar's eyes narrowed in a moment of consideration. "I think a few days in the bowels of *infrinn* will keep him occupied, don't you?"

"Father, why take the risk?"

"Risk for who? Do you believe he will survive?"

Tor chuckled and shook his head. "No, he won't."

"Fetch Griswold. He will enjoy this assignment." When Tor left, Dagar went back to a table covered with implements in various stages of construction. He picked up a pair of shackles and fiddled with the lock. In disgust, he tossed it aside. "They must be lethal!"

"I keep telling you, Rune is undermining your effort. You must take sterner measures with him," said Ram.

Griswold arrived. Even before formulating his plan of revolt, Dagar considered Griswold an imposing and intimidating warrior whose darker features and bulk made Armus look lean and friendly.

"Tor said you wanted to see me."

"Return to duty. I'll join you later," Dagar instructed Ram. He waited until Ram left. A sly smile appeared, as he casually leaned back against the table. "I have a delightful assignment for you involving Avatar." He saw Griswold smile in anticipation. "Make sure he doesn't follow my trail too easily. He's grown cocky and I want to teach him a lesson."

"You mean he's better than you anticipated and want him to pay for that."

Dagar glared at Griswold. Not many dared to speak so brashly to him. Whereas he was clever and skilled in the area of deception and planning, Griswold was stronger, and no fool. "He was last seen near the house and expressed interest in the occupants. Make certain he doesn't discover who is there. Cause a sufficient delay, yet don't stop his pursuit or hurt him too badly. I want to administer his final lesson. One Kell won't expect or forget. Take some of the pets with you."

Griswold's smile turned wicked. "Mortal child's play." He left in one direction just as Tor hurried in from another direction.

"You need to deal with Barrion now!" Tor announced.

"Why?"

"Vidar's been nosing around."

Dagar snarled. "Not enough he sends his insufferable protégé to keep an eye on me, now he's using other Trio Leaders."

"He's the captain. Did you expect less after his suspicions were aroused?"

Dagar ignored the question to ask, "Where is Barrion now?"

"At our station, last I heard."

"Keep an eye on things here." In long, hasty strides, Dagar left the room in the direction Griswold had taken.

A small well-built and furnished house served for Dagar and his Trio Mates in conducting business with the mortals. A flash of white light appeared. It faded to reveal Barrion, a Guardian warrior lean in feature and limbs with copper hair and jade eyes. He jerked with surprise to find someone waiting for him.

"Dagar. What are you doing here? I thought you were at the meeting."

"Where have you been?"

"Tending to business. Since you're not around much someone needs to deal with provincial matters." He noticed the way Dagar watched him, sizing him up. Whether for a verbal or physical attack was uncertain, especially the way the Leader acted lately.

"What do you know about the beating?" Dagar demanded.

"It's not the first time. Many mortals in the province are on edge. In fact, most are now wary of Guardians. Some wonder if it is the reverse of Radnor with rogue Guardians roaming the countryside waiting to prey upon helpless mortals." Barrion purposely mentioned the name of the infamous battle to watch for a reaction.

Both were involved. Both came away with differing views. He felt regret despite understanding the necessity for such brutal actions. Dagar viewed brutality as opportunity. However, back then Barrion didn't know what that meant. As anticipated, the Leader sneered and his eyes narrowed in offense.

"You can't keep this up much longer, Dagar."

"Or what? You'll tell Kell like you did Vidar?"

"I told Vidar nothing! I danced around his questions." Barrion snorted a mock laugh. "Although I'm surprised it took Tor this long to tell you since you send him to spy on me. Not the way a Trio should operate. Mates suspicious of each other?"

"Perhaps if you'd agree to help rather than be at odds with us there could be trust between us again."

"I am helping! While you prepare to play demigod, I'm keeping the province secure along with shielding your activities from nosy questions. Just because I disagree with you, doesn't mean I'll betray you. Try trusting that!"

A heavy moment of silence passed before Dagar spoke. "Very well. I trust you. Razi is at the house since her time is near. Go keep an eye on him."

Barrion nodded in agreement. "Consider it done."

Chapter 7

WREN STOPPED AT THE TREE-LINE. SHE SENSED AVATAR HAD been there. In fact, she stood where he did, a mile and a half from the manor house. Whether he went to the house and spoke with the mortal occupants or moved onto another destination, she could not discern since she wasn't alone for long.

"Fancy meeting you here," said Ridge. "This must be our lucky day. First we're graced by the presence of a renowned warrior and now the great archer's protégé."

"I take it you've spoken to Avatar."

"And pointed him in the right direction." Ridge proudly smiled.

Wren chuckled in surprise. "Are you saying he was off course?"

"Hardly," he groused. "The trail went to Midessex. What are you doing here?"

"Vidar's instructions."

Now, Ridge displayed surprise, only laced with frustration. "He told you to follow Avatar? Are we all growing suspicious of each other?"

"No! What Avatar discovered concerned Vidar, and he wanted me to find him. Dax went to explore the caves near the Highlands."

"Avatar didn't mention anything about caves. Then again, Hunter didn't let him speak much. Although Avatar said he wasn't expecting the sense to lead him here," Ridge spoke with dismay.

Wren noticed his tone of despondency yet continued with her inquiry. "Who lives in the manor?"

"A wealthy merchant, but it's rarely occupied."

"Then why is smoke coming from a chimney?" She pointed to the house.

"I'll find out." He started to leave, but stopped when she followed. "Wait here."

"I have instructions."

"So did Avatar, which angered Hunter when he mentioned them."

"That's the second time you sounded upset when speaking about Hunter, why?"

Ridge shook his head. "No time to explain. Please, wait."

True, she and Ridge tended to clash simply due to their similar natures and temperaments. Passing off his obvious despondency seemed unusual. Despite her curiosity, something in his expression told her not to press the issue. "Very well. Ten minutes."

Ridge ran toward the house.

Tegan sat in the drawing room taking a much-needed respite from Haggar. A nice fire burned in the hearth to chase away the chill. Although Guardians weren't affected by the weather, she enjoyed a few relaxing moments in front of the fire.

In truth, her life as a physician hadn't been too tedious or demanding. After a thousand years of dealing with mortals, she grew tried of the whiny, fragile and fickle creatures. They were both envious and jealous of her healing skills. Few showed enough potential to receive personal training by a Guardian, at least in her opinion. Eldric leaned more favorably toward the mortals. Four centuries earlier, he instituted a five-year training program pairing the more gifted mortals with a Guardian physician. Leaving Melwynn at Dagar's request to help a dying mortal, gave her the perfect opportunity to quit her Guardian duties to join him in his real purpose. Little did she realize Dagar actually wanted her to treat an ailing mortal female and not just a ruse to help her leave.

With Razi keeping close watch on his mother, Tegan had to be careful. She managed to place the final dosage of poison in Haggar's cup of medicine after he examined it. She could soon leave and assume her place as Dagar's prime physician. Providing he doesn't come up with another mortal for her to tend. She shook the thought from her mind.

The ringing of the front doorbell interrupted her solace. Perhaps the baker or grocer arriving. Not her concern, so she remained in the large cushioned chair with her feet up.

The rough clearing of a throat caught her attention and the steward said, "Excuse me, Doctor, you have a visitor."

Tegan became surprised at the individual accompanying the steward. She hadn't sensed a presence. "Ridge? What are you doing here?"

"I can ask you the same question. Last I heard you were at Melwynn."

She waved the steward away. "That'll be all, Harlen." Once the mortal was gone, she stood to confront Ridge. "I was summoned to care for a dying woman and just taking a moment's rest."

Ridge looked askew at her. "Sir Cedric's wife died three years ago, while his daughter is married and living in the South Plains."

She shrugged, stalling in an effort to recall the story Dagar concocted. "His niece, I believe. I didn't ask a lot of questions, I simply came as instructed."

"Is Sir Cedric here?"

"No. After I arrived, he left for important business."

"Leaving her to die alone?"

"I'm making her comfortable. There is nothing else to do. She barely knows anyone is near. Too painful for him to watch," she made excuse.

"Tegan!" a frustrated male voice called. Razi entered. He paused in surprise at seeing Tegan wasn't alone. "Who are you?"

Ridge appeared startled by Razi, yet recovered to reply. "I am Ridge, one of Hunter's Trio Mates, Guardians who look after the mortals of this province."

"I've heard of you," said Razi in a careful, guarded tone.

"May I inquire who you are, my lord?"

"Raz-"

Tegan coughed loud enough to interrupt the reply but Razi ignored her to finish his answer.

"Razi, Haggar's son."

"The dying woman?"

"Ay."

"*He* is why Sir Cedric left. She is in capable hands, mine and her son's," said Tegan with haste. She took Ridge's arm to steer him to the door. "Now, please leave— out of respect."

He pulled away. "I meant no disrespect. I'm sorry, my lord," he said to Razi.

"Apology accepted. Thank you for your concern toward my mother."

"My pleasure. If there is anything you need, Harlen knows how to send word." Ridge bowed to Razi. With an annoyed look at Tegan, the ranger left.

After slamming the door shut, Tegan confronted Razi. "It was foolish of you to come down!"

"I didn't know anyone was here. Besides, what harm can he do?"

"Didn't you see the way he looked at you? Your size and appearance made him suspicious. Remember, Dagar doesn't want that before it's time!" She roughly gestured. "Return upstairs."

Razi stiffened with insult. "I'm not a servant for you to order around. I came to fetch you to ease her discomfort. Or are you under orders to let her die in pain?"

Tegan covered her annoyance. Even being half-Guardian, Razi was strong and intelligent in his own right. He would someday be king. Despite a more sensitive nature, he proved the more clever of Dagar's sons. No good to anger him. "I'll do what I can, my lord."

Wren paced, impatient for Ridge's return. Ten minutes nearly passed and she considered her next move. She halted at sensing a presence. She accosted Ridge the moment he returned. "Well?"

"Well, is right. Something unusual is going on only I'm not sure of what."

"Does it involve Avatar?" asked a new voice.

Ridge began to whip out his quarterstaff to confront danger when Wren stopped him. She grinned and spoke over her shoulder. "You can come out now, Mahon."

Mahon flashed a roguish smile. "I made no attempt to hide my approach. Although you seem a bit agitated."

"For your benefit. I knew Ridge would succeed."

Ridge appeared skeptical so he asked Wren, "Can you tell him what I learned?"

"The occupant isn't the merchant."

His expression changed to impressed. "How did you know?"

"Easy. Since you didn't know who it was, it's not the merchant."

Ridge scowled at the simplicity. "Ask a foolish question."

"So who does occupy the house?" asked Mahon.

"I got two different answers, which one do you want first?" Ridge sent a challenging glare to Wren. She simply shrugged so he continued. "Tegan is here."

"Tegan?" she asked with surprised.

"Oh, good, you didn't know that! She acted evasive and defensive; claiming the dying woman she tends is Sir Cedric's niece. She said he left her for important business. That doesn't sound like Cedric at all. He's a very compassionate mortal."

"Did you speak to the woman?" Mahon asked.

"No, to her son. At least he says so, but by Tegan's behavior, I'm not so sure," he replied with skepticism.

"Why?"

Ridge's face displayed bewilderment. "He said his name is Razi. *If* he is her son, he is not like any mortal I've ever seen. He's not much shorter than Wren and me. How many mortals have you seen close to seven feet tall?"

"You're suspicion is based upon his height?" Wren scoffed.

"No! His whole appearance is striking, powerful and oddly familiar." Ridge hesitated with uncertainty before continuing. "If I didn't know better, I would swear he is part Guardian."

"Impossible!"

Ridge looked squarely at Wren. "You and Avatar both claim Dagar was here."

"Now, you're saying you suspect Dagar is this mortal's father?"

"I didn't say that."

"It's what you thought and implied."

"So you can read minds too?"

"Enough!" scolded Mahon. They reluctantly clamped their mouths shut at his command. "The questions are: Why is Tegan here when any mortal physician can tend to a dying woman? What would Dagar want with her, and who is Razi that Tegan covered for him? Most of all, what does all this have to do with the sense that brought Avatar here?"

Ridge continued. "Hunter wasn't pleased by Avatar's presence. After they argued, he ordered me to escort Avatar to the Midessex border. Hunter won't be happy to learn others are here and nosing around."

The reply intrigued Mahon. "What did they argue about?"

By his expression, Ridge tried to be discreet in reply. "Hunter doesn't like Avatar, or rather his brash mannerisms. He let Avatar know he didn't think much of him trespassing into the province without permission."

Mahon's frown and crossed arms showed he didn't appreciate the answer. "Avatar is following orders from Captain Kell. So am I!"

"Avatar said as much, and in no uncertain terms. Hunter countered that if Avatar were under his command he would be disciplined for insubordination. Then he ordered me to escort Avatar to the border."

"Rather harsh—"

Ridge seized Mahon to stop the warrior from further speech. "Hunter!" he whispered in warning just before the Trio Leader appeared.

"What's going on here?" demanded Hunter.

Ridge flashed a smile. "I'm entertaining guests."

Hunter's scrutinizing gaze passed to Mahon and Wren, lingering on Wren. "A little far south, aren't you?"

"Just passing through so I stopped to chat."

"And your excuse?" he asked Mahon.

"I make no excuses. I'm here on the captain's orders."

"At least one honest answer."

"I wasn't being dishonest," refuted Ridge. "I was entertaining them with my normal sense of humor."

"Right. Flippant and sarcastic. You need to work on your delivery," said Wren.

"Do you give lessons?"

Mahon laughed at the exchange, but Hunter was not amused. The Trio Leader pointed west, to which Ridge spoke to Wren and Mahon.

"Please, follow me. I'll show you both the way."

Without further words, they accompanied Ridge in making a wide arc around the house. When they reached the trees beyond the manor, Ridge paused to look back across the clearing. Hunter disappeared into the forest, opposite them. He must have watched them for several moments.

"I see what you mean," said Mahon.

With a despondent sigh, Ridge motioned to keep going. "I asked Avatar to tell Captain Kell about Hunter's strange behavior, only he wasn't sure when he would speak to the captain again."

"How long has this behavior been going on?" asked Wren.

"Several decades, only it's grown steadily worse the past year."

"Why not speak to Kell yourself?"

Ridge shot her a harsh look. "He's my Trio Leader and former mentor! I don't want to report him if there isn't anything to report. Cam and I have been unsuccessful in getting him to speak about what troubles him. With his rude behavior toward Avatar and now you two, it has gone beyond us."

"And you can't shield him anymore," said Mahon.

Ridge stopped to confront the warrior. "That's what Trio Mates are supposed to do, protect each other! Could you betray Avatar if he started acting out of character?"

Mahon didn't back down from the irate ranger. After all, he was the stronger of the two. His voice and expression were sympathetic. "I meant no offense. Merely stating your position. I would act as you in protecting Avatar. Unless …"

"Unless?" Ridge demanded. He took a step closer to Mahon. Wren seized Ridge, more for his protection than a threat to Mahon.

Undaunted by the anger, Mahon maintained a non-threatening posture in reply. "Unless reporting him would help to save him."

"He speaks wisdom, Ridge," said Wren.

The ranger was slow to nod his agreement.

"You escorted Avatar to the Midessex border, correct?" asked Mahon. When Ridge answered in the affirmative, Mahon continued. "I can find my way. Let Wren stay and help you discover what is troubling Hunter and who this large mortal is."

Ridge's temper again flared. "You mean spy?"

"No. Wren can make an objective observation. You and Cam are too close to Hunter to make an impartial judgment. If something is discovered, *she* can report it, shielding both of you from Hunter's displeasure."

"Ridge. Let me help you, help all of you," she said.

For a moment Ridge vacillated, so Mahon said, "You asked Avatar to report your concern. Why should this offer be hard to accept?"

Ridge's shoulders sagged, as all argument drained from him. "Ay." He turned to Wren. "I accept your help, and thank you," he said the last sentence to Mahon.

The warrior grinned. "Go. I can find my way."

"Jor'el be with you," said Wren.

"And with you both." Mahon ran southwest.

"Where do you want to start?" Wren asked Ridge.

"Find out the mortal's identity. The sense of familiarity is too striking and unsettling."

"Easy enough. Speak to the servants without Tegan's knowledge."

He shook his head. "Harlen, the steward, admitted me and he could say something to her about it."

"Who said you had to go?

"Tegan will sense you."

"Not if you cause a distraction."

"What excuse would I give for returning so soon?"

She just looked askew at him. "Mortals must eat. Tell her that in a gesture of goodwill, you bring meat. I'll even supply it by using a trap rather than shooting it to appear you caught it. How about a boar?"

"You are so irritating," he groused as he followed her into the woods.

At the manor house, Razi sat beside the bed reading aloud. His mother asked him to read from Verse to comfort her soul in remembering Jor'el. He spoke in soft, soothing rhythmic tones. Of course, Verse was not his father's favorite book. It contained the Almighty's laws and words of Wisdom for the mortals, thus never made available to him or Ram.

The act of reading reminded him of the times he happened upon Janel during surprise visits. She often read Verse when watching the sheep on a nice spring or summer's day. The first time she read aloud from the Sacred Book, he felt a surprise stirring in his heart and soul, something that touched him deep down. He wondered if his Guardian half responded to the Creator's voice or if the simplicity and certainty of her faith touched him. Whatever the reason, he now found new meaning to the words coming from his mouth as he read to his dying mother.

Noticing her eyes closed, Razi stopped. Concerned she might have passed, he placed the book on the nightstand to sit on the bed. "Mother?" He touched her face. He smiled in relief where her eyes opened. "I thought …"

"Soon," she spoke in a weak voice. "I'm glad you're here, but sorry Ram is not."

"I can send for him."

Her thin smile quivered. "He won't come. Too much of his father in him." She held his hand with her thin bony cool fingers. "Even as a young child, you were the more sensitive." Her eyes grew watery. "I wish we had more time together —"

"Please, save your strength."

"No, I must say this, and hope you can forgive me."

"There is nothing to forgive. You gave me life."

"As a plot of revenge, not for love. Oh, Razi, how can I make you understand, when all you believe is what he tells you? I once believed him and now I will pay the price. No, please, listen," she urged when he started to object. "I rejected my father because I thought he didn't love me rather wanted to control me. Now, at the end, I realize he did love me, that he wanted the best for me. I hurt him so."

"You don't have to tell me."

"I do. Confession is good for the soul. Remember that." She took a deep breath and began her story. "The first man I thought I loved was Curtis. I believed he loved me too. He just ruined my maidenhood to get back at my father after being condemned to the labor camp as justice for his crimes. Being the disgraced daughter of the Vicar, I became an outcast. That's when Dagar worked his wiles on me." She swallowed and licked her parched lips before continuing.

"Although I grew up around Guardians, Dagar swept me away with lavished attention. He is so good with words, clever and handsome beyond any mortal male." She smiled and reached to touch Razi's face. "You too are very handsome. The fact he was a Guardian didn't matter to me, though being the Vicar's daughter mattered to him." Scorn crept into her voice. "I didn't see it at the time because I was so desperate to be loved, or more rightly, what I thought was love. Only after he took you and Ram away did I reflect upon my life and what I had done." Her voice quivered with emotion, as she looked at him in fear. "By your birth, I gave Dagar the means to rebel against Jor'el. I let him use you both for his own evil purposes!"

"Ram and I are not without choices."

She gripped his hand with surprising strength for one so frail. She attempted to raise herself on her elbow. "What do you mean? You agree to help him destroy Jor'el and the Guardians? To conquer Allon?" Overcome, she fell back whimpering. "Merciful, heaven, tell me it's not true!"

"Mother, please, calm yourself."

She shook her head, agitated and in great fear. "Don't make my same mistake! Dagar doesn't love you or Ram! He never loved me. He isn't capable of love. All he ever wanted was power. Don't you understand?"

"I do."

She stared at him in horror. "And you agreed? Have you no love either?"

"No, I have not agreed," he said, frantically in trying to calm her. "And I do love. It is what brought me here."

She smiled, weak and tearful. "I am glad to hear someone loves me."

"Ay. It is a wonderful feeling when shared. It makes one's heart light. There is almost a sense of invincibility."

She studied at him. "You don't just mean me, do you?"

Razi became sheepish, conflicted about whether to speak of Janel.

Her voice now barely rose above a whisper. "If you have found true love, don't let it go. Fight for it, for you don't know how precious it is. I wasted my life searching only to find it in the person I wronged the most. Please, forgive me, my son!"

"I forgive you."

A fading look entered her eyes. Her words became breathy and forced. "Don't let your love slip away. Don't end up bitter and lonely like me ..." her voice trailed off.

Her last words echoed in his ears for a moment before he realized she became quiet. "Mother?"

Tegan entered. She approached the bed and placed a gentle hand on Haggar's neck. Her somber gaze told him the answer before she spoke. "She's gone."

Razi fought emotions as he laid Haggar's hand across her body. Tegan watched him, guarded. "I suppose you think it weakness to be touched by her death."

"That's not for me to say, my lord."

His gaze narrowed on her. "Have you ever cared about anyone or anything, Tegan? Other than ambition of being my father's prime physician?"

She tempered her reply. "Some emotions are not common to Guardians. However, I do care enough to be a good physician. A trait your father recognizes."

"Once he obtains his goal, we'll see how much he truly recognizes." He waved her away. "Make proper arrangements for her burial."

Tegan withdrew.

For several moments Razi stared at his mother. Learning her father's identity made the Vicar his grandfather. Not that the discovery changed his feelings for Janel or the fact they were now married. This was just a shock to him, as it will be to Janel the day she learns of his connection to Avram, her uncle. The irony was not lost upon him.

A flash of white light appeared in the room. Razi watched in wary anticipation. He relaxed at seeing Barrion.

"How is she?" asked the warrior.

"Dead."

Barrion held Razi by the shoulders. "I'm sorry. I would have brought you here more often if I could."

"I know. I appreciate the risks you have taken on my behalf."

"Small consolation for securing the future."

Razi smiled with tenderness as he picked up the book of Verse. "She asked me to read to her." In frustration, he spoke so only the warrior could hear. "Oh, Barrion, I don't know how much longer I can do this!"

Barrion replied in the same low, confidential voice. "Easy. *He* sent me to keep an eye on *you*." He smiled. "The best way to do so is to let your heart and conscience guide you." The smile faded. "The time is upon us. A choice must be made. For whom will you choose? Don't speak," he warned when Razi opened his mouth. "Keep it hidden here," he patted Razi's left breast. "Yet act as if it is known." His head snapped around to look at the door. "Someone is here! I shouldn't be seen. Take care, my prince."

"I will, and thank you."

Barrion grinned, stepped away and disappeared.

Tegan rushed in alert and ready. She must have sensed Barrion so Razi put off her inquiry with a question of his own.

"Why have you returned? Have you made the arrangements so soon?"

"Who was here?"

"No one."

"I sensed someone!" She closed her eyes.

He knew she meant to use her spiritual senses so he spoke a command in the Ancient, *"Tegan, sguir!"*

Her eyes snapped open. Every muscle became rigid at his command.

"You should know better than to question me."

Tegan stiffly bowed. "Forgive me, my lord. I am only looking out for your safety."

"My *health* is your concern, nothing else. Now, are the arrangements made?"

"Not all, my lord."

Razi continued to stare at Tegan. When needed, he could invoke his father's commanding mannerisms. She bowed and withdrew.

Chapter 8

AT TWILIGHT, RIDGE APPROACHED THE FRONT OF THE MANOR house with a dead boar slung across his shoulders. Soft lamplight showed from behind curtains. Unfortunately the snaring took longer for Wren than shooting it outright. This delay gave him some teasing triumph. However, he kept wondering if Hunter would arrive unexpectedly during the diversion. Maybe it would be easier to leave and speak his concern to Kell than play this mortal game of deception.

Despite understanding the growing necessity for such actions, deception went against Guardian sensibilities. More distressing was learning to be subtle and careful with his own Trio Leader, mentor and friend. Compared to Hunter, convincing Tegan about a second call in the same day should be easy. He hoped Wren acted quickly.

Ridge pulled the front doorbell cord and waited for a response. This time, Tegan opened the door. She greeted him in her usually surly manner.

"Ah, ranger! Two times in a day, how fortunate."

Ridge hoisted the boar to a more comfortable position on his shoulders. Not that the boar was heavy or uncomfortable, he just felt awkward in his covert role. He wished he had asked Wren for a sign of succeeding so he could make a graceful exit. He donned a smile in reply.

"I bring meat. With winter not far off, game will become scarce."

Tegan stiffened as if distracted. He had to act fast.

"Can she not have meat?"

"Unfortunately, she passed on."

At Tegan's renewed distraction, Ridge again spoke. "I'm sorry to hear that. Is her son still here?"

"Ay," she replied. This time Tegan looked over her shoulder.

Ridge spoke to get her attention. "Perhaps the boar can be used for the wake."

Tegan forced a grin of agreement. "Indeed."

"I can take it to the kitchen if you want to get back to your duties."

The physician frowned in obvious indecision. A male voice shouted from upstairs, which made Ridge pause in entering.

"Don't take the beast any further into the house," she scolded.

"Sorry, my mistake." Ridge narrowly missed Tegan slamming the door in his face. He reached the kitchen just in time to see the door closing. "Wait!" A balding man poked his head out. "Tegan told me to bring this to the kitchen."

"Fine looking boar."

"Thank you. Where do you want it?"

"On the table." The man pointed and commented, "It's not often we get two visitors in one night."

"Here now!" a woman scolded him.

"Oh, sorry," he muttered an apology.

Ridge hid a smile as he placed the boar on the table. "Don't worry. Guardians are the soul of discretion. You can offer some of the meat to the indigent or destitute. The onset of winter tends to bring them out."

"We'll do just that," she said with a sly smile. "Thank you."

Ridge touched his forehead in a salute as he left the kitchen. He took a leisurely pace in departing just in case Tegan was watching. Once in the wood, he quickly reached the rendezvous. Wren appeared serious in demeanor.

"You discovered his identity," he said.

"They gave very detailed *descriptions* that sound too familiar."

"Descriptions? More than one?"

Wren laid a hand on Ridge's shoulder. "*You must* speak to Kell."

With dreaded understanding, he said, "Hunter is involved."

"I believe he had you escort Avatar, Mahon and me in order to prevent us from going to the house."

"Why would he do that?" He couldn't keep the anger from his voice.

Wren heaved a shrug. "You can better answer that question. The servants believe the man is her son, at least from the few times he and his brother have visited."

A strange, eerie screeching sound began. Before both were completely armed with their weapons, four winged creatures pounced upon them. Their bodies had the shape of a reptile with small wings of scaly feathers and sharp, powerful talons. One knocked away Wren's crossbow. The shaft loosed and fired into the ground. She dodged the attack and drew her dagger. Talons snared her left shoulder, ripping her clothes while sinking deep into her flesh. She fell to her knees. She made a defensive swipe at the creature with her dagger. The blade made contact and it released her.

When the second creature leapt at her, Wren rolled away. It landed where she had been, angry and flapping it wings. It didn't take off, rather leapt at her again. Once more she rolled away. This time she stopped right next to her crossbow. The creature made for a third attack. Wren quickly notched an arrow and fired. The force sent it backward and impaled in a tree. From behind, the first one Wren wounded made an angry screech. Despite a deep gash in one side and the wing hanging useless, it leapt at her. She fired another bolt, instantly killing it.

The initial attack knocked Ridge off his feet. He managed to bat aside one of creatures with his staff. Another creature came at him. He couldn't move quickly enough to totally avoid the attack. He cried out in painful annoyance when sharp teeth scraped his neck. He scrambled to his knees where he bashed it squarely in the face with the end of the staff. He brought the staff down on its neck so hard he heard bones break. The creature went limp in death.

The first creature recovered from being swatted aside and came at Ridge. The ranger rose to his feet, yet swayed when trying to keep his balance. With an awkward swing of the staff, he sent it flying into the tree where the one Wren shot dangled. Stunned, it lay in a whimpering heap at the base of the tree.

Despite feeling unsteady, Ridge lifted the staff using both hands. One end pointed toward the ground. He shouted in the Ancient, *"Talamh uir sluig de namh!"* and stuck the ground with the staff. A large crack ran from the staff to the base of the trees. Both creatures fell into the crack. The earth closed in over them. The use of power made Ridge collapse in exhaustion.

Wren ignored her injury to examine the two remaining dead creatures. "What were they?"

"I don't know. I was going to ask you since I've never seen them before." Ridge tried to stand, but only managed to make it to his knees.

"How badly are you wounded?"

"Just a scratch on my neck from the fangs. Not sure why I feel weak and dizzy. Using my power shouldn't have drained my strength."

"I feel a bit weak myself," she groused. "If those were natural creatures we shouldn't be feeling this way."

"How could they not be natural?" he asked in confusion.

"If neither of us recognize them while we feel weak from relatively minor wounds. What else but unnatural?"

"Your wound looks worse than mine."

"We need to report this to Kell."

Ridge used his quarterstaff to stand. He screwed his eyes shut, and clenched the staff to stay on his feet. "I've never felt queasy before. I don't think I can dimension travel. I'm doing good to stand."

"I'll take you." She held his arm in support and said, *"Siuthad."* Instead of disappearing in dimension travel, both fell to their knees in pain. "That didn't work."

Ridge bent over and clenched his wounded neck. "You think! I feel worse than before."

"Whatever those creatures were, the wounds have decreased our strength and power."

"I guess we walk to the Fortress." Even using his quarterstaff, Ridge struggled to stand. "Should we take one of them with us?"

"Can you carry it?"

"Bad idea." He started walking.

Back at the manor house, Tegan kept busy with arrangements for Haggar's burial. If not for Razi's presence, she would have left to inform Dagar of the expected results. Haggar's death served as the signal to move forward with the final stage of the plan. Heaven knows what Kell will do when he learns of Dagar's sons. *Kell, no. Jor'el!* she thought.

One of the Almighty's mandates forbade Guardians from marriage to their own kind or mortals. Thus began the long held belief Guardians were sterile and incapable of producing offspring. She knew of three forbidden liaisons between Guardians and mortals in the past. None resulted in offspring. The Guardians involved received divine punishment while the mortals banished from Allon. Of course those liaisons happened between female Guardians and male mortals. This was first she knew of a male Guardian and a female mortal. Not that it would make a difference in the punishment when discovered. Of course, she made the decision to join Dagar fully aware of the ramifications.

Hunter arrived. More intrusion further soured Tegan's already crabby mood. With mourning servants milling about, she drew Hunter aside. She spoke in the Ancient to keep the conversation private.

"Well, this is a busy nights for visitors. Wasn't it enough that you sent your protégé bearing a gift?"

"Ridge was here?"

She warily eyed the Trio Leader. "I assumed you sent him."

"No. I ordered him to escort Wren and Mahon to the border."

"Why were they here?"

"Following Avatar."

"Avatar!"

"Be easy. I took care of everything."

"What is taken care of?" Razi's arrival startled them. He understood the Ancient.

"My lord. I didn't know you were here," said Hunter, switching back to Allonian.

Razi repeated his question. "What is taken care of?"

"A small wrinkle in the plan. Nothing to be concerned about." The answer didn't satisfy Razi so Hunter discreetly explained, "The captain's aide is nosing about."

"Does my father know?"

"I told him. He said he would take care of everything."

"Time draws near, my lord. We can't take any chances," said Tegan.

"My mother just died, so don't speak to me of chances!"

"Have you informed Dagar of her death?" Hunter asked Tegan.

Razi was quick to reply. "He will be informed when all is settled here."

Hunter locked eyes with the young half-breed. Indeed, Razi had Dagar's sense of command. "I understand, my lord. Would you like me to inform him? When all is completed here, of course."

Razi cracked a sly smile. "No. For now, help Tegan with the arrangements. Afterwards, you can take me back and *I* will tell him."

Hunter inclined his head in acknowledgement. "As you say, my lord."

Razi moved to leave yet paused at the bottom of the stairs. "Oh, and, Hunter. Don't try anything behind my back. Both of you." His harsh gaze shifted between them.

"Ay, my lord," they said in unison.

Razi went upstairs.

"I understand why Dagar favors him to be king over Ram," said Hunter.

"Ay. Ram is brawn while Razi the brains. I recognized the difference when they were boys. However, Razi has one downfall, he is emotional."

"And you play upon his weakness."

She heaved a careless shrug. "Not if he does what he is told. If he exhibits the same weakness he did with his mother, I will act." She leaned close to Hunter to speak in sarcastic tone. "Report *that* to Dagar."

"You think he sent me to watch you?"

Her hands went to her hips. "I would be foolish to think otherwise."

Hunter cocked a wry grin. "This may come as shock, but he didn't send me. I'm here on my own. This is my province and I do care for those in it."

"Then look after your own Trio Mate. When he came here a second time, he wasn't alone."

"Cam?"

Tegan shook her head. "I couldn't get a specific sense, but another Guardian."

Hunter spoke with regret. "I hoped to spare Ridge, but I don't think I can avoid it any longer."

"When all is revealed, we can't let sentiment get in the way."

He shot her a challenging look. "So will you secretly poison Eldric or kill him face-to-face?"

Tegan shoulders squared and lifted her chin. "I will do what is necessary when the time comes. So will you, if you value your existence. If not, Dagar will destroy Ridge and Cam before coming after you." She turned on her heels not seeing his angered reaction.

A short time later, servants left the gravesite. Razi remained at the mound of earth. Although he did not have the opportunity to know his mother well, her death hit him hard. He held the book of Verse. His mother's final urgent words gripped his heart. Without knowing it until now, his life mirrored hers in the desire to find true and lasting love. Even Barrion told him to follow his heart. Of his father's associates, Barrion knew him the best and was the one he trusted the most.

Recalling the encouragement of his mother and Barrion, his heart and mind turned to Janel. A sense of guilt formed at the knowledge of his mother being denied the love he found. For her sake and his own, he couldn't let it slip away! Janel would not suffer the same fate as his mother. To prevent any adversity, he needed to return to protect her.

Razi glanced to where Tegan and Hunter waited. Despite siding with Dagar, Hunter was the more honorable of the two Guardians. Thus he felt certain Hunter would follow his command to keep silent. Tegan was too ambitious, and posed a dilemma of leaving without rousing suspicion. He learned well the art of invoking authority, and had no compunction of using it when necessary. He did earlier to cover Barrion's arrival. Doing so now would gain him time to reach Janel.

"My lord, are you ready to return?" asked Hunter.

"Ay, only not directly. I need some more time. I will ride to Midessex and from there you can help me return."

"Are you sure that is all?" Tegan sounded far from cordial.

"Guardians may have difficulty understanding or even experiencing grief, but mortals feel the loss when someone dies," Razi rebuffed.

"I didn't mean to question your grief, my lord." She motioned to the book of Verse. "Rather your new found interest."

"My *interest* is that this belonged to my mother." His angry, intense look passed from Tegan to Hunter. "We will meet at the meadow in five days." He gave Tegan a last snarl before marching off.

"Shouldn't I accompany you, my lord?" called Hunter.

"No!" Razi turned around to continue his rebuke. "How would it appear the Trio Leader left the province to escort me? The whole idea is not to draw attention to me before it is time, correct?" His glare made both Guardians agree. "Now, both of you stay here five days!"

"It only takes four days to reach the meadow," said Tegan.

Razi boldly approached the physician. "Tegan, this is last time you will dispute me or try my patience. I know my mother did *not* die naturally. You may have been under orders from my father, but heed this. When I become king, I will remember, and *you* know I am skilled in dealing with Guardians—permanently!"

For the first time, Tegan appeared anxious. "Ay, my lord." She bowed.

"Hunter! See she stays put!"

The Leader spoke an acknowledgement so Razi resumed his course in leaving.

"The bay horse is suited for distance travel. The pale one is too old," she called.

Razi heard but didn't respond. He hoped his act of utilizing the authority established by his father would keep Tegan at the house long enough to reach Janel. Recalling Janel's confidence in him because he was not like his father pricked him.

No, I am not my father's son, but I will use what I have learned to protect those I love. Please understand that, Janel.

Razi ordered the bay horse saddled along with provisions packed for a journey. He managed to put his mother's book of Verse in the saddlebag without anyone noticing. He spoke a few words of thanks to Harlen before departing. He determined to put as much distance as possible between himself and the miserable manor house before nightfall.

Chapter 9

ALTHOUGH GUARDIANS COULD OUTRUN HORSES AND COVER great distances without resting, wounds hampered their mobility. Wren and Ridge didn't reach the Fortress until late the following afternoon. Wren cradled her arm in what appeared to be an attempt to protect her shoulder. Ridge used his staff to walk and dragged his left leg.

Phoebe, Eldric's first assistant, made her way across the compound when she saw them enter the gate. She rushed over. "By the heavenlies, what happened?"

"To tell the truth, we're not sure what attacked us," said Wren.

"That's an angry wound," said Phoebe concerning the marks on Ridge's neck.

"It's gotten worse. My whole left side is numb."

"Guard, inform Captain Kell." Phoebe moved to support Ridge. Nearby, she spotted two Guardians warriors. "Ewert! Bailey!"

The warriors hastened to her summons.

"Carrying them would be best for their conditions." Phoebe took Ridge's staff when Ewert lifted the ranger. Bailey carried Wren. Neither objected to the assistance. In fact, Ridge looked on the verge of fainting.

Kell, Armus, Dax and Vidar arrived at the infirmary just after Wren and Ridge were made comfortable upon cots.

"Wren?" Concerned, Vidar moved to the bed.

She flashed a tired smile. "I'm still here."

"What happened?" asked Kell.

"Can't your questioning wait until I tend to their wounds, Captain?" chided Phoebe. She shooed Vidar away since his arrival interfered with treatment.

"Their wounds appear serious," chided Kell.

She shot him an irate glare. "Serious enough to warrant treatment before interrogation. Now, wait in the hall."

Kell squared his shoulders at the rough dismissal. Armus took hold of Kell to steer him from the room. "She has Eldric's manner, but knows what is best." Vidar also showed reluctance to leave, so Armus grabbed the archer on the way out. Dax followed.

In the hall, they met Ewert and Bailey. Kell immediately accosted them.

"Do you two know what happened?"

"No, Captain. Phoebe asked us to help bring them here," said Bailey.

"Ridge's condition appears worse than Wren," said Dax.

"I'm not sure whether to be grateful or not," complained Vidar.

"We won't know anything until Phoebe finishes treating them," said Kell. His face and voice disagreeable. "I must to speak to Eldric about her bedside manner."

It took a half an hour for Phoebe and another Guardian assistant physician to finish dressing the wounds. Once allowed back into the infirmary, Kell made his displeasure apparent by glowering looks. Phoebe stood her ground and returned the captain's withering stare.

Wren sat up on the cot with pillows behind her for cushioning against the wall. She wore a new shirt over her bandaged shoulder. Some color had returned to her face. Ridge lay on the cot. His complexion appeared unusually pale and tired.

Kell demeanor softened toward them. "What happened?"

Wren began the explanation. "We were leaving our observation of the manor house, the place where I followed Avatar, when unknown creatures attacked us." Her brows leveled in perplexed recollection. "A strange mix of reptile and bird, only it didn't fly rather jumped." She made a motion with her good hand to illustrate.

Kell and Vidar exchanged knowing glances, which made Armus ask Kell, "How did they get out?"

"You know what they were?" asked Ridge in a weary voice.

"Kelpies," said Phoebe. She remained near the beds.

"How do you know?" demanded Kell.

"In my training, I learned to treat all manner of injury and wounds. I suspected it when Ridge complained of how the effects grew worse and his left side is numb. Wren hasn't experienced the paralysis since she was skewed by talons and not bitten."

"What are kelpies?" asked Wren.

"Creatures of the cave," replied Kell.

Wren blinked at him in annoyance. "That doesn't explain anything, Captain."

"The cave is a nether dimension prison for Guardians that contains labyrinths and creatures not meant for this realm. Vidar reported that Avatar mentioned a cave deep underground. There are no such physical caves in Allon."

"Then why did you send me to the Highlands?" Dax asked Vidar.

"To keep you busy. You've become arrogant and careless. You could have gotten yourself and Wren seriously hurt when approaching Avatar without proper identification during his surveillance."

"Oow," said Armus in disapproval. "Not a good idea to sneak up on a warrior. We set traps."

Dax tossed Armus an abashed look. "He did set a trap." His shame multiplied at chuckles from Ewert and Bailey, who stood just inside the door. "I guess I was more concerned with impressing you than handling the situation correctly," he admitted to Vidar.

"I was impressed enough to request you for my Trio. Now, learn from this to keep your position."

"Ay, sir." Dax cast a sheepish look to Wren. "I'm sorry."

She kindly smiled. "Accepted. Although you're not responsible for this." She indicated her bandage shoulder.

"I still want to know how they got out," insisted Armus.

Kell's frown deepened. "My guess is Dagar has gained control of the cave. I won't know for certain until Avatar returns. I hope Mahon finds him in time to warn him not to go there."

"We pointed Mahon in the direction of Avatar," said Ridge.

"After your first encounter with Tegan and that mortal," said Wren.

"Tegan?" inquired Phoebe. Anger filled her face.

"Ay," said Ridge wary of Phoebe's vehement reaction. "Tegan said she was summoned to care for a dying woman, Sir Cedric's niece. I don't think so." He turned to Kell. "She acted evasive and defensive of him. But," his expression grew disturbed and anxious. "I don't believe he is fully mortal, Captain."

Kell's eyes narrowed in suspicion. "What do you mean?"

"The way he looked, his height." Ridge raised himself onto his right elbow, his voice urgent. "Maybe three, four inches shorter than Wren and I. He has the same lean, powerful build of a warrior with golden hair and a pair of the brightest blue eyes I've even seen on a mortal. By the heavenlies, Captain, I swear he is part Guardian."

"Kell—" began Armus.

The captain raised a stiff hand for silence, though his focus remained on Ridge. "Did you speak to him?"

"Ay, Captain. He said the dying woman was this mother and called her Haggar. His name is Razi. During this exchange, Tegan tried to interrupt with coughing or loud noises. Wren and I went back later to confirm what I learned."

"And did you?"

"Ay. Although the woman died between my first and second visit."

"We also discovered the identity of two other frequent visitors— Dagar and Hunter," said Wren with added emphasis on *Hunter*.

"They told you this?" asked Vidar, stunned.

Wren shook her head. "I came to the conclusion after hearing the servants' descriptions and answers to carefully worded questions. Add to that Ridge's suspicions of Hunter."

"What suspicions?" asked Kell

Ridge hesitant to answer, but the captain's prompting glance forced a reply. "Hunter's behavior has become erratic and abusive. Cam and I tried to deal with him privately, but Avatar's arrival changed that."

"How so?"

"To put it bluntly, Captain, Hunter doesn't like Avatar. He threatened him with discipline for insubordination, saying he wouldn't tolerate him like you do, then ordered me to escort him to the Midessex border."

Wren continued, "Apparently stating the fact that one is following your orders isn't good enough for Hunter. He accosted Mahon and me in the same manner, with the same result, being escorted by Ridge to the border. Only Mahon continued to follow Avatar while I stayed with Ridge to confirm the information. It was upon leaving we were attacked by those kelpies."

"This doesn't bode well," groused Vidar to Kell.

Seeing Ridge lay down and squirm to get comfortable, Phoebe stepped forward. "That's enough for now, Captain. They need to rest."

Kell motioned for Ewert, Bailey and Armus to accompany him in leaving. Vidar signaled Dax to stay before following the others. The ranger complied, and sat beside Wren's cot.

In the hall, Kell gave instructions to Ewert and Bailey. "Stand watch. Don't let anyone other than myself, Vidar, Armus, Dax and Phoebe into the infirmary."

"Ay, Captain." They acknowledged with a salute.

With brisk steps, Kell crossed the compound. Armus and Vidar remained close on his heels. He led them to the Vicar's private study.

"Kell," Avram greeted with a smile, which faded at noticing the sobriety of the Guardian captain. "This isn't a social call."

"Wren and Ridge are in the infirmary being treated for serious wounds. However, it is the news they bring that we must discuss."

"How were they injured?"

"A creature of the cave." Kell watched for Avram's reaction.

"What?" the Vicar said with alarm then spoke with understanding. "Dagar has taken control."

"That is my assumption. Unfortunately, the news they learned is of a more personal nature. Your daughter is involved."

Thunderstruck, Avram stared at Kell. "Haggar? How?"

"Remember you told Armus and me about Razi and your suspicions of his parentage?"

"Ay"

What he was about to say would strike the Vicar hard, but everything was coming together. Kell maintained a level voice. "Wren and Ridge learned a son was with his dying mother at a house frequently visited by Dagar. His name is Razi. Her name was Haggar."

Avram paled in shock. Fearing the Vicar would faint Armus helped him sit. He then fetched Avram a glass of wine.

"Wait!" said Vidar, also surprised. "Are you suggesting this Razi is the son of Avram's daughter and Dagar? Kell, that's impossible."

"The evidence is mounting. Avram confided to us his suspicions concerning a man name Razi, who married his niece. He said the resemblance to Dagar is too striking to ignore. His description matches the man Ridge also identified as Razi."

"Merciful heaven," murmured Avram with distress. "I married my grandson to my niece!"

"An act done in ignorance," said Kell.

Avram bolted up. "Unless he plans to use Janel like Dagar did Haggar!"

"Easy," soothed Armus.

Avram ignored Armus to seize Kell's arm. "You promised to protect her!"

"I will. Despite the growing evidence, it is still speculation in regards to Dagar. I would see this Razi for myself and interrogate him."

"Meanwhile, Janel may be in danger."

"A watch will be placed at the farm."

"At once," said Armus in acknowledgement of Kell.

"Wait!" began Avram, with alarm. This made Armus stop. The Vicar spoke to Kell while Armus lingered. "You said her name *was* Haggar. Is she dead?"

"Ay," Kell replied with sympathy.

Avram screwed his eyes shut and swallowed back his grief. "I thought she died long ago. Or at least somewhere I would never find her. Now the past comes back to haunt me."

"You're not responsible for her choices."

In regret, Avram shook his head. "Perhaps if I acted with more compassion and not allowed her to be turned away."

"The decision was handed down by Jor'el to the Council of Priests."

"Ay, ay." Weary and exhausted, Avram sat. "I understand the rationale and need for such discipline. It devastated my wife to learn what she did and with whom … if we acted with mercy maybe this would not have happened. Poor Janel. They seemed to be so much in love and innocent when they came to me." His voice cracked with regret.

Kell motioned for Armus to leave. This brought Avram to his feet. "I'll go with you to speak to Dolan and Janel."

"That's not a good idea," said Armus.

"This is my family we're talking about! I did nothing for Toby because I was told to let justice take its course—and see what happened to him! I will not sit by and watch my niece be used by a half-breed for some nefarious purpose."

Kell seized Avram by the shoulders to force the Vicar to look at him. His golden eyes shown with full command and authority as he spoke. "I told you for the purpose of easing your mind, not to send you headlong into causing trouble. Armus will set the watch. If Razi shows up at the farm, he will be brought to me for questioning. There is too much at stake to make a wrong move, especially if Dagar *is* his father."

Avram could not withstand the captain's eyes. He nodded as he looked away.

Kell released him. "I'm sorry I had to be harsh. Try to be at ease and trust us and Jor'el."

Avram's eyes grew misty as he spoke to Armus. "Don't let them come to harm."

"I won't," he said kindly before leaving.

Kell and Vidar also left. They didn't go far before Vidar spoke. "You may want to recall Mahon and Avatar."

Kell kept walking as he replied. "I can't."

"Why not? What happened to Ridge and Wren proves Dagar has command of the cave."

Annoyed, Kell drew Vidar into the nearest room to speak privately. "Avatar has to be very careful to go undetected while tracking Dagar. Summoning him is risky, because it could give away his position, which is why I sent Mahon. You know that!" Kell poked a finger into Vidar's chest.

"Circumstances have changed," Vidar stoutly rebuked.

"All the more reason to be cautious! Until we know for certain Dagar's plan, any misstep could bring more harm."

"Then what will you do?"

Kell closed his eyes. His brows furrowed with concentration.

"I thought you weren't going to summon them?" demanded Vidar.

Kell's eyes snapped up at the terse comment. The captain's rebuking glance made Vidar huff in annoyance.

From a flash of light, Gresham appeared. "You summoned me?"

"Avatar and Mahon are somewhere in Midessex on assignment."

"I know, I sensed their presence," snickered Gresham.

Kell ignored the humor. "Complications have arisen so I want you and your Trio Mates to find them and tell them to report back to me immediately! And Gresham," he added with heavy warming, "if they are not in this realm don't follow them, instead report back to me."

Gresham's expression showed he understood. "Ay, Captain." He stepped back and vanished.

"I can help Gresham," said Vidar.

"No. With the situation deteriorating, your skills maybe needed elsewhere. Return to the infirmary. I have some hard thinking to do."

Kell retreated to his office, leaving instructions not to be disturbed except for Phoebe or Armus. Jor'el's warning echoed in his mind *Proceed with the meeting, but be wary of what you discover in its wake.* If Jor'el knew about Dagar's progeny—

"*If*—? Of course he knows! But why not tell me? Would I have believed it? Do I believe it even now?" Kell paused at the window overlooking the compound. The daily activity of mortals continued unaware of anything. "Dagar, what have you done? Why produce offspring?"

Kell turned back to his desk and caught sight of a framed map of Allon on the wall of his office. He didn't require a map, since he knew every square mile. Everything was for décor when receiving visiting mortals. A sudden chill racked him. He hurried to stand before the map. His focus traced the path of the trouble from the labor camp to the Southern Forest manor and to Midessex.

He heard Jor'el's voice, not in his mind but in reality. "I told you to beware."

"A coup?" said Kell in disbelief then answered his own question, "Why else seize control of infrinn, if not to use its secrets against us? Wren and Ridge prove that." He shook his head trying to will away the deeply disturbing assessment. "Avatar will discover ..." He touched the map where he knew the cave to be located. His closed his eyes, his face taut in concentration. "Avatar, hear me! Don't go anywhere near *this* meadow." He looked up. "Please, Jor'el, let Mahon find him in time."

Chapter 10

AVATAR ONLY PAUSED TWICE TO GET HIS BEARINGS. Each time the sense continued to lead him southwest. It normally took five days for a mortal on horseback to travel from the Greenwood to Midessex. He reached it by twilight of the second day. Night or day didn't matter to Guardians, as darkness did not hamper their vision.

The sense he followed was definitely Guardian; only it shifted between Dagar and an unknown. Could the rogue be traveling with Dagar? Or following him? Did it pose a threat to the Trio Leader? The rogue already beat two defenseless mortal boys so very capable of violence. Why? There were so many questions. Avatar hoped finding Dagar would provide the answers.

If he's in a cooperative mood, he thought with wry snicker.

All his encounters with Dagar happened in the company of Kell or Armus, not individually and direct. Dagar's reputation was that of a very clever, intelligent and cunning warrior. His growing unrest and the resulting tension concerned Avatar, more due to Kell than his own feelings regarding Dagar. Anything troubling the captain, he took personally. If Kell hadn't given him the assignment, he would have volunteered.

Now in the wee hours of the morning, Avatar paused again to recheck the sense and direction. He got down on one knee, placed a hand on the ground, took a deep breath and closed his eyes. His brows furrowed as he stretched out his senses. The cave again, only this time closer. He felt a defensive perimeter shielding what lay behind. He needed to get a better idea of the cave, so he focused his energy to push

120

past the barrier. Suddenly, he jerked back in pain and fell onto his rump. A sense of overpowering evil accompanied the pain.

With wide-eye befuddlement, Avatar stared at the ground. "What is this place?" Did the sinister pain mean the rogue did something horrible to Dagar? Is it the other way around? Hard to tell. He did learn the trail turned due west. He took a moment to gather himself before continuing.

By dawn, Avatar crossed the River Bendix flowing from the Region of Sanctuary through the heart of Midessex. The river collected in a low spot to create Lake Alwin before proceeding into the Lowlands and finally to the sea. The sense grew stronger and colder with a deepening aspect of evil, unlike anything Avatar felt before. Somehow it involved Dagar. Whether a direct connection to the evil, or a victim of it had yet to be determined. Could his discovery affect all Guardians and mortals? Could it be stopped before inflicting serious damage? Kell would want to know; *he* wanted to know.

Avatar paused on a gentle rise overlooking an open meadow two miles wide. Stacks of lumber, brick and stone were located on the opposite side of the meadow. He saw no sign of workers. Perhaps a mortal intended to build a manor house. Did the sense of evil scare them off? Then again, were mortals capable of sensing what he did?

Avatar headed toward the stacks. Upon nearing the center of the meadow, a shivering sense of cold gripped him. Guardians weren't affected by weather. An overwhelming sense of evil accompanied the coldness. He recoiled, unsteady on his feet. His knees gave way and he fell hard upon them.

"What manner of power is this?" he said stupefied.

"Avatar!" he heard his name echo from all around.

He bolted to his feet and reached for his sword. "Who calls me?" he demanded, at seeing no one. "Identify yourself!"

"Find me if you dare, captain's favorite. Or stay back and watch him be destroyed!"

Avatar recognized the taunting voice. "Dagar! Show yourself."

Mocking laughter came from all around then diminished as if emanating from right under his feet. Avatar knelt to touch the ground but immediately withdrew his hand as if stung.

"The cave is here." Avatar's eyes narrowed in consideration. "You dare me to follow you by threatening Kell. Why? To lure me into a trap? Too easy to figure out. Still, I've seen your growing grudge against him for decades. Now you declare it! For that, I will follow and stop you!"

Mahon reached the top of the meadow rise. He grinned with pleasure at seeing Avatar on his knees investigating a spot of ground. It took him less than a day and a half to find his former mentor. Suddenly, Avatar vanished in dimension travel.

Mahon ran down the slope. An almost paralyzing sense of evil made him stumble onto all fours. He landed where he last saw Avatar. "By the heavenlies, what is this?" He took a deep breath to regain his composure. "Avatar!" he shouted, hoping his friend went someplace within earshot. No response.

Mahon brushed aside the dried grass and debris to look for whatever interested Avatar. A forceful sense of evil emanated from the ground and made him recoil. A shiver running through him, as his face filled with dread. "The cave! I'm too late!"

He gritted his teeth against anger at failing and possibly losing Avatar to some unseen evil. He placed both hands on the ground. Impulsive and foolish it might be …

Reappearing, Avatar found himself in a small damp chamber of the cave. He experienced unusual weakness from the travel. He clumsily sat on a rock to recover. Wherever the location, it was not easily accessible. He traveled to the Fringe and Heavenlies before but never felt this much drain in his power and spirit. He glanced about the room. The sound of dripping water lay just beyond the opening. He pushed himself off the rock to leave only to stagger sideways. "Strange," he muttered at the unsteadiness of his legs.

White light caught his attention. He drew his sword ready to confront whatever or whoever appeared from the light. "Mahon?"

Mahon swayed, unable to maintain his balance. Avatar caught Mahon to lessen the impact of dropping to his knees. He used his sword to keep his balance when Mahon's weight threatened to take him down too.

"Thank Jor'el. I thought I was too late," said Mahon wearily.

"Too late for what?"

Mahon swallowed back his fatigue and glanced around. "Actually, I am. At least you're in one piece. I don't think I've ever felt so weak."

Avatar helped Mahon sit on a boulder then sat beside him. "This cave is not easily accessible."

"Because it lies in a nether dimension. Kell sent me to warn you. I thought I succeeded when I saw you from the rise. Then you disappeared, so I followed."

"What warning?"

Mahon looked askew at Avatar. "Not to go into the cave."

Avatar laughed.

"Seriously! We may not be able to get out. According to Kell the cave is as an eternal prison for any Guardian who turns against Jor'el. There are creatures and labyrinths here for punishment, along with a safeguard to prevent escape. Kell fears Dagar may have gained control and sent me stop you from entering."

The sobriety of the message reflected in Avatar's change of expression. "Then you should not have followed me."

"I failed to warn you. I wouldn't let you suffer for my failure."

Avatar gripped Mahon's shoulder. "Your loyalty and friendship is appreciated. However, Dagar issued a challenge I cannot refuse. He seeks to use me, and this place, in his plan against Kell. I won't let him."

"Then why scold me for following to help you when you place yourself in harm's way to protect Kell?" chided Mahon.

Avatar grinned at the sentiment. "There is much at stake. Whatever Dagar is planning, it will affect everyone in Allon. Kell sent me discover his plan. Even if you had reached me in time, that is more important than personal safety. I would have sent you back to inform Kell of what I learned before coming here."

Insulted, Mahon stood, though unsteady. "I won't leave! I'm not your apprentice any more that I'm obliged to follow orders without question."

"You misunderstand. With both of us trapped here, Kell won't know. I would dispatch you with intelligence, not send you away like a pupil. You're a fine warrior. One I've been proud to tutor and call friend."

Mahon sighed and sat. "I guess I'm still trying to prove myself."

"Not to me, nor to Kell. Be as confident in yourself as we are."

"I was surprised and honored he dispatched me to find you."

Avatar chuckled. "Next to him or Armus, you're the only one who could find me."

Mahon proudly grinned. "Kell said the same."

An ear-piercing animal scream made them flinch.

"What was that?" asked Mahon, a bit nervous.

Avatar shook his head. "Nothing I've ever heard before. We need to find out." He readied his sword. "Are you up for reconnaissance?"

Mahon answered by standing to draw his sword.

Cautious and alert, Avatar led the way from the chamber and into a cramped tunnel. Their size forced them to duck or else scrape the top of their heads. Echoing made it difficult to gauge the direction of the scream, while the sound of dripping water grew distinct. Traveling further down the corridor, the sound of water faded while animal noises grew louder. The tunnel ended on a ledge overlooking a pit filled with cages. Most of the cages contained unusual creatures.

"Those must be the ones the captain meant," whispered Mahon.

Avatar took in every detail of the pit. "Being locked in cages suggests a keeper, who can contain and control them."

"Dagar?"

Avatar didn't immediately answer. He carefully moved to the edge of the ledge. He spoke quietly when Mahon joined him. "Dagar may be an Original and powerful, but I don't believe him capable of containing all those creatures alone. Vidar can only handle six at a time and he's the premiere archer."

"Are you suggesting he has help?"

"He must. Ridge told me of his concern for Hunter's recent shift in behavior."

"He said the same to Wren and I."

With a wry expression, Avatar looked along his shoulder at Mahon. "I thought you said Kell sent you to find me? Are you admitting Wren helped you?"

"No!" declared Mahon then lowered his voice. "I found her at the manor house. She said Vidar sent her to follow you while Dax went to search the caves along the Highland border. Vidar was with Kell when I received my assignment."

Avatar grinned. "I suppose I should be flattered by everyone's concern for my welfare. Come. I want to get a good look at these creatures." He made his way down a flight of carved out stone steps.

"What if the keeper returns?"

"That's why you're going to stand watch." At the bottom of the steps, Avatar motioned Mahon to the entrance opposite the stairs.

Mahon complied while Avatar began circumventing the room. The cages varied in size from small ones set upon rough-hewn wooden tables to large cells carved into the cave walls. The cells and several large freestanding cages were empty. In the small cages, crawled fuzzy worm-like creatures the size of a large cat. They oozed a slimy substance when moving. Razor sharp teeth-like appendages lined what appeared to be the mouth. Dark slits served as eyes. Drawing closer to the table for inspection, one reared up and sprayed goop in Avatar's face. Surprised, he backed away. He tried to wipe it from his eyes and face.

"Avatar?" Mahon joined him.

He grimaced and coughed. "That stuff is hideous in taste and smell!"

Mahon snatched a rag off a nearby table to hand to Avatar. Mahon crinkled his nose. "Aside from smelling awful, does it sting or hurt?"

Avatar wiped the goop off his face. "Hard to tell. The smell and taste is enough to turn the stomach. Is there another rag?"

Mahon found another. He took the fouled one and tossed it aside. "Do you want to look at any more creatures? Or should we find a place for you to freshen up?"

Avatar nudged Mahon back toward the entrance.

Mahon passed a cage containing a winged reptile creature. It leapt at the bars. One talon slipped through and barely missed his face. He jumped back and struck out in defense. His blade severed the creature's talon, making it scream in pain.

"Are you hurt?" asked Avatar.

"No, but I think we've seen enough—"

The same ear-piercing scream filled the chamber with deafening volume. They covered their ears in pain. Avatar braved a glance in the direction of the sound. A huge creature filled the entryway. Standing on two legs it rose taller than the Guardians, around nine feet tall. The body was shaped like a man with the scaly, armor-like skin of a lizard, the head of dragon, wings folded against its back and a spiked tail. It wore a sword at its side.

"What is it?" asked Mahon. He tried to withstand the painful sound.

The creature lunged forward, which sent them in opposite directions. Mahon dodged behind the wounded creature's cage. Avatar dove under a table. Using a massive hand, the beast overturned the table in an attempt to get at Avatar. Small cages flew across the floor or into the wall. A couple of cages broke open, freeing their occupants. The disturbance agitated the ones still confined. Avatar hurried to crawl away. His left pant leg became ripped when the beast tried to grab him.

"Hey!" shouted Mahon. The beast turned its attention towards him. Mahon threw his dagger, striking the beast high in the chest. A scream of painful anger sent Mahon stepping backwards to cover his ears.

Avatar gritted his teeth against the painful cry. He attacked. His blade sliced the creature's thick back hide. The beast's defensive swing caught Avatar in the chest and sent him flying across the room. He slammed into the wall where he collapsed into a huddled heap. His sword loudly clanked and echoed in the chamber.

Seeing the beast advancing on Avatar, Mahon had to think fast. One of the freed worm-like creatures crawled along the floor. He snatched the worm and ran to place himself between the beast and Avatar. He threw the worm at the beast's face. The worm wrapped itself around the beast's face, muffling any sound. It spewed slimy goop.

Mahon pulled Avatar to his feet. "Can you run?"

"Do I have a choice?"

"Run or face that."

The beast tore the worm off its face and began to eat it.

Avatar retrieved his sword then followed Mahon up the steps and into the tunnel. Mahon turned into what he thought was another tunnel. Instead, he slid down damp, slimy rocks into an icy cold pool of water. Avatar couldn't stop in time and followed right behind Mahon. Both swam across the pool to a small beach area where they climbed out.

"Your idea of escape?" complained Avatar.

"At least you're clean. Smell better too."

Avatar glanced up at hearing dripping. "This must be the water we heard earlier. The pool is fed from the surface."

"If this is in a nether dimension, how can water come from the surface?"

Avatar shrugged. "You said Kell told you Jor'el created this as a prison."

"So he makes air to breath, water to drink, a labyrinth to navigate and creatures to battle?" challenged Mahon.

"If there really is no way out, a Guardian would spend eternity fighting to stay alive while searching in vain for an escape."

Mahon sighed in resignation. "I thought of that when Kell described it. He said only a few of the Originals hold the key to the cave's secrets."

"Even knowing that, you came after me. I had no idea what I would be facing."

"I said I didn't want you to suffer for my failure."

Avatar gregariously smiled. "We won't fail. We'll find a way out."

"How can you be so sure?"

"Because we weren't sent here as prisoners. We've done nothing to be condemned. In fact, we were both on missions for the captain. The Almighty is aware of our orders so why keep us here for eternity?"

Mahon blinked in wonder. "I hadn't though of it that way."

Avatar laughed. "I guess you still need some lessons." He tugged on Mahon's shoulder to pull him to his feet. "Come."

Exiting from the beach area they entered another larger tunnel. Despite the wet clothes and coolness of the cave, neither suffered the ill effects of a chill. Even here, Guardians were immune to the elements.

"Can you sense Dagar? I can't," asked Mahon.

"That may be part of the punishment. Robbing our sense of each other while trying to survive."

For several moments they continued until hearing muttered voices up ahead. Some spoke in low, hushed tones, others sounded like they were in pain. Cautious, Avatar advanced toward the voices, Mahon at his back. Avatar stopped a few feet from an opening of what appeared to be a cavernous room. Crouching down to his knees, he signaled Mahon to wait. He carefully inched forward to the opening.

Avatar found himself overlooking a room about one hundred feet in diameter and nearly as tall. Hundreds of cells and cages filled the chamber, each containing a Guardian in various stages of suffering with instruments of torture scattered about the cavern. He became distressed at seeing Witter and Altari stretched out between chains. Both showed signs of horrible abuse.

Dagar and Tor appeared from the opposite side of the chamber. Avatar drew back slightly, but intensely watched them approach Witter and Altari. Dagar roughly assaulted Altari. Avatar bit his lip. Every muscle tensed at witnessing the assault. He couldn't hear clearly what

Dagar said, but the tone sounded taunting and caustic. Witter said something, which promptly received a vicious backhand from Dagar.

Avatar swallowed back a grunt of intense anger. When Dagar turned in his direction, he scrambled back into the tunnel. Fury and anguish of the sight made him labor with breath in an attempt to keep silent.

Mahon took note of Avatar's disturbance. "What is it?"

Avatar had difficulty answering, his words thick and hoarse. "Worse than even Kell knows." To stop Mahon from moving to the opening, he dragged Mahon away from the chamber.

Dagar smiled at seeing Avatar's retreat. "All is going as planned."

"I thought you sent Griswold to take care of him?" said Tor.

"Only delay him. Since he is here sooner than I expected, make certain he doesn't leave. At least not until I'm ready to use him to send the final message to Kell."

Tor grinned. "The labyrinth should keep him busy."

Dagar laughed and left. Tor went in the opposite direction.

Not until they returned to the beach did Avatar speak again, his voice still unsettled. "What I saw is hard to imagine, much less describe. A torture chamber, filled with Guardians, including Witter and Altari. Both badly suffering."

"What?" Shocked, Mahon looked back. "We have to free them."

Avatar seized Mahon. "Dagar and Tor are there!"

"Among the tortured?" asked Mahon in confusion. The intense direct look and the deliberate shake of Avatar's head made Mahon recoil. He barely voiced his question. "You believe they are responsible?"

"I saw Dagar assault them!" Avatar passionately exclaimed. His jowls tensed with grim determination. "We must leave and warn Kell."

"Kell said it be could hours to regain enough strength to dimension travel. It hasn't been that long, and *if* we can pass the safeguard."

Avatar grew frustrated, the sight weighing on him. "If a few Originals know the secrets of the cave can come and go, that means there are certain points of entry. A portal. We just have to find one."

"Perhaps where we arrived is one of those places."

Avatar took the lead; only he turned in the opposite direction of where they came. He felt Mahon follow him closely. The younger warrior made no initial objection to his change of direction. By Mahon's expression, he wanted to speak. However, this was already difficult enough. The knowledge of a rogue Guardian abusing mortals caused concern, but the reality of Guardian abusing Guardian rocked Avatar to the core! Again he glanced over this shoulder, not at Mahon, but to look further back.

"You're thinking about them, aren't you?" said Mahon in more of a statement than a question.

"Ay."

"Then why are we leaving?"

Avatar didn't want to discuss the subject any further, not until he could comprehend it.

"It's me. It's because I'm here. You wouldn't back down otherwise." Mahon grabbed Avatar to stop him. "You're still treating me like your apprentice, protecting me. You didn't even let me see the room."

"No! You're wrong." Due to distress, Avatar searched for the words to speak, to explain the situation. "Since I began tracking and sensing the cave, I felt deep, agonizing pain associated with it. That room brought to light a horrible reality of Guardians torturing Guardians!" He made a passionate gesture back in the direction then gripped his sword to contain his rising emotions. "You're right, I don't back down. And I admit you are a consideration, but *not* as my apprentice, rather my equal. Even with our combined skills and special powers we cannot hope to rescue them without great risk to all. Escaping and informing Kell is the best and safest way to help them and to stop Dagar! Remember, *that* is my assignment. To discover what he is up to before it's too late."

Properly chastened, Mahon cringed. "You're right. I'm sorry. I just hate the thought of failing by abandoning them."

"So do I. Again, you haven't failed." Avatar gripped Mahon's shoulder and flashed one of his famous wry smiles. "I take back what I said. I'm glad you followed me. Heaven knows what I would have done if alone when discovering the chamber. At least together, we stand a chance of surviving and possibly helping them."

"Providing we find a way out."

"Stop being so pessimistic."

The distant echo of metal striking something caught their attention.

"Doesn't sound like swordplay," said Mahon.

"Hard to tell with all the echoing, so let's find out."

The sound grew louder and more directional. Upon nearing an opening, the air felt warmer. They heard the unmistakable hiss of metal hitting water. Avatar silently drew his sword. Mahon did the same. Before going inside, Avatar motioned for them to separate. Swiftly, they took cover on opposites sides of the opening. The room served as a large forge. They hid behind the weapons shelves. There was another opening across the room and down a few steps.

A tall, brawny, tanned Guardian stood at the bellows with his back to them. He wore a leather apron over his bare chest. From the far entrance another individual arrived and approached the forge. Since the far entrance sat below the forge level it was hard to tell his height. He appeared shorter then the average Guardian height yet a very tall mortal—with decidedly familiar features, golden hair and goatee. Mahon gaped in surprise at Avatar, who waved for him to remain silent in order to pay attention to the exchange.

"The last pair of manacles were defective," he chided.

The Guardian paused in pumping the bellows. His voice sounded unnaturally raspy. "I told him I'm still working on it."

"Well, your work is suspect! The next set better work properly or you'll be missing more pieces. A hand perhaps?"

Even the Guardian's laugh proved grating. "Then who will Dagar get to create his little surprises? Another half-breed?"

He began to draw his sword making the Guardian raise the piece of hot metal he worked on. Snarling, the half-breed slammed his sword back into its scabbard. "Beware, when I inform him of your insolence." He left the way he came.

Mahon mouthed to Avatar, *"Half-breed?"*

Avatar feared he understood the inference. Rather than answer Mahon, he directed his attention to the Guardian. He didn't recognize the voice. Several names came to mind, those of lesser rank among the metal smiths. When the Guardian moved from the bellows to hammer the hot metal, he involuntarily spoke a name. "Rune!?"

The premier Guardian metal smith turned in the direction of the voice. His face was marred while his left eye appeared to have been removed by a searing poker. He wore no patch to hide it. "Who's there? Come out or I'll skewer you!" He gripped the piece of hot metal as he moved toward the rack where Avatar hid.

Avatar motioned for Mahon to stay put before he stepped out of his concealment.

Rune halted in surprise. "You?" In quick, anxious glances, he scanned the room. "How did you get here? Did Kell send you?"

"The *how* doesn't matter. The question is why are you with Dagar?"

Rune swung at Avatar. Metal sparked when meeting Avatar's blade.

In a quick move, Avatar disarmed him. "Don't do this, Rune!"

The metal smith snatched a heavy metal chain whip. He wickedly grinned. "This has a longer reach than your puny sword, warrior."

Avatar dodged to one side when Rune faked an attack with the chain. If he drew Rune away and exposed his back to Mahon, the metal smith wouldn't know what hit him. Another fake attack came and another avoiding movement to turn Rune closer to Mahon.

Just beyond Rune, Avatar noticed Mahon move into position. Another dodge should do it. Only the third wasn't a feigned attack. The chain narrowly missed Avatar's head as it smashed a shelf containing forging instruments. Avatar flinched into a protective position when a large hammer fell from the shelf and struck him in the left shoulder. The distraction gave Rune time to land a stunning blow across the back of Avatar's shoulders. He went sprawling to the floor. Rune landed a second blow that ripped the back of Avatar's uniform and sliced flesh. Semiconscious, Avatar didn't react.

"*An luths de fichead!*" shouted Mahon in the Ancient. With a surge of strength, he knocked Rune across the room. The metal smith crashed into a rack of pikes and became buried beneath the fallen weapons. The noise echoed off the chamber walls. Mahon dropped to his knees. "Avatar?"

"The noise will alert them." He reached for Mahon to help him up. Standing, he couldn't support his own weight and started to collapse. Avatar cried out in pain when Mahon caught him.

"Sorry." Mahon readjusted Avatar by placing his arm over his shoulders and held him up by his belt. "Can you walk?"

"Not well."

They heard the voices of alarm coming from the opposite opening. Avatar willed himself to move as Mahon helped him from the forge. Mahon half-carried, half-dragged Avatar through the tunnel until Avatar motioned to be let down due to pain. Finding an alcove, Mahon lowered him to sit. He knelt to examine Avatar's back.

"What did he strike you with to cause such injury and debilitation?"

"Stygian metal or spurean chain. I'm not sure which," Avatar replied between gritted teeth of pain.

"What?"

"Secret weapons Kell ordered Rune to develop. Not only will it cause injury to an adversary but also rend them immobile. I can tell Kell it works. Such a minor wound shouldn't be able to stop me."

"It tore your uniform and nearly ripped the hide off your back."

"My back doesn't feel bad. When struck, I felt intense burning and stinging through my whole body followed by queasiness."

"I wish I had some of Eldric's herbs. All I can do is use my shirt to bandage your wounds." Mahon smiled, a hint of mischief appearing. "Of course I could dunk you in the pool for cleansing."

Avatar's glare showed his disapproval of the idea.

"Right, swimming is out of the question. It's more important to learn the identity of that mortal and why Rune called him a half-breed?"

"I don't know if I want to consider the answer. Although I can't deny his looks are familiar."

Mahon snorted with irony. "I've heard how he's grown to despise mortals. Now he's using them to his advantage."

Avatar growled in great vexation. "This is getting worse! The sooner we're out of here the better." He used his hand on the wall to brace himself and rise. Mahon made ready to help if needed, but Avatar stood on his own. He bit back the pain of moving.

Mahon glanced up and down the tunnel. "I don't see anyone." He began to take Avatar's arm when the warrior jerked away and left the alcove. With a wry smile, Mahon followed.

Avatar moved in slow, halting steps. He stopped upon reaching an intersection of four tunnels.

"Is the wound so painful that you need to rest?"

"No." Avatar motioned to the tunnels. "This one leads back to the pool. That one goes back to the chamber where we first arrived."

"How can you tell?"

"I have a good sense of direction. Besides, I left a mark on it when we turned." He pointed to the wall. "Don't you remember anything I taught you about tracking?"

"I found you, didn't I? But, I disagree. We didn't turn from the first chamber. We went straight. The only turn we made was the one I took when we fled and ended up in the pool."

"Then how do you explain my mark?"

"Senility." Mahon traced his hand over the rock. "These are claw marks, and lower than your sword would make." Suddenly he cried out and reached for something behind him. "Get it off!" Mahon turned his back to Avatar, revealing a giant black and yellow spider.

Despite the pain of his wound, Avatar's sword proved fast and lethal. He stabbed the spider and removed it from Mahon's back without ripping his friend's uniform. "Are you all right?"

"Ay." Mahon glared at the dead spider. "I agree, the sooner we get out of here the better."

Mahon just finished speaking when another spider moved from the same tunnel. He and Avatar backed into the third tunnel. Soon the tunnel ended. They returned to the intersection. The second spider was gone, yet sound came from the tunnel they just left.

"Why do I think we found the labyrinth?" chided Mahon.

"Or are being driven to it."

"Then Dagar knows we're here."

Avatar shook his head. "If he saw anyone, it was me since you never looked into the chamber. Remember, this is a personal challenge."

"All right, so Dagar knows you're here. What's the difference?"

"*You* are an unknown factor. I'll lure them away while you escape."

"No, you saw the chamber, I didn't. You know about those weapons and are wounded. I'll cover for you to escape and tell Kell."

When sounds of an approached creature grew louder, Avatar shoved Mahon into another tunnel. "We escape together or not at all."

Mahon pulled up short at seeing more tunnel choices. "All we have to do is find our way out."

"If we jointly employ out tracking skill that shouldn't take too long."

"What exactly do you suggest we track?"

"Stand watch." Avatar took the hilt of his sword in one hand, the point in the other hand and knelt. He placed the sword on the ground, held it there and closed his eyes. Under his breath, he spoke a prayer in the Ancient. The sword vibrated under his hands. When it moved along the ground, he released the point but held onto the hilt. The point indicated a tunnel on the far left.

Mahon watched in wonder. "How did you do that?"

"A trick Armus taught me. He swore me to secrecy with instructions to use it only under dire circumstances. I think this qualifies."

"Does that mean you won't tell me the secret?"

Avatar stood, ginger in his movement. "Only if Armus releases me from my promise." They moved down the indicated tunnel.

"Where will this trick lead us?"

"I don't know. Part of the prayer is for Jor'el's direction. I guess we'll find out when we reach the end."

"If we reach the end," groused Mahon upon entering a large domed cavern. Five more choices of tunnel awaited them.

Again, Avatar performed Armus' secret move. Again his sword indicated a tunnel. This time when they reached another chamber they were faced with three choices. Avatar had to sit, careful not to let his back touch the wall.

Mahon squatted beside him. "More queasiness?"

Avatar swallowed back the sickness. "And weakness. As I recall, Eldric disapproved of the idea when Rune presented it. However, Kell agreed there could be a need for such weapons. He told Rune to make a few experimental samples for testing. It never went beyond that since one of Rune's apprentices succumbed to the effects."

"You mean it never went further until now."

"Ay. Who knows what other experiments he took to completion?"

The echoing of creatures' cries came from one of the two tunnel accesses behind them. This prompted Avatar to move to his knees, place his sword on the ground and speak the Ancient. The sword didn't move, so he spoke again, and with the same result, no movement.

"Why isn't it working?"

"I think it is by indicating the same direction we're heading." Avatar grabbed his sword by the hilt, leaving the point on the ground to use as leverage to stand. After taking a deep breath against the pain, he started down the tunnel. Mahon was at his heels.

The short tunnel ended at the base of the large cavern. A ledge about fifty feet from the base circled the cavern. Four tunnels led from the ledge to different parts of the cave. In the center of the cavern, a solid rock formation with carved out steps, rose past the ledge about twenty feet to a plateau. A white marble domed gazebo stood on the pinnacle.

Avatar smiled and slapped Mahon's arm. "I told you. A portal."

"Can you make the climb?"

"Watch me." Avatar began mounting the steps when winged reptile creatures emerged from each of the four tunnels on the ledge. On the same level behind them, a dragon-man creature appeared. It roared, showed fangs and drew its sword.

Mahon reached the bottom step. "Go on! I'll hold it off."

"No! I said we escape together."

"There are creatures up and down. Take your choice."

Avatar continued up to the portal. Mahon braced himself at the bottom awaiting the dragon-man creature's advance. When it moved, Mahon spoke the Ancient to summon his special power of the strength of ten Guardians. Both charged. The force of the clash sent both stumbling sideways. Mahon looked surprised since such strength should have downed the creature.

He snatched a glance to see Avatar fighting one of the winged creatures. The beast he faced roared in anger. It came at him again. This time Mahon ducked under the sword and came up behind it. He landed a savage blow to its back. The force sent the beast crashing into the wall. Mahon took a deep breath of recovery. The battle took all his added strength. Again he looked up.

Avatar had reached the landing near the top when another winged creature leapt at him. Both tumbled down the stairs to a lower landing. Avatar's sword fell to the cavern floor while he dangled from the ledge. The creature also fell. Short wings helped it glide and land at the bottom.

"Hang on!" Mahon raced toward the steps intent on helping when a large rock struck him in the back of the shoulders. He went sprawling across the floor, stunned. Something grabbed his collar and lifted him off the floor. The beast snarled. Saliva dripped from four-inch fangs and its breath was foul. Mahon pulled out his dagger. He buried it hilt deep into the beast's body. In reaction, it flung him aside.

"Mahon!"

Hearing Avatar's call, Mahon pushed himself to his knees. Avatar reached the top, with no signs of winged creatures. He waved at Avatar. "Go! I'll be right behind you." He retrieved his fallen sword before staggering toward the steps.

Avatar moved back. A flash of white light came from the top. Mahon suspected the portal had being activated. When he reached the first landing something metallic ensnared his ankles. Searing pain surged through his body from the point of impact. He fell from the steps. He lay dazed and winded on the cavern floor. At the sounds of boots, his eyes opened to see someone standing over him. Even in his injured state he recognized him.

"Griswold," he grunted.

"Fancy finding you here, Mahon the mighty." Griswold jerked Mahon to his feet.

Mahon winced at intense pain. Due to searing agony and weakness, resistance proved impossible. Griswold tugged on him like a rag doll.

"Felled by a piece of metal. Where's your mentor? Did he leave you?"

By the earlier light, Avatar got away safely, thus Mahon didn't reply to the taunting. His silence infuriated Griswold.

"You'll talk, sooner or later." Griswold barked a command in the Ancient to the wounded beast and dragged Mahon from the cavern.

Chapter 11

ON THE SURFACE, AVATAR REAPPEARED INSIDE ANOTHER PORTAL. He wasn't alone. One of the winged reptiles attacked when he entered the cavern portal. He and the creature fell out of the surface locked in a struggle. Unarmed, he used all his strength to hold its face away and not allow it to bite him. He cried out in pain when talon's ripped the front of his uniform and tore more flesh. Angry at another wounding, Avatar brought his feet up under the creature and heaved it off him. It slammed against a pillar of the portal. It flapped its wings in a motion to once again bounce. A ball of fire struck the creature, sending it backward into the portal.

Avatar turned in the direction of the fireball. Gresham, Jedrek and Virgil raced toward him. The twin warriors were Gresham's Trio Mates. Also with them came Auriel, a female warrior. Jedrek's sword remained pointed at the creature. Auriel and Virgil drew their weapons.

A badly seared creature rose to confront the new arrivals. When it made for another attack, a stream of ice froze one of its legs to the floor of the portal. A second, larger fireball exploded the creature. The intense flames and concussion damaged the portal.

"No!" Avatar ignored the pain of his injuries to scramble to the portal. Immolated pieces of the creature lay over the badly charred floor. Weakened by the explosion, several pillars cracked.

"Look out!" Auriel tackled Avatar. They tumbled form the portal just as the dome collapsed.

Avatar pushed away from her. Frantic and enraged, he confronted Jedrek. "What have you done?"

"We saved your life," said Jedrek, somewhat confused. He indicated himself and Virgil. The twin warriors were fair-headed; only Jedrek had amber eyes and Virgil crystal blue eyes. A symbol of their power, fire and ice respectively.

Avatar tried to move part of the fallen dome. Too weak in his injured condition, he collapsed to his knees. "Mahon was behind me. This is the only escape from the cave and you destroyed it!" He spoke between labored breaths of pain.

Stunned, Jedrek spoke with regret. "We didn't know."

"No, you didn't." Gresham knelt beside Avatar. "None of us knew. If we had, we would have taken greater care."

Avatar's anger turned to weary despair. He leaned against a fallen pillar. "I'm sorry, my friend, I failed you," he muttered in direction of the broken pieces.

"You're badly injured. Let us take you to Melwynn." Gresham gently helped Avatar to his feet.

"What are you doing here anyway?"

"Kell sent us to find you and Mahon. Complications have arisen that made him recall you."

"What complications?" Avatar spoke in a voice weak. His shrouded eyes showed he teetered on the brink of fainting.

"Let's get you taken care of first. Kell will explain once you are well enough."

※

Melwynn, Castle of the Guardians, was a sprawling structure of buildings carved out of solid rock in the foothills of the Highlands. The architecture consisted of intricate stonework with hundreds of rooms and large open terraces with impressive views of the surrounding countryside. Since dealing with mortals proved dangerous and frustrating, Melwynn served as a place of training, refreshment and recuperation. Guardians frequently came and went.

Kell hurried into the infirmary with Gresham trying to keep pace. Once inside, Kell spied Eldric at the far end standing beside a bed. Avatar sat propped up by pillows. Large bandages wrapped his entire torso. Avatar looked frustrated, scowling at the physician's verbal instructions. Avatar spotted him.

"Kell! Will you tell this overgrown babysitter, I'm fine and that I can leave when I want."

Kell smiled with relief at hearing the familiar bravado. He rushed to Melwynn fearful for Avatar's condition after hearing Gresham's report. "I didn't expect you to find you awake, much less talking."

"Don't be fooled. One of Rune's inventions nearly ripped the hide off his back while a kelpie gouged his chest," said Eldric.

"Rune?" Kell repeated with annoyed curiosity at the mention of the metal smith. "Did you see him?" he asked Avatar.

"Ay, he was wielding the invention," groused Avatar.

Kell made Avatar lean forward to examine his back. Avatar muffled a grunt of great discomfort. Kell tried to be gentle in looking underneath the bandage. In that brief glance, he saw significant damage. He eased Avatar back against the pillows.

"You're hurt worse than you want to admit," said Kell.

Avatar didn't reply, appearing on the verge of being sick. He closed his eyes to swallow back the queasiness.

"He's suffering from metal sickness. Any movement makes it worse," said Eldric.

Kell sat on the bed so Avatar didn't have to move to look at him. "What weapon did he use?"

Avatar opened his eyes. "I couldn't tell whether the chain was made of stygian or spurean metal. Either way, it rendered me briefly immobile and sick. If I were whole, Mahon would be with me. Or at least have had a chance to escape!" he chided Gresham.

"Jedrek and Virgil didn't know," said Gresham in stout defense.

"I assume Mahon defended you due to your injuries," said Kell.

"Ay. It's what allowed me reach the portal."

"Then he did nothing different than you would have."

"No," said Avatar with reluctance. "I'm just sorry he followed me into the cave. He said *you* sent him."

"In hopes of stopping you from going into the cave. Since you did, it sounds like he arrived too late. How did he know where you went?"

"He saw me a moment before I vanished. He felt he *failed* to warn me in time, so he followed. I failed in getting him out." Avatar heavily emphasized the word *failed*.

Kell didn't accept the explanation. "Neither of you *failed*. Mahon protected an injured comrade and you escaped to bring intelligence."

"If the beast didn't kill him, he's been captured and imprisoned with the others!" Avatar's passion rose, causing more discomfort, which he ignored with an angry sneer.

"Others?"

Avatar looked squarely at Kell. "It's worse than you can imagine, and a sight I will never forget. The thought of Mahon and Altari ..." He proceeded to describe the chamber, which distressed Kell, Eldric and Gresham.

"Merciful heaven," muttered Eldric.

"There is nothing merciful about it!" chided Avatar. His attention returned to Kell. "Dagar taunted and assaulted Witter and Altari, both of whom looked barely alive."

Kell golden eyes flashed with fury.

"I wanted to free them, but even with Mahon's help the risk was too great," Avatar's voice faulted.

Kell's own words sounded thick with emotion. "You did right in not acting. Describe this beast you mentioned."

"Which one? There were three different creatures inside some kind of holding room. A fuzzy worm the size of a large mortal family cat sprayed me with disgusting, stinging and smelly green goop."

"A gullet worm. The goop is for preparing its prey for eating."

"Wonderful, it thought I was dinner."

Gresham suppressed a laugh when Eldric slapped his arm.

Kell ignored them to continue his inquiry. "The other creatures?"

"Two reptile-like beasts with wings. The smaller one went around leaping on all fours. The other reminded me of the wyvern dragons of the Delta, only much larger. It stood on two legs like a man; nearly nine feet tall and armed with a sword. We barely got away from one in the holding room and later encountered another at the portal. The one Mahon battled, the last time last I saw him."

Kell's brows knitted in consideration of the description. "The smaller one is a kelpie. Its bite can cause paralysis. The second, I've never seen or heard of before."

"As I said, it reminded me of a wyvern on two legs and capable of handling a sword."

"When did you encounter Rune?"

"After the chamber. We thought to report back, as I reasoned that if the Originals could come and go there had to be an entry point permitting dimension travel or a portal. During our search, we discovered a room converted into a forge. Rune and I fought."

"With you getting the raw end of the fight," said Eldric.

Avatar glared at the physician. "Rune won't be waking up anytime soon after Mahon used his power to stop him." He became somber and reflective. "I told Mahon that we did nothing worthy of condemnation, so we weren't prisoners and could escape. Now, he might well be a prisoner."

"When the time comes, I will free them all," declared Kell.

"There's more," said Avatar in emphasis. He waited to continue until he had the captain's full attention. "Before my encounter with Rune, we observed him speaking to a large mortal he called *half-breed* in a insulting manner."

"Half of what?" asked Eldric.

"Guardian." Kell's answer surprised Eldric and Gresham while Avatar agreed.

"Ay. He resembled Dagar, only with a goatee instead of a full beard."

Kell became curious. "Goatee? Not clean-shaven?"

"No. He had facial hair like me. Why?"

Kell didn't hear the question as he muttered to himself. "There may be two of them."

"Two half-breeds?" asked Gresham.

Kell tilted his head as he considered. "Possibly." He rose to ask Eldric, "When will he be ready for duty?"

"I'm ready now." Avatar began to rise when Eldric stopped him.

"You're not going anywhere for at least a week."

Kell shook his head in dispute. "We can't wait that long."

Eldric wouldn't yield. "You see how badly he is wounded. It will take four, maybe five days for the wounds to heal. He needs two more days of treatment to regain his strength from metal sickness otherwise he'll be too weak to face anything."

Kell held the physician's gaze. "And *I* said, we can't wait that long! I need him at full strength in one day, whether by way of tonics or your power. Whatever Dagar is planning, we must be armed and ready."

The statement had its intended impact. "I'll see the treatments are successful, Captain."

"I'll be there whether the tonics work are or not," said Avatar.

"*You*, be a good patient!" Kell insisted.

"Ay, Captain."

Kell left the infirmary. In the corridor, he met Armus.

"I just heard about Avatar. How bad is he?"

Kell took a deep breath to calm down before replying. The visit caused more concern than just Avatar's injuries. "Much worse than he'll admit. I encouraged Eldric to have Avatar on his feet in a day, not the week he estimated."

Armus made a low whistle at the estimate. "A week. Will Eldric need to use his power?"

"Doesn't matter—"

"Kell." Gresham's call interrupted the conversation. "I hope you're not angry with Jedrek and Virgil. None of us knew about Mahon."

"Mahon?" asked Armus, only to be waved silent for Kell to reply.

"I'm not angry. I bear responsibility for issuing the assignment."

"Mahon was good warrior. He'll be missed."

"He's not vanquished!" snapped Kell.

Gresham colored with embarrassment at his miscue. "I meant—I'll return to Midessex." He made the Guardian salute and took his leave.

"What about Mahon?" asked Armus.

"Captured in the cave while helping Avatar escape." Kell placed a hand on Armus' shoulder to steer him onto a terrace for a private discussion. "Altari among those being tortured by Dagar."

The news stunned Armus. "Tortured?"

"Avatar discovered a chamber in the cave where Dagar does unspeakable things to fellow Guardians. He witnessed Dagar assault Witter and Altari." Kell grew grim in consideration. His voice became low. "I wonder how much it will take before he succumbs?"

Armus took notice of Kell's dreary countenance. "You doubt Altari's loyalty? But you said Avatar witnessed him being tortured."

Kell soberly shook his head. "Despite the discovery of his indiscretion, Altari considered his reassignment a demotion."

"In hindsight, putting he and Dagar together may not have been a wise choice."

"The orders came from Jor'el!" Kell argued then softened his tone when Armus stared at him in response to his temper. "Altari has behaved since. Although we didn't know about Dagar's progeny until recently, Altari's indiscretion happened thirteen hundred years ago. Fortunately, no offspring."

"Could he have influenced Dagar?"

Kell snorted a huffed chuckle. "No, Dagar's too clever and Altari too blunt for his own good. Dagar has his own plan." He sat on a terrace railing. The majestic vista of the Highlands stretched across the horizon. The view didn't interest him, as he glanced down in thoughtful concern.

Armus sat on the railing to get Kell's attention. "Don't hold yourself responsible for Altari. He made his choice then. If he does yield and joins Dagar, again, it is *his* choice."

"I know. Avatar reported more disturbing news. Rune *is* helping Dagar. He succeeded with his metal experiment and Avatar became his target. Thus the reason for the severity of his injuries and metal sickness."

"That's not good."

"No, it's not," said Kell in an emphatic tone. "I was surprised to find him awake much less in any shape to give a report. Although I'm deeply troubled to hear of the chamber and Mahon's capture, it shows how far Dagar has turned. He tortures fellow Guardians!" His features grew hard in an attempt to contain his fury. "If he had captured Avatar, I'm certain he would have vented his spleen without mercy, knowing full well how it would impact me— us—more than Altari!"

Armus quelled his own rising emotions. "Jor'el warned you."

"Hearing a warning and experiencing reality are very different."

"Doesn't change want we must do."

Kell bolted up. "Oh, it changes everything!"

Armus rose to confront Kell. "Not in serving Jor'el! Unless you will make this personal, which seems to be what Dagar wants."

"I won't fall for his cleverness. However, I must secure the Leadership and ranks against his further wiles." Kell heaved a heavy sigh of lament. "We will never be the same after this." He placed a hand on Armus' shoulder. "Let's return to the Palace."

Chapter 12

A T THE MANOR HOUSE, TEGAN BECAME CONCERNED AT THE FLASH of white light. Dagar appeared with Ram. At first Dagar didn't notice her apprehension, as he focused on Ram recovering from the dimension travel. Tegan fought against betraying her uneasiness when Dagar started speaking.

"The situation is accelerating. We came to fetch Razi to begin implementing the final phase. Has she died yet?"

She lost her nerve and avoided eye contact to answer. "Ay."

"Tegan?" he questioned with suspicion.

"He didn't want Hunter or I to tell you until he could, but he's gone."

"Where?"

She shook her head, wary of his reaction. "I don't know, my lord. He said he would meet Hunter at the *meadow* in five days then rode off."

"When was this?"

"Two days ago."

"And you failed to report it immediately?"

"He threatened us! And he is *your* son, the one you want us to pledge allegiance to when he is king. Are we to betray each other?" she argued.

Dagar fists clenched at Tegan's rebuff.

Ram intervened. "She's right, Father. You demand loyalty to Razi and me. He as king and I as his general."

Dagar's temper was slow to cool. "What about Barrion? I sent him to watch Razi."

Tegan shrugged in uncertainty. "I never saw him."

Dagar spoke over his shoulder before turning. "Hunter! Why aren't you following Razi?"

Hunter moved from the threshold into the room. "With everyone snooping around on Kell's orders, it's too dangerous to act freely. Also, leaving the province to enter Midessex could draw Gresham's notice."

"Have you seen Barrion?"

"No, but I have seen the results of some unnecessary activity in *my* province." Hunter's narrow gaze filled with bitterness. "Ridge and Wren were attacked by kelpies and went to the Fortress for medical attention. Now, how did the creatures escape the cave, do you suppose?"

"I sent some pets with Griswold to use against Avatar. I can't help the collateral damage," Dagar spoke with disinterest.

Hunter accosted Dagar. "The deal was to let me handle Ridge and Cam!"

Dagar's mahogany eyes flashed with anger. "You were supposed to keep anyone from learning who lived here! Not to mention letting Razi leave. What happened to your protégé is a result of your failure to keep to our deal. Tread lightly, ranger, or you won't live to see the plan fulfilled."

The sting of the threat played across Hunter's face.

"What about Cam?" Dagar demanded.

Hunter's voice sounded hollow. "I've taken care of him."

"How?"

"He is immobilized so leave it at that."

"Time is short!" snapped Dagar.

"I know," droned Hunter. "I sensed your presence and came to tell you, I'll be joining you when I bring Razi to the Cave."

"Funny you sensed my presence but neither of you saw Barrion!" Dagar's gaze narrowed with suspicion of the ranger and physician.

"I did sense a presence and rushed into her room, only *your* son said no one was with him," insisted Tegan in defense.

"I was tending to Cam and nowhere near the manor," said Hunter.

Dagar was slow to accept the reasons. "We can't wait for you to meet Razi," he chided Hunter.

"I'll find him," said Ram.

"Having the two of you roaming the countryside right now is not part of the plan!"

"You taught us to improvise. Isn't that what you did with Avatar and netted Mahon? You know I can find Razi."

Dagar made a curt wave. "Ay."

"Did you see which way he headed?" Ram asked Hunter.

"West."

"There is a horse in the barn, my lord," said Tegan.

"A mortal or spirit? He has a two-day head start."

"A spirit horse. I made certain to have one for my particular use but not obvious to mortal eyes. It's an old looking pale horse."

"Are you certain Razi didn't take the beast?" demanded Dagar.

"I suggested he take the bay horse for better travel. He did."

"Be quick." Dagar dismissed Ram.

Ram rode west from the manor house at breakneck speed. Razi's actions were not totally unexpected, just lousy timing. He suspected more than a dalliance when Razi went to the farm a second time and didn't return until late the next morning. He hoped his threat to inform their father would curtail Razi's behavior. Although, he understood his brother's more sensitive nature, the execution of the plan was at hand.

All their lives they relied on each other. Living mostly in the nether dimension with occasional time spent in the physical realm, did not make for a comfortable upbringing. It brought them closer than many brothers. Rivalry existed, though not in a vicious or undermining sense. When Dagar declared which one would be king and the other general, they accepted the decision without complaint or argument.

Being the larger and older twin, Ram took it upon himself to protect his *younger* brother. Razi used his clever wit and intelligence to help Ram. Not that he lacked intelligence, Razi simply acted faster in thinking on his feet and with verbal exchanges. At first, both were satisfied with their roles. However, since they saw their mother five years earlier and learned of her serious illness, Ram sensed a growing uneasiness in his brother.

Razi's disturbance became verbalized in private conversations about her treatment. Overtime, a restless impatience emerged. Razi made daring solo ventures from the nether dimension into the realm of mortals and Guardians. Seeing the girl, Ram suspected the reason. More importantly, it meant Razi had a compatriot among their father's associates since neither of them could bridge the dimensional gap. He had been unable to discover the being's identity. Of course, that didn't matter when covering for Razi's forays. It just grew frustrating when those trips increased and he needed to be more aggressive in protecting Razi from discovery.

Dagar viewed their mother's death as the last obstacle to begin the final phase of the plan. True, Ram suspected Dagar's involvement in facilitating her death, but felt no attachment. If her death disturbed Razi as deeply as he suspected, then Razi would head for the farm and the girl for solace. He must intercept Razi and convince him to return to avoid their father's wrath at such a crucial time.

<hr />

During the four-day ride, Razi took little time to rest when switching horses, and ate only when necessary. His Guardian half could forego sleep longer than most mortals, while possessing great physical endurance. Eating was something he couldn't put off like he had seen his father and other Guardians. Food may not be essential to a Guardian's survival, but his mortal side demanded sustenance. Still, he traveled as long as his stomach and energy would allow. With the execution of the plan at hand, he couldn't waste any time in reaching Janel and her family.

Passing the turn to the road leading to Temple and Fortress of Jor'el, he considered going to speak to Avram. What could he say? How would such a dramatic revelation be accepted? Would he be believed? No, if he protected Janel and the others, perhaps Avram would realize marrying her wasn't part of his father's master plan.

Razi's heart sank at the thought of Janel's reaction and possible rejection. Of course, that possibility existed from the beginning. It is why he went to the farm, to tell her she would be better off without him. Once there, he gave into his heart, confessed his love and married Janel. Hearing his mother's tragic tale further stirred his heart toward Jor'el, and also confirmed the choice of marrying Janel.

Something inside him always knew Dagar's attitude toward Jor'el and his fellow Guardians was wrong. After becoming involved with Janel, it deeply troubled him. Now, he could no longer be a part of the plan. His heart and conscience wouldn't allow it. Whatever the outcome with Janel and her family, he would not help his father.

The poor horse wobbled, nearly spent. Being a two-hour ride from Temple to the farm, he eased off to allow the animal some recovery. Nothing would be worse then for the horse to die out from under him along the road. *Only a little longer, please!* Razi thought. Words sprang to his mind that he felt compelled to speak.

"Seach Jor'el's deon, bi nas uire agus ruith!" He knew the Ancient language of the Guardians, but the words were surprising to hear coming for his lips. Razi repeated, *"By Jor'el's will, be refreshed and run."*

He invoked the power of the Almighty, and the horse responded by gaining speed! The initial surprise became replaced by a soaring spirit of hope in knowing he would reach the farm safely.

Turning off the main road, he passed a male laborer tending to his chores. He didn't pay close attention to the man. If he had, he would have noticed the laborer stand to his full height of seven feet and vanish.

Razi drew the horse to a stop at the back of the house. He leapt from the saddle and ran inside the kitchen shouting, "Janel!"

"Razi!" She left the food preparation table to greet him with an enthusiastic hug.

"Thank Jor'el," he said in relief. He held her close.

"Indeed. I prayed for you to return quickly." She went to kiss him but he stopped her and spoke in haste.

"Why? Has something happened?"

"No, silly. I missed you."

This time he didn't resist. He made it in time and reveled in her kiss.

"Well, look who's back?" Mace entered the kitchen from the yard. Kerwin came behind him. Both were soiled from work.

"I thought you were in the fields," she said.

"We were. In case you hadn't noticed, it's near supper time," said Kerwin.

Mace poked Kerwin. "Somehow I don't think it's ready."

Janel blushed. "You're wrong. Razi just arrived. I'm nearly finished. Now wash up. I won't feed you looking a mess." She went to the stove to fetch a large pot of stew. She set it on the table. Four places were ready for supper.

"Ah, Razi, this is a welcomed sight." Dolan entered from another part of the house. He carried papers. "I'm glad to see your errand didn't take too long." He put the papers on a sideboard before taking a seat sat at the head of the table. He motioned for Razi to sit on his right.

"Any word on Toby?" asked Razi.

Dolan smiled. "He is doing very well. My wife reports they should be home by the middle of next week."

"Sounds like a long time."

Dolan chuckled. He held up his cup for Janel to pour him some hot tea. She then filled cups for Kerwin, Mace and Razi.

Dolan continued speaking. "Apparently the Guardians at Melwynn are such gracious hosts Toby doesn't want to leave."

After pouring the tea, Janel placed an empty bowl in front of Razi. Kerwin and Mace sat at the table opposite Razi, leaving the chair next to him for Janel.

"After what he's been through can you blame him? A little rest and hospitality is most welcomed," said Kerwin.

"His sister will spoil him with attention when he returns." Dolan winked at Janel when she set a large platter of slice bread on the table.

"He could use spoiling after so harsh a year." Janel sat beside Razi.

"Shall we pray." Dolan offered a prayer of blessing and thanks.

Ram never switched mounts, as the spirit horse showed no fatigue from the long, fast journey. Turning off the main road to the farm, Ram saw Razi on a horse ahead of him disappear around a bend. The road ended. He didn't know if Razi stopped at the house or proceeded since he didn't see a horse near the front door. He knew the girl lived here. Maybe they had a rendezvous place beyond the house. He steered the horse behind a shed on the far side of the house to observe.

The animal pawed the ground. He ignored it to take up position at the corner. From this vantage point, both the front and back were visible. He spotted the horse Razi rode near the rear door. Going around back showed this was more than a passing fancy, which means Razi lied about it only being a dalliance.

And like a fool I believed you, even when I suspected more.

Ram acted against his better judgment in not confronting Razi more forcefully about putting an end to the relationship. Despite the pain Razi felt at their mother's death, if he had come to him instead of seeking the companionship of a mortal female … Ram couldn't finish the thought due to painful anger at Razi turning to another. This changed everything; not just their past relationship but also the future. Only one thing to do: confront Razi and hope what he had to say was worth the risk.

In the kitchen, they paused in eating at knock upon the back door.

"Come," said Dolan. To his surprise a very familiar looking tall man with a goatee walked in. He wasn't the only one surprised.

Razi bolted up from his seat. "Ram! What are you doing here?"

"Me? It's you who has some explaining to do," Ram spoke in a tight voice. His eyes darted at the others.

"Who is this gentleman, Razi?" asked Dolan.

"My twin brother." Razi moved beside Janel in anticipation of Ram's anger. His mind raced to find the words. Yet, how to explain in a few words what had taken him time to understand?

Dolan rose to address Ram. "Please, my lord, join us."

"This is not a social call." Ram's focus remained on Razi.

"I hadn't meant for you to learn this way," said Razi.

"Oh? You ran off and expected me to learn of your betrayal how?"

"I haven't betrayed anyone." The accusation cut Razi to the quick, which made his voice slightly quiver. Janel took his in hand in support.

"And the wench?" Ram sent a brief, enraged glare at Janel.

Razi assumed a protective posture. "My wife."

It took a moment for the pronouncement to sink in then Ram's temper to explode. "What?!"

The outburst brought Dolan to Razi's side. "Please, my lord, there is no need for anger. Let us discuss—"

"There is nothing to discuss!"

"Ram, please, I can explain!" Razi pleaded in an attempt to diffuse his brother's anger.

"No, you can't." Ram's entire being tensed. "I shielded your dalliance from Father, even lied to protect you and this is how you repay me? By marrying this wretched mort—"

"Calm down and listen to me!" Razi's loud objection interrupted Ram. He moved from Janel to take hold of Ram's arm with urgency of his plea.

Ram jerked away and reached for his sword.

"Don't!" Razi's voice cracked with emotion. "I won't fight you. Will you strike me down unarmed, brother?"

A battle of painful frustration raced across Ram's face.

Ram's reaction brought Kerwin and Mace to their feet and ready for defense. Dolan signaled them to remain calm. Janel covered her mouth in horrid surprise, as she watched Ram and Razi locked in a battle of wills. Neither moved until Ram stormed from the house.

"Ram!" shouted Razi in desperation.

Dolan stopped Razi from following. "He's too angry to listen right now."

Janel moved to comfort Razi. Although pale and distressed, her voice was compassionate. "Father's right. Perhaps when he has calmed down you can speak to him again." She steered Razi back to the table.

Razi plopped in the chair. He shook his head, his face forlorn. "No. He feels I betrayed him. He will not get over it anytime soon. I've made an enemy of my brother." He fought back tears.

She quickly sat beside him. "It may not be that bad."

Razi flashed a plaintive smile at her attempting optimism. "You don't know him like I do. As twins, we shared everything together since birth. We protected and supported each in all circumstances." He became contrite. "I did lie to him about you. Lying to my father to protect you, all of you, I can accept, but Ram," his voice faltered. "I used him wrongly and will regret it the rest of my life."

"We can't replace your twin, but we are your brothers now," said Kerwin.

Razi simply nodded, muted by emotions.

Dolan motioned for everyone to resume sitting. "Let us continue and perhaps we can come up with a plan to win him over." He gave Razi an encouraging smile.

Ram ran to his horse. The confrontation produced a disturbing revelation. Razi married her! He may not see it as betrayal, but that is the only word Ram could think of for such foolishness. Before mounting, he caught sight of a brilliant flash of sustained white light from around the corner. Such radiance meant the arrival of more than one Guardian. He peeked out from behind the shed. Armus, Avatar and three other Guardians arrive. Not good.

Inside, Razi picked at his food. He feared the inevitable confrontation. Sadly, reality proved worse than imagined. He jumped at another knock at the door.

Janel smiled. "He may be reasoned with after all."

Razi looked a touch apprehensive. "I hope so."

"Come," said Dolan at hearing the second knock.

Armus entered, followed by Avatar, who appeared pale and moved somewhat gingerly. Glowering silver eyes immediately found Razi.

"Lieutenant Armus. Lieutenant Avatar. This is a surprise," said Dolan.

Not to Razi, not the way this day was turning out. He had never met the formidable Guardian first lieutenant or the captain's aide. He only knew them from his father's colorful, degrading descriptions. Upon sight of them, he felt no fear, rather relief that the evitable had come.

"Master Dolan, we are here at the request of Captain Kell and Vicar Avram," Armus spoke in an official tone.

"Oh? Why?"

Armus turned to Razi. His direct look made Janel take Razi's hand.

"They're here for me, Papi. Right, Lieutenant?"

"Ay, my lord. The captain and Vicar wish to speak to you."

Razi stood only Janel did not release his hand. Instead, she asked Armus, "Why? What has he done?"

"It's all right, Janel. Our discussion is for the best." He made her release his hand.

Fearful, she turned to her father and brothers. This prompted Kerwin and Mace to stand, both warily eying Armus.

"Stay, brothers. For Janel's sake. I'll be fine," said Razi with a grin.

"Everyone is to come," Armus in his continued diplomatic tone.

While the statement concerned Razi, Avatar's severe features troubled him. The captain's aide had not said a word. The silver stare was meant as a deterrent to any thought of non-compliance. Not that Razi offered resistance while Armus' solo appearance was enough to unnerve most mortals. Razi's glance at Avatar was brief when he asked Armus, "Is their presence necessary?"

"Captain's orders. Now, please." He made a motion to depart. "All your questions will be answered in time."

"Papi?" asked Kerwin.

Dolan rose from the table. "Neither the captain nor your uncle would take such action if it were not important and absolutely necessary."

"That is correct," said Armus.

Razi held Janel's hand as exited the kitchen. Ewert, Bailey and the laborer from earlier waited in the backyard. Razi reckoned him to be a vassal Guardian in height and appearance.

"We'll fetch our horses," said Dolan.

"No need. We'll take you," said Armus.

"How?" asked Mace.

"Dimension travel," said Razi.

"What kind of travel?"

"The Guardian method of going from one place to another."

"All the way to the Fortress?" asked Kerwin in disbelief.

Armus chuckled. "We can go further. The captain's orders were for no delay. Now, Master Dolan, if you will stand beside Avatar and your daughter beside Elgin," he indicated the vassal. "Master Kerwin with Ewert and Master Mace with Bailey. I will take his lordship."

"A moment, please," said Razi when Armus took up position beside him. "In my saddlebag is a book I would like to bring. It belonged to my mother," he added at seeing their reluctance.

Armus nodded to Avatar, who stood the closest to the horse. Avatar fetched the book. For the first time, his expression changed to curiosity at discovering The Book of Verse. He handed it to Razi. Once Avatar had hold of the Dolan, everyone vanished.

Ram gripped the hilt of his sword. Hearing the exchange and Armus mention the captain's order, he immediately understood the ramifications. Razi *had* betrayed them! And not just with the girl! He needed to speak to his father. He returned to his horse. To his annoyance, Barrion held the reins.

"What are you doing here?"

"Stopping you. You will not report Razi to Dagar. What is happening is the best for him and for Allon." Barrion spoke the Ancient to send the horse away.

Ram drew his sword. "You've been helping him come and go."

"And his protector." Barrion drew his sword yet suddenly became alert to another presence. He barely turned in time to intercept the attack from behind. Dagar had the advantage. Dagar landed a savage blow that sliced into Barrion's torso. Barrion made a defensive swing to put distance between himself and Dagar.

"I knew it was only a matter of time before you acted." Dagar attacked.

Wounded, Barrion proved clumsy in repelling the attack. "You're too late, Dagar! Your sons are divided. And by it, you will fall!"

"Not before I destroy you." With an angry wave of his hand, Dagar sent Barrion hurling into the shed.

Ram joined his father in attacking Barrion. The wounded warrior struggled to his feet. He managed to turn aside both attacks. In a surprise move, Barrion wounded Ram deep in the upper sword arm.

Enraged at his son's injury, Dagar called upon his power in the Ancient. "*Astair de am bhais!*" With blinding speed he attacked. His sword plunged through Barrion's chest. He collapsed, breathed his last and vanished in the grey light of demise.

Ram's attention went from where Barrion had been to Dagar. "How long have you known about Barrion?"

"I suspected him for awhile. However, this last year he acted too cagey, even for him. A few weeks ago, Razi let his name slip and tried to cover. That helped me make the connection."

"Barrion isn't the only one responsible. A mortal female also turned him. In fact, he married her!" Ram sneered in bitter anger.

"What?"

Ram hurried to speak before Dagar's anger exploded. "That's not all. He is on his way to *Kell* in the company of Armus and *Avatar*."

Ever inch of Dagar's being quivered in rage. He let out a tremendous growl and plunged his sword into the ground where Barrion had been. "I didn't realize how influential Barrion had grown or I would have destroyed him sooner!"

They heard commotion coming from behind them. Agitated farm laborers pointed at them. Dagar retrieved his sword then snatched Barrion's sword and stuck it in his belt He grabbed Ram and they disappeared.

In the nether cave, Ram stood near an entrance of the reconditioning chamber, brooding. Dagar and Tor conversed nearby. No doubt Dagar spoke to Tor about the incident at the farm. Not a discussion he wanted to participate in until he could come to grips with the reality of Razi betraying them. Despite what he witnessed, he wanted to believe Armus and Avatar were just lucky in capturing Razi. However, the evidence proved too compelling that Razi walked away of his own volition. First he became increasingly moody then married a mortal female.

Barrion's statements made him consider that more lay beyond the female. He spoke of being Razi's protector and said what he did was for the good of Allon. The fact their father suspected Barrion made his belief more certain. No, the seeds of betrayal were planted before Razi met the girl. She and the death of their mother made those seeds blossom. Barrion's last words *"Your sons are divided and by it, you will fall"* drove the point home. The part gnawing at Ram was the fact he knew it, yet still covered for Razi! No more! He would not let the plan fail. Bolstered by wounded pride and conviction, he joined Dagar and Tor.

"When do we strike?" he asked in hard, gritty voice.

Dagar studied Ram. "His betrayal has not changed your mind?"

Ram boldly met his sire's gaze. "Only to make me more determined to succeed. You're not the only one who wishes he stopped Barrion earlier. That aside, Razi made his choice. I feel a fool for all the times I made excuses to help him. Now, he has turned his back on us for a mortal girl."

"This means *you* will be king."

Ram rose to his full height and squared his shoulders. "When I'm crowned, my first task will be hunt down all traitors."

Dagar cocked a smile of pleasure then quelled it. "I instructed Tor to send word for our troops to assemble. Go. Prepare yourself, my son and king."

Ram clapped his sword and left.

"What do you want me to do about Mahon?" asked Tor.

"Has he said anything yet?"

"No, I haven't had the time to get information from him."

Dagar glowered in momentary thought. "I must take care of some business first. Upon my return, *I* will deal with Mahon."

Chapter 13

INSIDE A LARGE AUDIENCE CHAMBER AT THE FORTRESS, the Guardians reappeared. They held onto the mortals in an effort to help them recover from dimension travel. Razi fared better than the rest in the fact that he remained awake. He took several deep breaths to recover.

"I never liked doing that," he commented.

"Take a seat, my lord. I'll fetch the captain and Vicar," said Armus, but Razi wouldn't release him.

Razi spoke in a low voice. "Doubtless you know who I am, so why keep calling me *my lord?*"

Armus cast a discreet glanced to the other mortals, who were now recovered and seated. "For their benefit. This will be a harsh blow for them to endure."

"One I wish could be avoided." Razi sighed when he looked at the Book of Verse he held. "I love Janel. Something my mother never found. This book belonged to her."

When Razi looked up at him, Armus saw a depth of sincerity he did not expect. Guardians could tell if a mortal lied, so under the circumstances, he found it surprising to see such honesty. Nor did Razi shy from his probing gaze, where most mortals cringed or shied away. Another uncommon reaction.

"Razi." Janel reached out her hand him.

Armus welcomed the distraction. He was at an unusual loss for words. After a watching Razi join Janel, he spoke to Avatar and the other Guardians. "Stay with them." He left.

Dolan moved to the sofa. "Son, what is this about?"

Razi's smile wavered at the question. "I don't know if after this you'll think me of as a son."

"Why? Does this have to do with your father and why you left us?"

"Ay," he droned. Janel tightened her grip on his hand, so he spoke to her in ardent desperation. "Please, no matter what happens, know I love you with all my heart! I never intended evil or harm to any of you."

"Of course, but why would you say that?"

"Remember I said when you learn my father's identity you may not think so kindly of me?"

"And I told you, you are not your father."

Razi kissed her hand while blinking back swelling tears at her unwavering confidence. The time for revelation arrived, and he fought against conflicting emotions. Hearing the door open, he stood in anticipation. Janel rose, still clasping his hand in both of hers.

"Uncle," she said.

Avram entered first, followed by Kell and Armus. For this occasion both Avram and Kell wore their official clothes. The Vicar's robes were lavish blue and silver while Kell's uniform included a gold breastplate emblazoned with the ancient symbol of Jor'el. From the shoulder clasps hung a short purple cloak. Instead of a belt, a purple sash held his scabbard. His gold eyes sparkled with full power and heavenly authority.

"Captain," said Razi in awe. He bowed to Kell.

"Have you two met before?" asked Avram.

"No, my lord Vicar," said Razi, still in awe of Kell. "I know the captain only by reputation. Seeing him in person, far exceeds what I've been told."

"There you have me at a disadvantage, for I have not heard of you," said Kell.

"I'm not surprised. My father," he began then balked, "well, you are well acquainted with him from the beginning, thus aware of his tendencies."

"So it is true. Dagar *is* your father," said Avram in restrained anger.

"Dagar?" Janel could barely utter the name.

"What's this? Avram?" asked Dolan in astonishment.

"I thought I recognized him when he and Janel came to be married, only I couldn't place him. She persuaded me. At the time I saw no harm, so I performed a private ceremony. Not until the following day when I saw Dagar at the Temple did I realize why Razi looked so familiar."

Kerwin's temper exploded. He seized Razi. "What hand did you have in condemning Toby?"

"None! I have no part in his administration of the province. Nor had I met Janel when it happened. From the moment she told me, I tried to reason with him and lessen the sentence."

Kerwin's anger wouldn't be cooled. "And the beating?"

"Again, I didn't know about it until Janel told me. I swear! My dealings with my father are not what you think. In fact, our relationship is hardly one between a normal father and son," he said in a mix of hurt and sarcasm.

"And your mother? What of your relationship to her?" Avram's expression was harsh and fixed as he spoke.

With sobriety, Razi replied. "Sad to say, we didn't have the opportunity to see her often after being separated as toddlers."

"We?"

"My twin brother Ram and I."

"Twins?" said Avram, stupefied. He spoke to Kell. "She had twins."

"How closely do you resemble each other?" asked Kell.

"Almost exact, only he is a little larger and has facial hair."

"So you were both taken from her and raised where?"

Despite the awkwardness of the situation, Razi had to deal directly and honesty. "The Cave mostly. Only a few times did we live on the surface." He watched for their reactions. Avram showed mildly curiosity, but no surprise. Kell's expression never wavered. Armus appeared expressionless. Avatar's silver eyes narrowed upon Razi.

"You were reared in a cave?" asked Mace in confused disbelief.

"It is not a normal cave," said Avatar.

163

Razi met the intimidating silver stare of the captain's aide. "No, it is not. My father wanted to keep our existence a secret until the time he chose to reveal us."

"Why would he do that?" asked Dolan.

Visibly distressed, Razi entreated Kell. "Please, Captain, can we discuss this in private? I will tell you everything."

Avram spoke to the contrary while indicating Dolan and the others. "They have a right to know since you included them in this by your marriage."

"I didn't know!" Razi insisted in a voice thick with emotion. He struggled to maintain his composure.

"You expect me to believe that?"

"I learned the truth two days ago when on her deathbed she confessed her part in the plot and asked my forgiveness."

"Plot?" asked Janel, able to speak for the first time.

Razi took a deep breath, closed his eyes and prayed, "Jor'el, please give me strength."

"You call upon the Almighty?" asked Avram.

Razi opened his eyes. "Willingly."

Janel took Razi's arm as she spoke to Avram. "Razi and I often speak of Jor'el and read from Verse."

Avram sent a conferring glance to Kell. This was the first noticeable change in Kell's expression from stone-faced to curiosity.

Razi held out the book to Avram. "This belonged to my mother. She asked me to read to her as she lay dying. I managed to take it when I left. I believe you should have it, sir."

The gesture struck Avram hard, and his staunch façade began to crack. With indecision, he hesitated in reaching for the book.

Razi kindly smiled. "I'm confident she would want you to have it. With great regret, she spoke about spurning the love you tried to show her and all that happened as a result. Please." He placed the book in Avram's hand.

Great emotion played across Avram's face. He looked inside at the first page. A whimper of distress escaped so he closed the book. In a choked voice he spoke. "I gave this to her on her thirteenth birthday. I hadn't realized she took it with her."

"Who?" asked Dolan.

Avram turned to face Dolan. "Haggar." Stunned, Dolan sat. Avram rushed to the chair and insisted, "I didn't know!"

"Nor did I, I swear!" said Razi.

"Know what?" asked Kerwin.

"Not long before you were born, Haggar, my daughter, was found to be a sinful woman. The Council of Priests sent her away for refusing to give up her wayward lifestyle. Her mother and I did all we could to persuade her before she was discovered with child. Alas, once they rendered the decision, we couldn't go against the Council or the Almighty. We never discussed her again. Until this incident, I thought she was dead since I heard nothing from her or about her."

"That makes Razi my nephew. The Almighty forbids such close marriage among family," chided Dolan.

Janel wept so Razi held her. He looked expectedly to Kell for the answer.

"Nephew a generation removed," said the captain. "The marriage was done in ignorance on all sides. It will not be held against any since the state of matrimony is sacred to Jor'el."

"Although I was ignorant of our relationship, it doesn't change my love for Janel," Razi said to Dolan. He then lifted her face to look at him. "Does it change your love for me?"

"I don't think so, but this is all so confusing. My cousin was your mother, Dagar your father and some kind of plot?"

"A plot of revenge! She against her father and Dagar against Jor'el."

"Why? Dagar is the Guardian of the Temple," said Dolan.

There was no turning back so Razi continued. "He pretends! All the while plotting to raise a rebellion to topple Jor'el and place my brother and I on the throne. A plot I want no part of! You are my heart not a

165

throne," he insisted to Janel. He turned with urgency to Kell. "My mother's death is the signal. Everything else is in place." Emotions propelled him to leave Janel and approach Kell. "You must believe me, Captain! Of all beings, he wants your death the most!"

With drawn swords, Armus and Avatar stepped between Kell and Razi. Ewert and Bailey seized Razi. He strained against their hold to make a declaration.

"*Feucba le teine!* I claim the right of *feucba le teine* from you, Captain!"

To this, Kell stepped between Armus and Avatar to confront Razi. His face hard-set and golden eyes bright with authority. "You are half-mortal, you would not survive!"

"I am half-Guardian, you cannot deny my request."

Kell's jowls tightened in an attempt to maintain his temper. "Bring him to the Palace!" He turned on his heels.

Armus motioned for Ewert and Bailey. They fell in behind him holding Razi between them. Avatar followed with his sword still drawn.

"Razi!" called Janel.

Elgin stopped her.

"No, let them come," said Avram gravely. "They need to learn the truth."

Elgin moved aside for Avram to escort Janel from the room.

"What is going to happen, Uncle?" she asked in a quivering voice.

"Trial by Fire. It is a right among Guardians to make a request of either their mentor or Captain Kell when their truthfulness, duty or loyalty is called into question. It is the ultimate test of a Guardians' heart and intent. And *only* done under the most dire of circumstances. For Razi to claim it, he is either foolhardy or the bravest man I've ever met."

"What is this trial?" asked Mace.

"As it states: Trial by Fire. The accused passes through divine flames to have the purity and intentions of the heart tested by Jor'el."

Terrified, Janel clung to Avram's arm.

"Have you witnessed this?" asked Dolan.

"No, but the end result will determine guilt or truthfulness. If he survives then everything he said is true. Jor'el will have confirmed it, leaving no room for doubt or future charges in the matter."

"You said *if* he survives," she stammered.

"Any falsehood in him or if the charges are true, the flames will consume him." When Janel wept, Avram stopped. He held her face to look directly in her eyes. "Search your heart, niece. If you truly love him, I will take you to the Palace. If you have any doubt of his integrity or love for you, I will have Elgin take you home now."

"If he didn't love me then why subject himself to such interrogation and ask for this test? You just spoke of his courage, so how I can, his wife, not do for him what he is doing for me?"

Avram embraced her. "Then let us pray he succeeds."

Kell led the way into the Throne room. Jor'el was not present so he waited until everyone assembled before seeking an audience. Despite the family's relationship to Avram, they had never been to the Throne room. All gazed in wonder at the gleaming white marble pillars and floor. Highly polished gold and silver lamp stands illuminated the room. The high arch ceiling towered above them while lavish stained glass windows sparkled in the sunlight. A single throne of magnificently crafted gold with inlaid jewels stood situated five steps above the floor.

More than their reaction, Kell watched Razi. The half-breed appeared duly impressed at the sight of his Guardian splendor. The effect was what he wanted. However, he did not anticipate the request. A bold, brash, and brave move, if it is proven true.

At first sight of Razi, Kell understood why Avram, Ridge and Avatar believed they recognized a Guardian, and specifically Dagar. No mistaking his father's identity or why he and his brother were kept hidden. When Razi approached him and declared that Dagar wanted his death, Kell may have looked impassive, but that was not how he felt. It's difficult to think of his friend and peer as an enemy. After Wren, Ridge and Avatar's injuries, Mahon's capture and learning about the torture of fellow Guardians that is what Dagar had become: his enemy—Jor'el's enemy. Razi's revelation of the plan was the final severance of any lingering feelings toward Dagar. When he meets Dagar again, it will be to face him in battle.

Kell flinched from his introspection when someone touched him on the shoulder. Armus. With everyone present, Kell approached the Throne and knelt. "Almighty Jor'el, grant us the honor of your presence for the task which brings us before you."

At the appearance of the heavenly haze of bright light, gasps of awe came from the mortals; a typical response from those who had never been in the Almighty's presence. The light settled into the form of a male seated upon the throne, obscured from full detailed view, with just the opalescent eyes clearly visible.

"Rise, Captain. I know why you have come," Jor'el's voice filled the room.

"Will you grant the request for Trial by Fire, Holy One?"

"Bring forth him who makes the request."

Kell signaled for Razi. Avatar brought him to Kell. Avatar bowed to Jor'el before stepping back to join Armus.

"This is he, Holy One. Razi, son of—"

"Dagar!" said Jor'el in anger. "The product of a forbidden alliance."

"Indeed, Holy One, but what blame do I bear since I had no part in my conception?" Razi spoke with such boldness, that he received a jerk on the arm from Kell.

"Why should I grant your request?"

"According to the law you established for Guardians, any may request the right of *feucba le teine* when their loyalty and integrity is in question. Although I am the product of a forbidden alliance, I am nevertheless, half-Guardian. I willingly answered questions put to me regarding my parentage. Still doubts remain as to my veracity and intent. In my heart there is no doubt. For the sake of others I make the request, and submit myself to your divine fire for testing."

"You renounce your father and embrace me?" Jor'el's eyes grew with intensity and focus.

"Willingly," replied Razi without hesitation.

"You do this to gain the love of a woman?"

"For love, ay. Not solely for my wife, but also for my mother's memory, my grandfather's honor, and my own heart's desire to make right what has been wronged."

"Then step into the flames!" Jor'el's voice boomed. His image transformed to a pillar of fire stretching from the floor to the ceiling.

Terrified, Janel seized Avram. Dolan paled in fear. Kerwin and Mace gaped thunderstruck at the change.

Kell released Razi and stepped back. Without looking to Janel, Razi stepped into the fire. The flames intensified to the point of obscuring him from the others. A loud scream emanated from the flames. Janel also screamed and buried her face in Avram's robes. The pillar exploded in a burst of brilliant orange light. The force sent everyone to the floor temporarily blinded and stunned.

Kell recovered his senses first. To his astonishment, Razi lie in a heap on the floor. He survived! Kell blinked in wonder when Jor'el's image settled onto the Throne. Razi stirred, so Kell helped him to his feet.

Razi squinted in trying to focus. "Kell? Where am I?"

"You are still before me, Razi," said Jor'el, his voice soft and kind. "You have passed the test. Your heart and intent are true. No one shall question you or speak false accusations against you. For your courage and strength to do what is right, you and your wife shall be blessed. Now, go and keep yourselves hidden until your father is dealt with. He will seek to destroy you, but I will protect you."

"Thank you, Holy One." Razi bowed. Jor'el vanished. With a befuddled look on his face, Razi tried to absorb it all.

Janel ran and embraced Razi. He held her close as she wept.

"Indeed, my daughter married a man of honor and courage." Dolan embraced the couple, unable to hold back tears. Mace, Kerwin and Avram joined him in showering affection on the couple.

"My lord, only twice has the fire been requested, but you are the first to survive. If ever you have need, call and I will respond," said Kell.

"Thank you, Captain. If it is any consolation, he didn't always hate you. According to Barrion, his attitude changed after Radnor."

Kell slightly flinched at the statement. He covered by speaking to Avram. "Take them out by the secret passage to your quarters so he can recover."

"He acts nothing like his brother when he confronted Rune," said Avatar.

Kell noticed Avatar's stricken pallor. "Are you all right? Or did the strengthening tonics not work?"

"They worked. Jor'el's power aggravated my wounds."

"Get Phoebe to change the bandages and dressing."

Avatar rolled his eyes. "I'd rather wait until they are safe."

Kell cocked a grin. "Very well. Take them to Melwynn. They can be reunited with Toby and Clare until I find a place for them. *And* Eldric can tell you, *I told you so* while treating your wounds."

"Ay, Captain," droned Avatar. He saluted and withdrew.

Armus chuckled but Kell's humor faded to pensive. "What's troubling you? Everything went very well."

"You heard what Razi said about Dagar."

"Ay. Do as he said, and take consolation that one of his progeny has returned to Jor'el."

"We can, but Dagar won't. This will intensify his hatred." Kell sighed in great vexation. "If I could undo anything it would be Radnor."

Armus held Kell's shoulder "Everyone involved was touched by what happened. Killing so many mortals goes against our duty to protect them. Thankfully there hasn't been a civil war since."

Kell stared sharply at Armus. "There will be war shortly. Led by a Guardian who knows what he's doing and not inexperienced mortals."

"Like then, we must defend Jor'el's honor and protect the mortal population from the few who would defile everything."

"It's the aftermath which troubles me not battle."

"You can't think about that. All you can do is fulfill the duty to which Jor'el appointed you and leave the outcome to him."

"Easier said than done since my duty also includes the welfare of all Guardians!" Kell abruptly left.

A few hours later, Kell stood in his office gazing out the window, contemplating the situation. Waiting proved the hardest part of command. It gave him time to consider, to plan and in some cases, to worry. Dagar's discontentment proved difficult enough to deal with but he cringed at hearing about the defection of others. Be it by choice or torture, neither factor bode well for the Guardians as a whole. A new disturbing reality had to be faced.

Kell didn't notice the last fading of twilight. In fact, he didn't move during his consideration. That was until Armus, Avatar and Vidar arrived.

"Reporting as ordered," began Armus.

"Are they safe?" Kell asked Avatar.

"Ay. I left them in good hands." He flashed a gregarious smile.

Kell recognized Avatar's familiar expression when being humorous or mischievous. He wasn't sure he wanted to accept this attitude at such a critical moment. Thus he inquired with guarded anticipation, "Who?"

"Eldric. By giving him charge of them, I didn't have to endure his babbling."

Kell couldn't stop a chuckle at the clever refining of his order. "What of your wounds?"

"Brooke bandaged them and gave me an extra-strong healing tonic. I should be fine by tomorrow."

"What is it you wanted to see us about?" asked Vidar.

Kell's momentary mirth faded. "By Jor'el's orders I sent Jarvis to inform Dagar that in light of the evidence, the Almighty is removing him from his position, effective immediately. He is to report to Jor'el for reassignment."

Avatar, Vidar and Armus showed expressions of shock and concern.

"You sent a vassal to strip a warrior of his position?" asked Armus.

"Jor'el chose Jarvis. I argued to go in his stead."

"Actually, you informing Dagar could be worse after what Razi said."

Kell's golden eyes flashed with insult. "I'm not afraid of Dagar!"

"I'm not implying fear. Simply speaking from a strategic viewpoint."

Ewert rushed into the room. "Captain! To the Throne room!"

Kell hurried to comply with Ewert, Armus, Avatar and Vidar behind him. He mounted the palace steps in two large strides and passed the Guardians standing watch before they could react. Rushing feet echoed in the chamber then halted as they determined the need for haste.

A figure lay crumpled on the floor before the Throne. Kell knelt on one side, Armus the other side; the rest encircled the injured individual. The savageness of numerous wounds to the head and face made him unrecognizable. By his size and clothes he appeared to be a vassal. He tried to speak; at least he made noise sounding like words. Kell leaned closer to hear.

"I tried to tell Dagar ..." the voice failed.

"Jarvis," stammered Kell in surprise recognition.

"I'll fetch Phoebe," said Avatar. He stopped when light filled the room. Jor'el assumed his place on the Throne.

They knelt, except Kell, who stood and spoke with distress. "It is Jarvis, Holy One."

"I know, and he has suffered enough. *Bi aig fois, dileas searbhanta.*" Jor'el waved his hand. Jarvis vanished. "He is now at peace."

The act stunned the others. With unusual fury, Kell confronted Jor'el. "I should have been the one to go! Jarvis didn't have to cease existing."

Concerned, Armus and Avatar restrained their impassioned friend from approaching the Throne.

"Kell," began Jor'el with sympathy. "Jarvis has not gone out of existence. I returned him to the heavenlies and his first estate. Only his physical manifestation is gone. You know Guardians can't die, only change forms when the physical ceases or their mission is complete. At any time I can recall him or leave him at peace."

"*I* should have confronted Dagar."

"By sending a vassal, *I* showed Dagar *my* willingness towards him."

"You said there is nothing more to tell him to change his mind."

The veiled head shook. "Nothing for *you* to tell him. I gave him one last chance to make the right choice. He refused." The eyes grew harsh and the voice commanding. "Go, Captain! Bring him back to face my justice. If you are unable, prepare for battle!" Jor'el vanished.

"He won't come easily so we're going with you as back up," said Armus of himself, Avatar and Vidar.

"Just stay well out of sensing distance."

"I can sight him with my bow without him knowing," said Vidar.

"To wound, not kill. Jor'el will deal with him."

<hr />

Dagar's administrative house was the only structure on a road leading from the nearest town north to the labor camp. Kell arrived on foot. He thought about dimension travel, but such arrivals were always more dramatic at night when light pierced the darkness. Besides, he didn't want to be vulnerable when reappearing should Dagar choose to react. He held the hilt of his sword ready as he stretched out his senses. Feeling no immediate danger or presence, he entered. He grew suspicious at finding several candles lit yet the empty interior.

"Dagar!" Kell shouted. No answer. No surprise. After what happened to Jarvis, he didn't expect to find Dagar waiting to be arrested.

Moving further into the room, Kell discovered a sword lying on a desk with a folded piece of paper under the hilt. He recognized Barrion's sword. His jowls flexed in anger and regret, for the yielding of a warrior's weapon meant Jarvis wasn't the only Guardian felled by Dagar.

"I'm sorry I didn't speak to you after Vidar told me your concerns."

Kell stuck the sword in his belt. He picked up the paper to read. He took a brief moment to compose his temper after reading. He closed his eyes to once more stretch out his senses in both the physical and nether dimensions. His face showed the effort it took to bridge the dimensional gap. His eyes snapped open followed by a loud growl of frustration at finding nothing. He left the house. Stepping onto the road, he waved his fist over his head in a signal to the others to stand down. A moment later, they joined him.

"I guess he's not here," said Avatar in his dry sarcastic humor.

Kell removed the sword from his belt. "He discovered you spoke to Barrion," he said to Vidar, "and left it for me to find, along with this." He gave the note to Avatar.

"*Next time come yourself so I can put my sword in your heart, Dagar,*" Avatar read aloud then crumbled the paper in his fist.

"I assume he left no trail to follow," said Armus.

"No, he covered it well." Kell's voice grew harsh in pronouncement, "This means war."

"Against our own kind," chided Avatar.

"To defend Jor'el and protect Allon!"

"I have no qualms about facing Dagar. Not after the cave. It is the thought of others that gives me pause."

"I understand. But you, me—all of us—must concentrate on our duty. Anything else is a distraction. Now, come, we have planning to do."

In a bright flash of light, all disappeared.

Chapter 14

MAHON LAY ON THE COLD STONE FLOOR OF A LOCKED CELL. Griswold left the chain on his ankles. Suffering the drastic draining effects of the metal, he understood how weak and sick Avatar felt. He didn't have the strength to fight or resist Griswold.

During his nine hundred years of existence, he only experienced the injury of a minor wound when repelling invaders. For the first time he felt ill. He swallowed back nausea in an attempt to withstand the burning and stinging radiating through his body.

He carefully sat up and tried get comfortable. He screwed his eyes shut against the pain. He took several very deep breaths of recovery before opening his eyes. Slowly and deliberately, he turned his head to survey the room. Some prisoners appeared to fare better, while a few looked on the brink of extinction. How long they had suffered was unknown. What fate awaited him? No, Avatar would return, and more than likely with reinforcements. If he could hold out until then, heaven help Griswold!

Across the way, Mahon noticed Witter and Altari engaged in what appeared to be a casual conversation. They wore black uniforms complete with swords. Neither showed signs of abuse or injury. How? Avatar said he saw them among the tortured. Both were Originals, with Witter being the former Trio Leader of the Southern Forest. Kell reassigned him to head the Region of Sanctuary's militia, or more rightly to keep an eye on Dagar. Altari served as Kell's aide for two centuries before becoming commander of the Palace Guardians. His promotion and reassignment happened after Avatar became the captain's protégé.

All of this Mahon knew, which confused him, considering what Avatar said earlier about what he now witnessed.

Maybe the energy drain affected his reasoning and made thinking difficult. That thought passed when Dagar joined Witter and Altari. All three approached his cell. If they were coming for him, they wouldn't find him showing pain. He assumed a relaxed position against the back rock wall, while masking the great discomfort caused by movement.

Dagar laughed. "Well done. Most can't bear to move when wearing the chains."

Mahon didn't reply. Rather he couldn't until the pain passed. Still, determination and stubbornness reflected in his glare at Dagar.

"If you answer my questions, I will have the chains removed."

This time Mahon chose not to answer and continued to stare at Dagar.

Dagar grinned in warped pleasure. "Cocky obstinacy. Well, it doesn't matter. Avatar won't survive to return for you."

To this statement, Mahon's eyes narrowed with suspicion.

"Oh, come, Mahon, you know what is going to happen. Silence won't prevent the inevitable." He snorted an ironic laugh when Mahon remained quiet. "Since you insist, I will tell you. War! That's right. War among the Guardians! Something once unthinkable will now be reality. A war Kell and the others will valiantly fight only to lose."

"You overestimate yourself. Jor'el will not permit defeat," said Mahon.

Dagar laughed with mockery. "Are you so naïve? I thought Avatar taught you better." He heaved a shrug of indifference. "Unfortunately, you won't be there to see the truth, unless you join me."

Mahon's laugh mimicked Dagar "Are you so naïve?" He leaned forward. Despite his boyish features being pale and worn, there was no mistaking the lethal gaze or the hard-bitten edge to his voice. "Keep me anywhere close to you, and you will see just how well I learned a mere second before I kill you."

Dagar flinched at the declaration then recovered with a sneer. "You will remain for me to deal with after my victory!" He turned on his heels.

Witter and Altari began to follow when Mahon called, "Altari."

The warrior paused. At Witter's disapproving scowl, Altari spoke. "I'll be along shortly." He turned to Mahon. "What do you want?"

"Why are you helping Dagar?"

For a moment, Altari glared at him. He spoke with bitterness. "After you experience a century of torture ask me that question." He left.

"Altari!" shouted Mahon, only to be ignored. He groaned at the pain caused by shouting. "Jor'el, give me strength to endure," he prayed and wearily closed his eyes.

In the Cave's main chamber, Tor waited with Curtis. The mortal's nervous glance shifted around the cold confines of the cave. He swallowed back trepidation when Dagar arrived, alone.

"My lord." Curtis bowed to Dagar.

"Curtis. Do you know why you are here?"

"No, my lord," he said, trying to mask his apprehension.

"I told him that you wanted to see him, to test if he is worthy of your offer," said Tor.

Dagar grinned at the mortal. "How willing are you to prove your loyalty?"

"Whatever you ask, my lord."

The smiled turned gracious. "No, Curtis. Now is the time for you to choose and earn what I promised you. Any suggestions?"

Curtis fought a smile. "Ay, my lord."

"Proceed." Dagar took a casual seat to listen.

"My lord, the boy Toby is nephew to the Vicar. Mordecai sought to undermine you by his little deception. However, he forgot one important detail, I know where the boy's family lives."

"Where is that?"

"A farm two hours northwest of the Temple."

His interest piqued, Dagar sat forward to ask, "A farm you say?"

"Ay. Master Dolan is wealthy, and well respected in the province. He is also law abiding. If I were to arrive with a warrant for the boy, claiming he escaped from camp, he would be hard pressed to resist. If for some reason, he chooses *to* resist, I would have no recourse but to arrest the whole family. They could be leverage against the Vicar."

Dagar sat back in the chair to scrutinize Curtis. "As Guardian administrator of the province, I can accomplish the same thing."

"Of course, my lord. However," the mortal continued with some caution, "with the recent tension surrounding this rogue Guardian, your actions could be cause for concern among the populace. I am a mere mortal and would draw less attention. I took the liberty of writing a warrant from the Council of Judges complete with signature."

Dagar grinned with satisfaction. "You understand the situation very well, and came prepared. A forgery no doubt."

Curtis smiled. "I told your lordship you can depend upon me."

Dagar still smiled when he spoke to Tor. "Fetch Ram, Faxon and Farold." He returned his attention to Curtis. "Your plan has merit. Help yourself to some refreshment while we await the others."

Curtis approached the indicated table. He poured himself a cup of wine and took a sniff. Seeing Dagar watching, he smiled. "Will you join me as I toast your success, my lord?"

Dagar laughed. "You fear poison. What sense would there be in killing you?" He crossed to the table and took the cup from Curtis. He drained the cup in one long swallow. "Nothing to fear." He poured more wine in the cup and gave it to Curtis.

"To your success, my lord." Curtis saluted and drank.

Tor returned with Ram, Faxon and Farold; twins Guardians by the look of their similar features, flaxen hair and violet eyes.

"You sent for us?" asked Ram. Although by his curious glance, he wondered about Curtis.

Dagar took up the explanation. "This is Curtis from the labor camp. He's the mortal I told you about. He suggested taking the Vicar's family into custody for our use."

"And you agreed?"

"It has merit backed by sound reasoning. I want you, Faxon and Farold to accompany him."

"My lord," began Curtis with some hesitation. "I do not dispute you, however, these two are Guardians. I believe the same reasons would apply to their presence."

Dagar flashed a tolerant smile. "Did I forget to mention they are shape-shifters?"

"What are shape-shifters?"

Before Curtis' eyes the two Guardians took on the smaller, more distinct appearance of mortal soldiers.

"Do not be fooled by the change, they are still fully Guardian with the strength, power and perception natural to their station. They, along with my son, Ram, your future king, will accompany you," said Dagar.

Curtis looked in wonder at Ram. "You too are a Guardian?"

"Half-Guardian and half-mortal, and more powerful than you."

"I do not doubt that, my liege."

Ram flashed a toothy grin of pleasure.

Dagar continued his instructions. "Take horses and approach the farm like normal to present the warrant. If there is resistance, *Constable* Curtis has authorization to arrest the family. The presence of you three will prevent any thoughts of non-compliance or escape."

"Understood," said Ram.

<hr />

The journey took two hours from where Faxon and Farold brought them to fetch horses. As they approached from the north, Ram anticipated where they were heading.

"This farm of Master Dolan's, is it the large stone house around the next bend?"

"Ay, my liege. Are you familiar with it?"

Ram sneered his displeasure. "Let's just say my last visit was very unpleasant."

"I'm sorry to hear that, my liege."

Ram studied Curtis: an average looking mortal, nothing extraordinary or distinct about him. However, his father promised Curtis the position of Grand Master at court, the equivalent to Avram's office of Vicar. He expected more from what Dagar told him regarding Curtis. Still, the promising offer would not have been made if the mortal did not have some merit. No doubt this was a test. He would pay close attention should this mortal become his advisor.

"Hello, the house!" called Faxon. He rode ahead of Ram and Curtis with Farold in the rear. Receiving no answer, he called again.

The front door opened to reveal a rotund man of middle years. "May I help you, sirs?"

"Are you Master Dolan?" asked Faxon.

"He is not," said Curtis. "He is Orson, the steward."

"Curtis," said Orson, wary. "What brings you here?"

"Constable," he corrected. "Duty." Curtis dismounted, as did Ram. "Take me to Master Dolan."

Orson's eyes shifted in bewilderment from Ram to Curtis. "He is not here, *Constable*."

"Kerwin."

"He's not here either." Again he glanced at Ram.

"Mace? Clare?" Curtis asked. Each time he received a negative answer. His anger increased. "Where are they?"

"They went to the Fortress a couple of days ago with the Guardian lieutenant. The big one, only I forget his name."

"Armus," said Ram in disgust.

"Ay," agreed Orson, now staring curiously at Ram.

"What did the Guardian want with Dolan?" asked Curtis.

"They came to arrest Mistress Janel's husband."

Ram seized Orson about the throat. "The one who looks like me," it was more a statement than a question.

"Ay," he stammered in fear.

"How long have they been married?"

"I don't know exactly but they returned a night after we thought she disappeared. He left and returned a few days later. Then Lieutenant Armus, and some other Guardians arrived to take them to the Fortress."

Orson began choking under Ram's grasp. Curtis intervened to keep the steward from fainting.

"We have them, my lord! Dolan is an accomplice to aiding an escaped prisoner."

Ram shoved Orson aside to question Curtis. "What?"

Curtis quickly withdrew the warrant. "His son Toby. The entire family is implicated." He spoke to Orson with harsh formality. "I have a warrant issued by the Council of Judges to arrest Master Dolan on those charges, but apparently the Guardians of Jor'el preceded me. Once again they undermine our mortal authority and right to rule without interference. To prevent them from causing further insult, this farm is confiscated by order of the Council. If the Guardians of Jor'el object, they can take it up with the Judges!" He motioned to Faxon and Farold. "Clear everyone off the farm. If anyone resists, arrest them."

"Constable! Some of us never lived or worked any place else, what will we do?" Orson protested.

Curtis glanced at Ram. The latter's temper had cooled, and he looked very pleased. "His lordship will be an advocate for all who seek reparations from the Guardians at the appointed time. For now, everyone is to vacate. Your cooperation is appreciated."

"Ay, Constable. My lord." He bowed to them before returning inside.

Ram drew Curtis aside to speak. "You think and act quickly."

Curtis smiled in sardonic confidence. "Being trapped in a labor camp for over twenty years I took the opportunity to perfect ways of exploiting and frustrating those over me. Now I have a chance to get full, open revenge. As I told his lordship, I now tell you: you can depend upon me."

Ram smiled. He heartily patted Curtis on the shoulder. "Indeed. He will be as pleased as I am when this is reported."

Curtis frowned. "More dimension travel?" he asked in a low disconcerted voice.

Ram spoke in a confidential voice. "I don't like it either, but a necessity. When the farm is clear, we ride back to the safe house and proceed from there."

Time was difficult to gauge in the nether dimension. However, in the real world they just left, it was late afternoon. Ram and Curtis appeared satisfied.

"I take it all went well?" said Dagar.

"Not totally, but Constable Curtis is very resourceful and quick thinking."

Curtis bowed to Ram's description, making Dagar ask, "How so?"

Ram looked directly at his father. "It's the same farm where we encountered Barrion. The girl Razi married is the Vicar's niece."

Dagar's anger exploded. He knocked over the table upon which sat experimental models of torture devices.

Fear made Curtis jump back. "My lord? My liege?"

Ram signaled Curtis to remain calm, yet moved to shield him from Dagar's rage.

Not until Dagar destroyed nearly everything in sight did he stop. His breathing labored from activity and his eyes shown with lethal intent. "Did you know this?" he shouted at Curtis.

Terrified, he recoiled. "I don't know what you're talking about!"

"Father, he didn't know."

Dagar stared at Ram before saying, "You expect me to believe that?"

"You just introduced me to him before we left. He didn't react with a sense of familiarity, unlike the steward of the farm. He kept staring at me and knew who I meant when I asked about the person resembling me."

"You have another son, my lord?" Curtis dared ask Dagar.

"My twin." Ram continued his explanation to Dagar. "The steward told us about the Guardians' arrival, which Constable Curtis turned to our advantage."

"How?"

Ram gave an encouraging smile and nod for Curtis to speak.

Bolstered by the action, Curtis explained. "I took the opportunity to plant the seeds of doubt and mistrust against the Guardians of Jor'el. I showed him the warrant signed by the Council of Judges. I told him such action by the Guardians undermines mortal authority and our right to govern without interference. The steward protested about how the confiscation would displace the servants, to which I offered his lordship to act as advocate for their grievances against the Guardians at the appropriate time."

Dagar laughed. "Excellent! In one well-placed stroke you elevate Ram in their eyes and diminish the Guardians. Indeed you will be Grand Master." He casually placed an arm around Curtis' shoulders. "Come, we'll find you clothes more befitting your station and inform you of our plans." He then motioned to Faxon and Farold. "Clean up this mess."

Chapter 15

Lamps always remained lit inside Arundine. Being night, they were even more luminous. Kell stood on the platform near the high chair. Vidar waited at the threshold to allow him some privacy before the fateful meeting. Impatient concern made Kell gnaw on his lower lip. He dispatched Armus and Avatar to gather the Trio Leaders. Facing the first war among their members, he felt it important to reassure them with personal messages instead of an impersonal summons by way of vassals.

Since Razi's revelation and testing, Kell steeled himself against the inevitable. As he told Avatar, their duty was clear and they could not waver no matter the enemy. With determination, planning had to begin on how to face Dagar in combat.

When a flash of light splashed across the wall behind the platform, Kell turned. Armus. The lieutenant barely opened his mouth when light signaled another arrival. Avatar held his drawn sword and looked piqued.

"We have a serious problem!" he announced.

"What?" Kell asked, guarded and tense.

"Hunter isn't the only one siding with Dagar. I was forced to defend myself against Jayden." Avatar slammed his sword back in the scabbard.

"Sloan and Lilith have also turned," said Armus.

Astonished, Vidar rushed from the threshold. "What of their militias?" he asked, only to be met by grim expression from the warriors signaling the answer. "They went fully armed," he spoke with dread.

Kell's eyes flashed with anger at the news of further betrayal. "What about the others?"

"Valmar, Priscilla, Zanis, Raleigh and Gresham remain loyal," said Armus.

"So are Chase and Gulliver. The navy is intact," groused Avatar.

"Small consolation with our numbers divided," chided Vidar.

"At least we can contain Dagar to land."

"Escape is hardly in his plan."

"I know! I saw his plan displayed in cages and torture," Avatar hotly argued. Passion made him step too close to Vidar for Kell's liking. The captain separated them by jerking on each of their shoulders, nearly taking the smaller archer off his feet.

"Peace! There is enough division. I will not tolerate arguing."

"I'm sorry. I'm still jumpy from my fight with Jayden," Avatar apologized to Kell then made a submissive nod to Vidar. "My apologies."

The archer acknowledged the apology. "I'm also sorry. The Leaders are my peers."

After giving them a moment to calm down, Kell continued, first to Avatar and Armus. "Since planning here is now impossible, tell those remaining loyal to come immediately to the Fortress with half their militia. The rest are to remain in the provinces on alert along with any mortal forces they can muster." After sharp salutes, the warriors vanished. He turned to Vidar, his voice softened to sympathetic. "Collect your militia."

Vidar stepped back and vanished.

⁂

At the Fortress, Ridge and Wren were now recovered and released to return to duty. Ridge sat on the cot staring at the spot on the floor where Kell stood a moment earlier. The captain informed him of Hunter.

Wren sat beside him. "I'm sorry, Ridge."

He heaved a hapless sigh. "I fooled myself into hoping he wouldn't turn. That somehow he would come to his senses… As I said, I was foolish."

"It's not foolishness to hope for the best. I'd do the same for Vidar."

Still staring at the floor, Ridge shook his head. "It's more than Hunter. Kell didn't say it, but Cam isn't alive. Hunter wouldn't make the break and leave witnesses."

She held his shoulder. "You are alive, Ridge! *And* witness to his deception. Without you, Kell and the others wouldn't have been warned, and I may not have survived the kelpie attack. Thank you."

Ridge grinned. "The gratitude is mutual."

Wren smiled. "Come. We have duty. By doing so, Hunter and Dagar can be stopped and Cam avenged." She drew him to his feet and they left the infirmary.

Large, elaborate, gold streetlamps and gold lanterns hung at the entrances to buildings illuminating the compound. The light helped the mortals while also making a dazzling night display seen for miles in all directions.

At the armory, Wren and Ridge received new uniforms and weapons. Over her tunic she wore a thick leather vest buckled closed on the left side. The gold and maroon crest of the Northern Forest was embossed on the vest. Leather armbands covered the vulnerable parts of her hands and forearms, leaving only her fingers free to load and fire. She carried a full quiver of arrows, wore a new dagger yet retained her own crossbow.

Ridge also wore a leather vest; only he chose to keep it plain. He wanted no embossing or color to identify his unit since he alone represented the Southern Forest. He wore matching leather gloves and thick leather guards on his shins that covered the top parts of his feet. These helped to deflect quarterstaff blows or a badly aimed sword. The leather wouldn't help against arrows save to slow the impact and give him a chance for survival. Wren went bareheaded while he wore a metal helmet with a small brim and a leather chinstrap, again for defense against head blows. He carried his own staff, refusing to replace it when offered a new one by the armory sergeant. All rangers and archers dressed similarly, with each province having different embossing and colors for identification. Warriors were more ornate in their armor.

Upon leaving the armory, they met Vidar in the compound. His battle dress distinguished him as a Trio Leader and premiere archer. He wore a silver breastplate instead of a leather vest with the symbol of the Northern Forest painted on the raised image. He grinned.

"You both look well."

Wren smiled. "With your permission, I convinced Ridge to join us."

"Granted. Actually, I hoped to convince you to consider the option."

"Nice to know I'm wanted," said Ridge in a voice devoid of humor.

"More than you realize," began Vidar with unction. "I know Kell told you about Hunter, but did he mention the others?"

"What others?" asked Ridge, guarded.

"Sloan, Lilith and Jayden also joined Dagar. *And* took their militias. Our entire force is reduced by half."

Ridge stared at Vidar in disbelief. Wren stood speechless.

Vidar's touch on his shoulder shook Ridge out of his shock. "We have you to thank for informing us that this went beyond Dagar. Who knows how many more they could have convinced if left undetected."

Ridge's voice barely rose above a whisper. "I had no idea he was so persuasive. I wonder why Kell didn't tell me?"

"I'm sure Kell didn't want to overwhelm you. It's his nature to be protective, especially after what you've endured. However, since we're about to face a harsher reality than any of us would like, I thought you should know."

Ridge nodded, a bit absentminded in pondering the news.

"Join the others outside the south wall. I'll see you after the meeting.

Wren tugged on Ridge's arm to follow Vidar's instructions.

Instead of assembling inside the captain's office, Vidar went to the adjacent chamber. This served as a conference room complete with a table capable of seating fourteen. A large detailed map of Allon covered one wall with a map of the known world on another wall. Two double balcony doors flanked the second map. The floor-to-ceiling curtains were drawn aside with the doors opened for air and light from the compound.

A huge wrought iron chandelier hung over the table and illuminated the room. At one end of the room was a massive hearth devoid of fire.

Among the remaining Leaders, only Valmar was a warrior. His ornate armor stood out from the rest. A glorious mane of white hair made him appear the oldest while violet eyes shone shrewd and clear. Jade with gold accents highlighted the Highland Leader's polished silver armor. The hilt of his two-handed sword contained jade stones and gold filigree.

Over her flowing gown, Priscilla wore a gold plated bodice with no other adornment. Raleigh acted similar to Priscilla in his ability to control the elements. He was also less elaborate in his armament. Along with a plain breastplate of scarlet accents, he wore a helmet and gauntlets. Gresham had always been more ornate in his attire. His beautifully embossed leather breastplate, gloves of peacock blue and silver weren't out of place, nor were the plumes on his matching hat. Sea Guardians, Gulliver and Chase, didn't wear any form of armor, rather well crafted dark blue leather suits with silver accents. Gulliver wasn't a Trio Leader. He commanded the Guardian navy. Zanis wore a black and red breastplate to make a less visible target compared to Vidar's gold one. A sure and keen shot, he didn't like all the pomp of battle.

They didn't wait long before Kell arrived with Armus and Avatar. Kell wore his armor, minus the cloak. Armus and Avatar wore less ornate breastplates, along with finely crafted leather belts and scabbards.

"By now you are all aware of the situation. We face an undesired reality that must be quickly put down, or risk more than divided ranks."

"That goes without saying," groused Gulliver.

Kell didn't accept the salty sea Guardian's comment and chided, "Without a united Guardian leadership, the future of Allon and the Almighty's rule is threatened! Which is why I had you keep half your force in your provinces."

"May not be enough under the circumstances," said Valmar.

"I realize that, however we can't leave them vulnerable. Maintaining control of seven provinces is vital. Lose any more and the balance of power is turned."

"What about moving some of our forces into the turncoats' provinces to secure them before the conflict?" asked Gresham.

Kell shook his head. "Such a move may incite the mortals. Right now, I'm only aware of Guardian involvement. Any premature action could sway sentiment against us."

"This is as much to protect them."

"The latest actions of this rogue Guardian have caused unrest and suspicions. Opened and armed action will surely make matters worse. No, if any aggression is taken, it must first be by Dagar so we can be seen in a more favorable role."

"We were created to protect not inflict harm," added Armus.

Gresham became offended. "I wasn't suggesting harming the mortals, just securing the provincial seat of power. We can do so without conflict."

"Unless Dagar anticipates such a move and is prepared," said Vidar.

Much to his reluctance, Gresham agreed to the reasoning.

"We can make a preemptive strike," said Avatar. At Kell's disagreeable expression, he added, "I told you I would bring it up for discussion."

"The lad has a suggestion you disagree with?" asked Valmar.

"Let's just say, I'm not totally convinced."

"What is your suggestion, lad?"

Avatar received an impatient wave from Kell to proceed. Avatar crossed to the map of Allon. "Here, in Midessex, is the location of the Cave. The kelpies that attacked Wren and Ridge came from here. It is also where hundreds of our comrades are being held and tortured. If we can cut if off, Dagar won't have access to the creatures of infrinn, and we can free those suffering."

"You saw this *torture*?" asked Priscilla with some trepidation.

"Ay. Myself and Mahon," he replied, sneering at Gresham.

"Jedrek didn't know! Once and for all, you must stop holding him responsible."

"Responsible for what?" asked Chase.

"Destroying the portal through which I escaped. Mahon was right behind me but never made it," replied Avatar in a tight, grim voice.

"Jedrek saved your life from the kelpie!" said Gresham in further defense.

Avatar's jowls tightened, as he gripped the hilt of his sword to contain a reply. More rightly, it was Kell's admonishing grunt kept him from speaking.

"I'm sorry to hear about Mahon," said Chase. "I enjoyed getting to know him and having him in my militia. You trained him well."

"We'll lose more comrades before this is over," said Kell grimly.

"Why are you resistant to the lad's suggestion? It makes sense to cut the Cave off and prevent Dagar from calling upon its secrets. Few of us can control the creatures of infrinn," said Valmar.

"Ay, it would be to our advantage," agreed Zanis.

"For the same reason I am hesitant about moving into the turncoats' provinces, it may be anticipated. Dagar would not leave it unguarded after Avatar's escape," argued Kell.

"The Cave is in my province. A militia on maneuvers will not draw undo suspicion," said Gresham.

"From the mortals, perhaps, but Dagar might wonder," said Chase.

"By now Dagar knows we're preparing, so doing reconnaissance is normal. We can maintain a non-threatening posture for the populace," countered Gresham. He turned to Kell. "Lend me Avatar and some elite warriors."

"To launch a surprise attack, it would be better to dimension travel," insisted Chase.

"No," said Armus. "Such a large disturbance in the transverse would give away any surprise. Dagar's no fool. He would suspect our target."

"He might suspect that after seeing Avatar with Gresham on maneuvers, since he escaped and witnessed this torture," said Zanis.

"It's really no different than us knowing the compound is Dagar's target," said Avatar. "Either way we proceed, the main objective is to seal the Cave from being used against us."

Zanis and Chase acknowledged the validity of Avatar's argument.

Kell listened to the debate. He changed his focus from the others to Avatar. This made Avatar approach him to press his argument.

"Kell, please, if you saw …"

Kell's hand on Avatar's shoulder stopped further words. "I realize how deeply this affects you and you want to determine Mahon's fate, but it is too risky."

Avatar knocked Kell's hand away. "You ordered me to follow Dagar. That wasn't a risk? A risk I took without question. Or did you know where it would lead, *Captain?*"

Despite the ire rising in the golden eyes, Kell kept his voice level. "No! As soon as I did, I dispatched Mahon to warn you. Dagar could lure you into a trap to destroy your or turn you in some way."

"He did, and with a challenge I accepted."

"What?" Kell asked, taken aback by the statement.

"Foolish perhaps, but I had a task to complete in bringing *you* needed intelligence. Despite it all, even Mahon agreed it was worth the risk. A risk I would take again."

In sudden comprehension, Kell spoke in a tone for only Avatar to hear. "He used *me* to lure you."

Avatar didn't reply; he didn't have too.

"You don't want to take the risk again, do you, Kell?" asked Chase.

Kell was slow to take his focus off Avatar. "I don't want to give Dagar anymore prisoners. I want to stop him in one decisive stroke, and free those unfortunates."

"The lad's plan accomplishes the same by striking before he is fully armed and ready," said Valmar.

"Besides, if we sit back and wait for Dagar to make the first move then we're are simply reacting to him on his terms," said Gresham.

Kell tugged at his lower lip, as he considered the valid points.

Armus spoke, "If Dagar were alone in this, waiting may work, but losing nearly half our forces changes the situation. Granted, I agree about not making any moves to incite the mortals, but sealing the Cave isn't against mortals. It may prove vital to our success."

Kell looked askew at his second-in-command. "You agree? Why didn't you say so before?"

"Because Avatar needed to convince you and the others. He seems to have succeeded with them."

"Ay, we may gain the advantage," said Raleigh.

Priscilla shrugged. "I've never been one for military planning, but if what Avatar says is true about the torture of others, how can we not try?"

A thick apprehension hung over the room in awaiting Kell's response. He glanced from the leaders, to the map and finally to Avatar.

"Well? Have I convinced you, Captain?"

Rather than answering Avatar directly, Kell asked Gresham, "How many in your militia?"

"Two thousand with me, another three thousand spread throughout Midessex."

Kell returned to Avatar. "Take fifty warriors and go with Gresham for recon. Learn what you can and send me word—*but*," he stressed, his eyes narrowing in warning, "take no unnecessary reckless action without my authorization, is that understood?"

Avatar fought to keep a straight face as he replied. "Understood, Captain. Reckless actions only on your orders."

Armus coughed and placed a hand over his mouth to contain a laugh. Valmar and Gulliver weren't so tactful in laughing. Priscilla giggled; Zanis, Raleigh and Chase smiled.

"I'll make sure he doesn't step out of line." Gresham drew Avatar away from an irate Kell.

"Have Jedrek turn him into a block of ice if he does," quipped Gulliver.

"That's his twin, Virgil. Jedrek is fire."

"Then singe him for good measure," said the sea Guardian without hesitation.

"In the meantime, what do we do, Captain?" asked Raleigh.

"Pray they succeed, and prepare for deployment within the region. Dagar may use delaying or feigning tactics to divert attention. But make no mistake, *this* compound is his primary target!" Kell motioned to Zanis and Vidar. "Dispatch hunters and rangers to the provinces—"

"You said you didn't want to incite the mortals," argued Priscilla.

"For reconnaissance. I'm not going to be idle. We must have ears and eyes to respond quickly and decisively to any action."

"Hunters and rangers won't draw notice," said Zanis with a confident grin.

"And we thought just the wind blew foul with the hot air of boasting," snickered Gulliver to Chase while jerking his thumb at Priscilla and Zanis.

"Go! May Jor'el guide your actions." Kell dismissed them.

Armus remained. He spoke after the others left. "At least morale isn't lost under the circumstances."

"Let's hope it remains strong."

"With or without your authorization?" Armus finally laughed. "You did say *no unnecessary reckless action without my authorization.*" He mimicked Kell's voice.

Kell wasn't amused, rather grew pensive. "Hold onto your humor. I'll need some when I get back."

"From where?"

"Jor'el."

Crossing the compound, Kell spied various members of the provincial militias in the process of preparing. Near the armory, Avatar spoke to a group of warriors. He caught Avatar's eye, Avatar quickly turned away to continue speaking to the warriors. The meeting showed Kell that Hunter was correct about favoring Avatar as his aide and protégé. He manifested favoritism by over-protectiveness. In the past, he acted the same way towards Armus, only to be soundly confronted by his lieutenant about altering his ways. Whereas Armus was his peer and equal, Avatar was a subordinate. Thus, Avatar became clever at manipulating orders; like using Eldric to care for the Vicar's family to avoid treatment, or going into Dagar's trap. Bringing the suggestion of a preemptive strike before the Leaders was another ploy around Kell. True, the tactic annoyed him, but Avatar proved himself many times. Despite his strong inclination to shield those within his care, he had to stop being overprotective of Avatar, the same as he did with Armus.

The Guardian warriors on duty saluted Kell when he entered the Throne room. He assumed the position on one knee with head bent.

"Almighty Jor'el, grant me the honor of your presence for wisdom to complete the task which brings me before you." Kell waited with is head bowed but received no reply. Thus he repeated his request. Again no answer. He dared a glance at the Throne. "Are you withholding your presence due to anger?"

Jor'el's voice sounded from all around: firm, but not angry. "You seek an answer you already know. Guard your heart, Kell, for the task will not be easy and the cost great. Now, go."

"Will we be successful?" When met with more silence, Kell left. He came seeking reassurance, only Jor'el was right. He knew what must be done. The challenge came in the reality of dispatching Guardians to war against other Guardians. Now was not the time for second-guessing, doubt or wishing things different. Reality is what it is.

Armus waited on the portico. "That was quick."

"He told me to guard my heart against the cost of what must be done."

"Although caring deeply for others is an endearing quality, it is one Dagar has no qualms about exploiting. He tried by using Avatar and succeeded with Jarvis."

Kell looked to where he saw Avatar. He and the warriors were gone.

Armus followed his glance. "They left with Gresham." Kell continued to stare, prompting Armus to continue. "Kell, none of us go into this blindly. For the first time we do battle as Guardian against Guardian. Don't let Dagar see weakness."

Kell's jowls flexed and his eyes grew fierce. "When I face Dagar, it won't be weakness he sees."

Armus grinned at the bravado. "I mean, don't let him see weakness in ways he can hurt you." He gripped Kell's arm to continue. "If Avatar or I fall, you must not show any emotion other than raw determination to finish what must be done. Same as we must do if heaven forbid, you fall. Only in victory will there be peace and justice. So for those of us who do fall, it will not be in vain. And done in our ultimate service to Jor'el and the protection of Allon."

Kell snorted an ironic chuckle. "Sounds like a speech the captain should give."

Armus smiled. "Go ahead. I won't mind if you borrow it."

Kell chuckled as he steered Armus from the portico. "Let's see how the deployment of reconnaissance is going."

In the nether dimension's main chamber, Dagar, Tor, Hunter, Lilith, Sloan, Jayden, Griswold and Ram gathered around a table containing maps. Of the group, Hunter was the only non-warrior. Instead of the battle armor representing their various provinces, they wore all black armor and uniforms, with a few hints of scarlet. Lilith and Jayden wore swords slung across their backs rather than on their hips.

Lilith pointed to the map. "My forces are hiding along the mountain border between the North Plain and the Region all the way to the foothills of the Highlands."

"Half of my troops are poised on the border of Midessex. The other half I sent into the mountains of the South Plains," said Sloan.

"Too risky," said Griswold.

"Why? What is Raleigh going to do? I could cut him down before he conjures up a whirlwind."

"We have a secure line from the foothills to the River Bendix in the Lowlands." Tor traced his finger along the map. "Cutting off the western half of Allon."

Dagar looked to Hunter. "I'm assuming you secured your border?"

"Naturally. From the Greenwood to the coast."

"That leaves the Northern Forest and the Meadowlands for access of escape," said Ram.

Dagar huffed. "Kell will never retreat. Not while we threaten the compound."

"I can move my force to quickly secure the Meadowlands," said Jayden, motioning from his Delta province in the south.

"All of you realize we are discussing civil war against our own kind?" said Hunter.

Dagar folded his arms across his chest to glare at Hunter. "Having second thoughts, ranger?"

"No, merely speaking reality. We stand here coolly calculating our moves like we have no personal connection with those we are about to fight. In reality, we are taking up arms against our Creator and our comrades. Plan and fight we must, but let us not lose sight of those we have chosen to make our adversaries."

For a brief moment of grim silence, Hunter watched the faces of the others. His speech had little effect. A few stared mercilessly at him, namely Tor, Griswold, Ram and Jayden. Disquieted, Hunter looked away.

Lilith became alert. "I'm being summoned."

"Kell or Jor'el?" asked Hunter, trying to mask his nervousness.

"Alger," she said of her Trio Mate. She hastened from the chamber.

"Kell's making a move," suggested Tor.

"Possible. We'll await her return. Can you move undetected into the Meadowlands and secure the border from the river to Hunter's line?" Dagar asked Jayden.

"Using rangers and scouts, ay. It'll take time. Zanis isn't a patsy like Raleigh." Jayden moved to leave when Lilith rushed back. He stopped to hear her report.

"Gresham's force is leaving the compound heading south."

"Back to Midessex?" asked Dagar.

"That's the road they took. Avatar and some warriors are with him."

"Avatar," said Tor with delighted chuckle. "I wonder where they could be heading?" It was more a sarcastic statement than question.

Dagar widely smiled. "He'll have a warm reception waiting." He dismissed them. "The rest of you to your posts. Tor!" He left the main chamber with Tor at his heels and headed to the reconditioning chamber.

Dagar weaved his way through the cages in the reconditioning chamber. He stopped before Mahon's cell. The latter lay on the stone outcrop with his eyes closed. "Wake up, maggot!"

Startled, Mahon's eyes snapped open. He scowled at Dagar. "What do you want, traitor?" his voice strained by pain but filled with anger.

"I'm offering you a chance for freedom."

"On what terms?"

"An exchange. You for Avatar."

Mahon laughed, loud and mocking. "Go away and let me sleep." He closed his eyes.

Dagar shrugged. "Suit yourself. Avatar will be here soon, and I have a wonderful surprise planned for him."

Mahon opened his eyes. "What are you talking about?"

Dagar's smile turned vicious. "It has begun, Mahon, the battle for supremacy! Rather it will be once Avatar arrives with Gresham's force. No doubt to liberate the poor unfortunates," he spread his arms in gesturing to the cages and cells. "You will be the personal focus of his rescue."

"I'm no more important than the rest. Avatar knows that."

"You are important to me!" Dagar spoke in the Ancient while making a flick of his wrist. The cell door opened. He moved inside and jerked Mahon to his feet. The warrior gasped in pain at the sudden movement. "You will have a unique place in my plan."

"I won't serve as your bait!"

Mahon used all his strength to rip himself from Dagar's grasp. The action sent Dagar staggering backward. Unfortunately, in his weakness, Mahon stumbled into the bars. Searing pain from the bars racked his body, intensifying the burning sensation in his leg from the chains around his ankles. He fell to the ground unconscious. His face grew extremely pale and he barely breathed.

"Did that finish him?" Tor moved into the cell as Dagar examined Mahon.

"No, but close." Dagar seized the front of Mahon's doublet to jerk him into a sitting position. The warrior's head limply fell to one side. He grabbed Mahon's face. "You can't die on me yet, maggot!" His attempt to rouse Mahon failed. The younger warrior remained unconscious.

"He'll be no good like that," said Tor.

Dagar roughly released Mahon, who hit the ground hard. He spoke the Ancient and waved his hand over the chains ensnaring Mahon's ankles. The chains disappeared. "That should stop his life force from draining away."

"But will he regain his senses in time? The portal is ready. How will you lure Avatar without Mahon's help? He won't willingly enter the Cave a second time."

Dagar sneered with annoyance. "Send for Faxon."

"You know a shape-shifter can't assume another Guardian's identity."

Irate, Dagar bolted up. "He can imitate Mahon's voice! That may be all I need." In an act of frustration, he kicked Mahon's leg then marched from the cell. Tor barely exited the cell when Dagar spoke, waved his hand and the cell door slammed shut.

Chapter 16

A T MIDNIGHT, THEY RODE THROUGH *BEALACH DE FOIS,* the Pass of Peace. Gresham dispatched rangers to scout ahead. For this task, the leaders and warriors rode white spirit horses, which were larger and more powerful than mortal horses. Archers and rangers marched on foot. Most of Gresham's force consisted of archers and rangers. Only five hundred of the two thousand he brought with him to the compound were warriors. Add to that the fifty elite warriors with Avatar, for a total of five hundred and fifty. The remaining three thousand troops, Gresham strategically staged about the province. Only two hundred of those were warriors.

The number and type of Guardians assigned to each militia depended upon the province. In general, the number of troops ranged from five thousand to twenty thousand at any one time. This didn't include the Guardians at Melwynn or in the heavenlies for future use by Jor'el, only those dispatched to govern and protect the mortals.

With Midessex being in the heart of Allon, not as many warriors were required for defense. The West Coast, East Coast, Lowlands and Delta consisted mainly of warriors to act as a first line of defense to prevent invasion. The Meadowlands kept numbers similar to Midessex both in composition and size. Since the Northern and Southern Forests had some coastline, half the force consisted of warriors. The Highlands coastline lay too far north and had no seaports. Only one third of its forces consisted of warriors.

"How much further in this direction?" asked Avatar.

Gresham slyly grinned. "You can't tell me, he of the elite tracking sense?"

Avatar returned the crooked smile. "Since this is your province, I thought to give you the dubious honor of deferring to your expertise."

Gresham chuckled. "The portal or where you entered?"

"The portal. Dagar may repair it to use as a conduit. Much easier access than dimension travel."

"Several hours."

Jedrek moved his horse alongside Avatar. He, Virgil and Auriel rode behind them. "Again, we're sorry about the portal. We will be the first ones into the Cave to search for Mahon."

Avatar looked along his shoulder at Jedrek then further back to Virgil. In some ways, the twins reminded him of Mahon, being fair-haired with youthful features. They were the same age as Avatar at thirteen hundred years, and Trio Mates of the same rank. Jedrek served as Auriel's mentor. Gresham bestowed high favor upon Jedrek, just like he did with Kell and Armus. Thus Avatar found it difficult to hold a grudge at Jedrek's sincere apology.

"Second in the Cave, behind me. No—with me."

Jedrek smiled in relief. "Ay."

Auriel's short taunting laugh caught attention. "I thought all elite warriors were arrogant and unreasonable." Her gentle features, strawberry blonde hair pulled back in a long braid and vibrant jade colored eyes belied a fierce warrior. She wore the sword strapped to her back, along with a dagger at her right hip and a chakram on her left hip.

Avatar flashed a wry smile. "Sorry to disappoint you. Or rather, I should say, I'm happy to correct your warped opinion."

Jedrek, Virgil and Gresham laughed. Auriel forced a smirk at Avatar.

Gresham stopped laughing and pulled his horse to a halt. He stood in the stirrups as his eyes scanned the horizon.

"What is it?" asked Avatar.

Jedrek, Virgil and Auriel also became alert. "An uneasiness stirs the trees and ground," replied Virgil.

Auriel moved her horse between Avatar and Jedrek. "Don't you sense it, mighty one? Or should I say, feeble?"

Annoyed, Avatar chided Gresham. "I take it she flunked all the lessons in respect."

Gresham's focus remained ahead as he replied, "She's Jedrek's fault. I'm just the Trio Leader." He sat back in the saddle. "We need to hurry." He put up his hand in a signal. "Double speed!" He kicked his horse into a gallop.

Avatar pushed his horse to catch up to Gresham. "I meant the cause of the disturbance, not that I didn't sense something wrong."

"I know what you meant. Trespassers from the west."

"Lilith!" snarled Avatar.

They pressed on until Gresham drew them to a halt at the River Bendix. The water ran high and fast.

"This shouldn't be happening," said Gresham concerning the river.

Virgil explained the comment to Avatar. "The river doesn't become swollen until winter. This isn't natural."

"You expected less?" Avatar dismounted. "Ewert, Bailey!"

"Warriors to forge a river?" began Auriel in scoffing disbelief. "Wait. Don't tell me, Gulliver trained them?"

"Give her a remedial lesson in respect now!" Avatar ordered Jedrek.

Jedrek sent a firm hand-signal for Auriel to be silent.

Avatar didn't see the exchange as he gave instruction to Ewert and Bailey. "We need to cross."

Sly smiles appeared as they drew their swords. Ewert and Bailey moved to the bank of the angry river. They separated and moved a hundred yards up and down river. Facing each other, they raised their swords by the hilts with the blades pointing down. Together shouted in the Ancient. "*Talamah bi tioram!*" and drove the points into the ground.

Immediately, the earth quaked from the points of impact and continued across the river to the far bank. The water changed course. The reason became apparent when two large fissures ran the length of the riverbed. On Bailey's upriver side, the water poured into the fissure and emerged from Ewert's fissure on the downriver side to continue flowing. The riverbed between the two fissures became dry land.

Avatar vaulted into the saddle. With a wide satisfied smirk, he spoke to Auriel. "You were saying about warriors forging a river?"

"We could have dimension traveled across."

"And miss the opportunity to teach you a lesson in humility?" Avatar move his horse onto the dry riverbed. Gresham and Virgil followed.

"So speaks Kell's favorite about humility," she groused.

Jedrek drew his horse alongside Auriel for the crossing. "Softly! He *is* the captain's aide and a member of the High Trio."

"And he knows it."

He seized her arm to soundly scold her. "What we are about to face is more important than venting personal dislikes."

She sighed. "You're right. I'm just tense about the situation."

"We all are. Provoking Avatar won't help. Concentrate on why we are here and what we must do."

It took fifteen minutes for the entire force to cross the river. After the troop reached the other side, Ewert and Bailey withdrew their swords from the ground. The reverse happened. The fissures disappeared to allow the river to once more flow freely. The warriors disappeared and reappeared on the other side to join their companions.

The gray light of morning broke over the horizon. Gresham stopped the militia's advance in a small grove a half-mile from a wooded area.

"I don't sense trouble," said Avatar.

Gresham spoke with grave consideration. "No, I'm concerned that my scouts have not returned. We should have heard some news by now, especially from the west."

"I can dispatch more," said Jedrek.

"Too risky this close to the portal." Gresham turned his horse to face the troops. "We disperse into ranks. If Dagar is having Lilith bring her forces to protect the portal we should prepared. Four ranks; you to the south flank, Virgil to the north, Avatar and I in the center," he ordered Jedrek then said to Avatar, "Place your warriors among the ranks."

Avatar added his instructions to Jedrek. "Divide by platoons: Ewert and Bailey in the center with Gresham and I; Hearn to the south with you; Scully to the north flank with Virgil. Have Auriel stay in reserve to guard the rear. We don't want any uninvited guests."

Jedrek signaled to Auriel and Virgil. The three left to carry out the orders. It took a few moments for the militia to break into ranks. Once ready, they moved slowly toward the portal.

Avatar stirred uneasily in the saddle. His eyes focused on the horizon.

Gresham noticed the agitation. "The portal is just on the other side of the trees. We'll move into the clearing and let Virgil use the woods for a screen. Jedrek will swing further south."

Impressed, Avatar grinned. "I didn't realize a vassal could be so well versed in the art of war."

"I didn't get this job because of my looks, though they exceed most."

Avatar snickered in observance of Gresham. Indeed, his white hair and violet eyes made for a stunning contrast to his uniform of peacock blue and silver. "True, but how is only a dagger going to help?"

"Doubtless you don't know my power." He patted the dagger.

"Doubtless, you're right. I'm sure it matches your looks, ornate and garish."

Their humor ceased when they became alert. Avatar drew his sword and Gresham his dagger. Gresham used his weapon to wave Virgil into the trees then motioned Jedrek further south.

Even sinew of Avatar's body tensed in anticipation. Upon rounding the edge of the tress, he reined his horse. His brows furrowed in wary surprise. The portal had been repaired, but no signs of a posted guard or watch. He dismounted. When Gresham went to do the same, Avatar signaled in the negative. The leader remained mounted.

Avatar knelt to place a hand on the ground. He stared in great concentration at the earth. By the unusual sign of sweat forming on his face, it required tremendous energy to bridge the gap since Guardians didn't normally perspire. He grew pale while the veins on his forehead and neck became extended.

"Avatar?" asked Gresham with concern, only to be ignored. At least he thought so since the warrior didn't immediately reply.

"Pain, danger … Mahon?"

"Avatar, help!" Mahon's voice echoed, which made Gresham flinch to look around for the speaker.

Avatar cried out in pain a second before being thrown back about twenty feet. He lay stunned. Gresham dismounted to help Avatar. He paused when an eerie screeching became louder. The portal burst forth with brilliant beams of light, quickly followed by a seemingly endless number of kelpies.

The archers in Gresham's force loosed their shafts at the creatures. Balls of fire emanated from the ranks of warriors possessing such power. A few chakrams sliced through kelpies like a hot knife through butter. Due to the sheer number of kelpies, attacks against the Guardians proved successful in the form of gouging by talons or savagely bites.

"Firebearers, aim for the portal!" Gresham ordered.

"No! It's our only means of access," scolded Avatar.

"We're here to seal it, not use it!" Gresham shook off Avatar and tried to mount his horse.

Avatar wouldn't be put off and seized Gresham. "Dagar will kill them before that happens!"

Further conversation stopped at the unmistakable bangs of fireballs being discharged. Half a dozen simultaneously struck the portal causing a thunderous explosion. Flames engulfed the portal before disappearing, leaving scorched earth where it once stood.

Avatar's silver eyes flashed with anger. His hands clenched into fists.

"We had no choice," said Gresham in a firm yet compassionate voice. A passing arrow ripped deep into his left thigh sending him to his knees in pain. The abruptness of the incident startled his horse. The animal bolted away.

Avatar dodged arrows in an attempt to gauge the direction. An opposing force lined up a half mile across the meadow. "Lilith!" he bellowed in anger.

"Avatar," grunted Gresham. He tugged on the warrior's pant leg.

Avatar lifted Gresham and placed the leader's arm over his shoulder. They hurried from the field, dodging arrows and kelpies. Reaching the tree line, an arrow grazed Avatar's left arm, sending painful stinging down his arm. He tried to be gentle in lowering Gresham to sit behind the cover of a tree. An arrow impaled the ground near Gresham.

"That's no normal arrow. What is it?" asked Gresham.

"Stygian metal. Rune defected to Dagar." Avatar tried to rub the sting from his arm.

"Wonderful! When were you going to tell me this?"

"I thought Kell did. It was part of my report."

Gresham dragged his numb leg as he crawled for a better view of the battlefield. Lilith's arrows struck their targets. Guardians vanished in the dreaded gray light, signaling the end of their physical existence. "By the heavenlies, what has Rune done to us?"

"Delivered a Guardian's demise into Dagar's hand."

"We have no shields for defense, no counter measure! And blast it, I can't move!" He slapped at this leg thigh.

"It'll take time before you regain mobility. I'll assume command."

"What about your arm?"

"A grazing that stung, but no numbness. Stay under cover."

Avatar raced back into the fray. He ordered the employment of every known defensive maneuvers taught him, and some others by sheer instinct. Still, the kelpies and stygian arrows cut down Gresham's militia. A few times, Avatar managed to get off a bolt of lightning from his sword to strike down an individual kelpie or catch one of Lilith's careless archers; those who ventured from under cover. However, to fully utilize his special power in the open proved difficult.

Other Guardians employed their special skills. However, against new and unknown elements the effects varied. Sometimes a fireball destroyed a kelpie or one became encased in ice to be smashed by a ranger's staff or warrior's blade. Other times nothing phased the creatures. They had no defense against the arrows.

Finally, annoyed and frustrated, Avatar called Jedrek and Hearn. "Create a wall of fire while I take position. It's time to end this!"

"There are hundreds, will your power last?" asked Hearn.

"I don't know. But we have to keep them from escaping any further, even if it takes my life-force!"

Jedrek and Hearn spoke the Ancient. Between their swords, a wall of fire sprung to life to create a shield for Avatar.

Placing the pommel of his sword in front of his face, Avatar began speaking the Ancient to summon his full power of deadly lightning. "*An dealan-*" Suddenly the ground shook with such violence, it knocked them off their feet. The firewall vanished.

The ground beneath the portal caved in to create a vast gap in the earth. Tremendous roars, deep and resonating, emanated from the sinkhole. Three black billowing clouds of smoke rose from underground. The clouds stretched thirty feet into the air before moving onto solid ground. Shapes began forming, at first obscured by the cloud then became recognizable in size and threat. Three black hairy beasts stood fifteen feet tall with massive heads like bulls and the horns of a ram. The manlike torso had bulging arms and enormous hands that held huge axes. Their legs resembled those of bulls with cloven hooves.

Gresham watched in horrified shock, unaware that he had pulled himself to stand by using a tree. "Tartundeens? Impossible!" he muttered to himself then shouted, "Retreat! Retreat!"

The roaring of the beasts' drowned his orders. They swung axes, striking down four Guardians at time along with spirit horses. More arrows came from Lilith's archers. New kelpies rose from the hole.

Auriel arrived to help Gresham. She repeated his order to retreat. Finally, Jedrek and Virgil heard. They relayed the order to the ranks.

Avatar stood. Before he could respond to the order, he dove out of the way of an axe. It struck Hearn. The warrior vanished in gray light. Angered by the demise of a comrade, Avatar raised his sword to summon his power when someone grabbed him. Bailey. Ewert was with him.

"We must leave to tell Kell!"

Impassioned by the battle, Avatar surveyed the meadow. Few of Gresham's militia or his elite warriors remained. In fact, Auriel helped Gresham to vanish in the white light of dimension travel.

"Lieutenant!" urged Bailey.

Jedrek arrived in a rush. "Auriel and Gresham have retreated to the house. We should join them.

Avatar stared at the gaping hole where the portal once stood. They failed—he failed! The Cave stood opened to the real world. The sounds of defeat echoed around him. With barely a nod of acknowledgement, they vanished from the meadow in dimension travel.

Dagar, Tor, Griswold, Ram and Curtis appeared on the surface near the edge of the sinkhole. Dagar grimaced in pain. He took a deep breath. A talisman hung from a chain around his neck. Intricate knotting surrounded the emblem of an attacking raven.

"A bit taxing, controlling three tartundeens at once," he groused.

"A sound victory, Father," said Ram, proud and pleased.

Dagar flashed a grin. "There is more to come. Recall the tartundeens. I have another assignment for them," he said to Tor.

Tor frowned in trepidation of the order, but left to do as instructed.

"What about the kelpies?" asked Griswold.

This time Dagar's grin turned malicious. "Let them have some fun with the mortals, along with the gullet worms and drusi."

Curtis shuddered at the answer. "Why?"

"For the same reason you told the servants at Master Dolan's farm." Dagar placed friendly arm about the mortal's shoulders. "To further drive a wedge between the mortals and Guardians of Jor'el. If they are seen as responsible then after we achieve victory and control the beasts of *infrinn*, we shall be looked upon with favor and readily accepted."

Although by his expression, Curtis wasn't totally convinced he said, "I see your point, my lord. May I ask for how long this fun will be allowed to run loose?"

"Depends upon the successful completion of *your* part of the mission."

"Not complete. The portal was destroyed before Avatar took the bait," complained Ram.

"There are many meanings to the term *complete*. Gresham's forces were completely wiped out and Avatar made to look like a *complete* incompetent commander. Granted, not as satisfying as his demise, but it should take him down a notch or two in favorability. If not with Kell, then others, who won't be so quick to trust him or listen to him."

Lilith arrived, smug in attitude. "The arrows proved very effective. I'll have my archers gathering the wayward ones for later use. Although not many remained," she said with satisfaction and indicated the success.

A few seriously wounded Guardians remained. For the most part, the field lay empty save for the weapons left behind.

"What do you want done with the wounded?" she asked.

"Take them to the reconditioning chamber. If they survive their wounds, they'll wish they hadn't." Dagar walked to the sinkhole. Ram and Curtis accompanied him. "The hole is not too large and can be utilized when building our castle. Of course," he began with a delightfully wicked thought, "if Kell believes it is sealed that will be better."

"What do you mean?" asked Ram.

"Hiding in plain sight," said Curtis.

"Explain to him," Dagar said to Curtis concerning Ram.

"Similar to a hunter's blind. Utilizing the cover of nature around him, he waits in plain sight for his prey, which never knows the hunter's there. The castle will serve as a natural surrounding for the Cave, blinding those who would look for it but only seeing mortal power and authority."

"Along with ease of access," said Ram with a smile of understanding.

"Constable, I mean *Grand Master* Curtis, will serve you well," said Dagar.

Curtis nodded with a satisfaction. "My lord. My liege."

"Now for the next step." Dagar closed his eyes. After a moment, Witter and Altari appeared together from brilliant light. Both sat mounted upon black spirit horses. They held the reins of two more horses. Witter wore a talisman with the same symbol as on Dagar. "With these spirit horses you can cover the country in a matter of four days."

"How?" began an astonished Curtis. "It normally takes three weeks to travel from the Highlands to the Delta and ten days longer to go from coast to coast.

Dagar chuckled. "You'll see." From his doublet pocket, he pulled two more talismans identical to the one he wore. One was gold. He handed the other one to Curtis saying, "This will serve as your conduit to tap into Witter's power and," he continued speaking to Ram after giving him the gold talisman, "this will keep you connected to me. Make free use of them, especially you, Ram. The mortals must see you as strong and determined if they are to accept you as king."

After Ram and Curtis placed the talismans around their necks, they mounted.

Dagar continued with instructions to Witter. "Start in Midessex and make your way around Allon as needed." He stepped back to watch their departure.

Chapter 17

WITH AURIEL'S HELP, GRESHAM DIMENSION TRAVELED the short distance to the safety of the administrative house. He fainted when materializing so Auriel lowered him into a chair. She drew her sword when white light appeared in the room. It faded to reveal Jedrek, Virgil, Avatar, Ewert and Bailey. All showed signs of battle, soiled with slight wounds. She came off guard.

"Where are the others?" she asked.

Jedrek shook his head, the words difficult to speak. "There are no others. We're all that's left."

She paled in horror. "What? How can that be?"

"You saw what we faced."

Her distress turned to painful anger that she vented on Avatar. "This was your idea! You led us into a trap."

Avatar didn't speak, his silver eyes dulled by despair. His silence infuriated her. She punched him so hard he staggered sideways. The blow split open his lower lip. Even at the assault, he did not react or speak.

Jedrek seized Auriel, as she continued to pour her vehemence on Avatar. "Your bravado let Dagar open the Cave. Now Allon will be flooded with hellish creatures. You're arrogant, self-centered—"

"No!" snapped Gresham, sternly, and loud enough to be heard. Despite the grogginess on his face, he scolded Auriel. "Taking *our* troops to the portal was *my* idea not Avatar's."

"I suggested a preemptive strike." Avatar spoke in a hushed and pained voice.

"Fool!" Auriel jerked free from Jedrek, intent on striking Avatar again.

210

"Auriel!" Gresham pushed himself off the chair in time to catch her wrist and prevent impact. Again, Avatar made no defense.

Gresham held Auriel at bay. Every sinew in her body was tense and taut. "You scold him for taking the initiative to confront danger when all you've done is complain, insult and assault. Not once have you made a credible or intelligent suggestion. Perhaps I was wrong to allow Jedrek to promote you to militia commander. A warrior who can't control her emotions is not ready for such authority and responsibility!"

Dumbstruck by the rebuke, her whole body went slack so Gresham released her. "I—I'm sorry," her words thick with shock. At Jedrek's touch on her shoulder, she swallowed and spoke in a stronger voice. "It won't happen again, sir. I'll prove Jedrek was right."

"Start by apologizing to *Lieutenant* Avatar, your superior officer."

"That's not necessary," said Avatar. "I understand her anger and share her pain at the loss. You may have volunteered your troops, but it was my suggestion. That is how it will be reported to Kell, *my* plan failed."

Virgil voiced his frustration. "What of Dagar? Does he bear no blame? His desire to rule has led to war and released the creatures of infrinn!"

"Virgil's right," said Bailey. "One defeat doesn't mean the war is over. They took us by surprise. After reporting to the captain and reviewing what happened, weaknesses can be found."

"My arrogant, self-centered bravado," droned Avatar.

"No, weakness in Dagar's force. Surely the Originals know of ways to counter what he called forth. We didn't know, now the others will be informed because of this."

"Ay, we six survived for a reason," said Ewert.

Gresham nodded, thoughtful and deliberate. "Tartundeens are not impossible to defeat. It needs a uniting of powers while avoiding the axes to get close enough. Kelpies are a nuisance, only more vulnerable. Their sheer numbers surprised us."

"And the arrows?" chided Avatar.

The leader frowned. "That will take some thinking to counter. Did you see only Rune at the Cave? What of Stoker or Flint?"

"Just Rune. And he wasn't in the mood to converse when he struck me with a spurean chain."

"Rune was never one for conversation."

Commotion from outside caught their attention, which was promptly followed by pounding on the door and shouting, "Gresham!"

"Sounds like Baron Dyson. The mortal overlord of the area," he explained at Avatar's curiosity. He told Virgil to open the door.

Virgil barely laid hold of the handle when the door burst open. Five mortals rushed in. Dyson led the group, which was a sight for a short, wiry fellow wearing spectacles. He barely weighed a hundred pounds soaking wet.

"My lord. Is there a problem?" asked Gresham in a cordial manner.

Dyson's nervous agitation came spilling forth. "How can you even ask that with those—those creatures devouring almost everything and attacking helpless people?"

"What are you talking about?"

In his frazzled state, exaggerated hand and arm movements animated his words. "Creatures! Some with wings and hideous reptile features. Others are fuzzy, almost the size of a house cat, and oozing a stinking green slime."

"Kelpies and gullet worms."

"With the smallest, about so big." Dyson held his hand about seven or eight inches apart. "Looks like a cross between a rodent and insect that eats everything! When you try to pick them off, they jump on you and start biting, leaving red welts."

"I didn't see any such creature," said Avatar.

By Gresham's expression, he obviously knew the creature described. "Drusi," he said to Avatar then addressed the mortals. "As you see by our appearance we are trying to deal with situation, my lord."

"How long will it take?" asked Dyson, impatient.

"I'm not certain. I must report to Captain Kell about reinforcements."

"You mean you're powerless against these creatures?"

"I didn't say that. They took us by surprise," said Gresham with some reluctance.

The mortals grew more rattled and unnerved so Dyson demanded, "If you can't defend us and defeat these things then who can?"

"I didn't say I couldn't, I just need help," insisted Gresham. He took a step forward, which made his wounded leg collapse. Auriel caught him to keep him from falling. He fought back the pain.

Avatar intervened. "My lord baron, I am Lieutenant Avatar, Captain Kell's aide. I can assure you, help will come."

Skeptical, Dyson surveyed Avatar. "You appear to have suffered defeat also, Lieutenant. How much help is that?"

"The lieutenant saved my life." Gresham remained standing by leaning on Auriel's arm for support.

Dyson scowled in frustration. "Do something quickly!" He marched from the room. The other mortals tossed disgusted or annoyed looks at the Guardians on the way out.

"That went well," groused Ewert. Bailey poked him and sent a warning nod toward Avatar and Gresham. The Leader sat for Auriel to tend his wound. "Sorry, sir, lieutenant," said Ewert.

"We need to return to the compound," said Gresham.

"I'll stay and try to reassure Dyson and mortals," said Jedrek.

"No, we all go."

"Someone has to stay."

Gresham's temper exploded. "Don't you understand? Midessex is lost! Now Dagar is using the creatures of *infrinn* to prey upon the mortals and make us look incompetent."

A deep moment of silence followed before Auriel asked Gresham, "Can you endure the travel?"

Sneering with determination, he stood. "Ay." He placed an arm around her shoulder and she placed her arm in support of his waist. After a nod to the others, all vanished.

The meeting with Gresham did not satisfy Dyson and the others. They rode back to Dyson's manor house grumbling.

"By the time Kell gets here, it may be too late," one complained.

"Dyson! More of those worms are attacking your cows." A man pointed to a holding pen on the west side of the house. Three milk cows tried to avoid six gullet worms around their legs. One worm climbed up the hindquarters of a cow. It became frantic at trying to dislodge it.

"Infrinn spawn!" Dyson swore.

For a man no bigger than a scarecrow with glasses, Dyson acted quickly and with agility. He dismounted and seized a nearby shovel to smash the gullet worms. He had to be careful not to injure the cows. Several of his companions used either farm implements or the flat of their swords to deal with the worms.

Ram and Curtis arrived. Ram vaulted from the saddle. Curtis also quickly dismounted. Witter and Altari remained seated upon the large spirit horses.

"Careful! They can be dealt with and not harm the cows," said Ram.

"How? Unless your Guardian friends can do something," said Dyson.

"They are not Guardians, they are my body guards."

Dyson looked skeptically at Witter and Altari. "They appear large enough."

"It's the horses," said Witter, his gaze directly on Dyson.

"Right, the horses," agreed Dyson. The cry of an unsettled cow drew their attention back to the situation. One of his friends killed a gullet worm, which released a horrible stench that upset the cows even more. "Oh, by the Temple Towers, what a hideous smell!"

One man cried out when a gullet worm attached itself to his leg.

"By the powers, be off of him!" commanded Ram. He seized the gullet worm. The creature released the man. It squirmed in Ram's hands in an attempt to be free. "Be gone, creature of infrinn!" He tossed the worm to the ground. It vanished in a green puff upon impact.

The men became astonished. "How did you do that?" asked Dyson.

Ram didn't answer rather went to deal with the remaining worms. Curtis helped. Together the half-dozen worms vanished in a green puffs.

"By the heavenlies, how did you do that?" Dyson repeated.

"Exactly. There are powers in heaven accessible to mortals," said Curtis.

"There are?"

"Ay. We don't have to rely on the Guardians of Jor'el to protect us. We can do so ourselves."

"How?" asked another.

"The key is self awareness, my friend. To take our destiny into our own hands. That is something they don't want you do know."

"You mean the Guardians?"

"Ay. Just like governing, they want mortals to depend on them for everything." Curtis spoke with unmistakable scorn.

"They weren't able to stop these creatures from escaping infrinn," said Ram. "In fact, the province is crawling with such creatures. Where are the Guardians of Jor'el? Nursing wounded pride because of a few stinking worms."

Dyson glanced at his comrades with caution. "Gresham and the others were injured. But what you're saying is dangerous talk."

"Why? Are we mortals not intelligent, independent and self-sustaining beings?"

"Ay," said one.

Ram continued his probing questions. "Can we not grow, cultivate, build and create things with our own hands?"

"Ay," agreed another.

"So why not govern ourselves and deal with matter such as this without them?" Ram's keen blue eyes gazed at each man in the group.

"These were magical creatures," said Dyson.

Ram cocked a wry smile. "You saw what we did. You can do the same. If you want."

"How?"

Ram mounted his horse to depart. He spoke in a nonchalant manner. "Depends upon how much you want your freedom."

"I never felt trapped."

Ram laughed. "If you have to run to a Guardian every time you need something or want to make a decision regarding government what else would you call it but trapped?"

"Controlled, cajoled and otherwise treated as inferior." Curtis also mounted.

The statement annoyed three of the men. "How can we do as you say, become self-governing?" asked one.

"By taking control of Allon and doing like other countries, crown a mortal king," replied Curtis. He tossed a sly side-glance to Ram.

"Him?"

Ram straightened in the saddle, proud and confident. "I have seen the source of heavenly power. I am willing to challenge any and all Guardians for the right to live as we were meant to live. Why do you think I travel with bodyguards? They don't want a mortal ruling."

"Are you saying they would try to kill you?"

Ram grinned, sly and wide. "I'm still alive."

"What of Jor'el? He created Guardians to protect us," said Dyson.

Ram snorted a caustic laugh. "It is a secret even he doesn't want known. Why else subject us to their rule except to keep us ignorant?"

"Ignorant of what?"

"I've already told you, self-determination. Seize it, and live free as you were meant to. Or remain under Guardian domination, helpless to determine your own destiny. The choice is yours. I've made mine." Ram turned his horse. He, Curtis, Witter and Altari began to leave.

"Wait!" one called. "How can we know if or when you succeed?"

Ram smiled in great pleasure to Curtis before replying. "Oh, you'll know. The call to gather will go out when the time has come for Allon to enter a new age of mortal self-rule." This time when he turned to leave, there were no further questions.

Chapter 18

I N THE CAPTAIN'S OFFICE, VIDAR, VALMAR, ARMUS AND KELL LISTENED to the disturbing report about the battle in Midessex. Avatar stood ramrod straight, staring at some unseen spot on the far wall. Gresham did most of the talking. Auriel offered a few comments, which drew Avatar's attention from the wall to her. By her posture and tone she held back, and certainly not for his benefit, as told by catching her glance. She may not like him personally, but she tempered her words in the captain's presence. In some ways he couldn't blame her, since he keenly felt the failure. In others ways, he wanted to throttle her. When she stopped speaking and another spoke, Avatar's gaze returned to the wall.

A deep profound silence fell when the report concluded. Although it felt longer, the pause only lasted a moment before Kell addressed him.

"Avatar. You haven't said a word. I want to hear your account."

Despite Kell's benign tone, Avatar couldn't look at him. "I have nothing to say in my defense, Captain."

"Defense? Who is accusing you of anything?"

"My suggestion of a preemptive strike failed. The Cave is not sealed rather opened to the real world."

"Not your doing, lad." Valmar's grip on Avatar's arm made the younger warrior look at him. "Don't take blame that isn't yours. Dagar opened the Cave, not you."

"Valmar's right. I wouldn't be standing here; awkward as I am, if you hadn't saved my life." Gresham continued his speech to Kell. "When I became wounded, Avatar took command. He did everything he could to keep my force alive after *I* led them into battle. If there is any blame, it belongs to me. I suspected Lilith to be there, even sent out scouts. They

218

never returned. That should have been my first clue to trouble. I didn't proceed with caution like an elite warrior," he motioned to Avatar. "Midessex has fallen. As the province Leader, I bear responsibility."

"You're not alone in that," began Kell with soberity. "While you were gone, Raleigh reported the loss of the South Plains. Sloan managed to move in undetected and overwhelmed his remaining militia by utilizing some creatures of infrinn. At this moment, Zanis is trying to keep Jayden from invading the Meadowlands. Hunter's force is keeping Priscilla occupied."

"Dax is barely holding the Northern Forest," said Vidar.

Valmar snorted a sarcastic chuff. "I think the Highlands are too far north and remote for Dagar to worry about. Nixie reports no trouble."

"Small consolation," grumbled Auriel.

"It is more than small!" rebuffed Kell.

She snapped to attention, surprised at being heard.

With Auriel subdued, Kell's voice softened. "Go. Tend to your wounds. I'll have new assignments later."

While the others departed, Kell detained Avatar. He said nothing, just held Avatar by the arm. Avatar stiffened, as he braced for the encounter. Once alone, Kell spoke in a cordial tone.

"Relax. I am not going to scold you. Gresham is right, none of this is your fault."

"I proposed the plan."

"And *I am* captain. *I* could have prevented you from going. In fact, the total blame lies with me!" Kell paced, his agitation growing with each word. "As Trio Leader, Gresham can claim some responsibility for Midessex, but not you. As with Jarvis, *I* should have gone and not exposed either of you to Dagar's spleen. But no! *Again, I* let subordinates face him. Now two thousand are vanquished in one battle and the creatures of infrinn set loose!" In an outburst of tremendous rage, Kell knocked over a massive bookcase.

The unusual violent explosion of temper and crashing furniture made a surprised Avatar jump out of the way. Armus rushed in. Discovering the cause of the noise, he shut the door. Armus stood so that his bulk barred anyone from entering.

Oblivious to their reactions, Kell continued in high temper. "Well, no more! Dagar is mine!" He struck his chest in emphasis. "I will make him face justice for what he had done."

"Can we gather the books and repair the furniture first?" asked Armus casually.

"What?!" shouted Kell. Golden eyes flashed and nostrils flared in confronting Armus.

Remaining calm in the face of Kell's rage, Armus jerked his thumb at the smashed bookcase and books littering the office floor. "Your attempt to renovate."

Kell stared at the destruction his outburst caused. His brows furrowed in befuddlement. "I wasn't even aware I did that."

"I'd hate to be the foe when you are aware of what you're doing, Captain," said Avatar in awe.

"At least they can fight back. Smashing defenseless furniture is only good for redecorating," said Armus.

The humor brought an involuntary snicker from Kell. "I guess I got carried away. Still, I meant what I said! Take no blame in this and leave Dagar to me," he stressed to Avatar.

Avatar nodded then said, "Mahon is alive."

The news made Kell curious. "How do you know?"

"He called to me for help just before the portal opened."

"Did you see him?"

"No, I sensed his essence … and great pain."

"At least he's alive," said Armus.

"Ay. Once Dagar is dealt with, I will free him and the others. Now, tend to your wounds and get some rest." Kell steered Avatar around the debris to escort him to the door.

With Avatar gone, Armus knelt to begin picking up the books. "In a fit of rage Auriel gave him that split lip, and not the result of battle."

"She assaulted him? He didn't mention it. Why?"

"Apparently, she doesn't like Avatar. In case you missed her terseness in their visual exchanges whenever she spoke." Armus handed some books to Kell to pick up more.

Kell tossed them onto a nearby chair. He pulled Armus to his feet. "Explain."

Armus opened the door to summon Ewert and Bailey. The warriors couldn't help noticing the bookcase, yet made no comment. Or rather, Armus' shook his head for them to remain quiet about the debris. He spoke aloud.

"Tell the captain what happened between Auriel and Avatar."

"She was curt, disrespectful and spiteful towards him," said Bailey.

"That was before the battle," added Ewert.

"Why?" asked Kell.

Bailey shrugged. "We're not sure. When Avatar had enough of her belligerent attitude, he decided to teach her a lesson by having us use our power to clear the swollen river for crossing."

"How did that teach her a lesson?"

"In direct opposition to her scorn and impertinence regarding the skill of elite warriors to forge a river."

"So he had you two show her up. I'm sure that didn't set well," said Armus.

"No, and at first opportunity she made her true feelings known."

"I would have sent her across the room," groused Ewert.

"You don't have Avatar's self-control," said Bailey.

"Not self-control," Ewert replied to his counterpart then spoke to Kell. "The loss of the battle deeply affected Avatar. He didn't fight back or say anything when she punched him and called him an *arrogant, self-centered fool whose bravado led us into a trap.* To quote her colorful description of Avatar," he said to Kell's deep frown of disapproval. "He just stood there taking her verbal and physical abuse."

"Jedrek and Gresham physcially subdued her, while Gresham gave her a sound tongue-lashing. It wasn't until he told her to apologize, that Avatar finally spoke. He said there was no need for apology since he understood her anger. We tried to counsel him that she was wrong and none of it was his fault. He refused to accept it," said Bailey.

"Well, I believe I convinced him. Anything else?" asked Kell.

The warriors exchanged conferring glances before Bailey replied, "No, Captain, except to say, Gresham is right. If not for Avatar's leadership none of us would have survived the creatures of infrinn."

Kell dismissed them.

"Gresham or Auriel?" asked Armus after shutting the door.

Kell's look was sharp. "Which one do you think?"

"I'll fetch her."

Kell stopped Armus' departure. "Bring her to Eldric's private office. Mine needs cleaning."

⁂

Auriel marched in step behind Armus. She wasn't surprised by the captain's summons. She could imagine what Avatar told Kell in private. Her minor wounds were cleaned and bandaged though she still wore her soiled uniform having no time to change.

Kell inspected some books on a shelf in Eldric's office when they arrived. Armus announced her. Auriel snapped to attention when Kell turned to her. By his critical expression, she was in for a scolding. First she would listen to what Avatar told him before recounting her version.

"I heard a distressing report from Ewert and Bailey concerning insubordination, striking a superior officer and making false accusations."

"Ewert and Bailey? Not Avatar?" she said in surprise.

"*Lieutenant* Avatar," he corrected. "We haven't spoken about the incident."

"You detained him after our dismissal."

"To inquire about the battle. He made no mention of *your* inappropriate behavior."

She was surprised by the unexpected twist when Kell asked, "Why?"

"Why what?" she asked, baffled. "Why did I strike him?"

"Why do you dislike Lieutenant Avatar? Has he treated you with contempt or disrespect in front of others? Injured you in some way you have not reported? Some other offense perhaps?"

The questions came quick. Auriel tried to decipher them in some semblance of order. No, Avatar hadn't injured her or been offensive in any manner. She simply found him arrogant, insufferable and infuriating.

"You think those are acceptable excuses?"

Auriel became shocked to realize she verbalized the words, *arrogant, insufferable and infuriating.* "Did I say that, Captain?"

"You did." Kell crossed his arms, his golden eyes skeptical in their gaze. "You offer no better explanation? You are a militia commander. Such unwarranted behavior is unacceptable from one of your rank."

"Ay, Captain," she began apologetically. "Jedrek and Gresham told me the same. I lost my temper after the demise of my comrades. I lashed out, and I was wrong to do so."

Kell shook his head in dispute. "No, passion from combat I understand, but the reports of disrespect started *before* the battle. What reason do you give for then?"

Auriel's brows leveled in thought as she searched for an answer. She had already blundered. Yet the more she thought, the more she couldn't find a legitimate reason. "I don't know, Captain," she had to admit.

"I do."

Auriel braced herself when Kell moved to stand directly in front of her. His golden eyes unwavering as he began his assessment.

"You are young, nine hundred years old, and among the last group of Guardians created. Although a skilled warrior, you are passionate and quick to anger, both physically and verbally. You wore out your first mentor within a hundred years. And Scully is as patient and tolerant as they come. When pairing you with Jedrek, I thought his firm hand would moderate you."

"I have learned much from Jedrek, Captain, while I made amends with Scully centuries ago."

"However, after being on your own for several hundred years your bad habits have reemerged. Thus when Gresham approached me fifty years ago about you filling the vacancy in the Midessex militia, I agreed. I believed serving with Jedrek again could be the best thing to moderate you." Kell frowned in disappointment and made a short shake of his head. "Other reports have shown that not to be the case. With this latest incident of gross insubordination and striking a superior officer, I'm forced to take action."

Auriel stiffened in anticipation. "What action, Captain?"

"Once this campaign is over, you will be relieved of command and report to Lieutenant Armus for reevaluation."

Auriel gasped in alarm. "Oh, no, please, Captain! I already told Gresham I will change. What happened with Lieutenant Avatar will never be repeated, I swear."

Her plea didn't sway him. "The only way to know for sure, is for you to subject yourself to Lieutenant Armus and his instruction. If you are unwilling, there is always the final alternative; retirement from duty and return to the heavenlies."

"Lose my warrior status?" she murmured in dread. The thought was more horrifying than anything. True, the heavenlies was a place of peace and rest, but such a demotion meant failure. If she returned to the heavenlies, it would be as a warrior, vanquished in service. She gathered herself to attention. "I will do whatever Lieutenant Armus commands, Captain. I will prove I can be a disciplined and respectful warrior."

For a long moment, Kell studied her. "Start by apologizing to Lieutenant Avatar. Conduct yourself with respect and military courtesy from now on. Dismissed!"

"Ay, Captain." Auriel snapped a salute and left.

Armus remained. "Would you really demote her?"

"At present, I can't afford to be lax in discipline or allow discord among the ranks. If she so much as speaks a cross word or acts inappropriately toward Avatar or anyone, she is gone!"

"Understood. I'll tell Gresham and Jedrek privately."

"Not Jedrek. I hoped his firm hand would temper her. It's been the opposite. Her dominant nature has affected him. He may cover for her."

"She was his apprentice. He should know."

"I'll speak to him when the time comes—"

Vidar rushed in. "Trouble in the Northern Forest. Dax sends for immediate aid."

"Any details?" asked Kell.

Vidar shook his head. "Just serious enough to need urgent help."

Kell said to Armus, "I'll speak to Gresham. Take half your company and go with Vidar."

⁂

Avatar's most serious wound was the split lower lip. The impact of the stygian arrow upon his left arm proved minimal. He suffered a few minor scrapes and bruises that come with battle. Mostly he wanted to get cleaned up and changed from the soil of war.

As the captain's aide, he had a private room located over the barracks complete with a privy. Guardians didn't required sleep or privacy, yet such was the nature of physical existence among the mortals. The room was tastefully decorated. He had gathered a few personal mementoes during nearly four hundred years of serving as Kell's aide.

During his apprenticeship, he shared quarters with lower ranking warriors. He then billeted with Mahon for three hundred years as his mentor. After he replaced Altari on the High Trio, he got his own room. Gathering possessions wasn't of importance; simply used to give the room a homey feel for the mortals he dealt with. Such things made them feel at ease.

Avatar removed the more cumbersome part of his armor. He stripped to the waist in front of a table with a mirror. Also upon the table sat a basin and pitcher of water. Though physically leaner in bulk compared to Armus, every inch showed pure muscle and power. A bath would take longer and he didn't have time. Of course, he could just speak

225

and be clean. However, the act of washing felt soothing, almost cathartic in scrubbing away the stain of battle.

Splashing water on his face, he flinched at the stinging of his lower lip. The cut bled again. Phoebe put medicine on it to stop the bleeding. Cleaning must have washed it off. He used a towel to dab the blood away for examination. He hadn't seen the extent of the injury, only felt tenderness. The cut went fairly wide and deep, extending a little into his chin. It began to show the discoloration of bruising. Indeed, Auriel was strong. At a knock on the door, he stopped dabbing the cut to reply.

"Enter."

"Lieutenant."

In the mirror, he saw Auriel's reflection. "This a surprise." He turned to face her. "Come for more lessons or to view your handiwork?"

"I came to apologize."

Her expression and body posture told of some contrition. Mostly, she appeared awkward, which made him suspicious. "On your own, or under orders?"

She started to speak then balked to admit, "Orders from the captain."

Avatar dabbed the wound again and flinched at the sensitivity. "It would have been better if it were of your own accord. At least then I might believe you were sincere."

Auriel fought to keep her voice temperate. "Why must you always be critical? I came to apologize. Why can't that be good enough for you?"

"Me critical? An arrogant fool led by his bravado? Whose words are those?" Avatar challenged.

"Mine," she replied with restraint.

"And this?" He pointed to his lip.

"Me, again."

"So who is critical?"

"I am. I was," she corrected herself. "I want to change, which is why I'm apologizing."

"I thought you said you were under orders from the captain?"

"I did. I am, I just. Oh, you are infuriating!"

"Why?"

The question stymied her. "I don't know," she spoke in exasperation. She plopped into a chair. "I don't know why I have such a short temper, especially with you. You haven't done anything to me. Although I tried to think of an answer to Kell's same question of why? Nothing came to mind yet I managed to blurt out your attributes."

Avatar didn't comment on Auriel's breech of etiquette in speaking informally of Kell or sitting in the presence of a superior officer without permission. She seemed to be more arguing with herself than him. "Which attributes?"

"Arrogant, insufferable and infuriating," she droned.

"Ah, my more endearing qualities."

She involuntarily chuckled.

"Look, Auriel, I don't know what your problem is, whether it's just with me or others in general. You must curb your tongue and temper."

"The captain told me the same. I really want to." Agitated, she pushed herself out of the chair. "I enjoy being a warrior. I don't want to lose my position!"

"Oh," said Avatar with understanding. Kell didn't just scold her; he put her on notice. Only a handful of times had Kell demoted a Guardian. It greatly impacted that Guardian and his or her peers. "Well," he spoke in congenial tone, "I accept your apology, Commander Auriel." He used her formal title. "Let us consider this latest incident a non-issue and start over. Agreed?"

She smiled in relief. "Agreed, Lieutenant." She paused at the door with a wry expression on her face. "One question if I may, Lieutenant?"

"Go ahead."

"Do you always receive visitors half-naked?"

Avatar laughed. "Oww," he groaned and held the towel on his lip.

Auriel smiled. "Good day, Lieutenant."

"Gawd aay," he mumbled. He turned back to the mirror to examine his lip. Movement and shouting outside the window caught his attention. In the barrack's courtyard, Armus assembled one hundred warriors.

Avatar grabbed his sheathed sword and a shirt. He ran from his quarters to the courtyard. He donned the shirt as he went.

"Trouble?" he asked.

"A bit out of uniform, aren't you?" said Armus.

"I was cleaning up when I saw you. Why muster?"

"Trouble in the Northern Forest. Dax sent for help."

"I'll come too."

"No. This time you act as reserve."

Avatar stiffened at the statement. "Kell said it wasn't my fault."

"It wasn't. Who knows where Dagar will strike next? We can't commit all our forces at once." He patted Avatar's shoulder. "There will be plenty of fight to come. Take what rest you can, while you can. If I need help, I will send for you. By the way, your lip is bleeding." Armus moved to continue with his troops.

Avatar touched his wound. He saw Vidar, Wren and Ridge join Armus. Vidar spoke to Armus while gesturing toward the gate. Avatar caught Wren's gaze. She separated herself from the others to approach him. She fought against smiling.

"I heard Auriel got off a hit. Is that it?" She reached to touch his lip.

Avatar knocked her hand away. "Nothing I can't handle."

Wren's humor faded at hearing Armus' order for departure. "Any words of wisdom on what we might face?"

"Hard to tell if only Guardians, creatures of infrinn, or both. Whatever it is, Jor'el be with you, and keep your head down."

"I must see to aim," she said with bravado before leaving.

Chapter 19

WITH EVERYTHING HAPPENING SO FAST, THEY DECIDED TO dimension travel to the Northern Forest. Armus and Vidar's troops reappeared in bright flashes of white light just across the border on the south end of Lake Joram. The troops immediately dispersed into assigned fighting formations.

Vidar cupped a hand around his mouth to make a warbling bird call. After a brief moment, there came a response. They waited, armed and ready. They spied movement among the trees. A wounded and weary Dax arrived. He led twenty others. All sustained wounds.

"Thank Jor'el," said Dax in relief. "I didn't know if you'd make it in time." He staggered sideways in his attempt to sit on a log.

Wren knelt beside him. "How bad are your wounds?"

He replied with deep distress. "My wounds are nothing. We are all that are left!"

"Of seven thousand?" she gasped.

Vidar's jowls tightened. His copper eyes flashed like fire. "What happened?"

Dax fought his emotions to explain. "Kelpies came from everywhere, six tartundeens and hundreds of creatures I'd never seen before. Half-man, half-rabid wolf, standing nine feet tall and wielding massive clubs with spikes. Our arrows did little damage to the wolf creatures or kelpies. The warriors tried to deal with the tartundeens."

"We destroyed one," said a badly injured warrior.

"Did they use stygian arrows?" asked Armus.

Dax shooed Wren away when her administrations grew bothersome. "What are stygian arrows?"

"One of two metals Rune perfected that can down a Guardian, kill us even. The arrows helped destroy Gresham's entire militia."

Astonished, Dax rose to his feet. "Total defeat?"

"Ay. Avatar did what he could after Gresham became wounded, but they were overrun when Dagar opened the Cave to the real world. Now, we're seeing the results," said Armus grimly.

Stupefied, Dax sat. Wren moved beside him. She softly spoke. "Let me finish tending your wounds." He didn't respond, so she proceeded.

"Where did you encounter the creatures?" asked Vidar.

"South, near the Greenwood." Dax used his head to indicate the direction, not moving his arm due to Wren dressing his wounds.

"Lieutenant!" A ranger hurried over to Armus. "A massive force from the Greenwood is heading this way."

"How can they sense our arrival this far out?" asked Ridge.

"Considering our numbers, it would be hard to ignored such a large disturbance in transverse," said Armus.

"We're five times the distance for normal sensing," chided Vidar.

Armus glared at the prime archer. "There is nothing *normal* about what is happening! You lead a direct assault. I'll take five hundred archers, fifty warriors and attack from the rear. Wren, you and Ridge take five hundred archers, rangers and twenty warriors to the east. Dax, are you capable of more battle?"

The Trio ranger stood. "Just tell me what to do."

"Take the remainder of your troops, along with an additional hundred and secure the rear in the event of withdrawal. Go quickly, and Jor'el be with us all."

Vidar spread out his line before moving through the trees. They crossed several open meadows while moving toward the danger. A great, penetrating coldness brought them to a halt. It was not due to the crisp coolness of the day, rather an inner coldness.

A fellow archer showed signs of uneasiness. "Sir, what is it? Why is it so unnaturally still? No breeze stirs the trees and I hear no sounds of birds or creatures."

A ranger's eyes shifted about in wariness. "It's like everything has stopped and fled from this terrifying coldness."

"They're close," whispered Vidar, harshly.

"Why can't we see them?"

A deafening howling began. The volume rose to a frequency that forced them to cover their ears in pain. Some collapsed in distress. Before any could react in defense, the half-man, half-wolf creatures Dax described, rushed at them from every direction. Standing nine feet tall on two legs with the body of a man completely covered in fur. Their heads resembled wolves with snarling, drooling fangs. Large hands had sharp claws. With large spiked clubs, they swung at anything that moved.

Vidar managed to get off two shots before dodging a club aimed at his head. He didn't know if he initially hit anything. He reloaded and fired from his knees. A third time, he struck an attacking creature in the right shoulder. The creature continued toward him. Again Vidar ducked under the swinging club. This time he rolled into the legs of another creature. When it reached down to grab him, he smashed its hand with his crossbow. Vidar scrambled away on his knees.

The creatures came from everywhere, and the troops were not faring well. A few proved successful in fending off the attack while others disappeared into the gray light of demise. The warriors managed the best. The rangers held their ground. Archers had the most trouble being forced to use daggers in close combat having no chance to reload their bows. Several archers used arrows for weapons, thrusting them into the creatures when they couldn't shoot.

Briefly free from attack, Vidar began a rapid fire not possible by a mortal archer, getting off six shots. The arrows inflicted limited damage. Wounds slowed the creatures' advance. This allowed the warriors to kill or sever limbs of the beasts.

"Aim for the head and neck!" shouted Vidar. He proceeded to take down three creatures racing towards him.

Guardians spoke the Ancient to call upon their power in aiding the battle. Several archers followed Vidar's lead, resulting in the demise of numerous wolf creatures. The warriors fought with swords against clubs. Rangers used their staffs in pummeling the creatures to the ground where the earth swallowed them in a sinkhole. No sooner did they gain the upper hand against the wolf-men then an eerie screeching began.

Recognized the noise, Vidar shouted a warning. "Kelpies! Look to the trees!"

A kelpie leapt down upon Vidar. He managed to get off a shot that pierced the kelpie's wing. The force of the creature knocked him down. He lost his crossbow upon impact. He cried out when talons pinned him to the ground. He struggled to reach his dagger. The kelpie snapped at him. He barely avoided being bitten in the face. Instead, the kelpie caught his neck with a savage bite. He reacted by thrusting his dagger into the kelpies' chest. Before he could withdraw the blade to strike again, numbness overcame him. He couldn't feel his grip on the hilt. His arm fell limp to his side. Angry at the wounding, the kelpie went to bite him again. A quarterstaff sent it tumbling aside. Vidar couldn't move his head so he shifted his eyes to see Ridge kneel beside him.

"Don't try to talk. You won't be able to speak or move for quite some time. That's a worse bite than I received."

Vidar rolled his eyes and managed a questioning grunt.

"It's not going well, if that's what you're asking."

In distress, Vidar closed his eyes, a slight whimper escaping. He opened his eye at hearing Ridge speak. The ranger patted his chest; only he couldn't feel it.

"Don't worry too much, Armus is still out there."

Ridge had no idea what Armus faced. His five hundred and fifty troops of mostly archers and rangers, engaged five tartundeens, one hundred kelpies and numerous wolf men. The Guardian lieutenant did everything to keep his forces alive. Success came when the warriors utilized their full powers.

Armus' left sleeve became torn and the flesh gouged by the talons of a kelpie. Fortunately, it didn't bite him, thus no numbness. The headless carcass of the offending kelpie lay on the ground. Racing footsteps came from behind. Armus ducked to one side. The move allowed the attacker to pass. Armus swung his sword in defense and connected with steel. The swords hung together. This attacker was not a creature of infrinn.

"Tor!" said Armus in surprise. With an angry grunt, he shoved Tor aside.

"You should have stayed at the Fortress, Armus." Tor launched another attack. They exchanged a series of hard blows before Armus sent Tor stumbling sideways.

"You should have remained loyal!"

"I am. Loyal to my Trio Mate." Tor attacked again, with the same result. He lashed out. "Unlike what Kell did to Altari!"

"What?"

"Ay! Kell's former aide *chose* to join us in following Dagar."

"Only a fool follows one bent on evil!" Armus attacked.

Tor did all he could to contend with Armus' strength. Although Originals and warriors, Armus was more powerful than Tor. This time when they broke apart, Tor labored for breath.

"You call me fool?" he chided.

"Fool and coward! No true warrior attacks from the shadows or hides in dark caves. That's what you've become by following Dagar, nothing but a shadow warrior, a hollow form of what you once were."

Outraged by the insult, Tor threw his dagger at Armus. He shouted, "*Lorg agus milleadh!*" and raced into the trees.

Armus used his sword to deflect the dagger. He understood the command. He braced his feet with his sword ready. The ground shook from the heavy steps of the approaching tartundeen. He spied a fellow warrior nearly, one as brawny as he.

"Barnum! The tartundeen. Together!" Armus received an acknowledging wave. Simultaneously they spoke the Ancient to summon their power, "By Jor'el's strength I fight his enemies!"

Invigorated with the strength of twenty Guardians, Armus attacked the tartundeen from one direction. Barnum came from the opposite direction. The sheer force of their attack severed both legs of the beast above the knees. In falling, the flat of the tartundeen's axe caught Armus in the back. The force sent him hurtling down a ravine and into a shallow stream. For a moment he lay flat on his back in the shallow water, stunned due to the wind being knock from him. His head also hurt. He struggled to regain his breath. His sword lay a few feet away, knocked from his grasp upon impact with the ground.

The use of his power normally taxed his energy, but being smashed in the back made his whole body hurt. The splashing of water made him looked in the direction of the noise. A wolf-man. He tried to reach his sword but the creature jerked him to his feet. Fangs dripped with saliva when it roared in his face. Armus snatched his dagger from its sheath and drove it into the beast's side. Instead of loosening its grasp, the beast retaliated by slashing massive claws across Armus' chest. This ripped his tunic and left deep gashes his flesh. He cried out in pain.

The beast tossed Armus aside to deal with the dagger. Armus again he hit the shallow riverbed hard. His chest wound burned, but he couldn't remain down. He hissed in pain to push himself to his knees.

The beast withdrew the dagger and raised it to strike Armus. It stopped in mid-swing when something struck from behind. Enraged, it turned to deal with a new threat. A sword plunged upward and into its neck. With a wicked jerked, the withdrawing blade did more damage.

Armus moved out of the way when the beast fell beside him. He flinched to defend himself when someone grabbed his shoulder.

"Easy, Armus."

Armus blinked in surprise. "Razi? What are you doing here? Avatar took you to Melwynn."

Eerie howling sounds distracted Razi's answer. "We relocated. Now, no more questions. We must leave quickly." He helped Armus to stand.

"No, I must get back to the others."

"There are no others."

Armus shook loose of Razi. "What do you mean no others?"

Regret filled Razi's reply. "The attack either destroyed them or drove them off. I was surprised to find you still alive. Now, come! Before they return."

Shocked, Armus didn't move. "They can't be gone. Barnum, Vidar, Wren …"

"You are all that is left!"

The howling grew louder.

"*Madah-dune!* Quickly! Or how will you tell Kell?"

Armus bit back the pain to fetch his sword. They crossed the stream to the opposite side of where the battle took place.

For an hour, Armus followed Razi. Occasionally they ducked into cover to avoid detection. The region swarmed with enemy forces. They passed through narrow gorges until finally reaching a modest cottage deep in the Greenwood. Smoke rose from the chimney. Armus paused to observe the structure and to catch his breath. His injuries made the trek difficult and painful.

"Who lives here?" he asked.

"We do. Now, come inside. Night is near and the *madah-dune* will be hunting."

"Madah-dune?" Armus asked after entered.

Razi barred the door. "The creature I saved you from. One of my father's more successful experiments."

"Lieutenant Armus," began Dolan, first surprised then concerned. "You're hurt. Clare, medicine for his wounds."

"Mortal medicine won't work very well," said a weary Armus.

"Something to eat and drink, then," said Janel.

"Food isn't necessary, but something to drink would be nice." Stiff and painful, Armus sat at the table. He laid his sword on the bench beside him. Janel fetched a generous tankard of ale. He promptly drained the contents.

"More?"

"No, thank you." Armus glanced from her to Razi. "What are you doing in the Greenwood?"

"Eldric thought this would be a safe location within Vidar's province. Little did he realize my father's determination knows no bounds. Nowhere is safe in Allon, but we couldn't stay at Melwynn."

"Of course you could. Kell would insist."

Razi took a seat opposite Armus. "I'm a danger to the Guardians either at the compound or Melwynn. Hiding among the mortals or deep in the forest is the best chance for survival."

"And to receive Jor'el's blessing, I suppose," challenged Armus.

Razi grew frustrated. "Jor'el's blessing is something I never expected, and my new family is of great importance to me. But I'm not talking about *my* survival. I'm talking about *your* survival. My conception, my whole life was geared toward destroying the Guardians. You and Kell are among those my father seeks to kill. That is why we had to leave Melwynn. And why I can't help to stop him, though I wish to heaven I could! My presence would be detrimental."

Janel comforted Razi.

Despite the pain from his serious wounds, Armus sounded gracious in reply. "Your consideration is appreciated, though bittersweet. You know Dagar as he is now. Yet there was a time, he would have spoken similarly in defense of his comrades."

"Before Radnor."

"Ay," droned Armus. "That battle affected everyone who participated. Some had to be reassigned to less stressful duties, others sent back to the heavenlies because they could not tolerate being among mortals any longer. Dagar didn't display any of those troubles. At least not at first." Armus shifted in discomfort.

"Are you sure I can't get you some medicine for the pain or to salve your wounds?" asked Clare.

Armus cocked a weary smiled and shook his head. He continued speaking to Razi. "You said the madah-dune were one of Dagar's more successful experiments, how?"

"Over the centuries, he performed experiments on creatures from infrinn and animals from the real world. The madah-dunes are a result of crossbreeding, if you want to call it that. Although there is nothing natural in the process."

"So there are more?"

Razi shrugged. "I'm not sure. It's only been the last two years he told us the scope of his plans." He looked a bit shameful. "I tried to avoid it whenever possible. Even then I felt a growing sense of doubt about it all. Since meeting Janel, and experiencing my mother's death, all I wanted to do was get away. I didn't think about gathering intelligence. I'm sorry."

"I'm certain the lieutenant doesn't blame you," she said.

"No, of course not," said Armus, though difficult to keep the pain from his voice and face. "How did you come upon me?"

"By the unnatural noises I guessed what was happening. Hard to ignore living so close to what became a battlefield. Papi, Kerwin, Mace and I ventured out about a mile, no more. Whether we found something or not, when we reached our limit, we would return. That's what I was doing when I heard the madah-dune and saw you."

Armus listened, though obviously his wounds caused him great discomfort. "I need to get back to the compound." He used his sword to help him stand.

"Can you manage . . . What is it? Dimension travel?" said Kerwin.

"No, this bad, I walk."

"Then you won't get far in your condition."

"I have no choice." Armus turned for the door.

"Kerwin and I will accompany you," said Dolan.

"No, it is too dangerous."

Dolan hurried to the door. "We were planning to leave for the compound this evening."

"Why? Jor'el told you to stay in hiding."

237

"Jor'el told Razi and Janel to hide. We came along for safety. Besides, I'm not going to let Avram face this alone. Mace and Toby will remain. Kerwin and I have already packed what is necessary." He motioned toward two backpacks near the door. "And we are armed." He patted the sword at his side.

"You realize this could be taken as disobedience by Jor'el?"

Dolan softly smiled in dispute. "Are Guardians the only ones capable of understanding Jor'el or his will?"

"No, of course not," droned Armus.

"Then know we have prayed and considered our actions carefully. We are all in agreement with the decision."

"I trust Jor'el with the lives my husband and son, just like my brother," said Clare.

Armus frowned, more from pain and fatigue than consideration.

"Now, no more argument. We must get you back so your wounds can be properly treated." Dolan grabbed one backpack to put on. Kerwin took the other.

"We know a shortcut to the Region's border," said Kerwin.

***

Unable to find Armus, Barnum hurried back to the last place he saw Vidar and his troops. Signs of battle lay about in the form of dead kelpies, a few carcasses of wolf men and unfamiliar black arrows impaled in trees or protruding from the ground. No sign of Vidar or his troops.

Barnum went to investigate an arrow. He tried to yank it from a tree but withdrew his hand upon experience searing pain. Numbness radiated up his fingers to his hand. Hearing an approach from behind, he reached for his sword; only his numbed fingers couldn't grab the hilt.

"Barnum!" called a distraught female. He recognized Wren the moment she embraced him. "Thank Jor'el. I didn't know if anyone survived." Her upper left arm was bloodied from an open wound.

"You've seen no one else? Vidar?"

"No. You? Where is Armus?" She looked about, anxious and fearful.

"I don't know."

"He's gone?"

"No. I just don't know where he is."

Wren hastened from Barnum to begin a frantic search. "Armus! Arm—" From behind, hands seized her, covered her mouth and dragged her behind some brush. She struggled when a voice hissed in her ear.

"Be still!"

She relaxed in recognition. The hand removed from her mouth. "Ridge," she said in great relief.

"Wren?" called Barnum, careful and mindful of volume.

"Here," she replied in a harsh whisper.

Barnum arrived. He held the sword in his left hand, still unable to fully use his right hand. He lowered his sword at seeing Ridge. He complained to Wren. "You shouldn't have left like that. You could have run into trouble rather than a wayward ranger."

"For your information, my waywardness helped our fearless leader."

"Armus?" Barnum asked, hopeful.

"Vidar." Ridge motioned for them to follow him through the thicket. They stopped upon reaching the hiding place. Vidar sat propped up against a tree. He appeared pale with his arms lying limp in his lap.

Wren dropped to her knees beside him. "What happened?"

Vidar answered by rolling his eyes to Ridge.

"A kelpie," said the ranger. "Note the serious bite on his neck along with talon marks on his body. I wanted to wait to make sure all was quiet before taking him back the Fortress for treatment. That's when I heard you shouting for Armus."

Vidar grunted what sounded like a question to Barnum.

"When we cut the legs out from under a tartundeen, the axe caught Armus and sent him flying. I haven't seen him since."

With a whimper of despair, Vidar closed his eyes.

"I didn't see him disappear in grayness," insisted Barnum.

"There may still be hope," she added her encouragement.

"Not for Dax and the others. I'm sorry," Ridge said woeful.

Wren's eyes swelled with tears at the news. Vidar grunted to get her attention. "We have to get you back so Phoebe ..." She couldn't finish speaking. Instead she put up her crossbow to lift Vidar to his feet.

Barnum took Vidar from her. "I'll take him. You two are injured. It would be best to travel the distance together."

In the main chamber of the nether cave, Dagar leaned on the table to survey the map of Allon. Griswold and Hunter were with him.

Tor entered and announced, "The Northern Forest is ours."

"Vidar is defeated?" asked Dagar with guarded pleasure.

"Totally. And Armus."

"Armus?" echoed Dagar with amazement. "*You* took him down?"

Tor frowned. "Not exactly. I summoned a tartundeen after he insulted me by calling me a *shadow warrior,* a hollow image of my former self for following you."

"Shadow warrior?" repeated Dagar, intrigued. "Shadow warrior." He surveyed Tor, who was all dressed in black. Dagar laughed with delight.

Offended, Tor grasped the hilt of his sword. "I didn't like it when Armus said it so why are you laughing at me?"

Dagar tried to calm his mirth. "Don't you see the delicious irony? What he meant as an insult can be used to strike fear into the heart of our enemies. Tall, strong, fearless beings, arrayed in black from head to toe, seated high upon black spirit stallions." He laughed again, which made Tor scowl.

Hunter explained. "Witter reports all is going well with Ram. Some mortals swoon upon sight of him and Altari riding huge horses."

"Indeed. Why do you think I changed my uniform?" probed Dagar.

"To leave an impression," said Tor, now understanding.

Dagar grinned with wicked pleasure. "Ay! You shall be called *Shadow Warriors.* I'll make Kell aware of the name just before I kill him."

There was a moment of digesting the decision when Hunter asked Tor, "Do you know what became of Armus?"

"No, but I don't think even he can survive a tartundeen."

"And Vidar? Did you see him fall?"

"No, but I found none left."

Hunter spoke to Dagar. "We can't take any chances. The Northern Forest may have fallen but without confirmation of Vidar and Armus' demise, we must factor their survival into our battle plan."

"I tell you none were left!" insisted Tor.

Dagar replied in a temperate tone. "I believe you. However, Hunter is right. As precaution, we must plan as if they survived. With your recent success, we now command ten of the twelve provinces. With Ram and Curtis doing well in convincing the mortals, many will answer the call when the time comes."

"Why wait to launch our attack? Their pitiful numbers will have little effect on the battle," said Griswold.

Dagar impatiently waved the question aside. "If they believe they have a hand in changing the course of Allon, they will be more agreeable to accepting Ram as king." He again focused on the map. "Only the Highlands remain. Once taken, we will have totally isolated the Region."

"Valmar won't give up easy," said Hunter.

"Don't worry about Valmar. His force is thin on warriors," said Tor.

Hunter stiffened at the dismissive tone. "Rangers and archers won't simply fall over. They will make a stand."

"He means as reinforcements, not as defense when attacked, so take no insult." Dagar cocked a grin. "Time grows near to take the compound and end Jor'el's reign!"

Chapter 20

THE SPEED OF THE SPIRIT HORSES HELPED RAM, CURTIS, WITTER and Altari cover Midessex, the Southern Forest, and the East Coast in two days. This included stopping for similar encounters with mortals like Dyson and his companions. When defeating the creatures, the audience proved most attentive. Witter and Altari remained mounted to appear imposing.

In the Meadowlands, they came upon a commotion in the middle of a grain harvest. A group of twenty laborers with farm implements dodged and weaved as eerie screeching coming from somewhere in the crowd. Nearing the group, they saw two wounded kelpies being taunted by the workers.

"What's going on?" demanded Ram

"We're trying to kill these creatures," shouted one.

"Don't get too close! They've already killed Morris and wounded Sims," warned another man.

The kelpie with the broken wing snapped at the crowd, which made them back away. The kelpie with the missing leg made a lopsided lunge at the nearest man. It caught him by the hem of his pants.

At the man's outcry, Ram leapt down from his horse, drew his sword and severed the kelpie's head. Hearing the other kelpie scream in anger, Ram turned in time to dodge its attack. Using the back swing of his sword, he sliced it in half. The men watched in awe at the speed and strength of Ram dispatching of the kelpies.

"By the heavenlies!" said the saved man to Ram. "I thought only Guardians could handle such creatures."

Ram smiled with satisfaction. He used field rag to wipe off his blade. It was an unusual darker color metal.

Another cautiously surveyed Ram, who stood taller than all of them. "You are mortal, aren't you?"

"Ay," said Ram with a chuckle. "A mortal who has learned the secrets of the heavenlies. I am able to do what most Guardians can."

"Disappear?" asked a boy of fourteen.

"No. I am physical not spiritual. What Guardians can do in the flesh, I have mastered. As you just witnessed. So can my companion, Grand Master Curtis."

"Grand master of what?" asked the first.

"Of the new age of mortals," said Curtis.

"What do you mean *new age*?"

"Mortal self-determination and rule."

"You mean no more Guardians?" asked the second.

"Ay," began Ram. "Where were the Guardians while you dealt with creatures of infrinn? What if it happens again? Wouldn't you like to be able to deal with such creatures yourself?" He moved to the teenager to show the lad his sword.

"With a sword like yours?" asked the boy.

"Ay, among other things. Like making our own laws and not running to the Guardians every time we need something." Ram went to sheath his sword when the teenager asked:

"May I try your sword, sir?"

Ram deftly handed him the sword hilt first.

The teenager gaped in astonishment at the weight of the blade. He made several slicing motions. "It's so light. How could you kill the creatures with it?"

"I told you, I've learned the secrets of the heavenlies." Ram took the sword to sheath it. "Secrets Jor'el has kept hidden by way of the Guardians."

"The secret to self-rule," said the first.

Ram smiled with pleasure. "Indeed, my clever friend. By possessing such knowledge we can determine our own destiny and make Allon a nation to be feared and respected by the rest of the world."

"We are feared and respected now," said another.

Ram's countenance changed from pleasant to scorn. "No, Jor'el is feared while we mortals are looked upon as his servants, nothing more. The rest of world thrives by using their intelligence and industry. We languish behind them in every aspect of society."

"You've seen this?"

Ram glanced to Curtis. "You are man of commerce, tell them what you know."

Curtis dismounted. "How many of you own your own business or trade?"

One man raised his hand. "This is my farm."

Curtis shook his head and clicked his tongue. "One in twenty, not good odds. Do you supply or trade with anyone beyond the border of the Meadowlands?"

"No, not really. I do well enough locally to employ many." He motioned to the others. They nodded or verbally agreed.

Curtis continued. "You harvest grain so who supplies the building materials for your homes and barns? Is it local or brought in on the backs of those who populate the labor camps?"

"The camps are for criminals."

"Who makes such a determination? Mortals or Guardians?"

"We have mortal judges," said one.

"They make judgments based upon heavenly law, *not* mortal law. We are treated as if we can't decide for ourselves good from evil, right from wrong. Even the laws are made for us."

"My liege!" said Witter in warning. He steadied his agitated horse. He and Altari reached to draw their swords when the source for their concern appeared.

"What is going on here?" Hadley, a vassal Guardian and one of Zanis' Trio Mates arrived. He drew his dagger and glared at Witter and Altari. He waved at the mortals. "All of you get away from them!"

"Why? They've done nothing wrong. In fact, this one destroyed the creatures," argued the farmer, who indicated Ram.

Hadley ignored the farmer to remain focused on Witter and Altari. "Be gone, turncoats!"

Curtis seized the opportunity to step between Hadley and the warriors. "He calls us turncoats. Why? Because we mortals are tired of Guardian rule?"

"What?" Hadley asked in confusion. He used his dagger to indicate Witter and Altari while speaking, "They are in league with—" Hadley gasped with painful surprise, when Ram thrust his sword into his chest.

"You saw it! The Guardian attacked me! Lord Ram saved me!" shouted Curtis.

Ram withdrew the blade. Hadley collapsed, seriously wounded.

"Go, before Zanis and Zinna arrive!" the farmer urged them.

The men ushered Curtis and Ram to their horses. Heeding the warning, Ram, Curtis, Witter and Altari rode off.

The scene visibly upset the teenager. "What will we say to the magistrate? Has a mortal ever killed a Guardian?"

"He's not dead," said one.

Hadley lay on the ground semi-conscious.

"I've never even seen a mortal wound a Guardian!" said another.

"Everyone leave! Perhaps with the creatures near him they will assume it happened during an attack," said the farmer.

The workers quickly gathered their equipment and piled into the wagons to leave. The teenager lingered. He stared at Hadley with compassionate indecision.

"Jory! Come on," the farmer shouted from his seat atop a wagon.

"No. I can't just leave him." Jory knelt beside Hadley. He ignored the sound of the departing wagon to focus on Hadley. "Guardian? Can you hear me?"

Hadley's eyes opened. He tried to speak, but couldn't.

Jory stripped off his jacket then his shirt. Despite the coolness of the day, he didn't put his jacket back on, as he tied his shirt around Hadley's wound. The Guardian gasped in pain. "I don't know what else to do."

A flash of brighter white light signaled multiple arrivals. Hadley's head fell to one side, wary. Zanis arrived with his twin sister Zinna.

"By the heavenlies." Zanis dropped to his knees beside Hadley. "What happened?"

"I tried to stop the bleeding," said Jory in hasty concern.

"Kelpies." Zinna examined the creatures.

"Did the kelpies do this to you?" Zanis asked Hadley.

"No," said Jory and Zinna together.

Zanis turned his attention to Zinna when she joined them. "They were killed by a sword, not a dagger."

"A stranger killed the creatures, and did this to the Guardian," said Jory.

"Why?" asked Zanis. Hadley seized him to get his attention. Seeing Hadley's ashen features and blue lips, Zanis gathered him in his arms. "Bring the boy to the Fortress!" he said before vanishing with Hadley.

"The Fortress?" asked Jory in surprise.

"To explain what happened. If Hadley succumbs it will be murder."

"Murder? The other said the Guardian attacked him and that the tall stranger acted in defense."

"Is that what you saw?"

Jory bit his lip in consideration of his answer. Guardians' eyes could be commanding, prompting and sympathetic. He shied from her, vexed and uncertain.

"Jory," she softly began. "I know your parents named you after Jor'el, so tell me the truth."

The kindness in her voice and reference to his parents, made him look at her. "You knew my parents?"

Zinna smiled. "Ay. Because your father was a priest, my brother and I have kept watch of you since he and your mother died last year." She gently touched his face. "You have nothing to fear. Now, what happened? Did Hadley attack a mortal?"

"No. The other stranger stepped between Hadley and the two Hadley called turncoats."

"Turncoats?"

Jory shrugged. "Large men dressed in black on black horses. One had a scar on his face." He moved his hand to demonstrate where the scar was located. "Hadley did have his dagger out, and lifted it to point at the turncoats while speaking. That's when the one who killed the creatures plunged his sword into Hadley. A strange looking sword made of dark metal."

"Dark metal?"

"Ay. It was so light in weight I don't know how he killed the creatures with a single stroke."

"Were others around when this happened?"

"Ay. We were working in the field when the creatures attacked," he pointed to the kelpies. "The beasts killed Morris and wounded Sims. Two of the others took Morris' body and Sims back to the house while we dealt with the creatures. That's when they arrived."

"The two strangers and the turncoats?"

"Ay."

Zinna pursed her lips in consideration of what she heard. "So Hadley arrived just after the stranger killed the kelpies. Is that when he confronted the turncoats?"

"Ay. The others fled, but I couldn't leave the Guardian." Jory shook his head in befuddlement. "None of their talk made sense. Mortal self-rule. Defying the Guardians and Jor'el."

Disturbed by the statement she asked, "What?"

"The strong, tall stranger, who killed the creatures, claimed he discovered the secrets of the heavenlies that Jor'el has kept hidden. Of how the Almighty uses Guardians to hold mortals in subjugation."

Agitated and concerned, Zinna drew Jory to his feet. "You must come with me to the Fortress and repeat to the Vicar and Captain Kell what you just told me."

"The Vicar and Captain?" stammered Jory.

"It is imperative!"

Jory hesitated, appearing frightened. Zinna softened her tone to one of consoling and encouraging.

"Do you believe all your father taught you about Jor'el?"

"Of course. My father never lied."

"Nor do I lie in telling you those men and turncoats are the true threat to Allon."

Jory shrugged. "It didn't sound right what he said about Guardians and Jor'el. That's why I stayed to help Hadley when the others left.

Zinna kindly smiled and stroked his hair. "You did good. Now continue to do what is right and come with me. For your parents' sake."

He slowly nodded. "For them, I will go with you."

Zinna drew him to her side. They vanished in dimension travel.

✦

Kell met with Avatar, Zanis, Zinna, Priscilla, Gresham, Jedrek and Auriel in the antechamber of his office. They gathered to discuss the situation after Kell and the Vicar heard Jory's lengthy story. The boy remained in Avram's care since he could not return to the Meadowlands for fear of reprisal.

Curious, Priscilla spoke to Avatar. "You said Witter and Altari suffered torture. Now Kell says Hadley confirmed the boy's story about their identity. How is that possible?"

Avatar shrugged with uncertainty. "They must have succumbed and joined Dagar. Witter had the scar when I saw him."

"Descriptions from other encounters in Midessex also support Hadley's identification of Witter and Altari, along with what is being told the mortals," said Gresham.

"They use spirit horses to travel fast and wide to spread their lies," chided Jedrek.

"How can we counter them, Captain?" asked Zinna.

Kell didn't look at anyone, rather stared at the map of Allon. "I don't know if we can," he replied in a muted tone, almost under his breath. His golden eyes narrowed in concentration of the map. "Dagar is twisting our every move to suit his purposes and lay the ground work for mortals to rise and aid him. He learned well from their mistakes at Radnor. They wanted the same thing then, self-rule and determination. Without Guardian help, their rebellion was doomed. So would Dagar's plan fail if unable to sway the mortals against us by stirring the same unrest with false hopes and promises of a fake king."

"There must be something we can do, Captain?" said Auriel.

The door burst open. Wren and Ridge rushed into the room. Both appeared wounded and greatly distressed. "The Northern Forest . . . fallen! All gone! Dax. Armus ..."

"Armus?" repeated Avatar, stunned. He turned to Kell. The captain focused intensely on Wren in dreaded anticipation.

"We don't about Armus, Captain," said Ridge in haste. "All we know is Barnum couldn't find him after a battle with a tartundeen. Barnum saw no gray light."

Kell spoke in a husky voice. "Vidar?"

"The infirmary. A kelpie seriously wounded him. We fought numerous tartundeens, wolf-man-like creatures and these." Using his right hand, Ridge reached to pulled something off his left shoulder with difficulty. He brought out a quiver containing half a dozen black arrows. "I collected what I could."

Kell fiercely sneered at sight of the black shaft and feathers. He snatched the quiver from Ridge.

"Arrows?" asked Zinna.

"Stygian arrows!" chided Avatar. "They never stood a chance." When Zinna reached for the arrows, he seized her arm. "Don't touch them!"

"Ay," groused Ridge. "I still don't have full use of my hand, or much sensation in my left arm from gathering them."

"Unless Valmar can hold the Highlands, Dagar will succeed in isolating the Region from east, west and south," said Jedrek.

"And faster than any of us expected," said Zanis.

"Poor Dax," moaned Wren. She fought back tears.

Avatar spoke with compassion. "I'm sorry. I know what's it like to lose a friend. Multiple friends and comrades."

She just nodded, battling to maintain her composure.

"Avatar, tell Valmar to fall back and bring all his troops to the compound."

"What? Kell, no! That will give the Highlands to Dagar," argued Gresham.

"This compound is his prize!" snapped Kell. "Only by saving the Region can the rest of Allon be rescued. Lose it and Allon falls!" He made a curt dismissive wave for Avatar to depart. "The rest of you, return to duty. Wren, Ridge." He motioned for them to accompany him.

Indeed, everything happened quicker than anticipated. Hearing the report of the Northern Forest, Kell fought a sinking feeling regarding Armus' fate. His friend's words echoed his in mind, *If Avatar or I fall, you must not show him any emotion but raw determination to finish what must be done.* Oh, how easily spoken, yet so difficult to do. First learning of Altari's betrayal and now the possible loss of Armus.

"Captain."

The voice jolted Kell from his thoughts and stopped him in his tracks. He realized they arrived at the infirmary along with who spoke to him. "Barnum." He dismissed Wren and Ridge. "I'll be along shortly." He turned his attention to Barnum.

The warrior assumed a sympathetic expression as he asked, "Have you been told about Armus?"

Kell gripped the hilt of his sword. "Ridge mentioned a tartundeen. What exactly happened?"

"Ay. We called upon our powers, both striking at the same time and severing its legs. A defensive swing of the axe caught Armus and sent him flying into a ravine. I searched for him at the first opportunity. He landed in the stream at the bottom of the ravine so I know he survived the initial strike." Barnum pulled Armus' dagger from his belt where he tucked it. "I know because I found this in the stream bed. What I *didn't* find was his sword," he added at seeing Kell's jaw flex upon receiving his lieutenant's dagger. "He may still be alive."

"Did you find any other survivors?"

"Alas, no. Wren found me when she believed no one else survived." Barnum grew agitated. "Kell, our powers did little against those creatures! The archers barely stopped the kelpies. Against the wolf-men the arrows were like gnats biting them. It took Armus and I together to bring down a single tartundeen, while we had no defense against stygian arrows."

"I ordered Stoker and Flint to work on shields to deflect the arrows. With the few Ridge brought back, I'll see if they can forge such arrows for our use. As for the creatures of infrinn, the Originals will be giving quick lessons to the troops on how to handle the ones we are familiar with. This wolf-man creature is unknown." Kell clapped Barnum's shoulder. "Thank you for bringing me his dagger." He tucked it into his belt and entered the infirmary.

Phoebe, Wren and Ridge stood around Vidar's bed. Kell halted at the foot of the bed, taken aback by how pale and feeble the archer appeared.

Vidar cocked a lopsided smile. "Good to see you too, Kell."

"You can speak?"

"Thanks to my remedy," said Phoebe. "Not too long, Captain. He's weaker than these two; but thankfully, more cooperative," she said in a decidedly sarcastic tone about Wren and Ridge.

Kell suppressed a grin to say, "I won't tax him." He took a seat on the cot to speak to Vidar. "I'm sorry. I should have sent more troops."

Vidar made a feeble attempt to shake his head. "We didn't have time to wait for improvements in weapons or tactics before responding. Dax needed help. Armus—" He closed his eyes to compose his emotions. He opened his eyes when Kell took hold of his arm. "I'm so sorry, Kell."

Kell's expression turned hopeful in showing Vidar Armus' dagger. "Barnum found this in a stream at the bottom of the ravine where the tartundeen's strike sent him. But *not* his sword."

"No sword?" asked Vidar, his voice stronger and curious.

Kell grinned. "No. So he may have survived the strike and is still armed."

"Is that what you sense? That Armus survived? I couldn't move, much less seek out his essence."

Kell shook his head. "I just learned of it a few moments ago. I haven't had the chance to make an attempt." He held up the hilt of the dagger. "According to Barnum's report, and finding this, there is a very good possibility."

Vidar grinned. "I always thought his thick head would save him."

"Providing that's where he was struck," quipped Avatar. He appeared beside the cot. "I spoke to Valmar and he's falling back," he said to Kell.

"Falling back? Why?" Vidar sat up in shock then suffered pain for moving.

"Easy." Wren helped to ease him back against the cushions.

"On my orders. The compound is Dagar's goal. It *must* be held!"

Vidar grew agitated. "Then all who fell in Midessex and the Northern Forest fell for nothing!"

"No!" said Kell stoutly. "It's not *nothing* to fall in the line of duty. With it came vital intelligence we can use to defend the compound. Then launch a campaign to retake the provinces. Be assured, I will not allow their sacrifice to go unavenged."

"Captain," came a stern warning from Phoebe.

Kell gave her a wave of acknowledgement then spoke in a softer tone to Vidar. "Rest and recover, my friend. When you are well enough, I need you to teach the archers how to deal with the creatures of infrinn."

"Wren knows. I taught her long ago."

Kell rose to confront Wren. "Why didn't you say something before?"

She heaved an abashed sigh. "I didn't want to assume by boasting."

"Since when has modesty been one of your traits?" teased Avatar.

"Since seeing you get a fat lip for arrogance!" she shot back. Instead of receiving his usual bantering response, he scowled with offense. "Avatar—" she began apologetically, but he left.

"Report to the armory to begin the lessons," Kell told her and left the infirmary.

"Wren," began Ridge, sympathetically.

She hurried from the room.

"She's unusually upset. She'll come to around when this is over," said Vidar.

"Good, because I don't like seeing her so upset. It's too difficult to deal with. Like an emotional mortal female."

"Oh, don't let her hear you say that, or she'll use you for target practice."

"Now, that would be more like her." Ridge roguishly smiled. "I'll let you rest."

Wren made her way to the armory in a roundabout manner. She tried to find Avatar to apologize. She didn't know what made her lash out when he teased her. She realized why he reacted the way he did only after speaking. Being contemporaries in age, they frequently saw each other due to Vidar's status and close association with Kell and Armus. She and Avatar developed their own relationship based upon mutual sarcasm and good-natured rivalry. Occasionally they got on each other's nerves, but nothing personal or intentional.

"Wren!"

She whirled about at hearing her name. It didn't register in her ear that a female had called to her until she saw Auriel. "Oh, it's you."

Auriel's brows leveled at the sour tone. "I came to say I'm sorry about what happened. I understand what it's like to lose so many comrades."

"Is that why you did it? Because you know what it's like?" chided Wren.

"Do what?"

"Hit Avatar. You felt pain so you had to give it?"

The forcefulness of the accusation momentarily stymied Auriel. "No, it was an unguarded reaction brought on by the passion of loss. I already apologized to him. Must I apologize to you too?" she said in her usual biting manner.

Wren fought her temper at arguing since dealing with Auriel delayed her from her original course. She attempted to move around Auriel only she didn't get far when the warrior seized her.

"I asked you a question, be good enough to answer."

Wren's green eyes flashed with anger at the assault. "Let go of me."

Auriel did so, yet continued in a patronizing tone. "Why are you so defensive about Avatar? He's not your Trio Mate."

"He is my contemporary and a good friend. You may be a militia commander, but you are younger than both of us, and have a bad habit of showing disrespect."

"I came to offer sympathy not be scolded!"

"You have a funny way of offering sympathy and apologies," said Avatar. He appeared from behind Auriel and moved to stand beside Wren. "Being easily insulted and correcting the person you approach is a serious flaw you need to quickly correct or you may not get another chance."

Auriel forced herself to assume a more contrite posture. "You're right, Lieutenant. Thank you for pointing it out." She gave them each a formal salute before departing.

"I suppose I'm wrong in saying I feel sorry for Jedrek having such a difficult apprentice," said Wren.

"If she doesn't change, he may not have to put up with her."

"What do you mean?"

"Kell put on her notice for this." He pointed to his lip.

"Oh," she said, comprehending. Wren snatched a glance in the direction Auriel departed. "Don't report what passed between us. I'd like to give her another chance."

"That's why I warned her. I don't want her demoted for a cut."

"About that. I've been looking for you to apologize."

"I wasn't in the mood to listen so I've been avoiding you. Until I heard your gracious defense of me." He wryly grinned.

She spoke with befuddlement. "I don't know why I lashed out."

"I do. It's the same reason Auriel struck me: pain and grief."

"No, not like Auriel!" she insisted. "Ay, the pain and grief part," she admitted at his contrary look. "She has a mean streak. You and I just tease each other. There is no meanness or intent to harm. I'm truly sorry, Avatar. I've lost enough friends today, I don't want to lose one due to my stupidity."

Avatar smiled, broad and amiable. "I know. This whole situation is making all of us edgy and act out of character," he said with a certain provoking, teasing tone.

In mock anger, Wren placed hands on her hips. "Meaning what, Lieutenant?"

"Meaning, next time I prefer you hit me rather than get emotional. I can handle that since you don't hit as hard as others."

"It would hurt if I used you for target practice."

"Speaking of, your class is waiting and I'm needed elsewhere." He made a short, amused salute before leaving.

Chapter 21

O VER THE COURSE OF THE NEXT FOUR DAYS, THE GUARDIANS' numbers increased to twenty-nine thousand. Kell positioned them around the Temple Plain. They practiced new methods of dealing with the creatures of infrinn. They also reinforced the walls and battlements. Day and night smoke rose from forging fires as Stoker, Flint and armament Guardians worked feverishly to restock the armory and make new weapons to Kell's specifications. Without access to the main forge in the heavenlies the progress proved slow and frustrating.

Since Guardians required little sleep, Kell worked non-stop in the anteroom. He constantly received reports from mortal commanders of the Temple and Palace Guards. A few malcontents left when word of sentiment swaying against the Guardians spread among the mortal ranks. Most of the soldiers stayed true to their sworn oath. Still, the mortals only numbered one thousand since Allon relied heavily on the Guardians for protection and not a mortal standing army. Guardian scouts and commanders also provided intelligence.

Kell sought several audiences with Jor'el. Each time he received the same answer, do what is necessary. Not that he hesitated after losing thousands in two battles. However, he still wanted some form of hope. Something elusive when receiving reports and overseeing preparation.

Staring at the wall map hanging in the antechamber, he recalled the promise of protection and blessing Jor'el made to Janel and ... "Razi."

"No, I'm Avatar."

Kell flinched, unaware of Avatar's arrival. "Never mind. What is it?"

"You're needed in the infirmary. There is an unruly patient giving Phoebe a very difficult time. She says you are the only one who can reason with him."

"Why can't Vidar behave?" he complained.

Avatar flashed a mischievous smile. "Not Vidar."

"Oh?" asked Kell, suspicious. Avatar's glanced to Armus' dagger still on his belt. "Why didn't you say so?" Kell hurried from the room.

Armus sat on the examination table, bare-chested and grimacing in pain. Phoebe cleansed the deep claw marks that ran from his right shoulder across his chest. She already bandaged the wound on his arm. He seized her hand to stop her administration. "That's enough!"

"I must thoroughly cleanse the wounds. I don't know what type of creature did this. The claws may be poisonous."

"If they were poisonous I would know by now. It's been four days."

"Four days I've spent worrying," scolded Kell. His smile countered his tone. He clasped Armus on the neck. "By the heavenlies, don't ever do that to me again."

Armus winced at the greeting and forced a grin. "Not by choice."

"Were those wounds done by the tartundeen you and Barnum fought?"

"No, but I'm glad to hear Barnum survived."

"Ay, not many did."

"Vidar told me." Armus gingerly motioned to where the archer stood getting dressed.

"Are you cleared for duty?" Kell asked Vidar.

"No," said Phoebe at the same time Vidar said "Ay." He insisted to her, "Ay."

She huffed and returned to tending Armus. "Lift your arms so I can finish," she said in annoyance.

Armus followed her instruction then loudly hissed. "That's cold! Not to mention it hurts!"

"Oh, stop whining. Warriors are worse than mortal children when it comes to taking medicine."

Armus' regard of Kell turned sympathetic. "Tor told me to give you a message." He grunted and flinched in pain at Phoebe's continued care.

"To tell me he's joined Dagar. No surprise there."

"No—to tell you that *Altari* has joined Dagar."

"I already know that," groused Kell. "Zanis and Zinna reported him riding around with some mortals stirring up trouble. Along with Witter."

Armus sighed in relief when Phoebe finished with the salve. "You were right to be concerned about Altari's loyalty."

"They tortured him!" insisted Avatar.

Armus glanced to Kell. "You haven't told him?" He indicated Avatar.

Kell waved it off and changed the subject by asking, "Where have you been the past few days?"

"Making my way back here. I couldn't dimension travel and we had to move carefully."

"We?"

"Dolan, Kerwin and myself."

With annoyed curiosity, Kell asked Avatar, "I thought you left them with Eldric at Melwynn?"

"I did," said Avatar in surprised defense.

"He did," Armus spoke through clenched teeth while Phoebe wrapping a bandage around his chest. "Razi said Eldric thought hiding them in Vidar's province was a good idea. It's an isolated cottage in the Greenwood. Dolan and Kerwin insisted on coming to help Avram."

"Against Jor'el's instructions?"

"So I said, only they claimed the instruction was given to Razi. After prayerful consideration, everyone agreed Dolan and Kerwin should go." Armus shrugged, much to his painful chagrin. "Who am I to argue? I had to get back here and they offered to help. Which was good, since they knew a shortcut to the Region's border."

"The hidden pass?" asked Vidar. Now fully dressed, he joined them.

"I guess. I didn't ask, I just followed." Armus groaned and half-closed his eyes.

"Drink this." Phoebe gave Armus a cup containing a reddish liquid.

"What is it?" He hesitated with suspicion.

"Wine with poppy juice and comfrey. No more argument! You're in no condition to do anything else for a few days."

Armus drank the remedy.

Phoebe took back the cup. "You can use the archer's bed."

When Armus tried to move from the table, he nearly doubled over. Kell and Avatar caught him.

"What did this to you?" asked Avatar as they helped Armus into bed.

"Madah-dune. At least that's what Razi said Dagar calls them."

"There are no such creatures of infrinn," said Kell.

Armus gingerly moved to get comfortable, his speech weary. "Razi said Dagar experimented with creatures of infrinn and animals of the real world. The madah-dunes are one of the successes in crossbreeding or something like that." He sighed with relief as he lay down. He closed his eyes and fell asleep.

Kell drew Phoebe aside. "How long until he is recovered?"

"A week. The wounds are deep, but I'm more concerned for his strength. The time it took him to return for medical treatment taxed his lifeforce. I can give him strengthening tonics up to four times a day—" she stopped when Kell interrupted.

"Not good enough! I need him fully recovered by morning."

She became alarmed. "You know what that requires from me?"

He sternly regarded her. "You know what we are preparing to face?" It was more a statement than a question.

"Ay, Captain. We are stockpiling supplies. Yet you realize you can't ask me, Eldric or any physician to use our power to heal everyone who is injured. It would overtax us or kill us to use that much of our energy," she brashly countered.

"Of course not. However, if you are unwilling to heed a direct order regarding my second-in-command, I will summon Eldric and—"

"Very well! You don't need to pull rank. You'll have him back and spouting orders by morning."

Avatar followed Kell from the infirmary. At the first opportunity, Avatar pulled Kell aside. "What did Armus mean? Is there something I should know?" By Kell's expression, this wasn't a topic he wanted to discuss, so Avatar pressed him. "It has to do with Altari, doesn't it?"

"Ay," said Kell with reluctance.

Avatar scowled with great annoyance. "He joined Dagar because he's jealous. He still believes you favor me over him."

"What?" The statement and Avatar's bitter tone surprised Kell.

"Altari isn't the only one who thinks that. In fact, you practically shamed me in front of the Trio Leaders by refusing to even entertain my idea. Granted it didn't go as I hoped, but your action further added to my reputation of being shielded and protected by the *captain*."

Avatar's raised voice drew attention from others in the corridor. Kell snatched Avatar's arm. "We'll continue this in my office, Lieutenant."

With brisk strides, Kell led Avatar across the compound. He ignored any addresses along the way. Upon reaching the office, he left orders not to be disturbed. He closed the door hard.

Attentive, yet guarded, Avatar waited for Kell to speak. The captain's tone was firm.

"If you want to fault me for anything, it is to keep you and others alive! That was my concern regarding your plan, not to shame you or diminish your abilities."

"That's not what Altari and others see."

"Altari!" Kell huffed with annoyance. "Very well, I'll tell you what Armus meant. There is some truth to Altari's claim of *favoritism*, only not the way you think. Not in shielding or protection, rather in *friendship*." Kell took several pacing steps. "Armus and I were created as counterparts to work together. So naturally there is a strong bond. Altari was a separate creation, yet Jor'el appointed him as part of the High Trio."

"You didn't like the appointment?"

"Let's just say, Altari's personality made things difficult at times. He could be witty and compassionate. But he is also strong-minded and *standoffish*, as mortals would say. We functioned well together; at least I thought so. You remember how things were."

Avatar heaved a sheepish shrug. "I guess as your apprentice, I saw things a bit differently."

"How so?"

"As you said, the High Trio *functioned*. Even early on, I sensed Altari's begrudging attitude towards me. I couldn't place my finger on *why?* Only that he didn't like me being around."

"Why haven't you said anything until now?"

Avatar snorted a chuckle. "Back then, I dare not speak a word against an Original, *and* a member of the High Trio. Besides, what would I have told you? Altari doesn't like me? My task was to learn from you and Armus, not Altari. So I chose to ignore him. When I became your aide, he stated his disdain in no uncertain terms during a heated exchange."

Kell nodded. "I heard about it. His only reason for telling you was to take revenge on me."

"How? By making me feel guilty about losing his position?" chided Avatar.

"No, to make you discontent," insisted Kell. " His aim was to tempt you, to make you act wrongly like he did. His disobedience to Jor'el is what caused his demotion—not jealousy of you."

The statement confused Avatar. "I thought such disobedience meant immediate destruction or a permanent forfeiting of our station?"

"Depends upon the extent of the disobedience. I haven't always given you severe punishment, despite the times others believed *you* deserved it."

"True," said Avatar in abashed agreement. "What did he do?"

"He took a fancy to a mortal woman he believed was being unjustly treated by her husband. I learned of the relationship after the husband died. He claimed it was only a deep friendship. However, when the husband died, I wondered about Altari's involvement in his death.

However, I found nothing during my investigation to support anything other than natural causes." Kell's brows furrowed with uneasy remembrance.

"You still weren't convinced?"

"No. I felt there was more to the relationship." Kell sighed as he took a seat on the corner of his desk. A look of recollection deepened. "His reaction troubled me while his behavior grew cold and disdainful. Soon his deteriorating attitude began affecting his desire to fulfill his duty. Not good for a member of the High Trio. Fortunately, the relation didn't produce offspring, like what we face with Dagar. If it had, the punishment would have been worse."

Avatar spoke with confusion. "I still don't understand. Jor'el forbids such mortal-Guardian relationships. How was Altari not made an example? Or at least recalled to the heavenlies?"

Kell shrugged. "I questioned Jor'el at the time, but he chose to handle it different. He had me reassign Altari and spoke of appointing a new member to the High Trio. I thought he meant choosing from among the Originals. Unfortunately, news of Altari's indiscretion spread. Jor'el didn't want a tainted member. Thus, you were the first created of the second group of Guardians with no knowledge or opinion of Altari's actions. Once you completed apprentice training with us, and after mentoring Mahon, you were ready to take your place in the High Trio."

The explanation made Avatar very thoughtful.

Kell took hold of Avatar's shoulder to get his attention. "Don't let Altari's jealousy trouble you. It stems from something he never had and you had from the beginning—*my* friendship, and Armus. We are indeed *The* High Trio. Not just in name, both also in close friendship."

"I'm flattered." Avatar flashed one of his gregarious smiles. "And enlightened. You're overprotective of me so I *don't* act like him, and he's jealous of me because I *won't* act like him. Makes perfect sense."

Kell laughed, a good long belly laugh. He fought to catch his breath to speak. "Return to the infirmary and make sure Phoebe tends to Armus."

At sunset the following day, Kell stood on the highest point overlooking the Temple Plain. For centuries since Radnor, he tried to convince Jor'el to construct walls around the Palace. The Almighty resisted the suggestion. Jor'el wanted to remain open and accessible to the mortals. The makeshift defenses Kell ordered constructed would do little good. Activity really served more to keep morale high among the mortal soldiers, priests and servants. They wanted to help with the palace's defense.

Kell looked toward the Temple. Armus organized the mortal workers. Kell knew what he asked of Phoebe was dangerous to the physician. At such a crucial time, he could not be without his second-in-command. Fortunately, Eldric arrived from Melwynn to oversee Phoebe's recovery after using her power to heal Armus.

Kell noticed Eldric join him in his observation. By the prime physician's expression, he was about to receive a tongue-lashing. He thought to pre-empt it. "I hope Phoebe is feeling better today."

"She is."

He heard the sober tone and sighed. "I assure you, Eldric, it was not an easy request to make. You must understand; I had no choice."

"That's the same reason you gave me concerning Avatar."

Kell tried to keep his counter-point neutral. "You said you increased the strength of the tonics, nothing about having to use your power to heal him. If you did, then why was he still suffering the effects of the wounds when he returned to duty?"

Eldric frowned in annoyance. "I only used tonics. From what Phoebe said, Armus suffered injuries far worse than Avatar's."

"He did." Kell looked the physician squarely in the eyes. "Eldric, we are about to face a battle that has never happened before; Guardian against Guardian. I need everyone at full strength and ready for whatever must be done."

"I didn't come to speak to you about Phoebe, Armus or Avatar. The situation is worse than you realize."

"How so?"

"I could only gather a dozen physicians before a prohibiting force settled over Melwynn. When we reached the valley, we couldn't see the castle. It was gone, just the mountain remained ..." He stopped when Kell turned away. The captain's profile showed uneasiness. "Kell, do you know why Jor'el destroyed Melwynn?"

"Hidden, not destroyed. Jor'el prevented reinforcement at Radnor to protect the mortals from reaping the full measure of justice for their rebellion. He is now doing the same to us. There will be no help. We are all that he will permit to face Dagar."

"But this is far more dangerous to us and the kingdom!"

Kell didn't reply. His jowls tensed and lips pressed together.

The captain's posture disturbed Eldric. "Surely Jor'el will not sacrifice all of us who stand against Dagar?"

Kell lowered his head and spoke in a hoarse whisper. "I don't know."

"If you don't know, then we are doomed," said Eldric with finality. He moved to leave when Kell snatched his arm.

For a moment they regarded each other: Eldric expectant and Kell grave. "Jor'el will tell us in time. All we can do is what we know, and trust the outcome to the Almighty. Do you understand, Eldric?"

"I understand."

"Tell your comrades to be prepared. The ultimate maybe required of them—required of everyone."

"We shall be ready. I only pray it doesn't cost us everything."

"So do I." Kell released Eldric.

When Eldric was out of sight, Kell return to his observation. He anticipated Eldric's report about Melwynn, but dreaded it also. After losing so many so quickly, reinforcements would be welcomed. By his reckoning, twenty-nine thousand Guardians and one thousand mortals would face forty-five thousand Guardians in Dagar's force with an unknown number of mortals and creatures of infrinn.

Spreading his forces around the huge Temple Plain, stretched the defenses thinner than prudent. Vidar and Gresham manned the east flank, Zanis and Chase on the west flank with Valmar and Raleigh positioned to the north. He and Armus commanded the main line directly in front of the compound. Priscilla would hold in reserve while Avatar served as liaison to all fronts. Not a position Avatar wanted, but one Kell needed.

"How soon do you think before they come?"

Avatar's arrival and question made Kell annoyed at being so preoccupied as to not sense approach. Avatar didn't comment to his reaction, so he answered the question. "Tomorrow at the latest since by now Dagar should know I recalled Valmar and left the north open. How goes the preparation?"

"Well, all things considered."

Kell took note of sardonic tone. "A problem?"

"Not if you consider Priscilla's blustering a problem."

Kell chuckled. "She does have a way about her."

"A flighty windbag according to Gulliver."

"You didn't remind her of his opinion, did you? We need her winds."

Avatar flashed a wry smirk. "I may be considered impertinent by some, but I know my limitations. Battling the wind isn't a choice I'd make. Seriously, Kell, what are our chances? Has Jor'el replied to your repeated inquiries?"

"Guardians don't deal in chances and odds, we do our duty!" he snapped then heaved a deep sigh to regain his temper. "No, Jor'el hasn't spoken. In truth, there is nothing to say. Even with the superior heavenly knowledge we possess, Dagar and the others made their choice. Now, we must act as we were created, in the ultimate defense against our own kind. Besides, what could he tell us? Whether we will win or lose? The answer has no bearing on what must be done or the sacrifices it will take. We all know our duty from the moment we are created. This," he motioned to the defenses, "doesn't change anything."

"I meant for the mortals, not us. I can accept my demise in the line of duty. It is leaving those in our charge vulnerable that is difficult to accept."

Kell own vexation about the issue reflected in this face. "I understand. I always found them fascinating creatures. True, they are difficult at times, yet some are very dear to Jor'el."

"Do you think of any mortal in particular?"

"I can name many over the centuries, as can you, so don't play coy."

Avatar smiled.

Kell's grin faded when he spoke again. "However, they too made a choice. Perhaps not with the full knowledge we have. They know enough to distinguish right from wrong, good from evil. Avram, Dolan, Kerwin and a thousand others stand with us. We don't how many mortals Dagar has managed to sway. They cannot claim ignorance, and will face the consequences in the end. We can mourn for them and wish the situation different, but we must fight them as diligently as any enemy."

"It doesn't mean I have to like it," droned Avatar.

"Neither do I. Come. The sun is setting, and Avram will lead the evening prayers. We should join them, both for their sakes and our spirits."

Chapter 22

AROUND THE TEMPLE PLAIN, GUARDIAN SENTRIES STOOD WATCH, mindful that at any moment the enemy, former comrades, could arrive. The night had been unusually still with nocturnal animals strangely silent. Mortal soldiers waited alongside Guardians, nervous and jumpy in their vigilance.

The first gray light of dawn appeared in the eastern sky. The swooshing of something being thrown and the twang of archery broke the silence. Flames filled the sky, as fireballs headed toward the compound. The fireballs exploded when striking targets around the compound. Masked by morning darkness, black stygian arrows flew unseen until the last moment. The arrows took down mortals and Guardians alike.

Dolan, Kerwin, priests and scribes rushed to pump water or haul buckets to put out fires started by the attack.

Mounted on a white spirit horse, Kell rode to the front line outside the compound. Avatar accompanied him, also mounted. They moved to the group Wren commanded.

Kell shouted, "Rangers, shields up! Archers, prepare to return fire!"

"At what, Captain?" a female archer asked. "We can't see where the arrows or fireballs are coming from. They're everywhere."

Wren rebuffed the question. "You don't need to see, just sense. Elevate thirty degrees and fire!"

Pleased by Wren's response, Kell watched them follow her order.

Rangers held the newly forged protective shields in front of the archers. The archers fired over the shields.

"This is embarrassing, to hide behind pieces of metal," one ranger groused to Ridge. He flinched in surprise when two arrows struck the shield and bounded off with an echoing clank.

"You were saying?" Ridge drew back when the tip of an arrow pierced his shield. It lodged in it a mere few inches from his face. "That's not good." He looked around. The same thing happened to several other shields. "Wren!"

She rushed to Ridge at hearing his call. "What is it?"

"The shields are giving way!"

Wren bit her lip when other rangers and archers became injured or vanquished due to shield failure. "Turtle defense! Use stygian arrows! Pick your targets." She left Ridge to repeat the order along the line of archers and rangers.

The archers moved into positions between the shields to sense targets then came up to fire before resuming cover. This took more time than blanketing the enemy with a hail of arrows yet proved effective.

Dagar's forces continued the aerial assault with deadly effectiveness. The gray light of demise flared and flickered along the Guardian line.

"Kell?" said Wren in desperation at the losses.

The captain fiercely scowled. "Avatar! Tell Armus to have Carvel launch the fireball counter-offensive."

Avatar left to carry out the order.

Further down the line, Carvel stood his ground beside a lightweight ballista. Armus towered over the thin, wiry archer in height and bulk. Carvel chewed on his lower lip while watching enemy fireballs and stygian arrows coming closer to their line. Morning light grew stronger.

"They'll have our range soon," he urged.

"Hold fire until ordered. It'll do no good to waste ammunition." Armus spotted Avatar pressing his horse toward their line.

A fireball struck the ground in front of Avatar. It exploded in a burst of flame. The horse cried out. Both it and Avatar were tossed aside. The horse took the brunt of the blast and was killed. Avatar rolled several times before stopping. He didn't move. Armus raced over. He seized Avatar under the arms and dragged him to safety before another fireball exploded. Avatar's breastplate was badly singed and he appeared dazed.

"Are you all right?"

Avatar blinked several times. He held his chest and carefully rotated his shoulders. "Sore, but fine. Kell says to return fire."

"Carvel will be pleased to hear that. Stay down for a few moments to catch your breath." Armus returned and promptly issued the order.

The archer commander acted with precision. Ten ballistas fired.

Dagar sat upon a black spirit stallion. Ram and Curtis were also mounted. This time Curtis wore a black breastplate over his robes along with a helmet. He watched the battle with some trepidation.

"Having second thoughts, Grand Master?"

"No, my lord. Still, I admit it is difficult to watch. More for a sense of national pride than personal regret."

Dagar viewed the destruction inflicted upon the compound. "Allon is known worldwide for its unique government. We are changing that. From this day, a new national pride will emerge, Grand Master."

"Ay, my lord. And one I look forward to serving." He nodded toward Ram.

Griswold pulled his horse to a stop. "All is ready for our little surprise. I only have to return to facilitate the gathering."

"Do so," said Dagar.

Griswold dismounted then disappeared in dimension travel.

"Sloan! Release the wyverns!" Dagar smiled at Ram. "Your future army will now be recruited for reconditioning."

"Has it been successfully tested?"

Dagar shrugged. "Even if only some are transported and the rest vanquished, what difference does it make?"

Loud snarling screeches from above startled Avatar. He looked up from where he remained under cover. Flying over the trees on both the east and west flanks came a hundred wyverns, the man-like dragon creature from in the Cave. They carried something large and round.

"Wyverns!" Avatar shouted in warning.

The wyverns began dropping what they carried. Upon impact with the ground, the objects exploded with blinding white light and deafening noise. When the light disappeared, so did the Guardians in close vicinity of the light-bomb.

Avatar winced even though his ears were covered. In amazed horror, he watched the result of the attack. "By the heavenlies!" He ran to join Armus. "What happened? Where did they go?"

The sight also baffled Armus. "I don't know."

"Priscilla!" They heard Kell's voice above the battle. The captain pointed his sword skyward at the wyverns.

A fireball exploded nearby, making Avatar and Armus jerk in defense. The Guardians manning the ballistas cringed while mortal soldiers dove for cover.

"Continue firing. I didn't say stop!" Armus chided Carvel.

The archer barked orders to those manning the ballistas.

A wyvern dove toward them.

"Watch out!" Avatar seized Armus. They raced behind a makeshift defense just as the wyvern released the bomb. They placed their arms over their heads and screwed their eyes shut in a feeble defense. When the noise ended, they opened their eyes. The barricade still shielded them.

Armus glanced over the barricade. "Oh, no," he muttered and quickly stepped out from behind the barricade. Avatar joined him to see the ballistas destroyed, the mortals dead, and the Guardians—gone.

"Look!" Avatar directed Armus' attention toward the Fortress.

Priscilla stood on the highest battlement with her arms raised while speaking a loud command of the wind. The wyverns started having difficultly navigating against the contrary winds. The updrafts and down drafts she created finally made the creatures withdraw. Priscilla swayed then swooned. Another Guardian caught her, and carried her from the battlement.

"I hope she didn't go past her limit," said Armus.

Kell pulled his horse alongside them. "We might all have to push our limits this day. Can the ballistas be repaired?"

"I don't know. Carvel and the others ... I don't know," said Armus with uncertainty.

"We need them repaired, quickly if possible," he said to Armus, then to Avatar, "See how the others fared during the attack."

On the east flank, Vidar's force took the brunt of the fireballs and stygian arrows. Kell dispatched Wren, Ridge and Barnum as reinforcements. The sight of the wyverns heading for the flank only added to the chaos.

"Retreat to the defenses!" shouted Vidar.

"The flank will collapse if we retreat," argued Barnum.

"You have a better idea before I lose another force?" Vidar's unusually forceful rebuke made Barnum recoil, not from fear, but in resignation.

"Retreat!" Barnum added his order.

Wren and half a dozen archers continued cover fire for the retreat. Some black clad Guardians of Dagar's force ventured too close to her platoon. With wyverns returning to the flank, Vidar seized her arm, which made her lose aim. The shaft fired harmlessly into the air.

"Enough! I said, fall back."

"We can hold them!" she insisted.

A cry alerted them to an approaching wyvern carrying a bomb.

"Ridge! Get her out of here!" Vidar shoved Wren toward the ranger then turned to deal with the other archers. "Fall back! Hurry!"

The wyvern dropped its bomb. Vidar dove for cover.

The explosion knocked Ridge and Wren face first to the ground. Ridge landed on top to shield Wren. When the sound died down, he ventured a look. The wyvern headed back over the trees. He moved aside to let her up. When she gasped in alarm, he turned for a better view. There were no signs of anyone.

"Vidar!"

Ridge prevented Wren from rising. "He's gone. So are the others."

"No!" She broke loose to bolt away. Someone else grabbed her.

"Wren! Ridge, what are you doing? Get to cover!" Avatar practically dragged Wren toward the defenses as she fought his effort.

"No, Vidar!"

Avatar didn't want to hurt her, yet he continued to pull Wren to safety behind a wagon lying on its side. "What about Vidar?"

"The latest bomb took him and six others," said Ridge.

Wren struggled against the swelling tears with little success. "I told him we could hold to cover the retreat. He didn't listen!"

Avatar firmly held her by the shoulders. In an urgent yet sympathetic voice he said, "I'm truly sorry. However, there is no time for grief. When the time comes, I will mourn with you."

She sniffled, unable to answer.

This time Avatar held her face to look into her eyes. "Wren. We need your skills."

She swallowed back her emotions. "Ay."

"Stay with her," Avatar told Ridge.

Wren wouldn't release Avatar. "Where are you going?"

"To tell Kell. Don't worry; I'll be back. In the meantime, keep your head down and your aim true."

She armed her crossbow. "Anyone so much as twitches, I'll shoot."

Avatar cocked a wry grin. "That a girl." He ran back to the center.

* * *

In the reconditioning chamber of the nether cave, Griswold and a number of others gathered those Guardians successfully transported there by the bombs. Most were either wounded or unconscious from the forced dimension travel. They offered little resistance to the manhandling.

"A present for you!" Griswold shoved a semi-conscious Vidar into the cell adjoining Mahon's cell. The archer collapsed to the floor.

Surprised at seeing Vidar, Mahon waited for Griswold to leave before approaching the bars. He spoke in a low, hurried voice. "Vidar."

"Who calls me?" asked the archer, groggy and weak.

"Mahon."

"Mahon?" he repeated the name with some confusion. "Where?"

"To your left."

In slow, jerky movements, Vidar pushed himself to sit up. He managed a lopsided grin. "Avatar will be pleased to learn you're alive."

Mahon smiled. "Nice to be missed. How did you get here?"

Vidar heaved an uneven shrug. "I don't know. One moment I'm fighting, the next moment this creature dropped something from the air and—*Boom!* White light, deafening noise. Now, I wake up here. By the way, where is here?"

"The Cave."

"Wonderful, he created a forced dimension travel weapon." Vidar groaned and held his head.

"This is the chamber where it happens. Where Dagar tortures those he captures," said Mahon in a harsh, private whisper.

Vidar looked around at the chamber. "Charming." He then surveyed Mahon. "Have you been tortured?"

"Not aside from the ill effects of spurean chains. They've been too busy planning. Is that the fight you mean? Against Dagar?"

"Ay. He's attacking the compound."

"Merciful heaven," murmured Mahon, then to Vidar. "How goes it?"

With grim expression, Vidar shook his head. "Not well. Dagar's managed to utilize the secrets of the Cave to his advantage. Kell won't back down, so we mustn't give up hope." He looked at the cell. "Maybe we can escape and return to help."

"No, the bars and doors are made of stygian metal. I've tried speaking the Ancient like I've heard others do to unlock the cell door, but nothing. Somehow Rune altered the locks to respond only to certain individuals." He then looked across his shoulder to Vidar. "You're an Original. Avatar said Originals know the secrets of the Cave. Can you open the cell?"

Vidar moved to the cell door. Under his breath, he spoke the Ancient and made a twisting motion as if turning a knock. Nothing. He tried again, only with the same result. "You're right, he's done something to the locks."

"What about dimension travel? Can you leave the Cave? Avatar and I got in that way, but had to find a portal to leave."

"I should be able to come and go via dimension travel." Vidar put his hands up, spoke the Ancient and brought his hands together in a quick clap. Instead of disappearing, he was thrown backwards into the cave wall. For a moment, the archer didn't move.

"Vidar?"

"That didn't work either." He sat up.

"Why?"

Vidar blinked away the pain in his head. "I don't know. I understand Rune altering the locks. But how the entire Cave can be blocked from dimension travel is a mystery."

"So only one way dimension travel." Mahon groused as he watched other Guardian victims from the forced dimension travel being imprisoned. "If we can somehow leave the cells, I know the location of the portal."

Vidar shook his head. "It was destroyed during a battle between Gresham's forces and Dagar, when he opened the cave."

"Then we're trapped."

"Kell won't leave us here. He'll find a way. We must survive until he comes."

***

Kell didn't back down even though the merciless onslaught continued for the rest of the day. The shields failed, the ballistas destroyed and they ran out of stygian arrows. Stoker and the forge

Guardians tried to create new weapons, which proved difficult while under fire. Kell resorted to having Guardians combine their powers to repel attacks.

Raleigh, Wyndy and five other element Guardians called upon the whirlwinds and minor cloud bursts to keep control of the sky. This prevented more aerial assaults from wyverns, fireballs and arrows. Unfortunately, both the east and north flanks retreated to the Fortress. Priscilla remained in the infirmary. It would take a day or two before she recovered her strength.

At sundown, the assaults stopped. Kell and Armus stood behind the last line of defense directly in front of the Fortress gate. They surveyed the shrunken battlefield.

"I wonder what he's waiting for. Wouldn't take much to finish us," said Armus.

Kell drew Armus away from the line. "Such an assessment doesn't need to be spoken aloud."

"Openly or in private, it is reality. We are down to ten thousand Guardians and only one hundred mortals. Vidar is among those gone," he said, which made Kell wince. "Another day and Dagar will succeed—unless Jor'el intervenes. Why doesn't he?"

"I wish I knew. We must trust there is a reason."

"A reason for defeat?" said Armus brazenly.

Kell draw Armus further away and out of earshot of anyone. "You must keep your tongue! Have we served together so long for you to question and doubt?"

"No, but—"

"No buts! Doubts and questions are what drove Dagar to think more highly of himself and brought us to this! I would rather go down believing and fighting than doubt and succeed. I hoped you would be with me in this."

The rebuke brought a pained expression to Armus. "I am. I didn't mean to sound otherwise. I was simply stating reality. I'm sorry."

Avram arrived, badly soiled from battle and his face stricken with grief. "Kell."

"What is it?"

"I don't ask favors or take advantage of my position. However, Kerwin died from his injuries. I came to ask if you could spare a Guardian to take Dolan home. I fear the grief will inhibit his recovery and I want to spare my sister more heartache."

"I'll take him," said Armus.

"No," said Kell.

"What? Kell, please! If ever you granted me a favor, do so now," pleaded Avram.

"I meant for Armus not to take him. I will take Dolan home when this is over. In the meantime, you know of the secret vault beneath the Temple?"

"Of course I do."

"Take Dolan and the other mortals there to wait until this is over."

"I won't hide from Dagar!"

Kell grinned at the bravado. "Your courage and loyalty is commendable. If you notice, despite all this destruction, the Temple is not scarred." He turned Avram's attention to the Temple as he continued speaking. "Nor will a stone be touched. For it is decreed in heaven that as long as Allon exists and there are faithful ones among the mortal population, the Temple will not fall. All who seek refuge will be spared."

"Dagar's aim is to topple Jor'el and I'm the Almighty's Vicar."

Kell's smile grew sly. "With your presence, a remnant remains, so Allon will continue. Thus thwarting Dagar's desire for total dominance. If he violates the decree, he forfeits everything and ends his own existence."

Armus added, "An old warrior's saying, *keep your friends close and your enemies closer.* What better way to keep tabs on you than to have you in the open?"

"A thorn in his side," said Avram with an understanding smile.

"A *divine* thorn," said Kell. "Now you and others take refuge. You will know what has happened when I come to fetch you."

Bolstered by the suggestion, Avram hurried to do as commanded.

"Shrewd of you to take liberties with the Almighty's words," said Armus with a wry snicker.

"I didn't take liberties. Merely making certain that some of the faithful remain for Jor'el to keep his promise. Ask Hueil if you take issue with my tactic."

"No one can find him."

"Has he fallen?"

Armus shrugged. "Possible. Although, Hueil was never one to get involved in squabbles. He could just be hiding out.

⁕⁕⁕⁕⁕

Since light for visibility and warmth was for the benefits of the mortals, once they were safely hidden, Kell ordered the fires extinguished. Under the cover of darkness, a cloaked and hooded figure darted from the Guardian rear lines behind the palace toward the west flank. The timing had to be right to avoid the Guardian sentries. It was. From the cover of the trees the figure made a bold approach of Dagar's forces. Lilith and two warriors accosted the figure with drawn swords.

"Halt!" she commanded

Immediately the figure raised arms. He spoke in a male voice. "I'm unarmed."

"Identify yourself."

Carefully the figure removed the hood. "Hueil. Scribe of Jor'el."

"Well, well, how quaint. Did he send you with a message?"

"What I have to say is meant for Dagar's ears only."

She accosted him. "You always have been bold. Be warned, *scribe*, boldness can end your existence this day."

Hueil smirked. "Take me to Dagar, or jeopardize all this."

"Bring him!"

The two warriors seized Hueil, even though he offered no resistance. They brought him to where Dagar enjoyed a meal. Or rather, while he watched Ram and Curtis eat.

Lilith wore a rakish smile. "An interesting turn of a events. You have a visitor from the other side." She waved for the warriors to escort Hueil to the table.

Dagar reclined in his chair. A crooked smile of irony appeared. "What brings you here, scribe? Getting a little hot at the compound?"

"No, a little too restrictive for my liking. Something you should be familiar with." Hueil motioned to a chair at the table. "May I?"

"Depends on your reason for coming."

"To warn you. However, if I'm not welcomed, I'll take my warning elsewhere." Hueil turned to leave when the warriors blocked his path.

"Although I didn't issue an invitation, I'd hardly let you walk away." Dagar waved the warriors to seize Hueil.

"No need for violence, Dagar. I came here willingly, I should be allowed to leave willingly."

"Are you so naïve to believe I give a whit about you?"

"No," began Hueil, soberly. "You've shown you don't give a whit for your kind. What you do give a *whit* about is information. And *I* have information vital to you."

"Let's hear the information and I'll be the judge if it's worth letting you live."

Hueil jerked against the warriors. They wouldn't release him, so he spoke in frustration to Dagar. "I trusted you enough to walk away from Kell and the others. The least you can do is guarantee I survive or the information dies with me."

Dagar stood to accost Hueil. "I have ways of prying information out of stronger Guardians than you. Take Witter and Altari for example." He motioned to the warriors, who stood behind the table. "You, scribe, wouldn't survive a week. So take my offer of judging the information or vanish on the spot." He whipped out his dagger and held it at Hueil's throat before the scribe could react.

For the first time Hueil appeared nervous. "Very well. You know I take the words directly from Jor'el and transcribe them for the mortals. A recent passage Jor'el dictated brings me here. One that will impact what you are doing."

"How so?"

"Your victory will actually lead to your ultimate defeat."

"Don't talk in riddles, scribe. Say what was dictated."

Hueil quoted,

> " ' *When the great enemy*
> *Has gathered together his minions,*
> *Uneasy shall lie his crown,*
> *For when peace has come to his camp*
> *They shall behold him who is to come,*
> *To lay at the feet of Jor'el,*
> *The subduing of the great enemy.*
> *And with him shall be a shining multitude*
> *Whose light shall gleam with heavenly radiance.*
> *Blood shall stain Allon.* ' "

Dagar laughed, loud and mocking. "Blood is already staining Allon."

"A future prophecy, Dagar. In the end Jor'el will have his way. You might want to reconsider."

Dagar glared, incredulous "Surrender? Is this the information you bring, scribe?" He pressed the dagger to Hueil's throat.

Despite the prick of his throat, Hueil spoke in a tight, grim voice, "As a friend, I came to save you from a humiliating and ultimate end! Will you slit my throat as payment?"

Dagar studied Hueil for a moment. "Your information has proven useful."

"How?" asked Ram.

"Well, he did say *his crown*. Meaning you will become king. So my plan will succeed."

"To fail in the end," warned Hueil.

Annoyed, Dagar held his blade in front of Hueil's face. "When will this *end* come about? Can you tell me the timing, scribe?"

Hueil's brows knitted. "No, only in the future, not a precise time."

"Who is this person who will take it from me? Do you know?" He again played with the dagger in front of Hueil's face.

"No," began Hueil, nervous. " But what does it matter? The heavenly radiance refers to the Guardians."

Dagar sneered with intense hate. "By the time this battle is over, there will be no more Guardians of Jor'el only my Shadow Warriors!"

"Shadow Warriors?" asked Hueil with confusion.

Dagar used his dagger to motion toward Witter and Altari. "Shadow Warriors. So named in a scornful denouncement by Armus. Wonderfully ironic to use, don't you think?"

"If you say so."

"I do!" he shouted in Hueil's face, which make Hueil recoil a step." Dagar huffed a mocking laugh. "As a result of this discussion, I have judged your information. In part it is useful, though mostly irritating for its incompleteness. As such I deem your punishment—"

"Father, if I may make a suggestion."

Dagar gave Ram a tolerant wave to proceed.

"I agree with your assessment concerning the value of the information. The punishment you inflict will be merciful compared to what Kell will do to a *known* traitor."

Wary, Hueil eyed Ram. "Kell doesn't know I'm here."

"Oh, he will," said Ram with deadly certainty.

Fearful, Hueil confronted Dagar. "You don't agree, do you? I came here as your friend! I didn't betray you to Kell, why betray me to him?"

For a moment Dagar's considering gaze shifted between Ram and Hueil, finally coming to rest on the Hueil.

"Dagar!" Hueil insisted in desperation.

The mahogany eyes narrowed, as Dagar glared at Hueil. "You have until morning to leave the area. After which your coming to me will be made known." He stepped closer to Hueil, his voice low and lethal. "Regardless of the outcome, either I or Kell will find you, scribe."

Hueil pulled up his hood. A firm hand from Dagar stopped his departure.

"On foot. Any use of power to give away our position and you forfeit your life immediately."

Hueil nodded, so Dagar released him. Hueil raced into the darkness.

Chapter 23

THE FIRST DAY'S BOMBARDMENT INFLICTED HEAVY DAMAGE TO the Fortress and palace. During the night, the remaining Guardians made what repairs they could. An unspoken sense of gloom hung over their efforts.

Early on the morning of the second day, Auriel found Jedrek standing watch on one of the remaining Fortress battlements. He stared at the enemy line. For a moment he appeared not to notice her arrival. She knew better, and waited until he acknowledged her presence.

"Are you just going to stand there or did you come for a reason?" he said, still not looking at her.

"For a reason. I tried to find you last night to say how sorry I am about Virgil." She saw his pain in his tightened jowls and level brow. "May I ask how? Gresham didn't know. Did it happen during the bombardment?"

Jedrek screwed his eyes shut. "No. A skirmish sent us retreating. It is a sight I won't ever forget."

"Of course not, he was your twin."

"No, I mean the ones responsible." Lethal, glaring amber eyes looked sideways at her. "Mab, Burl and Rane. Gresham's former Trio Mates and militia commander. The ones we replaced."

The shock left her momentarily speechless. "I've heard their names, but have never met them."

Jedrek snorted in annoyance as he turned back to survey the field. "Count yourself fortunate. They were replaced because of their dismal attitudes and lack of diligence in performing their duty. I'm not surprised they joined Dagar." His caustic tone grew somber as he continued. "I tried to reach Virgil when a kelpie pinned him, only they arrived first and the kelpie left. They dragged him into the forest. I heard a scuffle then saw a flash of light …" his voice faltered.

"Did you see Virgil disappear?"

Jedrek shook his head. "Just light. In my spirit, I felt great pain."

"Could it be pain of injury and not demise?"

He shrugged. "I've tried all night to discern his sense. I haven't been able to shake a feeling of doom."

"Most have felt the same sense this night. It may not be Virgil." She tried to encourage him.

"I hope he listens to you." Gresham mounted the final step of the battlement. "Will you, lad? We need all our a faculties, power and strength this day. You can't be distracted."

Jedrek squared his shoulders and gripped the hilt of his sword. "I won't be distracted. Jor'el double my strength to avenge Virgil, and defend the Almighty's holy honor. This needs to be stopped!"

The screeching of wyverns pierced the cool morning air.

"You'll get that chance." Gresham drew his dagger. Jedrek and Auriel drew their swords.

"Stand fast!" they heard Kell shout. He and Armus rode from the Fortress to the main line.

Stoker and the forge Guardians worked through the night to repair the five remaining ballistas and create large, lethal projectiles. Shields from the previous day's battle were lashed together to make a wall and canopy to protect the ballistas. A small gap served for firing. Kell placed Wren in command of the ballistas.

Two hundred archers flanked the weapons. A thousand rangers stood behind the archers in a line stretching from the Temple to the end of the palace grounds. Behind the rangers, five hundred warriors assembled. Some sat upon spirit stallions. Similar defenses were arrayed on the east, west and north flanks, only these had no ballistas. Kell wanted those directed at Dagar's main line. Weather Guardians helped the other flanks. Kell hoped their abilities would serve either as an aid in defense or a distraction for the enemy. Spreading ten thousand around the perimeter of the entire compound made for difficult choices.

"Let's hope our little surprises work," said Armus.

"Avatar!" shouted Kell toward the Fortress.

The second lieutenant waited on the highest remaining battlement. He drew his sword and called in reply. "Ready!"

The ear piercing call of wyverns caught everyone's attention. The creatures flew over the treetops carrying more bombs.

"How many of those things does he have?" chided Armus. He drew his sword.

Kell didn't answer. He held his sword over his head, stood in the stirrups and looked back at the Fortress. He lowered his sword.

At the signal, Avatar shouted to those manning the projectiles on the battlement. "Counter measures! Fire at will!" He used his sword to point at the wyverns.

From strategic places on the battlements, projectiles fired at the wyverns. It proved successful in hitting the creatures or the bombs, encasing them in a tar-like substance. A few doused creatures released their bombs to make a hasty retreat. They fluttered in a sporadic pattern or spiraled toward the ground.

Once on the ground the wyverns fought rangers and warriors. Being covered in the tar-like substance seemed to diminish the wyvern's strength and mobility. They only inflicted minor damage before being overcome and killed by the Guardians.

The bombs not encased in tar, exploded upon impact. The same devastating effect happened to any nearby Guardians. The bombs coated with tar, didn't explode. Some tar-doused wyverns managed to stay in the air. They turned back still holding their bombs. Fortunately, this aerial attack was short and not as lethal as the previous day.

Kell issued orders to Wren. "The ground assault may be next. Be prepared to fire at first sign of movement."

She acknowledged and relayed instructions. "Load and stand ready!"

A trumpet sounded from the direction of Dagar's line. Painfully loud howling came from everywhere, as if surrounding the compound.

"Madah-dune!" warned Armus.

A thousand wolf men raced from the trees. A barrage of stygian arrows covered the advance. A new weapon was launched at them. This bomb exploded with paralyzing noise that rendered Guardians incapable of reacting.

An explosion killed Kell's horse. Weight of the animal pinned his left leg beneath it. Stunned and ears ringing, made it difficult for him to get free. A rising growl alerted Kell. A madah-dune raised a massive club ready to strike. Kell partially lifted the horse to use as a shield against the spike club. The force of the beast's blow sent the horse back on top of him. He cried out in pain at feeling his leg being crushed. The madah-dune reared back for another strike.

Twang! Twang! Thud, thud! Two bolts impacted the back of the beast's head and neck. Dead, it fell forward onto the horse. Kell loudly snarled in anger at the added weight of the dead wolf man.

Wren appeared beside Kell. "Are you hurt?"

"Only if you count having the foul smell of this thing in my face!" Kell let out a growl of effort in his attempt to lift the horse and wolf man. It suddenly got lighter as both were pushed aside. Armus. Kell took hold of Armus' outstretched hand to stand. He put all his weight on his right leg.

"Is your leg broken?" asked Armus.

Kell moved his left leg to stand on both feet. "Sore, but not broken."

"Tartundeens!" came Avatar's warning from the battlements.

"Any more ammunition for the ballistas?" Kell asked Wren.

"No," she said, fearfully watching the advancing tartundeens.

"Do what you can to keep them from reaching the palace!"

Setting her jaw, she raced back to the archers shouting, "By twos, aim for the head and face. Fire while saying *By Jor'el's command, stop!*"

Kell and Armus ran toward the Fortress. They were halfway when another trumpet made them stop. Along the front line and from the trees emerged black clad warriors mounted on black spirit horses. Tor rode in the lead.

Tor raised his sword and shouted. "Shadow Warriors! For Dagar and King Ram!" He lowered his sword. "Charge."

"Go! Get Avatar and reinforce the line," snapped Kell. He gave a hard nudge on Armus' arm.

"Where are you going?"

"To the palace to await Dagar."

From a flash of light, Dagar appeared on the Palace portico. He used his special power of blinding speed to take down the two warriors and two rangers standing guard before they knew what hit them. He rushed into the Throne room. For all the destruction and debris inside and outside the compound, the Throne room remained gloriously intact.

No sign of Jor'el. Then again, Dagar didn't expect the Almighty. He did, however, expect to see Kell. "Slipping in your duty aren't you, Kell? Well, it wouldn't matter. The prize is mine," he spoke to no one. A delightfully malevolent smile appeared as he mounted the steps to sit upon the Throne. He laughed.

"Dagar!" Kell arrived, sword in hand.

The laughing became replaced by a cynical smile. "You're too late, Kell. It's only a matter of time before I'm victorious. You can save yourself by leaving."

Kell stepped further into the room and assumed a defensive stance. "The only one who will be leaving is you, either as my prisoner or vanquished."

In one swift movement, Dagar leapt in the air toward Kell. He did a somersault and swung his sword. Kell sidestepped to deflect the blow aimed at his head. Dagar retaliated. For a moment their blades hung together. Kell recognized the darker color of Dagar's sword to be stygian metal. For Dagar to handle the sword meant the hilt and guard were of a non-conductive material to shield him from the effects of the metal. All this Kell realized in a glance. Several fierce blows were exchanged with loud clangs echoing in the chamber.

At one point, Dagar disengaged. He used a flick of his wrist to send a lamp stand hurling at Kell from the side. Kell jumped back to avoid the object. The crashing of the stand caused hot oil to splatter Kell He turned away in momentary pain. The flat of Dagar's sword caught Kell in the left shoulder and sent him flying across the room. He landed at the base of the Throne steps. His sword fell away on impact. Kell's left arm tingled. He could barely move his fingers, confirming the blade to be stygian metal.

When Dagar charged, Kell threw out his right hand. The blocking force knocked Dagar backwards into a pillar. Kell snatched up his sword, got to his feet and went after Dagar. Kell caught sight of the thrown dagger. By the time Kell knocked the blade out of the way, Dagar was on his feet. They exchanged another series of fearsome blows.

Kell's foot slipped on spilled oil, which made him stumble to one side. A hard, stunning blow from the flat of Dagar's blade numbed Kell's right hand. His sword fell to the floor. Kell whipped out his dagger by using his left hand. His fingers still felt weak, but capable of gripping. He slipped on the oil again while deflecting Dagar's attack. In falling to his knees, Kell thrust out. The blade found a chink in Dagar's armor. The blade buried hilt deep in right side of Dagar's chest under his ribs.

Enraged, Dagar called upon his power of deadly speed. The unarmed Kell couldn't counter the swift action. Dagar's sword plunged through Kell's breastplate just beneath the sternum. Jerking out the blade did more damage. Kell fell against a pillar. Seriously wounded, he labored to breathe and fought unconsciousness.

With angry determination, Dagar pulled the dagger out of his body. He staggered in pain. He raised the dagger to strike Kell when—

"Dagar!"

Jor'el's voice sounded from all around. The force of command made Dagar collapse to his knees and sent the weapon falling from his grasp. With intense hostility, he watched the swirling image of Jor'el appear.

The opalescent eyes flashed with rage. "You have desecrated this holy place by your willful act of rebellion and spilling the blood of your fellow Guardians. For acts of insurrection, you will face divine judgment."

"Killing me will only inspire my followers to hate you more!"

"You and your followers are doomed. From this desecration, shall rise a son after my own heart, and by whose hand you will fall. There shall also come a daughter, who shall restore the Guardians. Pride and arrogance have sealed your fate along with those who follow you. They are not without blame, and are unworthy of my presence until the time of cleansing."

Unseen, Armus entered while Jor'el spoke. He carefully made his way to Kell so as not to draw Dagar's attention. He balked at seeing the ripped open breastplate, which exposed the seriousness of the wound. No normal sword could have done this to captain's armor. Kell was unconscious. His face felt cool and his lips ashen. Not good signs! Armus lifted Kell in his arms.

The noise of rescue alerted Dagar. "No!" He seized the dagger and threw it.

In white light, Armus disappeared with Kell. A divine hand wreathed in haze, snatched the dagger in mid air. Jor'el brought it back to himself. The eyes focused intensely upon Dagar while the hand held the blade.

"Once you leave the compound, to the nether cave you shall be imprisoned until the appointed time. And this house will be rebuilt!"

The Almighty's image exploded in brilliant, immense and consuming light. It radiated from the room to engulf the palace and Fortress. Cries came from within the light. A tremendous explosion shook heaven and earth, sending Guardians to the ground, wyverns and kelpies disappearing from the sky, tartundeens and madah-dunes bursting into flames and vanishing.

When the light faded and the shaking stopped, everything became still. The Fortress and palace were reduced to rubble. Only the Temple remained standing in its splendor, not a single stone marred or scorched.

Avatar left the Fortress battlement per Armus' orders of reinforcing the line. He seized Wren to shield her when the explosion happened. The forced knocked them to the ground. After all grew still, Avatar rose to his knees to determine the cause. In wordless anguish, he surveyed the massive destruction.

A wounded Ridge, badly injured Gresham and weakened Priscilla hobbled over.

"What happened?" asked Wren in shaky voice of fear.

Avatar couldn't answer.

"Jor'el finally acted," said Gresham. He groaned, as he held closed the deep wound in his left side.

"He could have done better with the timing," groused Ridge. The bandage on his head showed fresh blood. His left arm hung limp.

Avatar made an impulsive hiss of alarm at seeing the Palace in ruins. The last time he saw Armus, he ran toward the Palace, saying something about Kell. A figure knelt amid the rubble in a crouched protective position. Avatar stood to get a better look, hoping to see Kell or Armus. His facial features hardened upon recognizing Dagar. He drew his sword with the intent of engaging Dagar. The appearance of Shadow Warriors stopped him.

"We're surrounded!" Priscilla recoiled a few steps.

"Be still!" warned Avatar. He gripped his sword in both hands, while his eyes made a visual count of the enemy. "Forty. Interesting odds. Wren, when I strike, you and Priscilla take Ridge and Gresham and leave."

"What? You can't stand alone," she said in protest.

His determination became tempered by an imploring glance. "We must save some. I'm the only remaining warrior in this group. *Please*, do as I say and leave."

Despite fear at Avatar's impending sacrifice, Wren made no further argument. She took hold of Ridge to support him for a quick retreat. Priscilla held Gresham. Before they could disappear in dimension travel they heard a whistle. Two Shadow Warriors held whistles to their mouths. The noise sounded similar to the concussion bombs that stunned them earlier. Gasping in pain, Wren, Priscilla, Gresham and Ridge fell to the ground.

Avatar gritted his teeth in distress against the noise. He placed the pommel of his sword in front of his face. He spoke the Ancient. "*An dealanach siuthad!*" and thrust the sword over his head. Mighty thunder resounded as shafts of deadly lightning flashed from his blade in all directions.

Some Shadow Warriors tried to flee. Others charged Avatar only to be stuck by the lightning and vanish in grey light. The concentration and effort of expending so much energy showed in the draining color of Avatar's face. The thunder and lightning continued until all the Shadow Warrior were vanquished. After the final clap of thunder, Avatar collapsed, unconscious.

Wren hurried to Avatar. She became fearful at seeing his deathly pale face. His skin felt very cool. "Avatar? Can you hear me?" Not receiving a response, she shook him by his shoulders and spoke in desperation. "Please, Avatar, answer me!"

"Did he go beyond he limit?" asked Priscilla in dreaded anticipation.

"He hasn't vanished, so he has some life force remaining," said Ridge. He leaned heavily upon his quarterstaff.

"Not for long, by the look of him," said Gresham, somberly.

In anxious consideration, Wren spoke to the others. "You two are wounded. Priscilla and I are not strong enough to carry—" Nearby movement caught her attention, making her momentarily anxious. At sight of a friendly face she called, "Barnum!"

He quickly joined them. "By the heavenlies, what happened to Avatar?"

"He used his power to save us from forty of the enemy. It may have been too much. We must get him to Eldric; only Priscilla and I can't carry him and also help Ridge and Gresham," Wren hastily explained.

"Eldric went to Melwynn. He said there is a temporary opening to return." Barnum lifted Avatar. "Can the rest of you make it?"

"Ay. Go!" Wren shooed him off.

"More of those warriors!" Priscilla pointed to the west.

Wren stuck Avatar's sword in her belt then waved Priscilla towards Gresham. "Quickly!" She grabbed Ridge, and in an instant, they disappeared in dimension travel.

In the midst of the Throne room rubble, Dagar remained on his knees. What he planned for years, he had achieved. Granted, not totally or to his satisfaction, especially when Armus escaped with a seriously wounded Kell. He tried to console himself with the thought that Kell would succumb. In actuality, he didn't hold out much hope since Kell was Jor'el's captain. He doubled over in pain. Kell managed to land a very serious blow.

"Father?" Ram aided Dagar to stand "How badly are you hurt?"

"Not enough to stop me from seeing you crowned." His sneer turned into a wicked smile. "We won. We chased away the mighty Jor'el and his Guardians. Give me your shoulder."

"A deep and nasty wound. How did it happen?"

"Kell," Dagar hissed. "I made certain he felt my sting harder."

Tor came running. He noticed the wound but didn't comment, rather gave a report. "There are survivors in the Temple. The Vicar and a hundred others."

"Kill them," said Ram.

"No!" snapped Dagar. "All will be lost if you do."

"Why? If we chased Jor'el away?"

"A heavenly decree." Dagar scowled with indignation. "Kell arranged this! I can't touch the Temple as long as a remnant of Jor'el remains. If I do, all is lost." He waved at Tor. "Give me your sash." The warrior complied. Dagar wrapped it around his wound to make it appears as part of his uniform. "Now to the Temple. I may not be able to touch the Vicar, but he will crown you king."

Shadow Warriors guarded Avram, Dolan and the mortals in the main Temple chamber. Curtis joined them. He showed no signs of battle. In his hands, he carried a large satchel.

Dagar flashed a mocking smile "Well, Vicar, you will be surprised to learn that Jor'el destroyed his own compound and deserted the mortals to my victory."

Avram wasn't fazed. "You deceive yourself, Dagar. Anyone familiar with prophecy knew this would come. Your days are numbered."

Ram seized Avram. "Do not speak impertinently to your conqueror. Or your king!"

"I see no king, only *my* half-breed grandson. Born of an unholy alliance."

Stunned, Ram stared at him. "What did you say?"

"Dagar didn't tell you? Your mother was my daughter—Haggar."

"It doesn't matter!" snapped Dagar with impatience. "You will crown your grandson king and bow to him in servitude! Haggar's final act of vengeance for a father who disowned her."

Ram shoved Avram toward the altar.

"Grand Master Curtis! Do you have the crown?" said Dagar.

"Of course, my lord." From the satchel, Curtis produced a gold coronet with ruby red stones and gave it to Dagar.

"Assemble the witnesses," said Dagar. He moved to the altar.

Curtis summoned the mortals outside the Temple, those who survived the destruction. In all, about two hundred were assembled. Most exhibiting uncertainty and caution, but held their tongues.

Ram spoke. "This is the day I promised you would happen. The age of mortal rule has begun. Jor'el is so disgusted by the thought of us taking control of our destiny he has abandoned Allon."

"Liar!" said Dolan. A Shadow Warrior clouted him to his knees.

"Peace," warned Avram.

Dolan scowled in reluctant agreement. He rubbed the back of his neck.

"Even the Vicar acknowledges the fact and will crown me king. Correct, Vicar?" said Ram.

"Correct," replied Avram without emotion. He took the crown Dagar gave him. "Do you swear by all in heaven that you will defend and govern rightly?" he asked Ram.

"I swear by the good will of the people of Allon to keep faith with them as they keep faith with me. Together, we shall raise Allon to a power to be reckoned with."

Some among the mortals agreed.

Avram tried to hide a smile as he said, "Then by *your* oath, I crown you king."

Being taller, Ram bowed his head to accept the crown.

"Long live King Ram!" Curtis began the cheering. The Shadow Warriors encouraged the mortals to participate.

"Now, go!" Dagar ordered those assembled. "Spread the word: a mortal is king. That Jor'el and his Guardians are defeated!"

At Tor's instructions, Shadow Warriors began to remove everyone from the Temple. The Vicar loudly protested the action.

"It is my right to live within these walls. And to keep any here who wish to remain!"

Tor looked to Dagar for confirmation or disagreement. Although slightly pale from pain, Dagar nodded. Tor released Avram.

The Vicar spoke to the men. "Those who wish to claim their right to remain may do so. If you do not, understand, you may forfeit the blessing of the Almighty.

For several moments, they argued for or against the choice. In the end, Dolan and sixty others remained inside the Temple. The rest left.

"Show them to the Vicar's quarters," said Dagar.

Tor and three Shadow Warriors no sooner left with the mortals then Dagar collapsed by sitting hard on the altar steps.

"Father? It is your wound?"

"No, my time has come. I must return to the cave," he chided.

"Why? We won."

"Jor'el's justice. You are king, while I am confined." He motioned to Curtis. "Through him and the talisman I will be in communication. Not in physical form will you see me again. Witter and Altari will remain to command the Shadow Warriors. Tor returns with me to act as liaison." Dagar gasped in serious pain. "Tor!" He seized Tor's arm to stand. "Quickly, before I succumb to the divine. Rule well, my son." Together Dagar and Tor vanished.

Unsettled by the abrupt departure, Ram sat on the altar steps. "I didn't think it would end like this. Him gone and me alone."

"You are not alone." Curtis sat beside him. "Perhaps that is why he recruited me and left Commanders Witter and Altari. He foresaw this and gave you companions."

"No. By his angry reaction this was unforeseen. He worked so hard. First I lose Razi, now him."

"My liege, do not despair. We can turn this to our advantage."

"How?"

"Few mortals know that Dagar is your father or Shadow Warriors are Guardians. We can claim that in his devastating departure, Jor'el punished the Guardians and killed your father. Dagar's loyal army is now under the leadership of Commanders Witter and Altari." Curtis motioned to the Warriors. "They will help you to establish the new era of mortal rule while I will serve as your royal advisor in forming the new government your father envisioned."

Ram nodded in acceptance. "I wish there was a way to establish direct contact rather than speak through you."

"It can be done," said Altari.

Curious, Ram rose. "How?"

"By establishing a connection to the real world. All that is needed is to bring a patch of earth from the Region to the Cave."

"It's still theory," said Witter in a tone of warning.

"So was the plan to overthrow Jor'el." Altari returned to Ram. "It would be best to have a permanent place for communication, like a castle."

"Ravendale."

Altari grinned. "Ay, Sire. It would make the connection close and direct."

"What about a temporary connection while the castle is being built?"

Altari thought for a moment. "A portable method can be crafted by Rune, I suppose."

"See both are done!"

Altari saluted and departed.

Later that night, inside a tent near the Temple, Ram and Curtis waited. Rune and Altari put together the makeshift device using some water and a piece of sod from the site of the Palace.

"Are you sure this will work?" asked Ram.

"I hope so, Sire. Witter is making something similar in the Cave. When you speak, we'll know," said Altari.

"What do I say?"

"Summon Dagar."

"Show me."

Altari stepped up to the device. "By the power of heaven, mighty Dagar, hear and answer one who seeks your presence."

The water around the sod began to boil. At the same time, the talisman Ram wore began to glow and it startled him.

"Be easy, Sire. That means it's working," said Altari.

The boiling water turned to steam that rose above the sod. In the steam, a fuzzy image of Dagar appeared. "I hear and respond. Who summons me? Ah, Altari."

"Actually, I was demonstrating for the king." The Warrior moved aside for Ram to approach the device.

"Father. You look better."

"That's a matter of opinion. At least this works. What has happened since I left?"

"Reports from various provinces say the Guardians are gone. Or at least nowhere to be found."

Dagar chuckled with delight. "Excellent. What of your wayward brother?" Contempt crept into his voice.

Ram tried to keep the pricked expression from his face. "Nothing yet. I swear, I will not give up looking, even if takes the rest of my life."

"What?" Dagar's attention was drawn aside by muttered words. "Father?"

Dagar impatiently waved at Ram while still looking to one side. When he turned back, he appeared decidedly put out. "Witter doesn't believe you'll find him. Something about the prophecy Hueil mentioned. He may be right. Ram?" His brows knitted as if looking for something.

"I'm still here."

"Ah, there you are. Witter says you intend to begin construction on Ravendale."

"Ay, along with a more permanent device for communication."

Dagar's image began to fade. "Move your headquarters to the building site and have Rune forge the device so we can communicate during construction." Dagar's image disappeared.

Ram sent a disapproving scowl to Altari.

"It's no longer theory. It does work," said Altari.

"Break down the encampment to head for Midessex."

"And the Vicar? What do you want done with him?" asked Curtis.

"Keep some Shadow Warriors here until he acknowledges who is supreme."

Curtis bowed and departed, as did Altari and Rune.

Chapter 24

SUSPENDED BETWEEN TIME AND SPACE, BETWEEN THE PHYSICAL world and the heavenlies, lay the Fringe. The grayish expanse continued endlessly in either direction. A bright white ceiling offered a view of the heavenlies. Though a glass-like floor the distant world below appeared in blurry shapes and muted colors.

From the light, Armus emerged, still carrying Kell. It took great effort to bridge the gap between the earth and heaven with an injured comrade. Armus collapsed to his knees in exhaustion. He managed to maintain hold of Kell. He carefully laid Kell on the glassy floor then relaxed with a groan of relief. It took a moment to catch his breath. He checked Kell's temperature. He felt cooler than before with traces of blue around the eyes and lips. All signs of being on the verge of succumbing.

Armus stood and looked up into the heavenlies. "Almighty Jor'el, I, Armus, Guardian of Allon, seek help on behalf of your captain. Hear me and answer!"

A swirling cloud of white majestically descended from the ceiling until the base of the cloud touched the glassy floor. A pair of opalescent eyes appeared in the cloud. "I know why you are here, Armus. Your loyalty and dedication to the captain is well known."

Armus knelt and bowed his head. "Dedication for your service, Mighty One."

The eyes kindly smiled. "Of course. I created you and Kell to act as one in many respects." The eyes shifted with compassionate to Kell then back to Armus. "Have no fear. I will not let my captain die."

A hand emerged from the cloud to touch Kell's forehead. "Awake, Kell. Your duty is not finished." The hand moved down the length of

Kell's body. The wound healed and his uniform became restored to perfection. Jor'el's hand retreated back into the cloud.

Kell gasped with the breath of life. His eyes snapped open. Baffled, he looked about. "The Fringe?"

Armus helped Kell sit up. "I brought you here since you were beyond Eldric's skill."

"I was, wasn't I?" said Kell in dreaded thought. Seeing Jor'el, he rose to his knees and bowed his head. "Many thanks, Mighty one."

"No thanks are needed, Kell. Your task is not complete. Now listen well before returning to comfort your comrades and bring news to certain mortals."

At Melwynn, Wren paced the infirmary. Eldric tended to an unconscious Avatar. Phoebe and Brooke, another physician, cared for Ridge, Priscilla and Gresham.

"Easy. Eldric knows what he's doing," Barnum tried to encourage Wren.

"How can you say that after what just happened? There aren't many of us left. If Avatar dies ..."

"Who said I am dying? I just needed a nap."

Wren hurried to the bed. She smiled in relief at seeing Avatar awake, albeit weak and tired. "Arrogant warrior," she teased. Suddenly, her teasing turned to horror when he disappeared. "Avatar? No!"

Armus and Kell rushed in from the terrace. "What happened?" demanded Kell.

At a momentary loss for words, Eldric shook his head. "I don't know, Captain. One moment Avatar was awake and speaking, the next he ... vanished. No light—"

Ridge vanished in the same manner as Avatar, which further stunned the others.

"Quick!" Kell shoved Wren toward the terrace. "Go to Arundine."

"What?" she asked in confusion.

Kell ignored her to keep speaking. "Gresham, Eldric, Priscilla ..." When Phoebe and Brooke vanish, Kell seized Priscilla and Wren. "Now!" They vanished in dimension travel.

Armus took Gresham and Eldric. Barnum left Melwynn on his own power. Everyone reappeared inside Arundine.

Wren jerked from Kell. "What is going on?"

"Jor'el's judgment."

His answer confused her. "I don't understand."

"That makes it unanimous," said Valmar. He, Zinna, Chase, Mona and Jedrek were already there.

"Ay, we don't understand either," said Mona.

"Armus brought me to the Fringe for healing," said Kell.

"You needed Jor'el's healing?" asked Eldric.

"Dagar nearly killed him when they battled in the Throne room. Realizing he was beyond your skills, I took him to the Fringe," said Armus.

Kell spoke with sobriety. "Once I was whole again, Jor'el told us the actions of Dagar and the others, has brought judgment upon all Guardians." He watched their bewildered reactions with dismay.

"Judgment? On those of us who remain loyal?" asked Valmar, perplexed.

Kell took a deep, steadying breath before proceeding to explain. "Jor'el withdrew his presence from Allon by destroying the Palace and Fortress. As a result, the majority of Guardians are banished. Only we few remain to keep watch. Which is why I had to get you and the others from Melwynn before it became sealed," Kell said the last sentence to Wren. "Arundine will also be hidden when we are finished here. To the mortals, the Guardians will pass into legend."

"What about Avatar, Phoebe, Ridge and the others? Are they...?" asked Wren, unable to finish her question.

"Recalled to the heavenlies."

"So they're alive," she said in relief.

"Ay," said Kell with a kind smile.

"How can twelve of us defend Allon?" said Chase.

"Jor'el left enough to watch each province in a limited capacity."

"Limited means diminished strength and abilities. And with little to no contact with the mortals," said Armus.

"That's rather difficult to accept," said Valmar.

Kell's jowls tensed with great distress as he continued. "There is more. Because of the others, Jor'el has decreed that any Guardian who kills another Guardian in cold blood will face immediate judgment. Their names will be blotted out from existence, and all memory of them wiped away. It will be as if they never existed."

The silence that followed the captain's statement was profound. Overcome by the new reality, Priscilla sat. Mona's knees almost gave way, so Jedrek steadied her.

Barnum found courage enough to speak. "What about the Shadow Warriors? Will they face this same judgment?" Sarcastic pain laced his words.

"Dagar and the rest have forfeited their station and become enemies of Jor'el. They will face eternal punishment once they cease to exist. Jor'el said this decree is to prevent further rebellion among our ranks," said Kell.

"So we must stand by and let them wreck havoc?" chided Chase.

"No!" said Kell in stout reply. "Despite restrictions, when faced with an enemy, we are still permitted to act in defense. This now includes Dagar, Shadow Warriors, or any other individual the Dark Way employs. It is cold-blooded murder among *our* ranks which will receive the harshest punishment." Seeing they still reeled from the news, Kell flashed a small smile. "There is hope. A time will come when we shall be restored."

"When?" asked Jedrek.

Kell shook his head. "I don't know. Jor'el promised a son will rise up to take back Allon from the darkness, while a daughter will help restore us to our rightful place. Until then, we keep watch."

"Not all is lost," said Armus with some encouragement.

"Now for your assignments," began Kell. "Valmar, the Highlands are still yours. Gresham, Midessex, Armus, the Meadowlands, Mona, the North Plains, Zinna, the South Plains, Wren, the Southern Forest, Barnum, the Northern Forest, Jedrek, the Delta, Eldric, the Lowlands, Chase, still the West Coast, and you, Priscilla, the East Coast. I will watch the Region of Sanctuary. Now go, and Jor'el be with you until the appointed time."

Kell watched the silent, somber departure. It didn't surprise him that Armus was the last to leave. The signs of Arundine's sealing began the moment Armus crossed the threshold. Vines and overgrowth sprung up from the floor winding their way around the pillars to the ceiling. Kell hurried outside. The same canopy of nature climbed up the walls. When he could see no longer see the dome, he vanished in dimension travel.

In the cottage of the Greenwood, the evening meal had been consumed and relaxing the order of the day. However, complete relaxation was hard to achieve with two missing from their numbers. They didn't speak much about Dolan and Kerwin. The reality was too unpredictable and the future uncertain.

White light filled the main room. Mace, Razi and Toby reached for their weapons. Janel and Clare withdrew to a corner in fearful anticipation. From the light appeared Kell, and holding onto an unsteady Dolan.

"Dolan!" Clare greeted her husband in tears of relief and joy.

Mace, Razi and Toby put down their weapons.

"Kell. This is a surprise," said Razi.

"I'm sure it is," said Kell in a sober tone that made Razi concerned.

"Wait. Where is Kerwin?"

Dolan shook his head unable to speak at seeing the fear of realization in Clare's eyes.

"I'm sorry," said Kell. "Be assured, his spirit is in the heavenlies with Jor'el."

"With Jor'el?" asked Razi. He sat, as the harsh realization struck him. "He succeeded."

"For now," said Kell.

"What do you mean?"

"Ram is crowned king, while Dagar imprisoned in the Cave. As a result of rebellion among the Guardians and the mortals, Jor'el withdrew his presence and banished the Guardians until the appointed time of restoration."

"No Guardians in Allon?" asked Toby, in wary skepticism.

"He means the good Guardians, not Shadow Warriors," said Dolan.

"What are Shadow Warriors?" asked Mace.

Razi stared at Kell. "The Guardians my father turned to his Dark Way."

"Ay. They will be dealt with at the appointed time," said Kell.

"When will that be?" asked Janel.

Kell tenderly smiled at her. "It is for the child you carry to tell of the time and season."

"I'm with child? We have only been married a few weeks."

"It only takes one time," snickered Dolan.

Razi stood beside Janel. "You said our child will tell? You mean he will be a prophet?"

"Ay. You shall call him Elias, for he shall restore the Almighty's written word that was destroyed upon departure. From your descendants will come a king to rekindle desire for the Almighty. From his lineage, Jor'el will raise up a son who will take back what your father stole, along with a daughter, who will restore the Guardians. What Dagar meant for evil in your conception, Jor'el will use for his purposes. So do not give up hope." Kell smiled.

Overwhelmed, Razi stood momentarily speechless. "I ... I don't know what to say. I never expected anything like this."

Kell's hand on Razi's shoulder made him look up at the captain. "Continue to remain faithful. Now, I must go."

"Will you return when the child is born?" asked Janel.

"I cannot say. But know this: the *Vicar* is looking forward to hearing of the child's birth. Discreetly of course. You must remain hidden while Ram lives."

"Avram is alive," said Clare in relief.

"And more feisty then ever," snickered Dolan.

"Peace be to this house, now and forever." Kell bowed to Razi and disappeared.

Explore the Kingdom of Allon

www.allonbooks.com

Featuring:

- Read excerpts of Allon books
- News and Events
- Photos and Videos
- Links to:
    - o Blog
    - o Facebook – The Kingdom of Allon Page
    - o Newsletter
    - o Contact Shawn Lamb

www.ingramcontent.com/pod-product-compliance
Lightning Source LLC
Chambersburg PA
CBHW070831250626
47159CB00003B/726